Crashed

BOOK THREE

K. BROMBERG

Cover art created by **Tugboat Design**
Copy and Line editing by **The Polished Pen**
Proof Edit by **Amy Tannenbaum**
Formatting by **Champagne Formats**

Except for the original material written by the author, all songs, song titles, and lyrics mentioned in the novel Crashed are the property of the respective songwriters and copyright holders.

ISBN: 978-0-9894502-5-6

Also by K. Bromberg

The Driven Series
Driven
Fueled
Crashed
Raced (Driven reading companion)
Aced

Driven Novels
SLOW BURN
SWEET ACHE
DOWN SHIFT

UnRaveled

Dedication

To Mom and Dad ~

Thank you for teaching me that life isn't about how you survive the storm, but rather how you dance in the rain.

And I'm finally dancing…

Prologue

THWACK. THWACK. THWACK.

The resonating pain in my head pulses to the sound assaulting my ears.

Thwack. Thwack. Thwack.

There is so much sound—loud, buzzing white noise—and yet it's eerily fucking quiet. Quiet except for that damn thwacking sound.

What the hell is that?

Why the fuck is it so damn hot—so hot I can see the heat coming in waves off of the asphalt—but all I feel is cold?

Motherfucker!

Something to the right of me catches my eye—mangled metal, blown tires, skins shredded to pieces—and all I can do is stare. Becks is going to throttle me for fucking up the car. Shred me to pieces just like my car strewn all over the track. What the fuck happened?

A trickle of unease dances at the base of my spine.

My heartbeat accelerates.

Confusion flickers at the far away edges of my subconscious. I close my eyes to try and push back the pounding that's suddenly playing percussion to my thoughts. Thoughts I can't quite grasp. They sift through my mind like sand through my fingers.

Thwack. Thwack. Thwack.

I open my eyes to try and find that goddamn sound that's adding pressure to the pain ...

... pleasure to bury the pain ...

Those words whisper through my mind, and I shake my head to try to comprehend what's going on when I see *him*: dark hair in need of a trim; tiny little hands holding a plastic helicopter; a Spiderman Band-Aid wrapped around his index finger that's spinning the pretend rotors.

Spiderman. Batman. Superman. Ironman.

"Thwack. Thwack. Thwack," he says in the softest of voices.

So why does it sound so loud then? Big eyes look up at me through thick lashes, innocence personified in that simple grace of green. His finger falters on the rotor as his eyes meet mine, cocking his head to study me intently.

"Hi there," I say, the deafening silence reverberating through the space between us.

Something's off.

Completely not fucking right.

Apprehension resurfaces.

Hints of the unknown whirl around my mind.

Confusion smothers.

His green eyes consume me.

Anxiety dissipates when a slow smile curls up the corner of his little mouth smudged with dirt, a lone dimple winking at its side.

"I'm not supposed to talk to strangers," he says, straightening his back some, trying to act like the big kid he wants to be.

"That's a good rule. Did your mom teach you that?"

Why does he seem so familiar?

He shrugs nonchalantly. His gaze runs over every inch of me and then comes back to meet mine. They flicker to something over my shoulder, but for some fucking reason I can't seem to drag my eyes from him to look. It's not just that he's the cutest fucking kid I've ever seen ... No, it's like he has this pull on me that I can't seem to break.

A little line creases his forehead as he looks down and picks at another superhero Band-Aid barely covering the large scrape on his knee.

Spiderman. Batman. Superman. Ironman.

Shut the fuck up! I want to yell at the demons in my head. They have no right to be here ... no reason to swarm around this sweet looking little boy, and yet they keep swirling like a merry-go-round. *Like my car should be around the track right now.* So why am I taking a step toward this polarizing little boy instead of preparing for the ration of shit Becks is going to spew at me, and by the looks of my car, that I obviously deserve?

And yet I still can't resist.

I take another step toward him, slow and deliberate in my motions, like I am with the boys at The House.

The boys.

Rylee.

I need to see her.

Don't want to be alone anymore.

I need to feel her.

Don't want to be broken anymore.

Why am I swimming in a sea of confusion? And yet I take another step through the fog toward this unexpected ray of light.

Be my spark.

"That's a pretty bad owie you got there ..."

He snorts. It's so fucking adorable to see this little kid with such a serious face, nose scattered with freckles scrunched up, looking at me like I'm missing something.

"*Thanks, Captain Obvious!*"

And a smart-ass mouth on him too. *My type of kid.* I stifle a chuckle as he glances back over my shoulder again for the third time. I start to turn to see what he's looking at when his voice stops me. "Are you okay?"

Huh? "What do you mean?"

"Are you okay?" he asks again. "You seem kind of broken."

"What are you talking about?" I take another step toward him. My fleeting thoughts mixed with the somberness of his tone and the concern etched on his face is starting to unnerve me.

"Well, you look broken to me," he whispers as his Band-Aid wrapped finger flips the propeller again—*thwack, thwack, thwack*—before motioning up and down my body.

Anxiety creeps up my spine until I look down at my race suit to find it intact, my hands patting up and down to calm the feeling. "No." The words rush out. "I'm okay, buddy. See? Nothing's wrong," I say, sighing a quick breath of relief. The little fucker scared me for a second.

"No, silly," he says with a roll of his eyes and a huff of breath before pointing over my shoulder. "Look. You're broken."

I turn, the calm simplicity of his tone puzzling me, and look behind me.

My heart stops.

Thwack.

My breath strangles in my chest.

Thwack.

My body freezes.

Thwack.

I blink my eyes over and over, trying to push away the images before me. The sights permeate through a viscous haze.

Spiderman. Batman. Superman. Ironman.

Fuck. No. No. No. No.

"See," his angelic voice says beside me. "I told you."

No. No. No. No.

The air finally punches from my lungs. I force a swallow down my throat that feels like sandpaper.

I know I see it—the chaos right before my eyes—but how is it possible? How am I here and *there*?

Thwack. Thwack. Thwack.

I try to move. To fucking run! To get their attention to tell them

I'm right here—that I'm okay—but my feet won't listen to the ricocheting panic in my brain.

No. I'm not there. Just here. I know I'm okay—know I'm alive—because I can feel my breath catch in my chest when I take a step forward to get a closer look. Fingertips of dread tickle over my scalp because what I see ... that can't be ... it's just not fucking possible.

Spiderman. Batman. Superman. Ironman.

The gentle whir of the saw pulls me from my ready-to-rage state as the medical crew cuts the driver's helmet down the center. The minute they split it apart, my head feels like it explodes. I drop to my knees, the pain so excruciating all I can do is raise my hands up to hold it. I have to look up. Have to see who was in my car. Whose motherfucking ass is mine, but I can't. It hurts too goddamn much.

... I wonder if there's pain when you die ...

I jolt at the feel of his hand on my shoulder ... but the minute it rests there, the pain ceases to exist.

What the ...? I know I have to look. I have to see for myself who is in the car even though I ultimately know the truth. Disjointed memories fracture and flicker through my mind just like pieces of the splintered mirror in that fucking dive bar.

Humpty fucking Dumpty.

Fear snakes up my spine, takes hold, and reverberates through me. I just can't do it. I can't look up. *Don't be such a pussy, Donavan.* Instead, I look to my right into *his* eyes, the unexpected calm in this storm. "Is that ...? Am I ...?" I ask the little boy as my breath clogs my throat, apprehension over the answer holds my voice hostage.

He just looks at me—eyes clear, face serious, lips pursed, freckles dancing—before he squeezes my shoulder. "What do you think?"

I want to shake a fucking answer out of him but know I won't. Can't. With him here at my side amidst this whirling chaos, I've never felt more at peace and yet at the same time more scared.

I force my eyes from his serene face to look back at the scene in front of me. I feel like I'm in a kaleidoscope of jagged images as I take in the face—my fucking face—on the gurney.

My heart crashes. Sputters. Stops. Dies.

Spiderman.

Grey skin. Eyes swollen, bruised, and closed. Lips lax and pale.

Batman.

Devastation surrenders, desperation consumes, life sputters, and yet my soul clings.

Superman.

"No!" I yell at the top of my lungs until my voice falls hoarse. No one turns. No one hears me. Every fucking person is unresponsive—my body and the medics.

Ironman.

The body on the gurney—*my body*—jolts as someone climbs on the stretcher and starts compressions on my chest. Someone fastens the neck brace. Lifts my eyelids and checks my pupils.

Thwack.

Wary faces. Defeated eyes. Routine movements.

Thwack.

"No!" I shout again, panic reigning within every ounce of me. "No! I'm right here! Right here! I'm okay."

Thwack.

Tears fall. Disbelief stutters. Possibilities vanish. Hope implodes.

My life blurs.

My eyes focus on my hand hanging limp and lifeless off of the gurney—a single drip of blood slowly making its way down to the tip of my finger before another compression on my chest joggles it to drip on the ground beneath. I focus on that ribbon of blood, unable to look back at my face. I can't take it anymore.

Can't stand watching the life drain from me. Can't stand the fear that creeps into my heart, the unknown that trickles into my subconscious, and the cold that starts to seep into my soul.

"Help me!" I turn to the little boy so familiar but so unknown. "Please," I beg, an imploring whisper, with every ounce of life I have in me. "I'm not ready to ..." I can't finish the sentence. If I do then I'm accepting what is happening on the gurney before me—what his place beside me signifies.

"No?" he asks. A single word, but the most important one of my fucking life. I stare at him, consumed by what is in the depths of his eyes—understanding, acceptance, acknowledgment—and as much as I don't want to leave the feeling I have with him, the question he's asking me—to choose life or death—is the easiest decision I've ever had to make.

And yet, the decision to live—to go back and prove like fucking hell that I deserve to be given this choice—means that I'll have to leave his angelic little face and the serenity his presence brings to my otherwise troubled soul.

"Will I ever see you again?" I'm not sure where the question comes from, but it falls out before I can stop it. I hold my breath waiting for his answer, wanting both a yes and a no.

He tilts his head to the side and smirks. "If it's in the cards."

Whose fucking cards? I want to yell at him. God's? The Devil's? Mine? Whose fucking cards? But all I can say is, *"The cards?"*

"Yup," he responds with a little shake of his head as he looks down at his helicopter and back up to me.

Thwack. Thwack. Thwack.

The sound becomes louder now, drowning out all noise around me, and yet I can still hear the draw of his breath. Still hear the pounding of my heart in my eardrums. Can still feel the soft sigh of peace that wraps around my body like a whisper as he places his hand on my shoulder.

All of a sudden I see the helicopter—Life Flight—on the infield, the incessant sound of the rotors—thwack, thwack, thwack—as it waits for me. The gurney shunts forward as they start to move quickly toward it.

"Aren't you going?" he asks me.

I work a swallow in my throat as I look back at him and give him a subtle, resigned nod of my head. "Yeah …" It's almost a whisper, fear of the unknown heavy in my tone.

Spiderman. Batman. Superman. Ironman.

"Hey," he says, and my eyes come back into focus on his perfect fucking face. He points back to the activity behind me. "It looks like your superheroes came this time after all."

I whirl around, heart lodged in my throat and confusion meddling with my logic. I don't see it at first, the pilot's back is to me, helping load *my* stretcher in the medevac, but when he turns around to jump in the pilot's seat and take the joystick, it's clear as day.

My heart stops.

And starts.

A hesitant exhale of relief flickers through my soul.

The pilot's helmet is painted.

Red.

With black lines.

The call sign of Spiderman emblazoned on the front of it.

The little boy in me cheers. The grown man in me sags with relief.

I turn back to say goodbye to the little boy, but he's nowhere to be found. How in the hell did he know about the superheroes? I look all around for him—needing the answer—but he's gone.

I'm all alone.

All alone except for the comfort of those I've waited a lifetime to arrive.

My decision's been made.

The superheroes finally came.

Chapter One

Numbness slowly seeps through my body. I can't move, can't think, can't bear to pull my eyes from the mangled car on the track. If I look anywhere else, then this will all be real. The helicopter flying overhead will really be carrying the broken body of the man I love.

The man I need.

The man I can't lose.

I close my eyes and just listen, but I can't hear anything. The only thing in my ears is the thumping of my pulse. The only thing besides the blackness that my eyes see—that my heart feels—is the splintered images in my mind. Max melting into Colton and then Colton fading back to Max. Memories that cause the hope I'm grasping like a lifeline to flicker and flame before dying out, like the darkness smothering the light in my soul.

I race you, Ryles. His voice so strong and unwavering fills my head and then dissipates, glittering through my mind like ticker tape.

I double over, willing the strangling tears to come or a spark to fire within me, but nothing happens, just lead dropping through my soul and weighing me down.

I force myself to breathe while I try to fool my mind into believing the past twenty-two minutes never happened. That the car never cartwheeled and pirouetted through the smoke-filled air. That the metal of the car wasn't cut apart by somber-faced medics to extricate Colton's lifeless body.

We never made love. The single thought flits through my head. We never had the chance *to race* after he finally told me the words I'd needed to hear—and that he'd finally accepted, admitted to, and felt for himself.

I just want to rewind time and go back to the suite when we were wrapped in each other's arms. When we were connected—overdressed and underdressed—but the horrific sights of the mangled car won't allow it. They have scarred my memory so horribly for a second time that it's not possible for my hope to escape unscathed.

"Ry, I'm not doing too good here." They're Max's words seeping into my mind, but it's Colton's voice. It's Colton warning me of what's to come. What I've already lived through once in my life.

Oh God. Please no. Please no.

My heart wrings.

My resolve falters.

Images filter in slow motion.

"Rylee, I need you to concentrate. Look at me!" Max's words again. I start to sag, my body giving out like my hope, but arms close around me and give me a shake.

"Look at me!" No, not Max. Not Colton. *It's Becks.* I find it within myself to focus and meet his eyes—pools of blue fringed with the sudden appearance of lines at their corners. I see fear in them. "We need to go to the hospital now, okay?" His voice is gentle yet stern. He seems to think that if he talks to me like a child I won't shatter into the million pieces my soul is already broken into.

I can't swallow the sand in my throat to speak, so he gives me another shake. I've been robbed of every emotion but fear. I nod my head but don't make any other movement. It's utterly silent. There are tens of thousands of people in the grandstands around us, and yet no one is talking. Their eyes are focused on the clean-up crew and what's left of the numerous cars on the track.

I strain to hear a sound. To sense a sign of life. Nothing but absolute silence.

I feel Becks' arm go around me, supporting me as he directs us out of the tower on pit row, down the steps and toward the open door of a waiting van. He pushes gently on my backside to urge me in like I'm a child.

Beckett scoots in next to me on the seat and pushes my purse and my cell phone into my hands as he fastens his own belt and then says, "Go."

The van revs forward, jostling me as it clears the infield. I look out as we start to descend down the tunnel, and all I see are Indy cars scattered over the track completely motionless. Colorful headstones in a quiet graveyard of asphalt.

"*Crash, crash, burn …*" The lyrics of the song float from the speakers and into the lethal silence of the van. My blank mind slowly processes them.

"Turn it off!" I shout with panicked composure as my hands fist and teeth grit, as the words embed themselves into the reality I'm unsuccessfully trying to block out.

Hysteria surfaces.

"Zander," I whisper. "Zander has a dentist appointment on Tuesday. Ricky needs new cleats. Aiden has tutoring starting on Thursday and Jax didn't put it on the calendar." I look up to find Beckett's eyes trained on mine. In my periphery I notice some of the other crew seated behind us but don't know how they got there.

It bubbles up.

"Beckett, I need my phone. Dane is going to forget and Zander really needs to go to the dentist, and Scooter ne—"

"Rylee," he says in an even tone, but I just shake my head.

"No!" I yell. "No! I need my phone." I start to undo my seat belt, so flustered I don't even realize it's in my hand. I try to scamper over him to reach the sliding door of the moving van. Beckett struggles to wrap his arms around me to prevent me from opening it.

It boils over.

"Let go of me!" I fight against him. I writhe and buck but he successfully manages to restrain me.

"Rylee," he says again, and the broken tone in his voice matches the feeling in my heart taking the fight out of me.

I collapse into the seat but Beckett keeps me pulled against him, our breathing labored. He grabs my hand and squeezes tightly, the only show of desperation in his stoic countenance, but I don't even have the wherewithal to squeeze it back.

The world outside blurs, but mine has stopped. It's lying on a gurney somewhere.

"I love him, Beckett," I finally whisper.

I'm driven by fear...

"I know," he says, exhaling a shaky breath and kisses the crown of my head. "I do too."

... Fueled with desperation ...

"I can't lose him." The words are barely audible, as if saying them will make it happen.

... Crashing into the unknown.

"Neither can I."

The whoosh of the electric doors to the emergency room is paralyzing. I freeze at the noise.

Haunting memories flicker from the sound, and the angelic white of the hallways bring me anything but calming peace. It's odd to me that the slideshow of fluorescent lights on the ceiling are what flash through my mind—my only possible focus as my gurney was rushed down the hallway—medical jargon sparred between doctors rapidly, incoherent thoughts jumbling, and the whole time my heart pleading for Max, for my baby, for hope.

"Ry?" Beckett's voice pulls me from the panic strangling my throat, from the memories suffocating my progress. "Can you walk in?"

The gentleness in his tone washes over me, a balm to my open wound. All I want to do is cry at the comfort in his voice. The tears clog my throat and burn my eyes and yet they never well. Never fall.

I take a fortifying breath and will my feet to move. Beckett places an arm around my waist and helps me with the first step.

The doctor's face flashes through my mind. Stoic. Unemotional. Head shaking back and forth. Apology in his eyes. Defeat in his posture. Remembering how I wanted to close my eyes and slip away forever too. The words "I'm sorry" falling from his lips.

No. No. No. I can't hear those words again. I can't listen to someone telling me I've lost Colton, especially when we've just found each other.

I keep my head down. I count the laminate tiles on the floor as Becks leads me toward the waiting room. I think he's talking to me. Or to a nurse? I'm not sure because I can't focus on anything but pushing the memories out. Pushing out the despair so maybe just a sliver of hope can weasel its way into its vacated spot.

I sit in a chair beside Beckett and numbly look down at the constantly vibrating phone in my hand. There are endless texts and calls from Haddie, ones I can't even think to answer even though I know she's worried sick. It's just too much effort right now, too much everything.

I hear the squeak of shoes on linoleum as others file in behind us, but I focus on the children's book on the table in front of me. *The Amazing Spiderman.* My mind wanders, obsesses, focuses. Was Colton scared? Did he know what was happening? Did he call out the chant he told Zander about?

The thought alone breaks me and yet the tears don't come.

I see surgical booties in my periphery. Hear Beckett being addressed.

"The specialist needs to know exactly how impact was made so we best know the circumstances. We've tried to catch a replay but ABC stopped airing it." No, no, no. Words scream and echo through my head and yet silence smothers me. "I was told you'd be the person who'd most likely know."

Beckett shifts beside me. His voice is so thick with emotion when he begins to speak that I dig my fingers into my thighs. He clears his throat. "He hit the catch fence inverted ... I think. I'm trying to picture it. Hold on." He drops his head into his hands, rubs his fingers over his temple, and sighs as he tries to gather his thoughts. "Yes. The car was upside down. The spoiler hit the top of the catch fence with the nose closest to the ground. Midsection against the concrete barrier. The car disintegrated around his capsule."

The collective gasp of the thousands of people in response still rings in my ears.

"Is there anything you can tell us?" Beckett asks the nurse.

The unmistakable noise of metal giving under force.

"Not right now. It's still the early stages and we're trying to assess everything—"

"Is he going to be ..."

"We'll give you an update as soon as we can."

The smell of burned rubber on oiled asphalt.

Shoes squeak again. Voices murmur. Beckett sighs and scrubs his hands over his face before trembling fingers reach over and pull the hand gripping my leg free and clasps it in his.

The lone tire rolling across the grass and bouncing against the infield barrier.

Please just give me a sign, I beg silently. Something. Anything. A tiny little thing to tell me to hang on to the hope that's slipping through my fingers.

Ringing cell phones echo off of the waiting room's sterile walls. Over and over. Like the beeps on the life supporting machines that filter out into the waiting room. Each time one silences, a little part of me does too.

I hear the hitch of Becks' breath a moment before he emits a strangled sob that hits me like a hurricane, shredding the paper bag I have preserving my resolve and faith. As hard as he tries to push away the onslaught of tears that threaten him, he's unsuccessful. The grief escapes and runs down his cheeks in silence, and it kills me that the man who has been the strength for me is now crumbling. I squeeze my eyes shut and will myself to stay strong for Beckett, but all I keep hearing are his words to me last night.

I shake my head back and forth in a panicked disbelief. "I'm so sorry," I whisper. "I'm so, so sorry. This is all my fault."

Beckett hangs his head momentarily before wiping his eyes with the palms of his hands. And the gesture—pushing away tears like a little kid does when ashamed—wrings my heart even more.

I can't help the panic that flutters as I realize that I'm the reason Colton's here. I pushed him away and didn't believe him—made him tired the night before a race—and all because I was stubborn and scared. "I did this to him." The words kill me. Rip my soul apart.

Beckett lifts his red-rimmed eyes from his hands. "What are you talking about?" He leans in close, his conflicted blue eyes searching mine.

"Everything ..." My breath hitches and I pause. "I messed with his head the last couple of days, and you told me that if I did, it was on me—"

"Ryl—"

"And I fought him and left him and we stayed up so late and I put him in that car tired and—"

"Rylee!" he finally manages in a harsh tone. I just keep shaking my head at him, eyes burning, emotions overloading. "This is not your fault."

I jolt as he puts his arms around me and pulls me into him. I fist my hands into the front of his fire suit, the coarseness of its fabric rough against my cheek.

"It was a crash. He drove into it blind. That's racing. It's not your fault." His voice breaks and falls on deaf ears. His arms are around me, trapping me, and claustrophobia threatens. Suffocation claws.

I stand abruptly, needing to move, to release the unease scavenging my soul. I pace to the far end of the waiting room and back. On my second pass the little boy in the corner chair scoots off his seat to pick up a crayon. The lights on his shoes flash red and grab my attention. I narrow my eyes to look closer, to take in the inverted triangle with the S in the center.

Superman.

The name feathers through my subconscious, but my attention is drawn to the television as someone changes the channel. I hear Colton's name and I suck in a breath, afraid to look but wanting to see what they're showing.

It seems like the whole room stands and moves collectively. A mass of red fire suits, faces conflicted with emotion, focus on the screen. The announcer says there was a crash that halted action for more than an hour. The screen flashes to the image of the cloud of smoke and cars careening off of each other. The angle is different than ours was on the track and we are able to see more, but as Colton's car comes into the turn, the broadcast cuts the footage. All of the shoulders around the television sag as the crew realizes that what they were anxiously anticipating will not be shown. The segment ends with the announcer saying that he is currently being treated at Bayfront.

I see Colton's lifeless body on the gurney, Max's beside me in his seat. The similarities of the situation knock the wind out of me, pain without end. Memories colliding.

I turn to see the Westins walk into the waiting room. Colton's regal and commanding mother looks pale and distraught. I swallow the lump in my throat, unable to tear my eyes from the sight of them. Andy supports her gently, guiding her to sit down as Quinlan grips her other hand.

Beckett's at their side in a flash with his arms wrapped around Dorothea and then Quinlan in quick but meaningful embraces. Andy reaches out and grabs Beckett in a longer hug, teeming with heart-wrenching desperation. I overhear a choked sob and almost break from the sound of it.

Watching the whole scene unfold causes memories to flicker through my mind of Max's funeral. A miniature pink casket laid atop a full-sized black casket, both blanketed with red roses, remind me of the words I can't hear again: *ashes to ashes, dust to dust.* Makes me remember the hollow, empty hugs that do nothing to comfort. The ones that leave you feeling over-sensitized, raw when you've already been scraped to the core.

I start to pace again amidst the hushed murmurs of "how long until there is an update?" Faces usually so strong and energetic are etched with lines of concern. And when my feet stop I'm looking into the eyes of Andy and Dorothea.

We just stare at each other, faces mirrors of each others' disbelief and anguish, until Dorothea reaches a trembling hand out for mine. "I don't know what ... I'm so sorry ..." I shake my head back and forth as words escape me.

"We know, sweetheart," she says as she pulls me into her arms and clings to me, both of us holding each other up. "We know."

"He's strong," is all Andy says as his hand rubs up and down my back to try and comfort me. But this—hugging his parents, all of us comforting each other, the tear-stained cheeks and muffled sobs— makes it all too real. My hope that this is all a really bad dream is now shattered.

I stagger back and try to focus on something, anything, to make me feel like I'm not losing it.

But I keep seeing Colton's face. The look of absolute certainty as he stood amid all of the chaos of his crew—the same crew that sits around me, heads in hands, lips pulled tight, eyes closed in prayer— and admitted his feelings for me. I have to stop to try and catch my breath, the pain radiating through my chest, in my heart, just won't stop.

The television pulls at me again. Something whispers through my mind and I turn to look. A trailer for the new Batman movie. Hope reawakens as my mind reaches into its depths—into the past hour.

The Spiderman book on the table. The Superman shoes. The Batman movie. I try to rationalize that this is all just a coincidence—that seeing three of the four superheroes is a random occurrence. I try to tell myself that I need the fourth to believe it. That I need Ironman to complete the circle—to be the sign that Colton will pull through.

That he will come back to me.

I start searching, eyes flitting around the waiting room as hope looms and readies itself to blossom, if I can just find the final sign. My hands tremble; my optimism lies beneath the surface cautious to raise its weary head.

There is sound toward the hallway and the noise—the voice—causes every emotion that pulses through me to ignite.

And I'm immediately ready to detonate.

Blonde hair and long legs breeze through the door and I don't care that her face looks as devastated and worried as I feel. All of my heartache, all of my angst rears up and is like a rubber band snapping.

Or lightning striking.

I'm across the room within seconds, heads snapping at the growl I let loose in my fury-filled wake. "Get out!" I scream, so many emotions coursing through me that all I feel is a mass of overwhelming confusion. Tawny's head whips up and her startled eyes meet mine, her enhanced lips set in a perfect *O* shape. "You conniving bit—"

The air is knocked out of me as Beckett's strong arms grab me from behind and yank me back into his chest. "Let me go!" I struggle against him as he grips me tighter. "Let me go!"

"Save it, Ry!" He grunts as he restrains me, his reserved yet firm drawl hitting my ears. "You need to save all of that fire and energy because Colton's going to need it from you. Every goddamn ounce of it."

His words hit me, punch through the holes in me, and sap my adrenaline. I stop struggling, his grip around me still iron clad, and the heat of his breath panting against my cheek. "She's not worth it, okay?"

I can't find my words—don't think I'm capable of coherency at this point—so I just nod my head in agreement, forcing myself to focus on a spot on the floor in front of me, rather than on the long legs off to the right.

"You sure?" he reaffirms before slowly letting go and stepping in front of me, forcing me to look into his eyes, to test if I'll be true to my word.

My body starts trembling, held captive to the mixture of anger, grief, and the unknown coursing through me.

My breath hitches as my lungs hurt with each breath. It's the only hint of the turmoil I feel inside when I meet the kindness edged with concern in Beckett's eyes. And I feel so horrible that he's here trying to take care of me when he loves Colton and is reeling from the unknown just as much as I am, so I force myself to nod. He mimics my action before turning around, his body blocking my line of sight to Tawny.

"Becks …" She sighs his name and her voice alone chafes over my exposed nerves.

"Not a fucking word, Tawny!" Beckett's voice is low and guarded, audible only to the three of us despite the numerous pairs of eyes watching the confrontation. I see Andy rise to his feet from the other side of the room as he tries to figure out what's going on. "I'm letting you stay for one reason and one reason only … Wood is going to need everyone he has in his corner—behind him if he …" he says, choking on the words, "when he pulls out of this … and that includes you, although right now after the stunt you pulled between him and Ry, *friend* is a very loose term when it comes to you."

Becks' words take me by surprise. I hear the noncommittal sound she makes before a momentary silence hits … and then I hear her start to cry. Quiet, sorrowful whimpers that break through the hold

19

on me that Beckett's voice couldn't.

And I snap. My reassurance to Becks that I'd save my strength vanishes right along with my restraint.

"No!" I scream, trying to push Beckett out of the way and take a swing. "You don't get to cry for him! You don't get to cry for the man you tried to manipulate!" Arms close around me from behind, preventing me from landing my punch, but I don't care, reality's lost to me. "Get out!" I shout, my voice wavering as I'm dragged away from her stunned face. "No!" I struggle against the restraining arms. "Let me go!"

"Shh-shh-shh!" It's Andy's voice, Andy's arms that are holding me tight, trying to soothe and control me at the same time. And the only thing I can focus on—can grasp onto as my heart races and body shakes with anger—is that I need a *pit stop*. I need to find Colton. I need to touch him, to see him, to quiet the turmoil in my soul.

But I can't.

He's somewhere close, my rebellious rogue unable to let go of the damaged little boy within. The man who has just started healing is now broken, and it kills me that I won't be able to fix him. That my murmured words of encouragement and patient nature won't be able to repair the immobile and unresponsive body that was loaded onto that stretcher and rushed to somewhere within these walls—so close yet so very far away from me. That he has to rely on strangers to mend and heal him now. Strangers that have no idea of the invisible scar tissue that still lingers beneath the surface.

More hands reach out to touch and soothe me, Dorothea's and Quinlan's, but they're not the ones I want. They're not Colton's.

And then a terrifying thought hits me. Every time Colton is near, I can feel that tingle—the buzz that tells me he's just within reach— but I can't feel anything. I know he's physically close, but his spark is nonexistent.

Be my spark, Ry. I can hear his voice say it, can feel the memory of his breath feather over my skin … but I can't *feel* him.

"*I can't!*" I shout. "I can't be your spark if I can't feel yours, so don't you dare burn out on me." I don't care that I'm in a room full of people, being turned around and encircled into Dorothea's arms, because the only one who I want to hear me, can't. And knowing that causes desperation to consume every part of me not already frozen with fear. I fist my hands into the back of Dorothea's jacket, clinging to her while I plead with her son. "Don't you dare die on me, Colton! I need you dammit!" I shout into the now sterile silence of the waiting room. "I need you so much that I'm dying right here, right now without you!" My voice cracks just like my heart, and as much as Dorothea's arms, Quinlan's hushed murmurs, and Andy's quiet resolve helps, I just can't handle it all.

I push away and stare at them before I stumble blindly down the hall. I know I'm losing it. I'm so numb, so hollow, that I don't even have the energy to argue with Beckett and refire the hatred I feel for Tawny. If I'm to blame for Colton being here, then she sure as fuck needs to share some of that blame too.

I turn the corner to head toward the bathroom and have to push myself to move. I press my hands against the wall for support or else I'll collapse. I remind myself to breathe, tell myself to put one foot in front of the other, but it's nearly impossible when the only thought my mind can focus on is that the man I love is fighting for his life, and I can't do a goddamn thing about it. I'm hopeless and powerless.

I'm dying inside.

My guiding hands hit a doorjamb, and I stagger between its frame and into the nearest stall, welcoming the cocooning silence of the empty bathroom. I unbutton my shorts, and when I shimmy them over my hips, my eyes catch sight of the checkered pattern on my panties. My body wants to quit, wants to slide to the floor and sink into oblivion, but I don't. Instead, my hands grip onto the belt loops of the shorts still hanging off of my hips. I can't catch my breath fast enough. I start to hyperventilate and get dizzy, so I brace my hands against the wall but nothing helps as the panic attack hits me full force.

You can bet your ass that's one checkered flag I'm definitely claiming.

I welcome the memorized sound of his voice. I let his rumble permeate through me like the glue I need to hold my broken self together. My breath drags in ragged rasps between my lips as I try to hold onto the memory—that incredible grin and the boyish mischief in his eyes—before he kissed me one last time. I bring my fingers to my lips wanting to make a connection with him, fear of the unknown weighing heavy in my heart.

"Rylee?" The voice jolts me to the here and now and I just want her to go away. I want her to leave me intact with my memory of the warmth of his skin, taste of his kiss, possession in his touch. "Rylee?"

There's a knock on the stall door. "Mmm-hmm?" is all I can manage because my breathing is still forced and irregular.

"It's Quin." Her voice is soft and uneven, and it kills me to hear the break in it. "Ry, please come out …"

I reach forward and unlock the door, and she pushes it open looking at me oddly, her tear stained face and smudged mascara only emphasizing the devastation looming in her eyes. She purses her lips and starts laughing, in a way that's borderline hysterical so when it echoes off of the tile walls around us all I hear is despair and fear. She points to my half-shoved down shorts and checkered panties and keeps laughing, the tears staining her cheeks an odd contrast to the sound coming from her mouth.

I start laughing with her. It's the only thing I can do. Tears won't come, fear won't abate, and hope is wavering as the first laugh falls from my lips. It feels so wrong. Everything is just so wrong and within an instant, Quinlan—the woman who hated me at first sight—reaches out and wraps her arms around me while her laughter turns into sobs. Gut wrenching hiccups of unfettered fear. Her tiny frame shakes as her anguish intensifies.

"I'm so scared, Rylee." It's the only thing she can manage to get out between hitches of breath, but it's all she needs to say because it's exactly how I feel. The defeat in her posture, the fortitude of her grief, the strength in her grip reflects the fear that I'm not able to express, so I cling to her with everything I have—needing that connection more than anything.

I hug her and soothe her as best as I can, trying to lose myself in the role of patient counselor I know so well. It's so much easier to assuage someone else's despair than to face my own. She tries to pull away, but I just can't let go. I don't have the wherewithal to walk out the doors and wait for the doctor to report news I'm terrified to hear.

I fasten my shorts and look up to meet my own reflection in the mirror. I can see the haunting memories flickering in my eyes. My mind flashes to a shattered rearview mirror, sun reflecting on its blood-specked, jagged edges as Max gurgles his last breath. And then my mind grasps onto a happier memory with another mirror. One used in the heat of passion to demonstrate why I'm enough for Colton. *Why he chooses me.*

"C'mon," she whispers, breaking my trance as she releases me but moves her hand down to wrap around my waist. "I don't want to miss an update."

Chapter Two

TIME HAS STRETCHED. EACH MINUTE feels like an hour. And each of the three hours that have passed feels like an eternity. Each swoosh of the doors has us all startling and then sinking back down. Empty Styrofoam cups spill over the wastebasket. Fire suits have been unzipped and tied around waists as the waiting room grows stuffy. Cell phones ring incessantly with people searching for updates. But there's still no news.

Beckett sits with Andy. Dorothea has Quinlan on one side of her and Tawny on the other. The waiting room is full of hushed murmurs and the television plays background to my thoughts. I sit by myself and except for the constant texts from Haddie, I welcome the solitude so I don't have to comfort or be comforted—the schizophrenia in my mind only getting louder with each passing second.

My stomach churns. I'm hungry but the thought of food makes me nauseous. My head pounds but I welcome the pain, welcome the drum of it to count to as I try to speed up time. Or slow it down—whichever is to the benefit of Colton.

The electronic beep of the door. The squeak of shoes. I don't even open my eyes this time.

"I have an update on Mr. Donavan." The voice jolts me. Feet shuffle as the guys stand and an understated anxiety hums through the room in anticipation of what is going to be said.

Fear grips me. I can't stand. Can't move. I'm so petrified of the words that are going to pass through his lips that I force a swallow down my throat but remain paralyzed with trepidation

I squeeze my hands, gripping them into the bare flesh of my thighs, trying to use the pain to bury the memories. Willing the past to not repeat itself—to not trade one wrecked car with a man that I love for another.

He clears his throat and I suck in a breath—praying, hoping, needing some kind of scrap to hold on to. "Let me just say that scans are still ongoing at this point but from what we can tentatively see, it's obvious that Mr. Donavan has suffered a sudden deceleration injury with an internal organ disruption from the force in which he hit the catch fence. The injury occurs because the body is forcibly stopped but the organs inside the body remain in motion due to the inertia. From what we can tell …"

"English, please," I whisper. My mind tries to comprehend the medical jargon, knowing that if I wasn't swimming in this fog of uncertainty, I'd be able to process it. He stops at my comment and even though I can't lift my eyes to meet his, I say it louder this time. "English, please, doctor." Fear overwhelms me. I cautiously lift my eyes to meet his, the crew turning to look at me while I stare at the doctor. "We're all very worried here and while you may understand what you're saying, the terminology is scaring the shit out of us…" my voice fades and he nods kindly, "…our minds are too overwhelmed to process this all right now … it's been a long wait for us while you've been with him … so can you please just tell us in simple terms?"

He smiles gently at me but his eyes are grave. "When Colton hit the wall, the car stopped—his body stopped—but his brain kept going, slamming into the skull surrounding it. Fortunately he was wearing a HANS device which helped to protect the connection between his spine and his neck, but the injury he sustained is serious nonetheless."

My heart races and my breath labors as a million different possible outcomes flicker through my mind.

"*Will he ...?*" Andy moves into my view facing the doctor and asks the question he can't complete. Silence descends upon the room and the nervous shifting of feet stops as we all wait for the answer with baited breath.

"Mr. Westin, I presume?" the doctor asks as he holds out his hand to a nodding Andy. "I'm Dr. Irons. I'm not going to lie to you ... your son's heart arrested—stopped twice during transport."

I feel as if the bottom of my soul has dropped out with those words. *Don't leave me. Please don't leave me.* I plead silently, willing the words to hit him somewhere within the confines of this hospital.

Andy reaches out and squeezes Dorothea's hand.

"We were able to get his heart regulated after a bit which is a good sign as we were afraid that possibly his aorta had torn from the force of the impact. At this point in time we know that he has a subdural hematoma." The doctor looks up and meets my eyes before continuing. "This means that the blood vessels ruptured and the area between his brain and the skull is filling with blood. The situation is twofold because Colton's brain is swelling from the trauma of hitting his skull. At the same time, the pooling blood is putting pressure on his brain because there is nowhere for it to escape to relieve said pressure." Dr. Irons scans the eyes of the crew surrounding him. "At this time he's more stable than not, so we are prepping him for surgery. It's imperative that we go in and relieve the pressure on his brain to try and stop the swelling."

I watch Dorothea reach over and cling to Andy for support, the obvious unconditional love for her son pulls on my every emotion.

"How long is the surgery? Is he conscious? Were there any other injuries?" Beckett speaks for the first time, rapidly firing off the questions we are all thinking.

Dr. Irons swallows and steeples his fingers in front of him while meeting Beckett's eyes. "As for other injuries, just minor ones in comparison to the head injury. He is not conscious nor has he regained consciousness at this time. He was in the typical comatose state we see with these injuries—mumbling incoherently, struggling against us—in very sporadic bouts. As for everything else, we'll know more when we get into surgery and see how bad the bleed on the brain is."

Beckett exhales the breath he's been holding, and I can see his shoulders slump with its release, although I'm unsure if it's in relief or resignation. None of the doctor's words have made the dread weighing down the pit of my soul lessen any. Quinlan steps forward and grabs Becks' hand as she glances over at her parents before asking the one thing we all fear. "If the swelling doesn't stop with the surgery..." her voice wavers, Beckett pressing a brotherly kiss onto the top of her head in encouragement "...what ... does that mean? What I'm trying to say is you're talking brain injury here so what is the prognosis?" Her breath hitches with a swallowed sob. "What are Colton's chances?"

The doctor sighs aloud and looks at Quinlan. "At this time, before we go into surgery and see if there is any damage, I'm not comfortable giving one." The strangled gasp that comes from Andy breaks the silence. Dr. Irons steps forward and places a hand on his shoulder until Andy looks up and meets his eyes. "We are doing absolutely everything we can. We are very practiced in this sort of thing and are giving your son every benefit of that training. Please understand that I'm not giving a percentage because it's a lost cause, but rather because I need to see more to know what we're up against. Once I know, then we can establish a game plan and go from there." Andy nods subtly at him, rubbing a hand over his eyes, and Dr. Irons looks up and scans the faces of everyone in the room. "He is strong and healthy and that's always a good thing to have on our side. It's more than obvious Colton is loved by many people ... please know I carry that knowledge into the operating room with me." With that he gives a tight smile then turns and leaves the room.

Upon his departure, no one moves. We are all still in shock.

All still letting the severity of his words slither into the holes poked through our resolve. People slowly start moving and shifting as thoughts meld and emotions attempt to settle.

But I'm unable to.

He's alive. Not dead like Max. Alive.

The dull ache of relief I feel is nothing compared to the sharp stab of the unknown. And it's not enough to assuage the fear seated deep in the depths of my soul. I start to feel the leeching claws of claustrophobia burn over my skin. I blow out a long breath trying to abate the sweat beading on my upper lip and sliding down the line of my spine. My breath slips from my lungs without replenishing my body.

Images flicker again. Max to Colton. Colton to Max. Blood tricking slowly from his ear. At the corners of his mouth. Flecking in specks across the shattered car. My name strangling on his lips. His pleas scarring my mind. Etching them like a brand marked to haunt me forever.

The sprinkling of unease turns into a downpour of panic. I need fresh air. I need a break from the oppression that is smothering this goddamn waiting room. I need color and vibrancy—something full of vigor and life like Colton—something other than the monochromatic colors and overwhelming memories.

I push myself up and all but run out of the waiting room ignoring Beckett's call after me. I stagger blindly toward the exit because this time the whoosh of the doors calls to me, offers a respite from the hysteria siphoning my hope.

You make me feel, Rylee …

I stumble through the doors, the memory feathering through my soul but hitting me like a sucker punch to the abdomen. I gasp loudly, pain radiating through my every synapse. I draw in a ragged breath, needing something, anything to help recoup the faith I need to face the reality that Colton might not make it through the surgery. The night. The morning.

I shake my head to rid the poison eating my thoughts when I turn the corner of the building and am thrown into a maelstrom. I swear there are over a hundred cameras that flash all at once. The roar of questions thunders so loudly that I'm blasted by a tidal wave of noise. I'm surrounded immediately, my back pressed against the wall as microphones and cameras are shoved in my face documenting my slowly depleting grip on reality.

"Is it true they're issuing Colton his last rites?"

Words trap in my throat.

"What is the status between you and Mr. Donavan?"

Anger intensifies but I'm overwhelmed by the deluge.

"Is it true that Colton's on his death bed and his parents are at his side?"

My lips open and close, my fists clench, eyes burn, soul tears, and my faith in humanity crumbles. I know I look like a deer in the headlights, but I'm trapped. I know that if I thought I felt the claws of claustrophobia inside, I feel the cinch of my windpipe as the hands of the media squeeze the air from me. My breath comes in short sharp bouts. The blue sky spins above as my mind warps it into a lazy eddy, blackness starts to seep through as my conscious fades.

Just as I am about to sink into the welcoming oblivion, strong arms wrap around me and prevent my crash to the ground. My weight slams into Sammy's like a freight train, and memories spear through my mind of the last time I fell into the arms of a man. Bittersweet images flicker of lost auction paddles and jammed closet doors. Vibrant green eyes and an arrogant, self-assured grin.

Rogue. Rebel. Reckless.

Sammy's voice breaks through my clouded mind as he chastises the press. "Back off!" he grunts as he supports my dead weight, arm around my waist. "We'll give an update when we have one." Flashes reignite the sky.

Again, the whoosh of doors, but this time I don't cringe. The beast on the inside is much more palpable than the one outside. My breath begins to even some and my heart decelerates. I am pushed down into a chair, and when I look up Sammy's eyes meet mine, searching for something.

"What in the hell do you think you were doing? They could've eaten you alive," he swears. It is such a flagrant show of emotion from the otherwise stoic bodyguard that I realize my mistake in going outside. I'm still finding my footing in Colton's very public world; and then I feel horrible because while I've been in the waiting room surrounded by everyone, I realize Sammy's been out here by himself making sure that we're left alone and undisturbed.

"I'm sorry, Sammy," I breathe an apology. "I just needed some air and … I'm sorry."

Concern lingers in his eyes. "Are you okay? Have you eaten anything? You almost fainted there. I think that you need to eat some—"

"I'm fine. Thank you," I say as I stand slowly. I think I surprise him when I reach out and squeeze his hand. "How are *you* doing?"

He shrugs nonchalantly, although the gesture is anything but. "As long as he is okay, then I'll be fine."

He nods at me as he turns to reclaim his post at the hospital doors before I can say anything else. My eyes track his movements for a moment, the callous comments from the press reverberating through my mind, while I build up the courage to walk back to the waiting room.

I close my eyes for a moment. I will myself to feel anything other than the numbness that consumes my soul. I try to pull from my depths of despair the sound of his laugh, the taste of his kiss, even his stubborn nature and staunch resolve—anything to cinch together the seams of my heart that Colton's love stitched backed together.

Not inconsequential, Rylee. You could never be inconsequential.

The memory whispers through my mind and is like flint re-sparking to life tiny flickers of hope. I take a deep breath and will my feet to move forward down the long corridor to where everyone else waits impatiently. I am just passing the nurses station when I hear Colton's name mentioned by two nurses whose backs are facing me. I slow my stride, trying to catch any bit of information I can. I try to force my mind from fretting that we're being lied to about the gravity of the situation, when I hear the words that punch the air from my lungs.

Makes my heart stop.

Causes a shiver to ricochet through my body.

"Who's in OR One with Mr. Donavan?"

"Dr. Irons is lead on the case."

"Well hell, if there's anyone I'd want operating on me in this circumstance, it sure as hell would be *Ironman*."

Spiderman.

I gasp, the nurses turn to take notice of me. The taller of the two steps forward and angles her head at me. "Can I help you miss?"

Batman.

"What did you just call Dr. Irons?"

Superman.

She looks at me, a slight crease in her brow. "You mean our nickname for Dr. Irons?"

Ironman.

All I can do is nod my head because my throat chokes with hope. "Oh, he's known around here as Ironman, sweetie. Do you need something?"

Spiderman. Batman. Superman. Ironman.

I just shake my head again then take the three steps toward the waiting room, but sag against a wall and slide down to the floor, as I become overwhelmed with hope, overpowered by the presence of Colton's beloved superheroes.

A childhood obsession now turned into an adult's grasp on hope.

I rest my face on my bent knees as I cling to the notion that this coincidence is more than just that—a coincidence. I rock my head back and forth, their names falling from my lips in a hushed chant that I know for the first time ever has been uttered with absolute reverence.

"Colton used to say that in his sleep as a little boy." Andy's voice startles me as he slides down the wall next to me, a heavy exhale falling from his lips. I shift some so I can look over at him. He looks years older in the hours since the race started this morning. His eyes hold a quiet grief and his mouth tries to lift in a soft smile but fails miserably. The man I've only known to be full of life has been sapped of his exuberance. "I haven't heard that in forever. Actually forgot about it until I just heard you say it." He chuckles softly, reaches out and pats my knee as he stretches his legs out in front of him.

"Andy ..." His name is a murmur on my lips as I watch him struggle with emotion. I desperately want to tell him about the signs—the random occurrence of his son's dearly loved superheroes—but worry he'll think I'm losing my grip on reality just as I fear Beckett thinks I am.

As I worry I might be.

"I'm surprised he told you about them. It used to be this secret code he'd chant as a little boy when he had a nightmare or was scared. He would never elaborate ... would never explain why those four superheroes were so comforting to him." He looks over at me, the soft smile falling. "Dottie and I could only ever imagine what he was hoping those superheroes would save him from ..."

The words drift between us and settle in questions we both want to ask but neither say aloud. What does Andy know that I don't and vice versa? He dabs the back of his hand at his eyes and exhales a shaky sigh.

"He's strong, Andy ... he's going to be ... he has to be okay," I finally say when I trust the resolve in my voice.

He just nods his head. We see a set of doctors running past us and my heart lodges in my throat, worried it's because of Colton. He scrubs a hand over his face and I watch the love fill his eyes. "The first time I ever saw him, he broke my heart and stole it all with one, single look." I nod my head at him to continue because more than anything I understand that statement, for his son did the same thing to mine.

He captured it, stole it, broke it, healed it, and forever owns it.

"I was on set working in my trailer on a scene rewrite. It had been a long night. Quin was sick and had been up all night." He shakes his head and meets my eyes for a moment before looking back down to focus them on the band of his watch that he's fiddling with. "I was late for a call time. I opened the door and almost tripped over him." He takes a moment to will the tears I see welling in his eyes to dissipate. "I think I swore aloud and I saw his little figure jolt back in unmistakable fear. I know he scared the shit out of me, and I could only imagine why a child would have that type of a reaction. He refused to look at me no matter how gentle I made my voice."

I reach over and take his hand in mine, squeezing to let him know that I know Colton's demons without him ever revealing them. I may not know the specifics, but I have seen enough to get the gist.

"I sat on the ground next to him and just waited for him to understand that I wasn't going to hurt him. I sang the only song I could think of." He laughs. "*Puff the Magic Dragon*. On the second time through, he lifted his head up and finally looked at me. *Sweet Christ* he stole my breath. He had the hugest green eyes in this pale little face and they looked up at me with such fear … such foreboding … that it took everything I had not to wrap my arms around and comfort him."

"I can't imagine," I murmur, going to withdraw my hand but stopping when Andy squeezes it.

"He wouldn't speak to me at first. I tried everything to get him to tell me his name or what he was doing, but it didn't matter. Nothing mattered—my missed call time, the wasted money, nothing—because I was mesmerized by the fragile little boy whose eyes told me they'd seen and experienced way too much in his short life. Quinlan was two at the time. Colton was so small in stature compared to her that I guessed he was about five. I was shocked later that night when the police told me he was eight years old."

I force the swallow that's stuck in my throat down as I listen to the first moments in Colton's life when he was given unconditional love. The first time he was given a life of possibilities rather than one of fear.

"I eventually asked him if he was hungry and those eyes of his got as big as saucers. I didn't have much in the trailer that a kid would like, but I did have a Snickers bar and I'll admit it," he says with a laugh, "I really wanted him to like me … so I figured what kid couldn't be bribed with candy?"

I smile with him, the connection not lost on me that Colton eats a Snickers before every race. That he ate a Snickers bar today. My chest tightens at the thought. Was that really only hours ago? It feels like days.

"You know Dottie and I had talked about the possibility of more kids … but had decided Quinlan was enough for us. Well, I should say that she would have had more and I was content with just one. Shit, we led busy lives with a lot of travel and we were fortunate enough with one healthy little girl, so how could we ask for more? My career was booming and Dottie took parts when she wanted to. But after that first few hours with Colton, there wasn't even a hesitation. How could I walk away from those eyes and the smile I knew was hiding somewhere beneath the fear and shame?" A tear slips over and down his cheek, the concern for his son, then and now, rolling off of him in waves. He looks up at me with gray eyes filled with a depth of emotions. "He's the strongest person—man—that I've ever met, Rylee." He chokes on a sob. "I just need him to be that right now … I can't lose my boy."

His words tear at places so deep inside of me, for I understand the anguish of a parent scared they're losing their child. The deep seated fear you don't want to acknowledge but that squeezes at every part of your heart. Sympathy swamps me for this man that gave Colton everything, and yet the numbness inside me incarcerates my tears. "None of us can, Andy. He's the center of our world," I whisper in a broken voice.

Andy angles his head to the side and looks over and studies me for a moment. "I fear every time he gets in that car. *Every goddamn time* … but it's the only place I see him free of the burden of his past … see him outrun the demons that haunt him." He squeezes my hand until I look back up to see the sincerity in his eyes. "The only time, that is, until recently. Until I see him talk about, worry about, interact with … you."

My breath catches, tears well for the first time but don't fall. After having Max's mom, Claire, hate me for so long, the unspoken approval from Colton's father is monumental. I hiccup a breath, trying to contain the tornado of emotions whirling through me.

"*I love him.*" It's all I can manage to say. Then it's all I can think about. I love him, and I might not ever get to really show him now that he's admitted to feeling the same way about me. And now I stand on the precipice of circumstances so out of my control that I fear I might not ever get the chance to.

Andy's voice pulls me from my rising panic attack. "Colton told me you encouraged him to find out about his birth mother."

I look down and draw absent circles on my knee with my fingertip, wary that this conversation can go one of two ways: Andy can be grateful that I'm trying to help his son heal or he can be upset and think I'm trying to drive a wedge between them.

"Thank you for that." He exhales softly. "I think he's always been missing a piece and maybe knowing about her will help fill that for him. Just the fact he's talking about it, asking about it, is a huge step..." he reaches out and places an arm around my shoulder and pulls me toward him so my head rests on his shoulder "...so thank you for helping him find himself in more ways than one."

I nod my head in acknowledgment, his confession causing words to escape me. We sit together like this for some time, accepting and pulling comfort from each other when all we feel is emptiness inside.

Chapter Three

I

T's a perfect day. Blue sky overhead, sun warming my cheeks, and not a thought on my mind. The waves crash into the sand with a soothing crescendo, roll after roll. I come here often, the place we had our first official date, because I feel close to him here. A memory, something to hold onto when I can never hold onto him again.

I wrap my arms around my knees and breathe it all in, accepting that sadness will always be a constant ache in my heart and wishing he were here beside me. But at the same time, I know I haven't felt this at peace since he's been gone. I might be turning a corner in my grief—at least that's what the therapist thinks—since it's been days without the blind panic and strangling screams that consume my thoughts and skew my grip on reality. I think that maybe after all of this time, I might be able to move forward—not on—but forward.

The lone car in the parking lot to my right catches my eye. I'm not sure why. Maybe it's because the car is parked near where Colton parked the Aston Martin on our first spontaneous outing—the most expensive beach date ever—but I look, my heart hoping what my mind knows is not possible. That it's him parking the car to come join me.

I turn to look just in time to see a figure walk up to the passenger side and lean over to talk to the driver through the open window.

Something about the person causes me to rise from the sand. I shield my eyes from the sun's glare and study his profile, suddenly feeling that something is off.

Without thinking, I start walking toward the car, my unease increasing with each step. The stranger straightens up and turns to face me for a second, the sun lighting his dark features and my feet falter, breath lost.

My dark angel standing in the light.

"Colton?" My voice is barely a whisper as my brain attempts to comprehend how it's possible that he's here. Here with me when I saw them load his unresponsive body on the stretcher, kissed his cold lips one last time before they laid his casket to rest. My heart thunders in my chest, its beat accelerating with each passing second as the hope laced with panic starts to escalate.

And although my voice is so soft, he tilts his head to the side at the sound of his name, his eyes filled with a quiet sadness, lock onto mine. He starts to raise a hand but is distracted momentarily when the passenger door is shoved open. He looks into the car and then back to me, resignation etching the magnificent lines of his face. He hesitantly raises his hand again but this time finishes the wave to me.

I bring my fingertips to my lips as the grief rolling off of him finally reaches across the distance and collides into me, knocks the breath clear out of my lungs. I feel his absolute despair instantly. It rips through my soul like lightning splitting the sky.

And in that instant I know.

"Colton!" I say his name again, but this time my desperate scream pierces through the quiet serenity of the beach. Seagulls fly at the sound but Colton slides into the passenger seat without a second glance and shuts the door.

The car slowly heads toward the parking lot's exit, and I break out into a full sprint. My lungs burn and legs ache but I'm not fast enough. I'm not going to get there in time and can't seem to make any progress no matter how fast I run. The car turns to the right, out of the lot onto the empty road, and is angled to head past me on its way south. The blue metallic paint shimmers from the sun's rays and what I see stops me dead in my tracks.

It feels like forever since I have seen him like this. All-American, wholesome with blue eyes and that easy smile I love all too much. But his eyes never break from their focus on the road ahead.

Max never even gives me so much as a second look.

Colton, on the other hand, stares straight at me. The combination of fear, panic, and resignation etched on his face. In the tears coursing down his cheeks, the apologies his eyes express, in his fists pounding frantically against the windows, in his words I can see him mouth but can't hear him plead. All of it twists my soul and wrings it dry.

"No!" I yell, every fiber of my being focused on how to help him escape, how to save him.

And then I see movement in the backseat and am knocked clear to my knees. The gravel biting into them is nothing compared to the pain searing into the black depths of my core. And although I'm hurting more than I ever thought imaginable, a part of me is in awe—lost in that unconditional love you never think is possible until you experience it for yourself.

Ringlets frame her cherubic face, bouncing with the car's movement. She smiles softly at Max, completely oblivious to the violent protests from Colton in the seat in front of her. She twists in her car seat and looks toward me, violet eyes a mirror reflection looking back at me. And then ever so subtly, her rosebud lips quirk up at one corner as childhood curiosity gets the best of her and she stares at me. Tiny fingertips rise above the windowsill and wiggle at me.

I have to remind myself to breathe. Have to force the thought into my head because she's just singlehandedly ripped me apart and pieced me back together. And yet the sight of her has left me raw and abraded with tomorrows that will never be.

That I can never get back.

That were never mine to keep.

And from my place on the ground, my soul clinging for something to hang onto before being swallowed into the darkened depths of despair, I yell at the top of my lungs the name of the only person that can still be saved.

"Colton! Stop! Colton! Fight damn it!" My voice falls hoarse with the last words, sobs overtaking and despair overwhelming me. I hang my head in my hands and allow myself to be dragged under and drowned, welcoming the devastating darkness for the second time in my life. "No!" I scream.

Invisible hands grab me and try to pull me away from him, but I struggle with every ounce I can muster against them so I can save Colton.

Save the man I love.

"Rylee!" The voice urges me to turn away from Colton. No way in hell am I walking away again.

Never.

"Rylee!" The insistence intensifies as my shoulders are shoved back and forth. I try to flail my arms but I'm being held tight.

I awake with a start, Beckett's aqua blue eyes staring intensely into mine. "It's just a dream, Rylee. Just a dream."

My heart is racing and I gulp in air but my body doesn't seem to accept it. I can't grab my next breath fast enough. I bring a trembling hand up and rub it over my face to gain my bearings. It was so real. So impossible, yet so real … unless … unless Colton is …

"Becks." His name is barely a whisper on my lips as the remnants of my dream gain momentum and I start to understand why Colton would be with Max and my daughter.

"What is it, Ry? You're white as a ghost."

The words strangle in my throat. I can't tell him what my mind is processing. I stutter trying to get the words out when we are interrupted.

"The family of Colton Donavan?"

Everyone in the waiting room stands and moves to congregate

near the entrance of the waiting room, where a short woman in scrubs stands untying her surgical mask. I stand too, fear driving me to push my way to the forefront with Becks clearing the path ahead of me. When we stop next to Colton's parents, he reaches his hand over and grips mine. It's the only indication that he's as scared as I am.

Her eyes take in the lot of us and she shakes her head with a forced smile. "No, I need to speak to his immediate family," she says. I can hear the fatigue in her voice and of course my mind starts racing faster.

Andy steps forward and clears his throat. "Yes, we're all here."

"I see that, but I'd like to update his immediate family in private as per hospital protocol, sir." Her tone is austere yet soothing, and all I want to do is shake her until she says "screw the rules" and gives me an update.

Andy shifts his eyes from her to glance over at all of us before he continues. "My wife, daughter, and I may be Colton's immediate family, but everyone else here? They're the reason he's alive right now … so in my eyes, they are family and deserve to hear the update at the same time we do, hospital protocol be damned."

A look of slight shock flickers across her features and in this moment I can see why all those years ago the police officers in the hospital didn't question Andy when he told them Colton was going home with him for the night.

She nods slowly at him, lips pursed. "My name is Dr. Biggeti and I teamed up in the operating room with Dr. Irons on your son's case." In my periphery I see most of the guys nod their heads, bodies leaning forward to make sure they hear everything. Dorothea steps up next to her husband, Quinlan on the opposite side, and grabs his hand like Becks is clutching mine. "Colton made it through surgery and is currently being moved to the ICU."

A collective gasp fills the room. My heart thunders at an accelerated pace and my head dizzies with the news. He's still alive. Still fighting. I'm scared and he's scarred but we're both still fighting.

Dr. Biggeti puts her hands up to quiet the murmuring among us. "Now there are still a lot of unknowns at this point. The bleeding and swelling were quite extensive and we had to remove a small section of Colton's skull to relieve the pressure on his brain. At this time, the swelling seems to be under control but I need to reiterate the words *at this time*. Anything can happen in these cases and the next twenty-four hours are extremely crucial in telling us which way Colton's body will decide to go." I feel Beckett sway next to me and I detangle our hands and wrap my arms around his waist, and take comfort in the fact we are all here, feeling the same way. That this time I'm not alone in watching the man I love struggle to survive. "And as much as I have hope that the outcome will be positive, I also need to prepare you for the fact that there may be possible peripheral damage that is unknown until he wakes up."

"Thank you." It's Dorothea who speaks as she steps forward and grabs a surprised Dr. Biggeti in a quick embrace before stepping back and dabbing the tears beneath her eyes. "When will we be able to see him?"

The doctor nods her head in compassion at Colton's parents. "Like I said, right now they are getting him situated and checking his vitals in the ICU. After a bit, you'll be able to see him." She looks over toward Andy. "And this time, I must follow hospital policy that only immediate family be allowed to visit with him."

He nods his head.

"Your son is very strong and is putting up one hell of a fight. It's obvious he has a strong will to live ... and every little bit helps."

"Thank you so very much." Andy exhales before grabbing Dorothea and Quinlan in a tight embrace. His hands fist at their backs and expresses just an iota of the angst mixed with relief vibrating beneath his surface.

As the doctor walks away her words hit me, and I close my eyes to focus on the positive. To focus on the fact that Colton is fighting like hell to come back to us. To come back to me.

All of us—crew and family—have been moved to a different waiting room since we were taking up all of the space in the emergency area. This one's on a different floor, closer to the ICU and to Colton. The room's a serene light blue, but I'm nowhere near calm. Colton is near. The thought alone has me hyperventilating. I'm not immediate family so I'm not going to get to see him.

And that alone makes every breath an effort.

Leaves every emotion raw, nerves bared as if my skin has been peeled back and exposed to a fire hose.

Each thought focused on how much I need to see him for my own slipping sanity.

I stand and face a wall of windows overlooking a courtyard below. The parking lot beyond is swarming with media trucks and camera crews all trying to get something more on the story than the station next to them. I watch them absently, the mass becoming one big blur. *You were a spark of solid color to me in a world that's always been one big mixed blur of it …*

I'm so lost in my thoughts that I jolt when someone places their hand on my shoulder. I turn my head and meet the grief-stricken eyes of Colton's mother. We stare at each other for a moment; no words are spoken but so much is exchanged.

She's just come from seeing Colton. I want to ask her how he is, what he looks like, if he's as bad as the images I have in my mind. I open my mouth to speak but close it because I can't find the words to express myself.

Dorothea's eyes well and her bottom lip trembles with unshed tears. "I just …" she starts to say and then drifts off, bringing her hand to her mouth and shaking her head. After a moment, she begins again. "I can't stand seeing him like that."

My throat feels like it's closing as I try to swallow. I reach my hand up to my shoulder and squeeze hers, the only solace I can even remotely offer. "He has to be okay …" The same words I've uttered over and over today that fix nothing, but I say them nonetheless.

"Yes," she says with a determined nod as she takes in the circus of the parking lot. "I haven't had nearly enough time with him. I missed the first eight years of his life, so I'm owed extra ones for not getting the chance to save him sooner. God can't be that cruel to rob him of what he deserves." She looks over toward me on her last words, and the quiet strength of this mother fighting for her son is unmistakable. "I won't allow it." And the commanding woman that had slipped momentarily is back in control.

"Mom …" The sob is hiccupped as Quinlan re-enters the waiting room. We both turn to face her as she walks toward us, all eyes in the room on her. I watch Dorothea's face shifts gears as she goes from fierce protector to maternal soother. She pulls Quinlan into her arms and kisses the top of her head, squeezing her own eyes shut tight as she whispers words of encouragement that she fears are lies.

I feel like a voyeur—wanting my own mother more than anything right now—when Dorothea looks up at me over the crown of Quinlan's head. Her voice is a hushed murmur but it stops my breath. "It's your turn now."

"But I'm not …" I don't know why I'm so shocked that she's giving me this opportunity. The rule follower in me bristles, but my traumatized soul stands at attention.

"Yes, you are," she says, a tight smile on her lips and sincerity flooding her eyes. "You're helping make him whole—the one thing I've never been able to do as a mother and that kills me, but at the same time the fact that he's found it in you …" She can't finish the sentence and tears well in her eyes, so she reaches out and squeezes my hand. "Go."

I squeeze it back and nod at her before I turn to go to the man

I can't live without, fear mixed with anticipation streaks through me like fireworks on a pitch black night.

Chapter Four

I STAND OUTSIDE OF THE intensive care unit and prepare myself. Fear and hope collide until one big ball of anxiety has my hands trembling as I turn the corner to stand at his doorway.

It takes me a moment to gain the courage to raise my eyes and take in the broken body of the man I love. The images in my head are worse—bloody, bruised, total carnage—but even those couldn't have prepared me for the sight of Colton. His body is whole and unbloodied, but he lies there so motionless and pale. His head is wrapped in white gauze and his eyelids are partially closed, the whites of his eyes showing somewhat from the swelling of his brain. He has tubes coming out of him every which way, and the monitors beep around him constantly. But it's not the sight of all of the medical equipment that breaks me—no—it's that the life and fire of the man I love is nonexistent.

I shuffle toward the bed, my eyes mapping every inch of him as if I've never seen him before, never felt him before. Never felt the thunder of his heart beating against my own chest. I reach out to touch him—needing to desperately—and when I hold his hand in mine, it's cold and unresponsive. Even the calluses I love—the ones that rasp deliciously over my bare skin—are not there.

The tears come. They fall in endless streams as I blindly sink down into the chair beside the bed. I grip Colton's hand with two of mine, my mouth pressed to our joined hands, my tears wetting his skin. I cry even harder when I realize the all too familiar Colton scent that feeds my addiction has been replaced by the antiseptic hospital smell. I didn't realize how much I needed that scent to be there. How much I needed that small, lingering piece of the man I love to remain when everything else has changed so drastically.

Incoherent words cross my lips and muffle against our entwined hands. "Please wake up, Colton. Please," I sob. "You can't leave me now. We have so much time we need to make up for, so many things that we still need to do. I need to cook you horrible dinners and you need to teach me how to surf. We need to watch the boys play little league and I need to be in the grandstands when you win a race." The thought of him getting back in a car makes my heart lodge in my throat, but I can't stop thinking of all the things we still have left to experience together. "We need to eat ice cream for breakfast and eat pancakes for dinner. We need to make love to each other on a lazy Sunday afternoon, and when you walk in the door, I'll push you up against it because we just can't get enough of each other. I haven't had my fill of you yet ..." My voice fades as I close my eyes and rest my forehead against our hands, Colton's name a repeated prayer on my lips.

"You know, I've never been as angry with him as I was last night." Beckett's voice jars me from my scattered focus.

I look up through blurred eyes to see him leaning against the doorjamb, arms crossed over his chest, and his eyes focused on his best friend. I know he's not expecting a response from me—and frankly, I'm hoarse from crying so I give him the only answer I can manage, an incoherent murmur before turning back to look at Colton.

"I've been pissed at him plenty of times, but last night took the cake." Becks breathes a long, frustrated sigh, and then I hear his feet shuffle across the floor. He sits down in the chair opposite me and hesitantly reaches out to squeeze Colton's free hand. He looks over toward his friend's impassive face before holding my gaze across the lifeless body of the man we love. "When I knew Colton was willing to let you walk away without telling you the truth or putting up a fight..." he shakes his head in disbelief as tears swim in his eyes "...I don't think I've ever been so pissed off or wanted to throw a punch at someone as much as I did when he told me to leave your room."

"Well, we were both being stubborn asses," I concede, wishing that we could be back in that hotel room—repeat the day—so that we just could stop fighting and I could wrap my arms around him a little tighter, a little longer. I wish I could rewind time so I could warn Colton of what was going to happen at the track. But I know it wouldn't matter. My reckless rebel thinks he's invincible and would have climbed into the car anyway.

I look back up at his face and he's anything but invincible now. The sob rises in my throat, and I try to hold it back but fail miserably.

"He's so used to thinking he's not worth any of the good fortune that's come his way. He's never given me specifics, but I know he thinks he doesn't deserve any better than what he was from, wherever he came from. He thinks he's not enough for you and—"

"He's everything," I gasp, the truth in my words resonating clear within my soul.

A ghost of a smile turns up the corners of Beckett's mouth despite the sadness in his eyes. "I know, Rylee." He pauses. "You're his lifeline."

I lift my eyes from Colton to meet his. "I don't know how that's going to help him now. I left him last night after you walked out of the room," I confess, staring again at our two hands intertwined, guilt consuming me. "After what he said to me, I kept thinking, *I can't be with him anymore under these circumstances.* I thought I could stick around—help him heal everything that's broken—but I couldn't stand around and be cheated on, so I left."

"You did the right thing. He needed a taste of his own medicine. He was being an ass and was using his fear to fuel his insecurity … but he went after you, Ry. That in itself tells me he knows how much he needs you."

"I know." My voice is almost a whisper and is drowned out by the incessant beep of the machines. "I'd gladly walk away from him again and never look back if it would prevent us from being here right now."

I say the words without any conviction because I know deep down that wherever Colton is, I would never be able to stay away from him.

We sit for a bit, each battling our own thoughts when Becks stands abruptly, his chair scraping across the floor and shattering the antiseptic silence in the room. "This is fucking bullshit. I can't sit and look at him like this." His voice is thick with emotion as he starts to walk out.

"He's going to pull through, Becks. He has to." My voice breaks on the last few words, betraying my confidence.

He stops and sniffles before turning around to look at me. "That fucker is stubborn in everything he does—everything—he better not disappoint me now." He shifts his attention to Colton and strides to the side of the bed, the grief turning into anger with each passing second. "It's always got to be about you, doesn't it, Wood? *Self-centered bastard*. When you wake the fuck up—and you will wake the fuck up because I'm not letting you go out like this—I'm going to kick your ass for making us worry."

He reaches his hand out and, in contradictory fashion to his gruff words, lays a hand on Colton's shoulder for a brief moment before turning and walking out of the room.

I'm left alone with the man I love, the weight of the unknown pressing down upon us but hope finally starting to bleed through the edges of the pain.

Chapter Five

COLTON

I CAN FEEL THE CAR—THE engine's rumbling in my chest that tells me I'm alive—before I even see it slingshot out of the backside of the turn. I focus on my hands. They're shaking, fucking trembling. I can't hold onto the wheel, to my thoughts, to anything at all. The wheel shudders beneath my goddamn fingers. Fingers that can't quite grip to control the chaos unraveling around me.

The confidence I own in a place that's always been my salvation is gone. Dust in the motherfucking wind.

What the hell is going on?

The sound of metal giving—fucking shredding—mixed with the squeal of rubber sliding across asphalt echoes all around me. Jameson's car slams into mine. And with the impact—the jolt of my body, the theft of my thoughts—my memories crash and collide like our cars do.

The thought of Rylee sucker punches me first.

The bright ray of light against my goddamn darkness. The sun shining through this crash-crazed haze of smoke. The one and only exception to my fucking rule. How can I hear her sobs through my headset and yet see her doubled over in shock from a distance? Something's messed up here. Like bat-shit crazy messed up.

But what? How?

And even though there's all this smoke, I can still see her face clear as day. Violet eyes giving me something I don't deserve—motherfucking trust. Begging me to let her in, to let her help heal the parts of me forever damaged from a past I'll never outrun—never escape—even when slamming head first into the damn wall.

I see my car rise above the smoke—above the goddamn fray of broken trust and useless hope—and I lose my breath and my chest feels like it's exploding, detonating like the shrapnel of memories embedding themselves so deep in my mind I can't quite place where they land. Even though I'm watching it, I can still feel it—the force of the spin, the strain on my muscles, the need to hold tight to the wheel. My future and past coming down all around me like a goddamn tornado as I roll out of control struggling to fight the fear and the pain I know is coming next.

That I can't ever escape.

Debris scatters … on the track and in my head.

Collateral damage for another poor fucking soul to deal with. I've had more than my share of it. I choke on the bile that threatens—the soul siphoning fear that stabs into my psyche—because even mid-flight, when I should be free from everything, *she's* still there. *He's still there.* Always a constant reminder.

Colty, when you don't listen, you get hurt. Now go be a good boy and wait for him. When you're naughty, naughty things happen, baby boy.

The crunch of metal, his masculine grunt.

The smell of destruction, his alcoholic stench.

My body banging into the protective cage around me, his meaty fingers trying to take me, own me, claim me.

Tell me you love me. Say it!

I love you. I love you. I love you. I love you.

I welcome the impact of the car because it knocks those words off my tongue. I can see it, feel it, hear it all at the same time as if I'm everywhere and nowhere all at once. In the car and outside of it. The resonating, unmistakable crunch of metal as I become weightless, momentarily free from the pain. Knowing that once I've spoken those *three words* only hurt can come.

The fucking poison will eat at me piece by piece until I'm the nothing I already know I am.

The goddamn fear will paralyze me—fucking consume me—dynamite exploding in a vacuum chamber.

My body slams forward but my shoulder harnesses strangle me motionless, like Rylee urging me to move forward. Like the memory of *him* holding me back—unforgiving arms trapping me as I fight against the blackness he fills me with. Against the words he forces me to say, forever fucking up their goddamn meaning.

The impact hits me full force—car against barrier, heart against chest, hope against demons—but all I see is Rylee stepping over the wall. All I can see is *him* coming at me while she's walking away.

"*Rylee?*" I call out to her. Help me. Save me. Redeem me. She doesn't turn, doesn't respond. All my hope is fucking lost.

... I'm broken ...

I watch the car—feel its movement encompassing me—slowly come to a stop, the damage unknown as the darkness consumes me.

... and so very bent ...

My final exhale of resistance—from him, for her—as the fight leaves me.

Spiderman. Batman. Superman. Ironman.

"We're losing him. He's crashing!

... I wonder if there's pain when you die ...

"Colton, come back. Fight goddammit!"

Chapter Six

MINUTES TURN INTO HOURS.

Hours turn into days.

Time slips away when we've lost too much of it as it is.

I refuse to leave Colton's bedside. Too many people have left him in his life, and I refuse to do it when it matters the most. So I ramble to him incessantly. I speak about nothing and everything, but it doesn't help. He never reacts, never moves ... and it kills me.

Visitors drift in and out of his room in sporadic bouts: his parents, Quinlan, and Becks. Updates are given in the waiting room where some of the crew and Tawny still gather daily. And I have no doubt that Becks is making sure Tawny keeps her distance from me and my more than fragile emotional state.

On the fifth day I can't take it anymore. I need to feel him against me. I need that physical connection with him. I carefully move all the wires to the side and cautiously crawl on the bed beside him, placing my head on his chest and my hand over his heart. The tears come now with the feel of his body against mine. I find comfort in the sound of his heartbeat, strong and steady beneath my ear, instead of the electronic beep of the monitor I've grown to rely on as a gauge of his momentary status.

I snuggle into him, wishing for the feel of his arm curling around me, and the rumble of his voice through his chest. Little bits of comfort that don't come.

We lie there for awhile and I'm fading off into the clutches of sleep when I startle awake. I swear it's Colton's voice that is pulling at me. Swear I hear the chant of superheroes, a tumultuous sigh on his lips. My heart races in my chest as I reacquaint myself with the foreign surroundings of his room. The only thing familiar is Colton next to me, and even that's a small comfort to the riot in my psyche because he's not the same either. His fingers twitch and he moans again, and even though it's not the words that awoke me, deep down I know he's calling to *them*. Asking for the help to pull him from this nightmare.

I don't know how to soothe him. I wish I could crawl inside of him and make him better, but I can't. So I do the only thing I can think of, I start singing softly, his dad's comments ringing in my ears. I thought I'd forgotten the words to the song I'd heard long ago, but they come to me easily after I struggle through the first few.

So in this cold and sterile environment, I attempt to use lyrics to bring warmth to Colton by singing the song of his childhood: *Puff the Magic Dragon*.

I don't even realize I've fallen asleep until I jolt awake when I hear the squeak of shoes on the floor and look up to meet the kind eyes of the charge nurse. I can see the reprimand about to roll off the tip of her tongue but the pleading look in my eyes stops her.

"Sweetie, you really shouldn't be up there with him. You risk the chance of pulling a lead out." Her voice is soft and she shakes her head when I meet her eyes. "But if you want to while I'm on shift, I promise not to tell." She gives me a wink, and I smile gratefully at her.

"Thank you. I just needed to …" My voice trails off because how do I put into words that I needed to connect with him somehow.

She reaches over and pats my arm in understanding. "I know, dear. And who's to say it won't help pull him from his current state? Just be careful, okay?" I nod in understanding before she leaves the room.

I'm left alone again in the darkness with the eerie glow from the machines illuminating the room. Still snuggled into his side, I angle my head up and press my lips to that favorite place of mine on the underside of his jaw. His scruff is almost a beard now, and I welcome the tickle of it against my nose and lips. I draw him in and just linger in the feel of him. The first tear slips out quietly and before I know it, the past few days come crashing down around me. I am lying holding on to the man I love—still afraid that I might lose him—overcome with every form of imaginable emotion.

And so I whisper the only thing I can to express the fear holding my soul hostage.

Spiderman. Batman. Superman. Ironman.

My tears subside over time, and I slowly succumb to the clutches of sleep again.

I awake disoriented, eyes blinking rapidly at the sunlight filtering in through the windows. Murmured voices fill my ears but the one that surprises me the most is vibrating beneath my ear.

Awareness jolts me when I realize the rumble is Colton's voice. In a split second my heart thunders, breath catches, and hope soars. My head dizzies as I sit up and look at the man I love, all others in the room forgotten.

"Hi." It's the only word I can manage as my eyes collide with his. Chills dance over my flesh and my hands tremble at the sight of him awake and alert and aware.

His eyes flicker over my shoulder before coming back to rest on mine. "Hi," he rasps as my elation soars. He angles his head slightly to observe me, and even though confusion flickers over his face, I don't care because he's alive and whole.

And he's come back to me.

I just sit there and stare at him for a moment, pulse racing and the shock of him awake robbing my words. "*Iron-Ironman ...*" I stutter, thinking that I need to go get the doctor. I don't want to move. I want to kiss him, hug him, never let him go again. He just looks at me as if he's lost and understandably because he's just woken up to a frantic mess and the only thing I say is the name of a superhero.

I start to shove off the bed but he reaches out and grabs my wrist. "What are you doing here?" His eyes search mine asking so many questions that I'm not sure that I can answer.

"I—I—you were in an accident," I stutter, trying to explain. Hoping the trepidation snaking up my spine and digging its claws into my neck are just from the overload of emotions over the past few days. "You crashed during the race. Your head ... you've been out for a week ..." My voice fades as I see his eyes narrow and his head angle to the side. I can see him trying to work through the memories in his head, so I give him the time to do that.

His eyes glance back over my shoulder again, and it's now that I remember there were voices in the room—more than one person—but something about the look on his face makes me afraid to look away. "Colton ..."

"You left me." His voice is broken and heart wrenching, filled with disbelief.

"No ..." I shake my head, grabbing onto his hand as fear starts to creep into my voice. "No. I came back. We figured it out. Woke up together." I can hear the panic escalating in my tone, can feel the pounding of my heart, the crashing descent of the hope I'd just gotten back. "*We raced together.*"

He shakes his head gently back and forth with a stuttering disbelief. "No, you didn't." He looks back over my shoulder as he pulls his hand from mine and holds out his now free hand to the person behind me. "You left. I chased you but couldn't find you. She found me in the elevator." The smile I'd been silently needing, wanting to reaffirm our connection, is given ... but not to me.

The air punches from my lungs, the blood drains from my face, and a coldness seeps into every fiber of my soul as the smile I love—the one he only reserves for me—is given to the person at my back.

"Colton couldn't remember everything, *doll.*" The voice assaults my ears and breaks my heart. "So I filled him in on all of the missing pieces," Tawny says as she comes into view, scrunching up her nose with a condescending smirk. "How you left and we reconnected." She works her tongue in her mouth as the victorious smile grows wider, eyes gleaming, message sent loud and clear.

I won.

You lose.

The bottom drops out of my world, blackness fading over my vision, and nothingness left to contend with.

Chapter Seven

I AWAKE WITH A START. My lungs are greedy for air and my mind reaches to cling to anything real through its groggy haze. The scream on my lips dies when I realize I'm in Colton's room, alone, with him beside me. My head is still on his chest and my arm still hooked around his waist.

I blow out a shaky breath as my adrenaline surges. It was a dream. *Holy shit, it was just a dream.* I tell myself over and over, trying to reassure myself with the constant beep of the monitors and the medicinal smell—things I have grown to hate but welcome right now as a way to convince myself that nothing has changed. Colton's still asleep and I'm still hoping for miracles.

Just ones that don't involve Tawny.

I sink back down into Colton, my nightmare a fringe on the edge of my consciousness that leaves me beyond unsettled and my body trembling with anxiety. I'm so lost in thought—in fear over both nightmares—that as the adrenaline fades, my eyes grow heavy. I'm so lost to the welcoming peace of sleep that when a hand smooths down my hair and stills on my back, I sink into the soothing feeling of it in my hazy, dreamlike state. I nestle closer, accepting the warmth offered and the serenity that comes with it.

And then it hits me. I snap my head up to meet Colton's. The sob that chokes in my throat is nothing compared to the tumble in my heart and awakening in my soul.

When our eyes meet I'm frozen, so many thoughts flitting through my mind, the most prevalent one is that he came back to me. Colton is awake and alive and back with me. Our eyes remain locked and I can see the confusion flicker through his at a lightning pace and the unknown warring within.

"Hi there," I offer on a shaky smile, and I'm not sure why a part of me is nervous. Colton licks his lips and closes his eyes momentarily which causes me to panic that he's been pulled back under. To my relief he reopens them with a squint and parts his mouth to speak, but nothing comes out.

"Shh-Shh," I tell him, reaching out and resting my finger on his lips. "There was an accident." His brow furrows as he tries to lift his hand but can't, as if it's a dead weight. He tries to angle his eyes up to figure out the thick bandages surrounding his head. "You had surgery." His eyes widen with trepidation and I mentally chastise myself for fumbling over my words and not being clearer. The monitor beside me beeps at an accelerated pace, the noise dominating the room. "You're okay now. You came back to me." I can see him struggle to comprehend, and I wait for something to spark in his eyes but there is nothing. "I'm going to get the nurse."

I reach out to pull myself off the bed and Colton's hand that's lying on the mattress clasps around my wrist. He shakes his head and winces with the movement. I immediately reach out to him and cradle his face with one hand, his skin paling and beads of sweat appearing on the bridge of his nose.

"Don't move, okay?" My voice breaks when I say it, as my eyes travel the lines of his face searching to see if he's hurt anything. *As if I would know if he had.*

He nods just barely and whispers in an almost absent voice, "Hurts."

"I know it does," I tell him as I reach across the bed and push the call button for the nurse as the hope deep within me settles into possibility. "Let me get a nurse to help with the pain, okay?"

"Ry …" His voice breaks again as the fear in it splinters in my heart. I do the only thing I know might reassure him. I lean forward and brush my lips to his cheek and just hold them there momentarily while I control the rush of emotions that hit me like a tsunami. Tears drip down my cheeks and onto his as the silent sobs surge through me. I hear a soft sigh and when I pull back, his eyes are closed and his mind lost to the blackness behind them once again.

"Is everything okay?" The nurse pulls me from my moment.

I look over at her, Colton's face still cradled in my hand and my tears staining his lips. "He woke up …" I can't say anything else because relief robs my words. "He woke up."

Colton comes in and out of consciousness a couple more times over the next few days. Small moments of lucidity among a haze of confusion. Each time he tries to talk without success, and each time we try to soothe—what we assume from his racing heartbeat—are his fears, in the few minutes we have with him.

I refuse to leave, so fearful that I'll miss any of these precious moments. Stolen minutes where I can pretend nothing has happened instead of the endless span of worry.

Dorothea has finally convinced me to take a few moments and head to the cafeteria. As much as I don't want to, I know I'm hogging her son and she probably wants a minute alone with him.

I pick at my food, my appetite nonexistent, and my jeans baggier than when I first arrived in Florida a week ago. Nothing sounds good—not even chocolate, my go to food for stress.

My cell rings and I scramble to get it, hoping it's Dorothea telling me Colton's awake again, but it isn't. My excitement abates. "Hey,

Had."

"Hi, sweetie. Any change?"

"No." I just sigh, wishing I had more to say. She's used to this by now and allows the silence between us.

"If he doesn't wake anytime soon, I'm ignoring you and flying my ass out there to be with you." Here comes Haddie and her no-nonsense attitude. There's no need for her to be here really. She'd just sit around and wait like the rest of us, and what good is that going to do?

"Just your ass?" I let the smile grace my lips even though it feels so foreign in this dismal place.

"Well, it is a fine one if I may say so myself ... like bounce quarters off of it and shit." She laughs. "And thank God! There's a bit of the girl I love shining through. You hanging in there?"

"It's all I can do," I sigh.

"So how is he? Has he come to again?"

"Yeah, last night."

"So that's what, five times in two days according to Becks? That's a good sign, right? From nothing to something?"

"I guess ... I don't know. He just seems so scared when he wakes up—his heart rate on the monitors sky rockets and he can't catch his breath—and it's so quick that we don't have time to explain that it's okay, that he's going to be okay."

"But he sees you all there, Ry. The fact you're all there has to tell him he has nothing to fear." I just give a non-committal murmur in response, hoping her words are true. Hoping that the sight of all of us soothes him rather than scares him into thinking he's on his deathbed. "What does Dr. Irons say?"

I breathe in deeply, afraid if I say it my fears might come true. "He says Colton seems stable. That the more often he wakes up the better ... but until he starts talking in full sentences, he won't know if any part of his brain is affected by everything."

"Okay," she says, drawing the word out so that it's almost a question. Asking me what I fear without asking. "What are you not telling me, Ry?"

I push the food around on my plate some, scattered thoughts focusing for bouts of time. I work a swallow in my throat before drawing in a shaky breath. "He says sometimes motor skills might be temporarily affected ..."

"And ..." Silence hangs as she waits for me to continue. "Put your fork down and talk to me. Tell me what you're really worried about. No bullshit. You're not a lesbian so stop beating around the damn bush."

Her attempt to make me laugh results in a soft chuckle turned audible exhale of breath. "He said that he might not remember much. Sometimes in cases like these, the patient may have temporary to permanent memory loss."

"And you're afraid he might not remember what happened, good and bad, right?" I don't respond, feeling stupid and validated in my fears at the same time. She takes my lack of a reply as my answer. "Well, he obviously remembers you because he didn't freak out when you were lying in bed with him the first time, right? He grabbed your hand, stroked your hair? That has to tell you he knows who you are."

"Yeah ... I've just found him though, Haddie, and the thought of losing him—even if it's in the figurative sense—scares the shit out of me."

"Quit thinking about something that hasn't happened yet. I understand why you're worried but, Ry, you've made it through some pretty random shit so far—Tawny the twatwaffle's antics included—so you need to back away from that ledge you're sitting on and wait to see what happens. You'll cross that bridge and all when it comes, okay?"

I'm about to respond when my phone beeps with an incoming text. I pull my phone from my ear and my heart rockets when I see Quinlan's text. *He's awake.*

"It's Colton. I gotta go."

Chapter Eight

COLTON

PAIN POUNDS LIKE A JACKHAMMER against my temple. My eyes burn like I'm waking up after downing a fifth of Jack. Bile rises and my stomach churns.

Churns as if I'm back in that room—dank mattress, crab weeds of trepidation blooming in me as I wait for *him* to arrive, for my mom to hand me over, *trade me* … but that's not fucking possible. Q's here, Beckett. Mom and Dad.

What the fuck is going on?

I squeeze my eyes shut and try to shake away the confusion, but all I get is more of the goddamn pain.

Pain.

Ache.

Pleasure.

Need.

Rylee.

Flashes of memories I can't quite grasp or understand blindside me before disappearing into the darkness holding them hostage.

But where is she?

I fight to gain more memories, pull them in and grasp them like a lifeline.

Did she finally figure out the fucking poison within me? Realize this pleasure isn't worth the pain I'll cause in the end?

"Mr. Donavan? I'm Dr. Irons. Can you hear me?"

Who the hell are you? Ice blue eyes stare at me.

"It may be tough to speak. We're getting you some water to help. Can you squeeze my hand if you understand me?"

Why do I need to squeeze his hand? And why is my hand not moving? How the hell am I going to drive in the race today if I can't grip the wheel?

My heart hammers like the pedal I should be dropping on the track right now.

But I'm here.

And last night I was there, with Ry. Woke up with her … and now she's gone.

… checkered flag time, baby …

It all zooms into focus at once. And then complete darkness. Checkered holes of black—polka dots of void—throughout the slide-show in my head. I can't connect the dots. I can't make sense of anything except that I'm confused as fuck.

All eyes in the room stare at me like I'm the side show at the goddamn circus. *And for his next act folks, he'll move his fingers.*

I try my left hand and it responds. Thank Christ for that.

My mind flashes back. Crunching metal, flashing sparks, engulfing smoke. Crashing, tumbling, free-falling, jolting.

… It looks like your superheroes came this time after all …

My mind tries to figure out what that means but comes up empty. Rylee's gone.

She doesn't love the broken in me after all.

I try to shake the bullshit lies from my head but groan as the pain hits me.

Max.

Me.

She left.

Can't do this again.

I can't believe I was selfish enough to even ask her to.

"Colton." The doc is talking again. "You were in a bad accident. You're lucky to be alive."

A bad accident? The flickering images in my head start to make more sense but gaps of time are still missing. I try to speak but my mouth's so dry all that comes out is a croak.

"You injured your head." He smiles at me but I'm wary.

Never look a gift horse in the mouth.

He may have given me life again, but the fucking reason for living isn't here. She's smart enough to leave because I just can't give her what she needs: stability, a life without racing, the promise of forever.

"The nurse is bringing you some water to wet your throat." He notes something on his tablet. "I know this might be scary for you, son, but you're going to be okay. The tough part's over. Now we need to get you on the road to recovery."

The road to recovery? Thanks, Captain Obvious—more like the speedway to Hell.

Faces fill my immediate space. Mom kissing my cheek, tears coursing down her face. Dad hiding his emotion but the look in his eyes tells me he's a goddamn wreck. Quin beside herself. Becks muttering something about being a selfish bastard.

This must be pretty fucking serious.

And yet I still feel numb. Empty. Incomplete.

Rylee.

After a few moments they slowly back away at my Mom's insistence to give me space, to let me breathe.

And the air I've just gotten back is robbed again.

I turn to look at the vague blur I notice in my periphery, and there she stands.

Curls piled on top of her head, face without makeup, hollow, tear-stained cheeks, eyes welled with tears, perfect lips in a startled *O*

64

standing in the doorway. She looks like she's been through Hell, but she's the most beautiful thing I've ever seen.

Call me a pussy, but I swear to God she's the only air my body can breathe. Fuck if she's not everything I need and nothing that I deserve.

Her hands are fiddling with her cell phone, my lucky shirt hanging off her shoulders, and I can see the trepidation in her eyes as they flit around everywhere but at me.

Breathe, Donavan. Fucking breathe. She didn't leave. She's still here. The neutralizer to the acid that eats my soul.

Her eyes finally find and lock onto mine. All I see is my future, my salvation, my singular chance at redemption. But her eyes? Fuck, they flicker with such conflicting emotions: relief, optimism, anxiety, fear, and so many more unknown.

And it's the unknown I focus on.

The unspoken words telling me all of this is tearing her apart. That it's not fair for me to put her through this again. But racing is my life. Something I need as much as I need the air that I breathe—ironic considering she's my fucking air—but it's the only way I can survive and outrun the demons that chase me. The black ooze that seeps in every crack of my soul making sure it can never be eradicated. I can't be selfish and ask her to stand by me when all I want is to be the most self-centered bastard on the face of the earth.

Urge her to go but beg her to stay.

But how can I let her go when she owns every single part of me?

I'll gladly suffocate so that she can breathe freely. Without worry. Without the constant fucking fear.

Be selfless for the first time ever when all I've been my entire life is self-serving.

I should have told her—got over the fear that consumes my soul—but I couldn't … and now she doesn't know.

… I Spiderman you …

Words scream through my head but choke in my throat. The words I don't know if I'll ever be healed enough to say.

She robbed me of that all those years ago.

And now I'll pay for it.

By letting my one fucking chance go.

Then I hear the sob wrench from her throat. Hear the disbelief and torment in that singular sound as her shoulders shake and her posture sags.

And I know what I want and what is best for her are two completely different things.

Chapter Nine

OUT OF NOWHERE THE SOB tears from my throat at the sight of him, lucid and groggily alert. My damaged man that is the most beautiful sight I've ever seen.

My heart tumbles even further if that's even possible. And we just stare as the noise and excitement in the room abates, everyone taking a step back and silently watching our exchange.

Yet my feet are frozen in place as I try and read the emotions racing rapid-fire through Colton's eyes. He seems apologetic and maybe unsettled, but there's also an underlying emotion I can't place that has trepidation eating at the corners of my mind.

A nurse whisks past me, brushing my shoulder and breaking Colton's hold on me. She brings the straw from a cup of water to his mouth and he sips eagerly until it's gone.

"Well, you're a thirsty one, aren't you?" she teases before adding, "I'll go get you some more but let's make sure this stays down before we waterlog you, okay?"

I try to quiet my hiccupping draws of breath but can't seem to calm my anxiety. I feel Quinlan's arm go around my shoulder as she sniffles herself, but I don't even acknowledge her. I can't bear for my eyes to focus on anything but the tear–blurred vision in front of me.

The nurse reaches over and takes a chart from Dr. Irons and leaves. I haven't moved yet. I can't seem to. I just stare at Colton as Dr.

Irons examines him: tracking his eyes, testing his reflexes, feeling the strength in his grip as he squeezes. I notice he asks Colton to repeat the grip test for his right hand a couple of times, and I can see panic flicker over Colton's features. I can't drag my eyes away. I trace over every inch of him, so very afraid I'll miss something—anything—about these first few moments.

"Well, all seems quite well," Dr. Irons says eventually after he examines him some more. "How are you feeling, Colton?"

I watch his throat work a swallow and his eyes close with a wince before opening them again. I take a step forward, wanting to help take the pain away. He glances around at everyone in the room while he finds his voice. "My head. Hurts," he rasps. "Hand?" He looks down to his right hand and then back up, confusion apparent in his eyes. "Happened? How long?"

Dr. Irons sits down on the edge of the bed next to him and begins to explain about the crash, the operation, and the amount of time he has been in a coma. "As for your hand, that could be a result of some residual swelling still in your brain. We'll just have to watch it and see how it progresses over time." Colton nods at him, concentration etched on his face. "Can you tell me the last thing that you remember?"

I suck in a breath as Colton blows one out. He swallows again and licks his lips. "I remember … knocking four times." His voice comes out, his vocal chords scraping over gravel.

"What else?" Andy asks.

Colton looks over at his dad and subtly nods his head at him before squeezing his eyes shut in concentration. "It's like snippets in my head. Certain things are clear," he rasps before swallowing and then opens his eyes to look at Dr. Irons. "Others … they're vague. Like I can feel them there but can't remember them."

"That's normal. Sometimes—"

"Fireworks on pit row," he cuts the doctor off. "Waking up *overdressed*." Colton's eyes lift and find mine with the words that let me know he remembers me, remembers my memorable pre-race wake-up call. A slight smile curls up one corner of his mouth looking so out of place against the pallid tone of his usually bronze skin.

And if he didn't own my heart already—if he hadn't tattooed every single inch of it with his unmistakable stamp—he just did.

I can't help the laugh that bubbles up and spills over. I can't stop my feet from moving and stepping up to the edge of the bed as his words fade and his eyes track my movement. My grin widens, my tears fall faster, and my heart swells as I feel relief for the first time in days. I reach out and squeeze his hand resting on the mattress beside him.

"Hi." It sounds stupid, but it's the first and only word I can manage, my throat clogged with emotion.

"Hi," he whispers, that lopsided grin I love ghosting his mouth.

We just stare at each other for a beat, eyes saying so much and yet lips speaking nothing. I lace my fingers with his and I see the alarm trigger in his eyes again when he tries to respond but his hand doesn't.

"It's okay," I soothe, unable to resist. I reach my other hand out and cup the side of his face, welcoming the feeling of the muscle in his jaw ticking beneath my palm. "You've gotta give it some time to heal."

Emotions dance at a lightning pace in the green of his eyes as he tries to comprehend everything. And in this moment the ache in my chest transforms from the fear of the unknown to sympathy over watching the man I love struggle with the knowledge that his usually virile, responsive body is anything but.

"Rylee's right," Dr. Irons says, breaking the connection between us. "You need to give it some time. What else do you remember, Colton? You woke up underdressed and knocked four times," he prompts, his face masking the mystification he must feel over not understanding the meaning behind these statements. "Then what?"

"No," Colton says, wincing when he shakes his head instinctively. "First knocking and then waking up."

My eyes snap up to Beckett's because of all people he'll understand that this is not the order in which the events happened. Dr. Irons notes the startled look on my face and shakes his head for me to remain quiet.

"Not a problem. What else do you remember about the day regardless of the order?" Colton gives him a strange look and the doctor continues. "Sometimes when your brain has been traumatized like yours has, memories have a way of shifting and changing. For some, the sequence of events may be off but they'll still be there. For others there are some memories that are completely clear and others that are lost. I have some patients who remember the day of their trauma perfectly fine but have a void of time during other times or events that have happened. Every patient is unique."

"For how long do these voids usually last?" Andy speaks up from the side of the bed.

"Well, sometimes for a little while and sometimes forever ... but the good thing is that Colton seems to have memories of the day of the crash. So it would seem that a small chunk of time has been lost for him. As days pass, he may realize he doesn't remember other things ... because really, until he is reminded of something, he doesn't even know he's missing it." Dr. Irons looks around the room at all of us and shrugs. "At this time it wouldn't seem far off to reason that you'll regain all of it, Colton, but I advise caution because the brain is a tricky thing sometimes. In fact—"

"The national anthem," Colton says, relief flooding his voice at reclaiming one more memory from the darkness within. I smile at him in encouragement as he clears his throat. "I ... I can't ..." Frustration emanates off of him in waves as he tries to remember. "What happened?" He blows out a breath and looks around at everyone in the room before scrubbing his left hand over his face. "You were all there. What else happened?"

"Don't force it, sweetie." It's Dorothea speaking. "Right, Dr. Irons?"

We all look over at Dr. Irons, who nods his head in agreement, but when we look back at Colton, he's fallen asleep.

We all breathe in a collective gasp. All fearing he's slipped back into a coma. All our minds racing into overdrive. Dr. Irons puts the brakes on our panic when he says, "This is normal. He's going to be exhausted the first couple of times he wakes up."

Shoulders relax, sighs are exhaled, and relief is restored, but our concern never completely abates.

"We know he seems to be—that his brain seems to be—functioning well so far," Quinlan says as she steps up to the bed. "What can we expect now?"

Dr. Irons watches Colton for a beat before he continues, meeting all of our eyes. "Well, each person is different but I can tell you that the longer it takes Colton to remember, the more frustrated he may become. Sometimes in patients their disposition changes—sometimes they have a temper or are more mellow—and sometimes it doesn't at all. At this point it's still a waiting game to see how all of this has affected him long term."

"Should those of us that were there fill in the blanks for him of what he can't remember?" Becks asks.

"Of course you can," he says, "but I can't guarantee how he'll respond to it."

I resume my seat bedside as Dorothea comes over to kiss me goodbye on the cheek before leaning over to press her lips to Colton's forehead. "We're just heading to the hotel to get some rest. We'll be back in the morning. Don't you dare give up." She steps back and stares at him for a beat more before smiling softly at me and leaving to join Andy and Quinlan in the hall.

I sigh out loud as Beckett gathers the remaining trash from our late night dinner we'd had while impatiently waiting for Colton to wake. I glance over from my book that I'm really not paying attention to and watch Becks' methodical movements. I can see the toll the past week has taken on him in the bruises beneath his eyes and the scruff on his usually clean-shaven face. He seems lost.

"How you doing?" I ask the question softly, but I know he can hear me because his body stops momentarily before he puts the last bit in the trash can and shoves it down.

He turns and leans his hip against a counter behind him and just shrugs as our eyes meet. "You know," he drawls out in his slow, reso-nating tone that I've come to love. "In the sixteen years we've known each other, this is the longest we've ever gone without talking." He shrugs again and stares out the window for a moment at the media trucks in the parking lot. "He may be a demanding smart-ass, but I miss him. Call me a pussy, but I kinda like the guy."

I can't help the smile that spreads on my lips. "Me too," I murmur. "Me too."

Becks walks over to me and presses a kiss to the top of my head. "I'm going to head back to the hotel. I've gotta take a shower, check in with my brother, and then I'll be back, okay?"

A growing adoration for Becks blooms within—the ever true best friend. "Why don't you stay there tonight and get a good night's sleep? In a real bed instead of the crappy chairs in the waiting room."

He chuckles derisively and shakes his head at me. "Pot calling the kettle black, huh?"

"I know, but I just can't ... and besides, I've been sleeping in these crappy chairs in here." I pat the seat of the one I'm sitting on. "At least this has more padding than those out there." I angle my head and watch him mull it over. "I promise to call if he wakes up."

He exhales loudly and gives me a reluctant look. "Okay ... but you'll call?"

"Of course."

I watch Becks leave and welcome the unique silence of the hospital room. I sit and watch Colton, feeling truly blessed indeed that he's here and whole in front of me—that he didn't forget me—when it could be so much worse. I send a silent prayer up as time passes, knowing I have to start following through with the various barters I made to the great beyond to get Colton to come back to me.

I field a couple of texts from Haddie, check in on the boys and see how Ricky's math test went today, before texting Becks good night and telling him Colton's still out.

The early morning hours approach and I can't resist anymore. I slip off my shoes, pull the clip out of my hair, and position myself in the only place in the world I want to be.

At Colton's side.

Chapter Ten

THE MORNING LIGHT BURNS THROUGH my closed eyelids as I try to rouse myself from the deepest sleep I've had in over six days. Instead I just burrow in deeper to the warmth beside me. I feel fingers brush across my cheek and I'm instantly alert, my body jolting with awareness.

"Morning." His voice is a whispered murmur against the top of my head. My heart floods with an array of emotions but what I feel more than anything is complete.

Whole again.

I start to move so I can look into his eyes. "No doctors yet. I just need this. Need you. No one else, okay?" he asks.

Seriously? *Is the sky blue?* If I could, I'd whisk him out of this sterile prison and keep him all to myself for a while. Forever or more if he'd let me. But rather than letting the flippant comment roll off my tongue, I just make a satisfied moan and tighten my arms around him. I close my eyes and just absorb everything about this moment. I so desperately wish we were somewhere else, anywhere else, so I could lie with him skin to skin, connect with him in that indescribable way. Feel like I am doing something to help heal his broken memory and damaged soul.

We lie there in silence, my hand over his heart and the fingers of his left hand lazily drawing lines up and down my forearm. There are so many questions I want to ask. So many things that run through my head, but the only one that I manage to say is, "How are you feeling?"

The momentary pause in his movement is so subtle I almost don't catch it, but I do. And it's enough to tell me that something's wrong besides the obvious.

"This is nice." It's all he says and that further solidifies my hunch. I give him a bit of time to gather his thoughts and work out what he wants to say because after the past few weeks, I've learned so many things, least of which is my inability to listen when it matters the most.

And right now it matters.

So I sit in silence as my mind wars with the possibilities.

"I've been awake for a few hours," he starts. "Listening to you breathe. Trying to make my right hand fucking work. Trying to wrap my head around what happened. What I can't remember. It's there. I can sense it but I can't make it come to the forefront ..." he trails off.

"What do you remember?" I ask.

I desperately want to turn, to look into his eyes and read the fear and frustration that is most likely marring them, but I don't. I give him the space to admit that he's not one hundred percent. To balance that inherent male need to be as strong as possible, to show no weakness.

"That's just it," he sighs. "I remember bits and pieces. Nothing flows though, except you were there in most of them. Can you tell me what happened? How the day went so I can try to fill in what's missing?"

"Mmm-hmm." I nod my head gently, smiling at the memory of how our morning started.

"I remember waking up to the best sight ever—you naked, on top of me." He sighs in appreciation that causes parts within me that have been ignored over the past week to stir to life. I don't even fight the smile that spreads across my lips when I feel his growing arousal beneath the sheet next to me. Glad I'm not the only one affected by the memory.

"Becks came in without knocking and I was pissed at him for that. He left and I do believe your jeans were on the floor and your back was up against the wall in a matter of seconds after the door was shut." We fall silent for a moment, that undeniable charge crackling between us. "Sweet Christ what I wouldn't give to be doing that right now."

I start laughing and this time when I shift myself to sit up and look at him, he allows me. I turn to face him and can't help the chills that blanket my skin when I lock eyes with his. "Now I don't think Dr. Irons would approve of that," I tease, silently sighing with relief that we feel like we are right back where we left off before the accident. Playful, needing, and each other's complement. I can't stop my hand from reaching out and lingering on his cheek. I hate the thought of not being in contact with him.

"Well," he says, "I'll make sure that's the first thing I ask Dr. Irons when I see him."

"The first thing?" I ask and swallow around my heart that's just somersaulted into my throat when he turns his face and presses a kiss into the palm of my hand. The simple action knotting the bow on the ribbon already tied around my heart.

"A man has to have his priorities." He smirks. "If one head's fucked up, at least the other one can be used to its *maximum potential*." He starts to laugh and winces, bringing his left hand up to hold his head.

Alarm shoots through me and I immediately reach out to push the call button, but his hand reaches out and stops me. And it takes a second for me to register that it's his right hand he's just used. I think Colton realizes it at the same time.

He works a swallow down his throat, his eyes shifting to watch his hand as he releases my arm. I follow his gaze to see his fingers tremor violently as he unsuccessfully tries to make a fist. I notice a sheen of sweat appear on his forehead below the bandage as he wills his fingers to tighten. When I can't bear to watch him struggle any more, I reach out and grab his hand in mine and start massaging it, willing it to move myself.

"It's a start," I reassure him. "Baby steps, okay?" All I want to do is wrap him in my arms and take away all of his pain and frustration, but he seems so fragile that I fear touching him, despite how much it would lessen the lingering unease that tiptoes in my head. My usual optimism has been put through the ringer these past few weeks, and I just can't seem to shake the feeling that this isn't the worst of it. That something else is lurking on the horizon waiting to knock us down again.

"What else do you remember?" I prompt, wanting to get his mind off of his hand.

He gives me his recollections of the day, little pieces are missing here and there. The details aren't too major but I do notice that the closer he gets to the start of the race, the bigger the voids are. And each piece of the puzzle seems to get harder and harder to recall, as if he has to grab each memory and physically pull it from its vault.

Giving him a moment to rest, I return from the in-suite bathroom to put away the mouthwash he'd requested. I find Colton looking out the window, shaking his head at the media circus below. "I remember being in the trailer. The knock on the door." His eyes angle over to me, salacious thoughts dancing within his glints of green as I return to my seat on the bed beside him. "A *certain* checkered flag I never got to claim." He purses his lips and just stares at me.

And resistance is futile.

It always is when it comes to my willpower and Colton.

I lean in, doing what I've wanted to do desperately. Giving into the need to feel that connection with him—to feed my one and only addiction—and brush my lips against his. I know it's ridiculous that I'm nervous about hurting him. That somehow the lascivious thoughts behind our innocent brush of our lips are going to cause pain to his healing head.

But the minute our lips touch—the minute the soft sigh escapes his mouth and weaves its way into my soul—I find it hard to think clearly. I withdraw a fraction, needing to make sure he's okay when all I want to do is devour the apple tempting me.

But I don't have to because Colton hands it to me on a silver platter when he brings his left hand to the nape of my neck and draws my mouth back down to his again. Lips part, tongues meld, and recognition renews as we sink into each other in a reverent kiss. We're in no hurry to do anything other than enjoy our irrefutable connection. The annoying beep of the monitors is overtaken by the soft sighs and satisfied murmurs signaling the affection between us.

I am so lost in him, to him—when I feared I might never taste him again—all I can think about now is how will I ever get enough of him?

I feel the tightening of his lips as he grimaces in pain and guilt immediately lances through me. I'm pushing him too hard, too fast to soothe my own selfish need for reassurance. I try to pull away but his hand holds my head firm as he rests his forehead against mine, noses touching, breaths feathering over each other's lips.

"Just give me a sec," he murmurs against my lips. I just nod my head slightly against his because I'll give him a lifetime if he asks.

"These headaches come on so quick it feels like a sledgehammer hits me," he says after a moment.

Concern douses the flames of lust instantly. "Let me get the doctor."

"No," he says, pounding his left hand against the bed making the rails shake. "This place brings me back to being eight." And the argument that was about to roll off the tip of my tongue dies. "Everyone looking at me with worried eyes and no one giving me answers ... except this time I'm the one who can't give answers."

He laughs softly and I can feel his body stiffen again with the pain. "Colton ..."

"Uh-uh. Not yet," he says again, stubbornly, as he rubs his thumb back and forth across the bare nape of my neck trying to soothe me when it should be the other way around. "I remember my interview with ESPN. Eating my Snickers bar." He gets a rather odd look on his face and averts his eyes momentarily. "Kissing you on pit row and then nothing for a bit," he says, trying to distract me from wanting to get the doctor.

"The drivers' meeting." I fill in. "Becks was with you then."

"Why would I remember eating a candy bar but not the meeting?"

And I draw the connection in my own mind with the missing information that Andy had filled in. Because the traditional good luck Snickers bar is tied to his past—the first chance encounter he had with hope in his life. "I don't know. I'm sure it will all come back to you. I don't think—"

"You were next to me during the anthem. The song ended ..." His voice fades as he tries to recall the next events, while mine catches in my throat. "I watched Davis help you over the wall, wanting to make sure you were safe while Becks started last minute checks ... and I remember feeling the weirdest sense of being *at peace* as I sat at the start/finish line but I'm not sure why ... and then nothing until waking up."

And the lingering tiptoe of unease that I'd felt earlier turns into a full-on stampede.

My heart plummets. My breath hitches. *He doesn't remember.* He doesn't remember telling me the phrase that's glued the broken pieces of me together. It takes every ounce of strength I have to not let the unexpected slap to my soul show in the stiffening of my body.

I didn't realize how much I needed to hear him say those words again—especially after thinking I'd lost him. How knowing he remembered that defining moment between us would mend together the last fissures in my healing heart.

"Do you?" His voice breaks through my scattered thoughts as he kisses the tip of my nose before guiding my head back so he can look into my eyes.

I try to mask the emotions that I'm sure are swimming there.

"Do I what?" I ask, forcing a swallow down my throat over the lie that clogs it.

He angles his head as he looks at me and I wonder if he knows I'm holding something back. "Do you know why I felt so *happy* at the start of the race?"

I lick my lips and mentally remind myself to not worry my bottom lip between my teeth or else he'll know I'm lying. "Uh-uh," I manage as my heart deflates. I just can't tell him. I can't force him to feel words he doesn't remember or make him feel obligated to repeat words that make him recall the horrors of his childhood.

... What you said to me—those three words—they turn me into someone I won't ever let myself be again. It triggers things—memories, demons, so fucking much ...

His words scrape through my mind and score a mark that only he will ever be able to heal. And I know as much as I want to, as much as it hurts me to suppress my need to hear it, I can't tell him.

I force a diminutive smile on my lips and meet his eyes. "I'm sure you were just excited about the start of the season and thinking that if your practice runs were any indication, you were going to be claiming the checkered flag." The lie rolls off of my tongue, and for a minute I worry he's not going to believe it. After a beat one corner of his mouth lifts up and I know he hasn't noticed.

"I'm sure there was more than one checkered flag I was focused on claiming."

I shake my head at him, the smile on my lips beginning to tremble.

Colton's face transforms instantly from amusement to concern at the unexpected change in my demeanor. "What is it?" he asks, bringing his hand up to cradle the side of my face. I can't speak just yet because I'm too busy preventing the dam from breaking. "I'm okay, Ry. I'm going to be okay," he whispers reassurances to me as he pulls me into him and wraps his arms around me.

And the dam breaks.

Because kissing Colton is one thing, but being encircled in the all-encompassing warmth of his arms makes me feel that I'm in the safest place in the entire world. And when all is said and done, the physical side to our relationship is earth shattering and a necessity no doubt, but at the same time this feeling—muscular arms wrapped around me, his heated breath murmuring reassurances into the crown of my head, his heart beating strong and steady against mine—is by far the one that will carry me through the tough times. The times like right now. When I want him so much—in so many ways—that I never realized were possible. That never even flickered on my radar before.

I'm crying for so many reasons that they start to mix and mingle and slowly fade with each tear that makes the all too familiar tracks down my cheeks. I'm crying because Colton doesn't remember. Because he's alive and whole and his arms are wrapped tight around me. I'm crying because I never got the chance to experience this with Max and he deserved it. I'm crying because I hate the hospital, what it represents, and how it affects and changes the lives of everyone inside for the good and for the bad.

And when the tears stop—when my catharsis is actually over and all of the emotions I've kept pent up over the past week abate—I realize what matters most is this, right here, right now.

We can get through this. *We can find us again.* A part of me worries deep down that he'll never remember that moment so poignant in my mind, but at the same time we have so many more moments ahead of us, so many ready for us to make together, that I can't feel sorry for myself any longer.

My breath hitches again and all I can do is hold on a little tighter to him, hold on a little longer. "I was so worried," is all I can say. "So scared."

"Spiderman. Batman. Superman. Ironman," he whispers in what seems almost a reflex.

"I know." I nod and pull back from him so I can look him in the eyes as I wipe away the tears from my cheeks. "I called to them to help you."

"I'm sorry that you ever had to." He says the words with such honesty that all I can do is stare into his eyes and see the truth within them. That his apology knows how truly scared I was.

I lean in and press my lips gently to his one more time, unable to resist. Wanting him to feel the sense of relief finally settling in my soul. Wanting to prove to him that I can be the strong one while he heals. That it's okay for him to let me.

"Well lookie here. Sleeping Beauty finally woke his ugly ass up."

We break from our kiss at the sound of Beckett's voice, heat flooding my cheeks. "I was just going to call you."

"Really? Is that what you were doing?" he teases as he approaches the bed. "Kiss a lot of frogs? Because it looks to me like the comatose prince here has you under his spell."

I can't hold back the laugh that bubbles up. "You're right. I'm not sorry at all." I reach out and squeeze the hand he offers me. "But I was going to call you next."

"No worries. I know you would have." He turns and looks at Colton, his smile the brightest I've seen since race day. "Aren't you a sight for sore eyes. Welcome to the land of the living, man." And I know he sounds tough, but I catch the break in his voice and the water beading at the corners of his eyes when he focuses on Colton. He reaches out and cuffs his shoulder. "Shit. That freakish-looking shaved patch on your head might just knock you back down to the realm of good looking people. How's it feel leaving the land of I'm-a-fucking-God?"

"Fuck off. This coming from the land of I'm-a-fucking-comedi-an?"

Beckett barks out a laugh with a shake of his head. "At least in my land we don't have to modify door casings to allow overinflated egos to walk through."

"This is the kind of welcome back to the world I get? I feel the love, dude. I think I prefer the drugs they're giving me to hold me under rather than wake up and listen to this shit." Colton squeezes my hand and his eyes dart over to mine before returning back to Beckett.

"Really? Because I may not have just awoken from a coma, but I assure you that the fuzzy feeling those drugs give you is nothing compared to being awake and the feeling of a warm, wet—"

"Whoa!" I hold my hands up and scoot off the bed, not wanting to hear where the rest of this conversation is going. The faint smell of last night's dinner in the trash gives me all the excuse I need to give them a moment alone. "That's enough for me, boys. I'm going to head down, stretch my legs, and take this trash out."

"Oh, Ry! C'mon ..." Becks says, holding his hands out to the side of him. "I was going to say bath. A warm, wet bath." He laughs loudly and then I hear Colton's laugh and I feel like the world that had been shifted off its axis has just been righted somewhat.

"Yeah," I chide as I pull the liner from the trash can. "I know I always use the adjectives warm and wet when referring to a bath." I shake my head and catch Colton's gaze for a beat. "Be back in a couple of minutes."

Chapter Eleven

MY HEART FEELS SO MUCH lighter as I walk down the corridor back toward Colton's room. I've texted his parents and Quinlan about him being awake again, and I'm sure they'll be here momentarily. I head to the end of the hall, where the staff of the hospital has so graciously placed Colton's room. His room is more private than most of the others so he can stay out of the sight of other hospital visitors. And there's less chance of the media getting a coveted picture of him.

I'm just about to enter his room when I realize he might want some water. I turn around, not paying attention, and almost run head on into the one person I have no desire to see.

Ever.

At all.

Tawny.

We both startle when we see each other. And of course I'm looking ragged from intermittent sleep and days' old clothes, while she is looking perfectly polished and camera ready. And I have to give her credit, she's kept her distance since Becks gave her the dressing down in the waiting room. But when she offers me up a consolatory smile, I don't care that it's not meant in her usual catty way, because all of the emotions I've pent up over the past few days erupt.

"What are you doing here?" I spit out between gritted teeth. If you could make revulsion a sound, my voice would definitely be laced with it right now. My fingernails dig into my palms, my hands fist, and every muscle in my body is vibrating with indignation.

It takes a minute for the shock to fade from her face, but when it does, I recognize the mask of superiority slip in its place.

"Colton's awake." She shrugs, a smirk ghosting over her pink painted lips. "He wants to speak with me privately," she says as she juts her chin out in case I didn't already know her disdain for me.

"Anything that's Colton's business, is my business."

"Keep dreaming, doll."

"Wipe the smug look off your face, Tawny."

"Are we feeling a little guilty for fucking with Colton's head the night before a race. Everyone knows you were playing your little games with him. That you made him tired. That you—"

The air whooshes out of her when my hands grip her arms and shove her up against the wall, fury sheathed in calm. "Let me make something perfectly clear to you, Tawny. I'm only going to say it once, but it's best you listen, understood?"

I watch her swallow, and her breath comes out in a shaky shudder as she nods. Her eyes flicker around the hallway but there is no one around to come to her rescue.

I lean in closer, fire in my veins and ice in my voice. "You are the reason that Colton is here. Not me. You. There's a special place in hell for women like you—women who fuck with other women's men—and if you keep your shit up, rest assured one of those spots is going to have your name written all over it." I squeeze her arms a little harder, a silent warning that I'm just getting warmed up.

"Here's how this is going to play out, just in case you haven't gotten that new watch and are still living in the past. Colton's no longer on the market. He's mine and I'm his. Is that clear?" I don't care that she doesn't respond because I'm on a roll and nothing's going to stop me. I see her eyes widen and I continue. "Second, if you ever try to insinuate or imply to anyone that there is anything more between you and Colton than a business relationship with family ties, you're going to have to deal with me … and I guarantee that it's not going to be pretty. You haven't seen anything yet, *doll*. I protect what's mine without a second thought to collateral damage." She tries to shrug her shoulders out of my grip, and that just causes me to lean in closer and squeeze a little tighter. "You will treat me with respect and keep your gaggle of whoring friends away as well."

Despite my hands holding her hostage, she regains some of her composure and responds. "Or what?"

I continue on as if she never speaks. "You will keep your relationship with Colton completely professional and will keep your tits and other *assets* out of his face. Is that clear enough or do I need to spell it out for you?"

I loosen my grip, message delivered, although I feel no better for it because Colton is still in the bed on the other side of the wall. Tawny eyes me up and down. "Oh I think you've made it crystal clear … too bad you don't get that Colton needs me in his life."

In a heartbeat I slam her back up against the wall, this time my forearm pushes against her chest and my face is within inches of hers. "Your expiration date was years ago, *sweetie*. I am all he needs. And if you attempt to show him otherwise, that very prestigious job of yours might just go bye-bye … so I'd definitely think twice before opening your mouth again." I start to walk away but turn back and glare at her, her eyes reflecting the anger in mine. "Oh, and, Tawny? Colton will not know about this conversation. That way you can keep your job and he can keep the notion that his childhood friend and college sweetheart really is the nice person he believes her to be, and not the underhanded bitch you really are."

"He'd never believe you. I'm still here, aren't I?" She says the words to my back, and I turn slowly trying to gain some semblance of control over the inferno of rage boiling just beneath the surface.

"Yeah, *for now*," I say with a raise of an eyebrow and a disbelieving shake of my head, "but the clock's ticking, *doll*." Tawny starts to speak but I cut her off. "Try me, Tawny. Try me, because there's nothing I'd rather do than prove to you how serious I am right now."

"Is there a problem here?" The voice jolts me out of my rage induced haze as I look over to the nurse from earlier, who's now leaving Colton's room.

I look from her and then back at Tawny for a second. "No problem," I say, saccharine lacing my tone. "I was just taking out the *trash*." I shoot Tawny one more warning look before I take the ten steps to Colton's room and enter it with a smile plastered on my face.

I breathe out in relief that Dr. Irons is busy examining Colton when I enter the room, because I need a minute to settle my thundering pulse and calm my fingers trembling from anger. Colton glances up and smiles softly at me before focusing back on the doctor and answering his questions.

I exhale the shaky breath I was holding and see Beckett angle his head as he looks at me, bemusement in his eyes as he tries to figure out why my cheeks are so flushed. I just shake my head at him, and at that moment, Dr. Irons decides to remove the bandage from Colton's head.

I have to withhold the gasp that instinctively wants to escape from my lips at the sight. There is a shaved patch of hair with a two inch diameter circle of staples on the upper portion of the right side of his skull. It's still swollen and the silver staples juxtaposed against the pink incision with the dark red of the dried blood make a ghastly contrast.

Colton must see the look on my face because he looks over at Beckett while Dr. Irons examines the incision and says, "How bad?"

Beckett just chews the inside of his cheek and twists his lips as he looks at it and then back at Colton. "It's pretty nasty, dude."

"Yeah?"

"Yeah," Beckett says and nods his head.

"Whatever." Colton shrugs with nonchalance. "It's just hair. It'll grow back."

"Think of the serious sympathy points you could get with Rylee though if you play it up."

Colton glances over at me and smirks. "I don't need any sympathy points with her." I'm about to speak when his gaze shifts over my shoulder. "Tawny."

My back bristles instantly but I try to smooth it down as best as I can. I've said my piece. I've given her enough rope to hang herself; let's just see if she chooses to swing or stand.

"Hey," she says softly. "It's good to see you awake."

I step to the side of the bed next to Colton—staking my claim in case I hadn't made it crystal clear earlier—and reach out to squeeze his right hand, noting its strength has still not returned.

"It's good to be awake," Colton replies as he winces at Dr. Irons' intrusive fingertips against his scalp and hisses in a breath of air. "Give me a minute, okay?"

"Sure."

We all stand there quietly watching Colton until the exam is over and the doctor steps back. "So what other questions do you have, Colton, because I'm sure you have some besides what we spoke about earlier?"

Colton looks over to me and I'm sure he sees the dare in my eyes because mirth begins to dance in his. He works his tongue in his cheek as his grin widens with a lift of his eyebrows.

"Not yet, young man." Dr. Irons laughs out in amusement as he guesses the question and pats him on the knee. I'm sure embarrassment stains my cheeks but I don't even care. "What I wouldn't give to be in my early thirties again," he sighs.

Colton laughs and looks over at me, eyes locking, sexual tension crackling, and the underlying ache starting to smolder. "At any time and in any place, sweetheart," he repeats the words back to me he'd said the night we met.

Everyone else in the room ceases to exist. My insides coil with craving from his words and the salacious look in his eyes. The muscle in his jaw tics as he stares at me for a beat before looking back at Dr. Irons. He shrugs in mock apology as a mischievous grin lifts one corner of his mouth.

"Sorry, Doc, but you gave me a rule and that just tempts me to break it that much more."

Dr. Irons shakes his head at Colton. "So noted, son, but the ramifications of ..." he continues on in warning about needing to watch the pressure of blood flowing through the major arteries in his brain while they heal, and thus certain strenuous activities can cause that pressure to be stronger than is safe at this stage of healing. "Anything else?"

"Yes," Colton says, and I don't miss the look that passes between him and Beckett. He pulls his eyes back to the doctor's and says, "When will I be cleared to race again?"

Of all the questions I had expected him to ask, it wasn't that. And of course I'm stupid for hoping that on the off chance Colton might not want to race again, but hearing him actually say it causes panic to course through me. As much as I try to hide the mini-anxiety attack his words have evoked, my body instinctively tenses, my hands jerking tight around his hand while my breath audibly catches in my throat.

Colton averts his eyes from Dr. Irons momentarily to look into mine. Obviously Dr. Irons senses my discomfort because he waits a beat before answering. And during that time, Colton's eyes convey so much to me but at the same time are guarding his deepest thoughts. The moment I start to catch more, he looks away and back to the doctor.

This immediately puts me on edge, and I can't quite place why. And that scares the shit out of me. The unknown in a relationship is brutal, but with Colton? It's a downright mindfuck.

My pulse is racing from Colton's question alone, and now I have to worry about the cryptic warning in his eyes? What the fuck is going on? Maybe like Dr. Irons said earlier, his emotions and disposition have been affected by the accident. I try to tell myself this is the reason—to play it off as such—but deep down I hear warning bells and when it comes to our relationship, that's never a good sign.

Dr. Irons snaps me from my turbulent thoughts with the clearing of his throat. And I fear how he is going to answer Colton's question. "Well …" He sighs and looks down at his iPad before looking back up to meet Colton's gaze. "Since I'm getting the sense that whatever I tell you *not* to do, will just encourage you to do it even faster—"

"You're a quick learner," Colton teases.

Dr. Irons just sighs again, trying to fight the smile tugging on the corners of his mouth. "Normally I'd tell you that getting back in the car is a bad idea. That your brain has been jarred around enough and even when your skull is fully healed, it will still have a weak spot where the bone has reconnected and that could be dangerous … but I know no matter what I say you're going to be back on the track, aren't you?"

I have no option but to sit down now because despite how calm I appear on the outside, my insides have just been shredded by Dr. Irons' correct assumption.

Colton blows out a long breath and looks out the window for a bit, and for just a moment I notice the chink in his armor. It's fleeting, but it's there nonetheless. He may never admit it, but he's scared to get in the car again. Scared to recall the moments during the crash that he can't remember right now. Afraid he might get hurt again. And he's so consumed by his thoughts that he doesn't notice that he's withdrawn his hand from mine.

"You're right," he finally says, and chills immediately blanket my body. "I will. I have no other choice … but I'll follow your advice and wait until I'm medically cleared. I'll have my doctors in California connect with you to make sure nothing is missed."

Dr. Irons swallows and nods his head. "Okay, well I'm going to bank on the fact that you're a sensible guy … well, as sensible as one can be that drives two hundred miles an hour for a living." Colton smiles at the comment. "I'll be back to check on you later."

Dr. Irons leaves and for a moment there is an awkward silence between the four of us. I imagine it's because all of us are secretly wondering what it's going to be like if—no *when*—he hops back in the race car, but no one says anything.

Dread weighs heavy on me, and I have no clue how I'm going to be able to handle it. How I'm going to be able to watch him climb inside a car nearly identical to the one he almost died in.

Colton breaks the startled silence. "Becks?"

"Yeah." Becks steps forward and stares at his friend.

"Make sure to tell Eddie that he needs to get my records from Dr. Irons so we can study my injury. See how we can make it complement the HANS even better."

I know Colton is talking about the top secret safety device he was wearing during the accident. The one that CD Enterprises is getting ready to submit for patent protection, so I'm not sure why Beckett's face falls. I watch his eyes dart over to Tawny momentarily, a flash of worry flickering through them, before looking back at Colton.

"What, Becks? What aren't you telling me?" Obviously Colton notices the reaction too.

Becks clears his throat and takes a deep breath. "You fired Eddie a couple of months ago, Colton."

"What? C'mon, Becks. Quit fucking with me and just get the records for him, okay?"

"I'm not fucking with you. A second set of schematics disappeared. With his gambling debts and other issues, too many factors pointed to him, so you fired him," Beckett says as Colton's eyes flicker around the room, his head toggling back and forth as if he's trying to comprehend what he's being told.

"Seriously?" When Becks just nods, Colton looks over at Tawny and she nods too. "Fuckin' A," he grits out as he rolls his shoulders and stares out the window for a moment before looking back at Beckett. "*Stealing?* I don't remember that at all." His voice is dead quiet and full of disbelief.

I reach out and squeeze his hand, causing him to look over and meet my eyes. "Hey, it's okay. It'll come back. It's only temporary," I say, trying to reassure him as best as I can.

"But … if I don't remember something like that, what else don't I remember that I don't even know about?" His eyes swim with confusion and he grimaces momentarily causing my heart to speed up with worry.

"Don't worry about it, dude. Think of all the crap you can claim amnesia on that normally you'd get shit for."

Thank God for Becks and his easygoing personality because even though I can still see Colton struggling as he tries to grasp everything, I can also feel some of the tension relax from his hand that I'm holding. I meet Becks' eyes, a silent thank you passing between us.

Tawny clears her throat softly and all of a sudden it's like we all snap from our private thoughts with the sound. Colton breathes in deeply and says, "Tawny, I need you to issue a press release right away."

"What would you like it to say?" Ms. Ever-efficient asks while walking to the bedside opposite me, as Colton gathers his thoughts. And with just the slightest glance my way, she refocuses on him and softens her voice. "Colton?"

"Yeah?" he answers, raising his eyes to meet the question in her voice.

She reaches out and squeezes his bicep, her eyes roaming over his wound before withdrawing her hand when he doesn't respond. "I'm so glad that you're okay."

I can hear the sincerity in her voice—know she means it—but it still doesn't make me like her any more.

"Coulda been a lot worse from what I'm told, so I'll get there." Colton takes a sip of water while his brow furrows in concentration. "Tell them I'm awake and have been for a day or so. I'm on the road to recovery and will be heading back to California within the week, once I'm cleared, and returning to the track in no time. Thank them for their support and prayers, and instead of any flowers or gifts, I'd rather they make a donation to Corporate Cares. The boys need it more than I do."

Tawny looks up from her phone where she's typing all of this and asks, "What about your memory loss?"

"None of their business," Colton says, glancing up at Becks again, a silent understanding passing between them. "That's all." Tawny lifts her focus from her phone and looks at Colton as if she doesn't understand. "You can go now," he says to her, and I have to hide the look of shock on my face at the unexpected dismissal.

Tawny's head snaps up as she shoves her phone in her purse. "Well, um, okay," she says, color staining her cheeks as she heads for the door.

"Hey, Tawn?" Colton's words stop her and the acid in his tone surprises the hell out of me.

"Yes?" she asks as she turns around to face the two of us side by side.

"After you issue the press release, you can get your stuff and head back home."

She angles her head and stares at Colton for a moment, confusion flickering over her face. "It's okay. It's better if I stay here and deal with the media—"

"No," Colton says. "I don't think you understand what I'm saying." Tawny's tongue darts out and wets her bottom lip as nerves start to eat at her. She takes a step toward the bed as he begins to explain. "We've known each other, what? Most of our lives? Long enough for you to know that I don't like being fucked with." Colton leans forward as her eyes widen and I hold my breath in disbelief at the ice in his voice. "You fucked with me, T. And more importantly you fucked with Rylee. *Now that?* That I most definitely remember. Game over. Pack your shit. You're fired."

I hear Beckett suck in a breath. At the same time Tawny sputters out, "Wh-what? Colton, you—"

"Save it." Colton holds up a hand to stop her and shakes his head in disappointment. "Save your ridiculous excuses and go before you make things any worse for yourself."

She just stares at him, blinking away the tears before glancing over at Beckett, spinning on her heels, and rushing out of the room.

I watch her leave, trying to fathom what it would be like to be in her shoes. To lose both your job and the man you've believed is yours.

And as I hear Colton breathe out a huge sigh beside me, I actually feel sorry for her.

Well ... *not really.*

Chapter Twelve

A MUFFLED SOUND PULLS ME from sleep. And I'm so tired—so wanting to sink into the blinding oblivion because I've had so little sleep over the past two weeks—that I keep my eyes closed and write it off as the purr of the jet's engine. But because I'm now awake, when I hear it a second time, I know I'm wrong.

I open my eyes, startled at what I see. The sight of my reckless bad boy—eyes squeezed tight, teeth biting his bottom lip, and face painted with the grief that courses down his cheeks—coming completely undone in disciplined silence. I'm momentarily frozen with uncertainty.

I'm uncertain because I've felt a disconnect between us in the past few days. On the one hand I felt like he was trying to push me away—keep me at arms' length—by keeping all discussions superficial. By saying his head hurts, that he needed to sleep, the minute I brought up any serious subject.

And then there were the odd moments when he thought I wasn't paying attention to him when I'd notice him looking at me from the reflection in the room's window with a look of pained reverence, one of longing laced with sadness. And that singular look always caused chills to dance over my flesh.

He hiccups out a sob and opens his eyes slowly, the pain so evident in them, my grown man scarred by the tears of a scared little boy.

He looks away momentarily and I can see him trying to collect himself but only ends up squeezing his eyes shut and crying even harder.

"Colton?" I shift from my reclined position, starting to reach out, but then pulling back in uncertainty because the absolute desolation reflected in his eyes. My hesitation is answered by Colton looking at my hand and shaking his head as if one touch from me will crumble him.

And yet I can't resist. I never can when it comes to Colton.

I can't let him suffer in silence from whatever is eating his soul and shadowing his face. I have to connect with him, comfort him the only way that has seemed to work over the past few weeks.

I unbuckle my seat belt and cross the distance between us, my eyes asking if it's okay to make the connection with him. I don't let him answer—don't give him another chance to push me away—but rather settle across his lap. I wrap my arms around him as best I can, nestle my head in the crook of his neck, and just hold on in reassuring silence.

Hold on as his chest shudders and breath hitches.

As his tears fall, either cleansing his soul or foreshadowing impending devastation.

Chapter Thirteen

"**I** DON'T NEED A GODDAMN wheelchair!"

It's the fourth time he's said it, and it's the only thing he's said to me since waking up on the airplane. I bite my lip and watch him struggle as he glares at the nurse when she pushes the chair once again to the back of his knees without saying a word to her difficult patient. I can see him starting to tire from the exertion of getting out of the car, and walking the five feet or so toward the front door, before stopping and resting a hand on the retaining wall. The strain is so obvious that I'm not surprised when he eventually gives in and sits down.

I'm glad I texted everyone ahead of time and told them to stay inside the house and not greet us in the driveway. After watching the effort it took for him to get off the plane and into the car, I figured he might be embarrassed if he had an audience.

The paparazzi are still yelling on the other side of the closed gates, clamoring to get a picture or quote from Colton, but Sammy and his new additions to the staff are doing their job keeping this moment private, which I'm so very grateful for.

"Just give me a fucking minute," he growls when she starts to push him, and I can see that a headache has hit him again when he puts his head in his hands, fingers bending the bill of his baseball hat, and just sits there.

I take a deep breath from my silent place on the sideline, trying to figure out what is going on with him. And after his silent breakdown on the jet, I know it's more than just the headaches. More than the crash. Something has shifted and I can't quite put my finger on the cause of his warring personalities.

And the fact that I can't pinpoint *the why* has my nerves dancing on edge.

Colton presses his hands to the side of his hat, and I can see the tension in his shoulders as he tries to brace for the pain radiating from his head. I walk toward him, unable to resist trying to help somehow although I know there's nothing I can really do, and just place my hands on his shoulders to let him know I'm there.

That he's not alone.

"I don't need a fucking nurse watching over me. I'm fine. Really," Colton says from his partially reclined position on the chaise lounge. Everyone left shortly after our arrival, everyone but Becks and me, realizing what a surly mood Colton was in. Colton's parked himself on the upstairs patio for the last thirty minutes because, after being trapped in the hospital for so long, he just wants to sit in the sun in peace. A peace he's not getting since he's been arguing with everyone about how he's perfectly fine and just wants to be left alone.

Becks folds his arms across his chest. "We know you're hardheaded and all, but you took quite a hit. We're not going to leave you—"

"Leave me the fuck alone, Daniels." Colton barks, annoyance evident in his tone as Becks steps toward him. "If I wanted your two cents, I would've asked."

"Well crack open the piggy bank because I'm going to give you a whole fucking dollar's worth," he says as he leans in closer to Colton.

"Your head hurts? You want to be a prick because you've been locked up in a goddamn hospital? You want sympathy that you're not getting? Well too fucking bad. You almost died, Colton—*died*—so shut the fuck up and quit being an asshole to the people that care about you the most." Becks shakes his head at him in exasperation while Colton just pulls his hat down lower over his forehead and sulks.

When Becks speaks next, his voice is the quiet, calculating calm he used with me when we were in the hotel room the night before the accident.

"You don't want sponge baths from Nurse Ratchet downstairs? I get that too. But you have a choice to make because it's either her, me, or Rylee washing your balls every night 'til you're cleared by the docs. I know who I'd choose and it sure as fuck isn't me or the large, gruff, German woman in the kitchen. I love ya, dude, but my friendship draws the line when it comes to touching your junk." Becks leans back, his arms still crossed and his eyebrows raised. He shrugs his shoulders to reiterate the question.

When Colton doesn't speak, but rather remains ornery and stares Becks down from beneath the brim of his cap, I step up—tired, cranky, and wanting time alone with Colton—to try and right our world again.

"I'm staying, Colton. No questions asked. I'm not leaving you here by yourself." I just hold up my hands when he starts to argue. *Stubborn asshole.* "If you want to keep acting like one of the boys when they throw a tantrum, then I'll start treating you like one."

For the first time since we've been out on the patio, Colton raises his eyes to meet mine. "I think it's time everyone leaves." His voice is low and full of spite.

I walk closer, wanting him to know that he can push all he wants but I'm not backing down. I throw his own words back in his face. Words I'm not even sure he remembers. "We can do this the easy way or the hard way, Ace, but rest assured it's going to be *my way*."

I make sure Becks locked the front door on his way out before grabbing the plate of cheese and crackers to head back upstairs. I find Colton in the same location on the chaise lounge but he's taken his hat off, head leaned back, eyes closed. I stop in the doorway and watch him. I take in the shaved patch that's starting to grow back over his nasty scar. I note the furrow in his forehead that tells me he's anything but at peace.

I enter the patio quietly, the song *Hard to Love* is playing softly on the radio, and I'm grateful that it masks my footsteps so I don't wake him as I set his pain meds and plate of food down on the table next to him.

"You can go now too."

His gruff voice startles me. His unexpected words throw me. My temper simmers. I look over at him and can't do anything other than shake my head in sputtering disbelief because his eyes are still closed. Everything over the past couple of days hits me like a kaleidoscope of memories. The distance and avoidance. This is about more than being irritated from being confined during his recovery. "Is there something you need to get off your chest?"

A lone seagull squawks overhead as I wait for the answer, trying to prepare for whatever he's going to say to me. He's gone from crying without explanation to telling me to leave—not a good sign at all.

"I don't need your goddamn pity. Don't you have a house full of little boys that need you to help fulfill that inherent trait of yours to hover and smother?"

He could've called me every horrible name in the book and it wouldn't sting as much as those words he just slapped me with. I'm dumbfounded, mouth opening and closing as I stare at him, face angled to the sun, eyes still closed. "Excuse me?" It's no match for what he's just said, but it's all I've got.

"You heard me." He lifts his chin up almost in dismissal but still keeps his eyes closed. "You know where the door is, sweetheart."

Maybe my lack of sleep has dimmed my usual reaction, but those words just flicked the switch to one hundred percent. I feel like we've time warped back to weeks ago and I immediately have my protective guard back up. The fact that he won't look at me is like kerosene to my flame. "What the fuck's going on, Donavan? If you're going to blow me off, the least you can do is give me the courtesy of looking at me."

He squints open an eye as if it's irritating him to have to pay attention to me and I've had it. He's managed to hurt me in the whole five minutes we've had alone together, and the fact that my emotional stability is being held together by frayed strings doesn't help either. He watches me and a ghost of a smirk appears, as if he's enjoying my reaction, enjoying toying with me.

Unspoken words flicker through my mind and whisper to me, call on me to look closer. But what am I missing here?

"Rylee, it's just probably best if we call it like we see it."

"Probably best?" My voice escalates and I realize that maybe we're both a whole lot exhausted and overwhelmed with everything that's occurred, but I'm still not getting what the hell is going on. Panic starts burgeoning inside me because you can only hold on so tight to someone who doesn't want to be held on to. "What the hell, Colton? What's going on?"

I push off the chair and walk to the ledge and look out over the water for a moment, needing a minute to shove down the frustration so patience can resurface, but I'm just plain worn out from the whiplash of emotions. "You don't get to push me away, Colton. You don't get to need me one minute and then shove me away as hard as you can the next." I try to keep the hurt out of my voice but it's virtually impossible.

"I can do whatever the hell I want!" he shouts at me.

I whirl back around, jaw clenched, the taste of rejection fresh in my mouth. "Not when you're with me you can't!" My voice echoes across the concrete of the patio as we stare at each other, the silence slowly smothering possibilities.

"Then maybe I shouldn't be with you." The quiet steel to his words knocks the wind out of me. Pain radiates in my chest as I draw in air. What the hell? Did I read this all wrong? What am I missing?

I want to tear into him. I want to unleash on him the fury I feel reverberating through me.

Colton deflects his eyes momentarily and in that moment, everything finally clicks. All of the puzzle pieces that seemed amiss over the past week finally fit together.

And it's all so transparent now, I feel like an idiot that I didn't put it together sooner.

It's time to call his bluff.

But what if I call it and I'm wrong? My heart lurches into my throat at the thought, but what other option do I have? I smooth my hands down the thighs of my jeans, hating that I'm nervous.

"Fine," I resign as I take a few steps toward him. "You know what? You're right. I don't need this shit from you or anyone else." I shake my head and stare at him as he grabs his hat, places it on his head, lowering the bill so I can just barely see his eyes that are now open and watching me with guarded intensity. "*Non-negotiable, remember?*" I throw my threat back at him from our bathtub agreement weeks ago, and with those words I see a sliver of emotion flicker through his otherwise stoic eyes.

He just shrugs his shoulder nonchalantly, but I'm onto his game now. I may not know what it is, but something's wrong and frankly this *been here, done that* bullshit is getting old. "Didn't you learn fucking anything? Did they remove the common sense part of your brain when they cut it open?"

His eyes snap up to mine now and I know I've gotten his attention. *Good.* He doesn't speak but I at least know his eyes are on me, his attention is focused. "I don't need your condescending bullshit, Rylee." He yanks the bill of his hat down over his eyes and lays his head back, dismissing me once again. "You know where the door is."

I'm across the patio and have flipped his hat off of his head within seconds, my face lowered within inches of his. His eyes flash open, and I can see the wash of emotions within them from my unexpected actions. He works a swallow in his throat as I hold my stare, refusing to back down.

"Don't push me away or I'm going to push back ten times as hard," I tell him, beseeching him to look deep within and be honest with himself. To be honest about us. "You've hurt me on purpose before. I know you fight dirty, Colton … so what is it that you're trying to protect me from?" I lower myself in the chaise lounge, our thighs brushing against each other's, trying to make the connection so he can feel it, so he can't deny it.

He looks out toward the ocean for a few moments and then looks back at me, clearly conflicted. "Everything. Nothing." He shrugs, averting his eyes again. "From me." The break in his voice unwinds the ball of tension knotted around my heart.

"What … what are you talking about?" I slide my hand into his and squeeze it, wondering what's going on inside his head. "Protect me? You ordering me around and telling me to get the hell out is not you protecting me, Colton. It's you hurting me. We've been through this and—"

"Just drop it, Ry."

"I'm not dropping shit," I tell him, my pitch escalating to get my point across. "You don't get to—"

"Drop it!" he orders, jaw clenched, tension in his neck.

"No!"

"You said you couldn't do this anymore." His voice calls out to me across the calming sounds of the ocean below despite the turbulent waves crashing into my heart. The even keel of his tone warns me that he's hurting, but it's the words he says that have me searching my memory for what he's talking about.

"What—?" I start to say but I stop when he holds his hand up, eyes squeezing shut as the cluster headache hits him momentarily. And of course I feel guilty for pushing him on this, but he's crazy if he thinks I'm going anywhere. I want to reach out and soothe him, try to take the pain away but know that nothing I can do will help, so I sit and rub my thumb absently over the back of his tensing hand.

"When I was out ... I heard you tell Becks that you couldn't do this anymore ... that you'd gladly walk out ..." his voice drifts off as his eyes bore into mine, jaw muscle pulsing. The obstinate set to his jaw asking the question his words don't.

"That's what this is all about?" I ask dumbfounded and struck with realization all at once. "A snippet of a conversation I had with Becks when I said I would have gladly walked away from you—done something, anything differently—if it would've prevented you from being comatose in a hospital bed?" I can see how his mind has altered bits and pieces of my conversation with Beckett, but he's never asked me about it. Never communicated. And that fact, more than the misunderstanding, upsets me.

"You said you'd gladly walk out." His repeats, his voice resolute as if he doesn't believe I'm telling him the truth. "Your pity's not needed nor welcome."

"You've been pulling away because you think I'm only here out of pity? That you got hurt and now I don't want you anymore?" And now I'm pissed. "Glad you thought so highly of me. Such an asshole," I mutter more to myself than to him. "Feel free to make assumptions, because in case you haven't noticed, they've done wonders for our relationship so far, right?" I can't help the sarcasm dripping from my voice, but after everything we've been through together—everything we always seem to come back to when all is said and done—I'm hurt that he even remotely thinks I'm going to want him any less because he's not one hundred percent.

"Rylee." He blows out a loud breath and reaches for my hand but

I pull it back.

"Don't *Rylee* me." I can't help the tears that swim in my eyes. "I almost lost you—"

"You're goddamn fucking right you did, and that's why I have to let you go!" he shouts before swearing out a muttered curse. He laces his fingers at the back of his neck and then pulls his elbows down, trying to staunch some of his anger. My eyes flash up to meet his, my breath choking on confusion. "I heard you on the phone with Haddie the other night when you thought I was asleep. Heard you tell her that you're not sure you'll be able to watch me get back in the car again. I can't be made to choose between you and racing," he says, anguish so palpable it rolls off him in waves and crashes into the desperation emanating off of me. "I need both of you, Rylee." The desolation of his voice strikes chords deep within me, his fear transparent. "Both of you."

And now I get it. It's not that he thinks I don't want him because he's hurt, it's that I won't want him in the future because I'll fear for every minute of every second that he's in that car, as well as the minutes leading up to it.

I had no idea he'd heard my conversation. A conversation with Haddie that was so candid, I cringe recalling some of the things I said, without the sugarcoating I'd use with most others.

I lift my hand to his face and bring it back to look at mine. "Talk to me, Colton. After everything we've been through, you can't shut me out or push me away. You've got to talk to me or we can never move forward."

I can see the transparent emotions in his eyes, and I hate watching him struggle with them. I hate knowing something has eaten at him over the past week when he should have been worried about recovering. Not about us. I hate that he's even questioned anything that has to do with us.

He breathes out a shaky breath and closes his eyes momentarily. "I'm trying to do what's best for you." His voice is so soft the sound of the waves almost drowns it out.

"What's best for me?" I ask in the same tone, confused but needing to understand this man so complicated and yet so childlike in many ways.

He opens his eyes and the pain is there, so raw and vulnerable they make my insides twist. "If we're not together … then I can't hurt you every time I get in the car."

He swallows and I give him a moment to find the words I can see he's searching for … and to regain my ability to breathe. He's been pushing me away because he cares, because he's putting me first and my heart swells at the thought.

He reaches up and takes the hand I have resting on his cheek, laces his fingers with it, and rests it in his lap. His eyes stay focused on our connection.

"I told you that you make me a better man … and I'm trying so fucking hard to be that for you, but I'm failing miserably. A better man would let you go so that you don't have to relive what happened to Max and my crash every time I get in the car. He'd do what's best for you."

It takes a moment to find my voice because what Colton just said to me—those words—are equivalent to telling me he races me. They represent such an evolvement in him as a man, I can't stop the tear that slides down my cheek.

I give in to necessity. I lean in and press my lips to his. To taste and take just a small reassurance that he's here and alive. That the man I thought and hoped he was underneath all of the scars and hurt, really is there, really is this beautifully damaged man whose lips are pressed against mine.

I withdraw a fraction and look into his eyes. "What's best for me? Don't you know what's best for me is you, Colton? Every single part of you. The stubborn, the wild and reckless, the fun loving, the serious, and even the broken parts of you," I tell him, pressing my lips to his between every word. "All of those parts of you I will never be able to find in someone else … those are what I need. What I want. You, baby. Only you."

This is what love is, I want to scream at him. Shake him until he understands that this is real love. Not the unfettered pain and abuse of his past. Not his mom's twisted version of it. This is love. Me and him, making it work. One being strong when the other is weak. Thinking of the other first when they know their partner is going to feel pain.

But I can't say it.

I can't scare him into remembering what he felt for me or said to me. And as much as it cripples me that I can't say *I race you* to him, I can show him by standing by his side, by holding his hand, by being strong when he needs me the most. By being silent when all I want to do is tell him.

He just stares at me, teeth scraping over his bottom lip, and complete reverence in his eyes. He sniffs back the emotion and clears his throat as he nods his head, a silent acceptance of the pleading in my words. "What you told Haddie is true though. It's going to kill you every time I get in the car …"

"I'm not going to lie. It is going to kill me, but I'll figure out how to handle it when we get to that point," I tell him, although I already feel the fear that stains the fringes of my psyche at the thought. "*We'll* figure it out," I correct myself and the most adorable smile curls one corner of his mouth, melting my heart.

He just nods his head, his eyes conveying the words I want to hear, and for now, it's enough for me. Because when you have everything right before you, you'll accept anything just to keep it there.

"I'm not any good at this," he says, and I can see the concern fill his eyes, etch across his features.

"No one is," I tell him, squeezing our linked fingers. "Relationships aren't easy. They're hard and can be brutal at times … but those are the times you learn the most about yourself. And when they're right," I pause, making sure his eyes are steadfast on mine, "they can be like coming home … finding the rest of your soul …" I avert my eyes, suddenly embarrassed by my introspective comments and my hopeless romantic tendencies.

He squeezes my hand but I keep my face toward the sun, hoping the color staining my cheeks isn't noticeable. My mind races with the possibilities for us if he can just find it within himself to let me have a permanent place there. The silence is okay now because the empty space between us is floating with potential instead of misunderstanding. And on this patio, bathed by sunlight, we're lost in thought because we're accepting the fact that there are tomorrows for us to experience together, and that's a good place to be.

As my mind wanders I see the plate of food and pain meds on the table next to us. "Hey, you need to take your pills," I say, finally turning toward him and meeting his eyes.

He reaches out and cups the side of my face, brushing the pad of his thumb over my bottom lip. I draw in a shaky, affected breath as he angles his head and watches me. "You're the only medicine I need, Rylee."

I can't help the smile spreading across my lips or the sarcastic comment that slides off my tongue. "I guess the doctors didn't mess with your ability to deliver smooth one-liners did they?"

"Nope," he says with a devilish smirk that has me leaning into him the same time he does, so that we meet in the center.

Our lips brush ever so gently, once then twice, before he parts his lips and slides his tongue between mine. Our tongues dance, our hands caress, and our hearts swell as we settle into the tenderness of the kiss. He brings his other hand up to cup my face, and I can feel it trembling as he tries to keep it there. I lift my hand up to hold onto the outside of his and help him hold it against my cheek. Desire coils deep in my belly and as much as I know I can't sate my body's yearning, per doctor's orders, it doesn't mean I don't want to desperately.

When we connect through intimacy, it's more than just the mind blowing orgasm at the hands of the oh-so-skillful Colton, but rather something I can't exactly put words to. It's almost as if, when we connect, there is a contentment that weaves its way deep down in my soul and completes me. Binds us. And I miss that feeling.

A sexy as hell groan comes from the back of his throat that doesn't help stem the ache I have burning for him. I reach my free hand out and run it up the plane of his chest, loving the vibration humming beneath my fingers as a result of my touch. Chills prickle my skin and it's not from the ocean breeze but rather the tidal wave of sensations my body misses desperately.

"Fuck, I'm dying to be in you, Ry," he whispers against my lips as every nerve in my body stands at attention and begs to be taken, branded, and remade his all over again. And I am so close to saying *fuck the doctor's orders* that my hand is sliding down his torso to slip beneath his waistband, when I feel his body tense and his breath hiss out.

I'm immediately swamped with guilt over my lack of willpower to take the temptation so readily at my fingertips and I switch to high alert. "A bad one?"

The grimace on Colton's face remains, eyes squeezed shut, as he just nods his head softly and shifts backward in the chair until he's reclined. I reach for the medicine and put them in his hands.

I guess I'm not the only medicine he needs after all.

Chapter Fourteen

I WANDER THE HALLS OF the Malibu house—worry over Colton, homesickness for the boys, and missing Haddie all robbing me of sleep. This has been the longest I've been away from any of them, and as much as I love Colton, I'm needing that connection with *my life*.

I need their energy that always lifts my soul and feeds my spirit. I've missed Zander's deposition, Ricky's first home run, Aiden being called into the principal's office for stopping a fight rather than starting one ... I feel like a bad mother neglecting her children.

Not finding solace, I climb the stairs for the umpteenth time to check on him. To make sure he's still knocked out from the cocktail of medications Dr. Irons prescribed on the phone earlier when Colton's headache would not let up.

I'm still worried. I think I subconsciously fear falling asleep because I might miss something he needs.

Then I think of Colton's revelations earlier before the headache hit, and I can't help the smile that softens my face. The knowledge that he was trying to push me away to protect me may have been misguided, but perfect nonetheless.

There is most definitely hope for us yet.

I walk toward the bed, Halestorm playing softly on the stereo overhead, and can't help the breath I hold as I sit down on the bed beside him. He's lying on his stomach, his arms buried beneath the pillow and his face angled to the side of the bed facing me. The light blue sheets have fallen down below his waist, and my eyes trace the sculpted lines of his back, my fingers itching to touch the heated warmth of his skin. My eyes roam over the scar on his head and note that the patch of hair is starting to grow in with stubble. In no time at all no one will even know the trauma beneath his hair.

But I'll know. And I'll remember. And I'll fear.

I shake my head and squeeze my eyes shut, needing to get control of my rampant stampede of emotions. I notice his discarded shirt on the bed beside him and can't help picking it up and burying my nose in it, drinking in his smell, needing the mapped connection in my mind to lessen the worry that's now a constant. It's not enough though, so I crawl into bed beside him. I lean forward, careful not to disturb him, and press my lips to the spot just between his shoulder blades.

I inhale his scent, feel the warmth of his heated flesh beneath my lips, and thank God that I get this moment again with him. A second chance. I sit like this for a moment, silent *thank yous* running through my mind when Colton whimpers.

"*Please no,*" he says, the juvenile tone in the masculine timbre is haunting, unnerving, devastating. "*Please, Mommy, I'll be good. Just don't let him hurt me.*"

He thrashes his head in protest, body tensing, arms bracing as the sounds he's making become more adamant, more upsetting. I try to wake him, take his shoulders and shake him.

"*Please, Mommy. Pleeeaaassseee,*" he whimpers in a pleading voice wavering with terror. My heart lodges in my throat and tears spring to my eyes at that eerie combination of little boy within the grown man.

"Wake up, Colton!" I shove his shoulder back and forth again as he becomes more animated, but the strength of the prescriptions that Dr. Irons had me give him are too strong to pull him from the nightmare. "C'mon, wake up," I say again as his body starts rocking, the all too familiar chant falling from his lips.

I hiccup a sob as he shifts again, voice silenced and rolls onto his back. He shifts a couple more times and I'm relieved that his nightmare seems to have left him. He still seems uneasy though, so I crawl up beside him and lay my head on his chest, leg hooked over his, and rest my hand on his frantically beating heart. And I do the one thing I can in hopes of soothing him, I sing.

I sing of little boys and imaginary dragons. Of believing in something unbelievable. Of forgetting and moving on.

"My dad used to sing that to me when I had nightmares."

His rasp of a voice scares the crap out of me. I didn't even know he had woken up. He places an arm around me and pulls me in closer to him. "I know," I whisper into the moonlit room, "and you were."

Silence hangs between us as he blows out a soft breath. I can tell his dreams are still on his mind, so I grant him the silence to work through them. He presses a kiss onto the top of my head and keeps his mouth there.

When he speaks, I can feel the heat from his breath as he murmurs into my hair. "I was scared. I remember the vague sense of being scared those last few seconds in the car as I was flipping through the air." And it's the first time he's admitted to me anything to confirm my fears in regards to the crash.

I run my hand over his chest. "I was too."

"I know," he says as his hand finds its way beneath the waistband of my panties and cups my bare ass, pulling me up his body so my eyes can meet his. "I'm sorry you had to go through that again." I can see the apology in his eyes, in the lines etched in his forehead, and I'm unable to speak, tears clogging in my throat at his acknowledgment of my feelings so I show him the next best way I know how. I lean in and brush my lips against his.

His lips part as I slip my tongue between them, a soft groan rumbling in the back of his throat, spurring me on to taste the one and only fix to my addiction. My hands run over his stubbled jaw to the back of his neck, and I take in the intoxicating mixture I've grown to crave. His taste, his feel, his virility.

His hands cradle my face, fingers tangled in my curls as he draws my face back momentarily so we're inches apart, our breath whispering against each other's and eyes divulging emotions we've previously kept guarded under lock and key.

I can feel the pulse of his clenched jaw beneath my palms as he struggles with words. "Ry, I …" he says and my breath catches. My soul hopes with bated breath. And I mentally finish the sentence for him, fill in the two words that complete it, complete us. Express the words that I see in his eyes and feel in the reverence of his touch. He works a swallow down his throat and finishes, "Thank you for staying."

"There's nowhere else I'd rather be." I can see the words I breathe out sink in and register as he pulls me toward him, guiding my body to shift and settle in a straddle over his lap while his mouth crashes to mine. *And it does crash.* A frenzy of passion explodes as my need collides with his desperation. Hands roam, tongues delve, and emotions intensify as we refamiliarize ourselves with the lines and curves of one another.

Colton runs his left hand down my back and grips the flesh on my hip as I rock over the ridge of his boxer-brief clad erection. Sensation swells within, creating an ache so powerful, so intense it borders on painful. My body craves the all-consuming pleasure I know only he can evoke.

I swallow his groan as I am engulfed in the emotion—the connection between us—in this moment. I feel Colton's right hand slide down to my other hip as he brings his hands to the sides of my tank top trying to pull it up and off. But when I feel his right hand fail to grasp the material, I quickly take control, not wanting it to affect this moment. I cross my arms over my front, grab the hem, and lift it over my head.

I sit astride him, bare except for a scant pair of panties, as his eyes scrape over the lines of my body, raw male appreciation apparent in his gaze. Unfettered lust. Undeniable hunger. He reaches back out to touch, to dance fingertips up my ribcage enabling him to guide my face back to his so that he can take, taste, tempt.

I moan at the feeling of my breasts pillowing against his firm chest, hardened nipples hypersensitive to the touch. Colton urges my hips back and forth again, and the sensation rocks me, nerves ready to detonate. I angle my body back, lost in the feeling when his mouth finds my breast, warm heat against chilled flesh.

I want him. Need him. Desire him like I never thought possible.

Our breaths pant and hearts race as we act on the instinct that has pulled us together since day one. And it's in this moment that I feel his hand flex and hear the warning of Dr. Irons flash through my head. I want to ignore him, tell it to go the fuck away so I can take my man again, pleasure him, own him as he owns me in every sense of the word. But I can't risk it.

I bring my hands down to my hips and lace my fingers with his. I break from our kiss and rest my forehead against Colton's. "We can't. It's not safe." The strain is apparent in my voice, expressing how hard it is for me to stop from taking exactly what we both want. Colton doesn't utter a sound. He just presses his hands into my hips as our labored breathing fills the silence in the bedroom. "It's too much exertion."

"Baby, if I'm not exerting myself then I'm sure as fuck not doing it right." He chuckles against my neck, stubble tickling my skin that's already begging for more of his touch.

I force myself to sit up so I'm farther away from the temptation of his mouth, but neglect to realize that my new positioning causes more pressure on the weeping apex between my thighs as my weight settles down on his erection. I have to stifle the moan that wants to fall from my mouth at the feeling. Colton smirks, knowing exactly what just happened, and I try to feign that I'm not affected but it's no use as he rolls his hips again.

"*Colton*," I moan, drawing out his name.

"You know you don't want me to stop," he says with a smirk and as he starts to speak again, I reach out and put a finger to his lips to quiet him.

"*This woman* is just trying to keep you safe."

"Oh, but you forget that the patient is always right and *this patient* thinks that *this woman*," he says as he draws my finger into his mouth and sucks on it causing desire to coil within, "needs to be thoroughly fucked by this man."

My legs tighten around him and I dig my hands into the top of my thighs as my body remembers just how thorough a fucking by Colton Donavan can be. And despite my resolve, my body screams take me, brand me, claim me. Own every part of me, right here, right now.

"Safety," I reassert, trying to regain some type of control over my body and the situation. Trying to think of his safety rather than the constant ache burning like a wildfire within me.

"Ryles, when have you ever known me to play it safe?" He smirks that devilishly handsome grin he knows I can't resist. "Please … let me exert myself," he pleads, but I know that beneath the playful tone is a man scavenging what's left of his restraint. "I'm dying to take the driver's seat and set the pace."

I can't help my laugh because his words cause a certain comment to come back to me. "When we first met, Haddie wondered if you fucked like you drive."

He snorts out a laugh, a mischievous grin gracing his lips and leaving that dimple I love. "And how's that?"

"A little reckless, pushing all the limits, and in it until the very last lap …" I let my voice trail off as I tease a fingernail over the midline of his chest, his muscles flexing as he anticipates my touch.

He angles his head to the side and his arrogant smile grows wider. "Well, was she right or do I need to take you for another spin around the track to refresh your memory?"

I love seeing the Colton I know, the Colton I missed, so vibrant that I decide to have a little fun—play him at his own game. He wants sex that I'm not going to give him, but that doesn't mean I can't put on a good show to tide him over. Give him a little something to ease the burn.

Or intensify the ache.

I run my fingers back down his chest and then to my parted knees and up and over my thighs. His eyes follow their wanton progression as they sit on top of the triangular swatch of fabric covering my sex. "Not sure I remember, Ace. It's been a while since I've seen you in action."

He sucks in a hiss of breath and the reaction drives me, spurs me to go one step further. I rub my hands over my naked stomach and up to cup my breasts already weighted with desire. I purposefully drag my teeth over my bottom lip, breathing out a soft moan as I pinch my nipples between my thumbs and forefingers, the sensation ricocheting through my every nerve. Colton's eyes darken, his lips part, and I feel his cock throb under my core at the sight of me pleasuring myself.

His reaction empowers me, allows me to have the courage and confidence to carry this out. A few months ago I would have never done this—touch myself so brazenly under the scrutiny of his stare—but he's done this for me, shown me that my curves are sexy; the body I used to readily criticize is something he desires, something that turns him on. *Is more than enough for him.*

And because of that knowledge, I can give him this gift with steady hands and complete confidence.

I let another moan fall from my mouth, and as much as I can see the desire swell in his green eyes, I can tell the minute he's on to me. The slow, lopsided spread of a smile turning up one corner of his deliciously handsome mouth. He just shakes his head subtly, mirth dancing over his expression as he shows me he's more than willing to play this game.

"Baby, if you're trying to get me to stop, then you shouldn't throw around comments like that."

He rolls his hips beneath me, his rock hard length pressing exactly where I ache for it to fill—where I'm silently begging for it to stroke—and feeds my pleasurable pain. I try to stifle the reaction on my lips, try to play coy, but it's no use when he does it again. My mouth falls lax, a satisfied purr comes from deep within my throat, and my hands fall without thought to press against the outside of my damp panties. Needing something to stifle the urge to take what I so desperately need, so desperately want.

Him.

When his hips settle, my fingers dig into the flesh of my thighs to prevent me from taking what I want—fingers ripping down boxer-briefs, taking his steeled length in my hands, guiding him into me, stretching me to sublime satisfaction—I gain enough composure to raise my eyes back up and lock onto his. To feign that I have a tight hold on the control that's begging to be snapped.

He reaches a hand up and draws a line down the middle of my chest at an excruciatingly slow pace. His smirk spreading to both corners when my nipples pebble from his touch, proving that despite my strong façade, I'm affected by him in every possible way.

"Well, if you think I fuck like I drive, you should see me drop the hammer and *race* you to the finish line."

I can't help the breath that catches in my throat. It has to be coincidence that he uses the term *race*—it is his profession after all—but every single part of me hopes momentarily that I'm wrong. That he's using the term to tell me he remembers. But as quick as the thought soars with hope, it burns out, shutters the breath in my lungs. So I do the only thing I can to help make me forget and help him remember.

It's time to give him the show I've been tempting him with.

As his eyes flicker back and forth between my eyes and my fingers, I spread my legs further apart wanting to make sure he can see everything I'm doing. My fingers slip just beneath the waistband of my panties and then stop, my own body aching for my touch as much as I can see he is by the look in his eyes and his own fingers rubbing together, itching to touch me himself. But he's still in control. Still so calm.

Time to test that restraint.

"I thought racing wasn't a team sport," I say from beneath my lashes. "You know, more of an every man for himself kind of thing." I make sure he's watching, make sure he sees my fingers slide a little farther south. And I know he does because his Adam's apple bobs as he works a swallow down his throat.

"Every man, yes," he finally says, his voice strained. "Racing can be a dangerous sport too, you know?"

"Oh really?" I respond.

I take it upon myself to give into the sweet torture of parting myself and rubbing the evidence of my arousal around so I can apply the much needed friction to my clit. And as good as it feels—the pressure, the friction, his hardened dick rubbing against me—nothing turns me on more than the look on Colton's face. Undeniable arousal and complete concentration as he watches movements he can't see but can only guess at through the silky red fabric.

I want more from him. I want that stoic restraint snapped, and so I give into the feeling, into the eroticism of the moment—of him watching me while I pleasure myself—and I do the one thing I know will help push him over the edge, pull that hair-string trigger I know he has so tightly wound. I lift my head back, close my eyes, and let "Oh, God!" slip from my lips.

"Sweet Jesus!" he swears, restraint snapped right along with the strings of fabric holding my panties together.

I keep my head back knowing he's watching me move my fingers—absorb the pleasure—because there is something unexpectedly liberating about him stripping my clothes so he can see. I am unbound, unashamed, and utterly his for the taking, both physically and mentally.

I feel my pulse quicken. Warmth spreads through me like a tidal wave of sensation that I willingly want to be drowned in. Colton groans out in front of me and I come back into the present, lift my head up, and open my eyes to find his trained on the delta between my thighs. I hiss a moan as I bring my hand out for him to see the evidence of my arousal glistening on my fingers. I struggle to control the burning fire spreading through me, igniting places I didn't even know exist and try to find my voice.

"Well, Ace, danger can be overrated. It seems I know how to handle a *slick track* perfectly well," I purr, unable to fight the smirk that plays as his fingers dig deeper into the flesh at my hips. I keep my eyes locked and taunting on his as I bring my fingers up to my lips and suck slowly before withdrawing them.

The muscle in his jaw tics. His dick pulses beneath me in reaction. His breath rasps out. "Slippery and wet, huh? Danger has never been more fucking tempting," he drawls before his tongue darts out and wets his lips as he tracks my hands sliding back down my torso, over my breasts, down my stomach, and back down to between my thighs. This time though, I spread my knees wider as I use one hand to part my cleft so he can see my other hand slide down between the swollen, pink flesh. I can see the struggle flicker across the magnificent lines of his face, watch the desire swamp him, and the knowing smile that curls up his lips somehow fits him with absolute perfection.

My handsome, arrogant rogue.

A little cocky.

A lot imperfect.

And completely mine.

"You know," he rasps, trailing a fingertip up one thigh, purposely missing my core clenching in anticipation before continuing down the other leg. "Sometimes in a race, in order to reach the finish line, rookies like you have to tag team to get the result you want."

I don't fight the smile that comes or hide the shudder of breath as his fingers leave my skin. I lean forward placing my hands on his chest and look straight into his eyes. "Sorry, but this engine seems to be doing just fine running solo," I say, scraping my fingernails in lines down his chest as I sit back up. His muscles convulse beneath my fingers proving that even though the arrogant curl to his lips remains, his body still wants and needs what I have to offer. I slip my fingers between my thighs again and deliver the line I'm hoping will push him over the edge. "I know exactly what it's going to take to get me to the finish line."

"Oh, so you like to race dirty, huh? Break all the rules?" he taunts, tossing the ball right back into my court.

"Oh, I most definitely can race dirty," I tease with a raise of my eyebrows before I reach a hand out, his eyes narrowing as I bring a finger, coated with my moisture, to his lips. His hand flashes up immediately and grabs my wrist, guiding my fingers into his mouth, the low hum in the back of his throat reverberating over me, through me, into me. And my own restraint is tested as his tongue swirls over them, my hips grinding down and rocking over him in automatic response. *Holy shit that feels like Heaven.* My nerves reach the fever pitch of ache as I rock back again, his hard to my soft, and all I can think about is the need coursing through me. The moisture pooling between my legs. The thought of his fingers on me, in me, driving me.

Fuck, I need him now. Desperately. So I do the only thing I can without downright begging. I deliver the last coherent dare I have left because all of my thoughts are jumbling in my head with this onslaught of sensation. I lean forward, the feather of my lips up his whiskered jaw line, and inhale his scent before I whisper, "Being a seasoned pro such as yourself, you just might have to show this rookie exactly why they say rubbing's racing."

I rotate my hips over the top of him and I can feel his teeth grind in willpower. I repeat the motion one more time, a satisfied exhale slipping between my lips as my body begs for more. "Big bad professional race car driver like you afraid to show a newbie how to drive stick, huh?"

I forgot how fast Colton can move, bad hand and all. Within a heartbeat he's pushed me so I'm sitting back up again. My feet have been pulled forward so they're flat on the bed on either side of his rib cage, and he pushes my knees as far out as they can go.

Bingo.

Fuse lit.

That razor thin edge of control snapped.

Thank God!

He must be mistaking the look on my face—the one of relief edged with desperation—as confusion because he says, "I'm shifting gears, sweetheart, because I'm the only one allowed to drive this car." I can hear the hum deep in his throat as he slides his hands up my thighs, stopping to sweep his thumbs up and down my tight strip of curls. A teasing touch that sends tiny tremors ricocheting through me, hinting at what's to come, the level of pleasure he can bring me to.

His fingers still and he drags his eyes up my body to meet mine, a smug grin ghosting his mouth. He holds my stare—almost as if daring me to look away—as he moves one hand to part my swollen flesh while the other tucks his fingers inside of me. My head falls back as I cry out at the feeling, fingers moving, manipulating, circling to stroke over the responsive bundle of nerves. He slides his fingers in and out, my walls clenching around him, gripping onto him in pure, carnal need. Greed.

I watch his face. See his tongue slip between his lips, the desire cloud his eyes, watch the muscles ripple in his arms as he works me into a fever pitch. Causes me to climb quickly because I'm so pent up—so addled with need—that the sight of him, the feel of him, the memory of him, pushes me over the edge.

My fingernails score down his forearms as my body tenses, pussy convulses, and the broken cry of his name fills the room around us. I fall forward, collapsing on top of Colton's chest as the heat spearing through me in waves liquefies my insides. Makes coherency a distant possibility. I want the feel of my skin on his. Need to feel the firmness of him against me and the security of his arms wrapped around me as I swim through the sensation he just flooded me with.

I pant out in short, sharp breaths as my body settles, his fingertips tracing lines up and down my spine. I can feel his soft chuckle against my chest. "Hey, rookie?"

I force myself to look up at him—to pull myself from my post-orgasmic coma. "Hmm?" is all I can manage as I meet the amusement in his eyes.

"I'm the only one that's allowed to drive you to the motherfucking checkered flag."

I can't help the laugh that comes out and bubbles over. He can claim my checkered flag any day.

Chapter Fifteen

"OH, BUDDY, I'M SO PROUD of you!" I fight back the wave of guilt that rolls over me. I missed helping Connor study for a test in his most dreaded subject—math. "I knew you could do it!"

"I just used that little trick you told me about and it worked!" The pride in his voice brings tears of joy to my eyes, and at the same time, grief over not being there.

"I told you it would! Now go get ready for baseball. I'm sure Jax is waiting for you already!" He laughs telling me I'm right. "I promise I'll see you a little later in the week, okay?"

"'Kay. I Lego you."

"I Lego you too, bud!"

I hang up and look out toward the patio as laughter filters in above the crash of the waves—years worth of friendship breaking though Colton's bad mood. I'm so thankful to Beckett for stopping by. I hear them belt out another laugh, and as much as I wish I was the one putting the smile on Colton's otherwise scowling face of late, I'm just grateful that it's there.

Beggars can't be choosers.

I watch them clink the necks of their beer bottles over something and I sigh out loud, wanting the tension between Colton and me to go away. I'm sure it's because we're both sexually frustrated. To need and want and desire when temptation is right beneath your fingers, but to not be able to take and devour, is brutal in every sense of the word.

And yes, his more than skillful fingers brought me a small ounce of the release I needed the night before last, but it's not the same. The connection was made but not cemented, because when Colton is in me, literally stretching me to every depth imaginable, I am also completely filled figuratively in every sense of the word. He completes me, owns me, has ruined me for anyone else ever again.

I feel closer to him right now—spending so much time with him—and yet further away. And I hate it.

I shake myself from my pity party and think how much worse things could be right now. I slip my shoes off and head out onto the deck for fresh air. I walk between Colton and Beckett's lounge chairs and sit in one of my own, facing them.

Behind my sunglasses I take in the sight before me, and I know there isn't another woman in the world that wouldn't want to be in my shoes right now. Both men are relaxed, clad in board shorts, ball caps, and sunglasses. I let my eyes roam lazily with more than ample appreciation for the defined lines of their bare torsos and fight the smile that wants to pull at the corners of my mouth.

"Well if it isn't Florence Nightingale," Beckett drawls in that slow, even cadence of his as he brings the bottle to his lips.

"Well I think if I was Ms. Nightingale, I'd be telling my patient, Mr. Donavan here, that he probably shouldn't be drinking alcohol with all of those pain meds running through his blood."

"More like Nurse Ratchet." Colton snorts, looking at me from beneath the shadow of his bill, green eyes running over the length of my legs stretched out on the chaise in front of me. A quick dart of his tongue over his lips tells me he wants to do a whole lot more than just look.

"Nurse Ratchet, huh?" I ask as I slide my foot up and down the calf of one of my legs trying to not feel insulted.

"Yep," he says, pursing his lips as his eyes watch me over the top of his beer bottle. "If she gave me what I really wanted, I'd be able to recover that much quicker." He raises his eyebrows at me, the suggestion in his eyes devouring me.

"Well shit," Beckett swears, "if I'm not trying to get the two of you back together, I'm fucking trying to keep you apart."

"*Fucking*," Colton drawls in Beckett fashion, "now there's a word."

Becks just snorts a laugh and rolls his eyes. "Definitely a good word indeed."

Colton breaks our eye contact for the first time and angles his head over to look at his oldest and best friend. "Rest assured, bro, when the doc clears me, nothing—and I mean nothing—is going to be coming between Rylee and me for a long *fucking* time, except for maybe a change of sheets."

My cheeks burn red at his frankness but my body clenches at the promise of his words. And I don't care that Beckett just heard because I'm focused on the words *long, fucking time.*

"So noted," Becks says as he takes another tug on his beer.

"I gotta take a piss," Colton says, shoving himself up from the chaise. As I've learned to do over the past days, I force myself to remain seated as Colton struggles momentarily with his lack of balance and the sudden dizziness that I know assaults him. After a few moments he seems steady and goes to place his beer bottle on the table next to him. About a foot from the table, Colton's right hand's grip gives way and the bottle clatters to the deck below.

Becks' eyes flash to mine momentarily, concern passing through them before he laughs and pretends not to notice. "Party foul!" he laughs. "I think Nurse Ratchet just might be on to something in regards to mixing all those drugs with that alcohol."

"Fuck off," he tosses over his shoulder as he turns toward the house. "Just for that I'm grabbing another!" I watch Colton walk into the kitchen, and when he thinks no one is looking, he looks down at his hand and tries to make a fist out of it before shaking his head.

"How's he doing?"

I turn to face Becks. "The headaches are coming less and less but he's frustrated. He keeps finding little things here and there he can't remember. And he's feeling confined." I shrug. "And you know how he gets when he feels confined."

Beckett blows out a loud breath with a shake of his head. "He needs to get back out on the track as soon as possible."

I stare at him, mouth lax. "*What?*" slips from between my lips, feeling a stab of betrayal at his words. This is his best friend. Doesn't he want to keep him safe? Keep him alive?

"Well, you say he's feeling confined ... the track is the one place he's always been free of everything," Becks says, holding my stunned stare. "Besides, if he doesn't get behind the wheel soon, he's going to let that fear he has eat at him, embed itself in his head, and fucking paralyze him so when he does actually think he can get back in the car, he'll be a danger to himself."

I'm an intelligent person and maybe if I weren't still surprised by Beckett's first comment, I would really hear what he's saying—see the whole picture—but I don't. "What are you talking about? Since he's been home all he's been grumbling about is getting back on the track."

He just chuckles and even though it's not condescending, I feel like my back is up against the wall here and grit my teeth at the sound. "Fuck yeah, he's scared, Ry. Scared out of his fucking gourd. If it's not his hand that he uses as an excuse, it will be something else ... and he needs to get over it. If he doesn't, the fear is just going to eat him alive."

My mind jogs back to the past week. Things Colton has said about racing. Actions that contradict the words he's saying, and I begin to realize that Beckett is right.

"But what about *my* fear?" I can't help the desperation that laces through my voice.

"You think I'm not scared? That it's going to be easy for me too?" The bite in Becks' voice has me turning to look at him. "You think I'm not going to relive those seconds over and over in my mind every time I buckle him in the car? Every time he flies down the chute?

Fuck, Ry, I almost lost him too. Don't think this is going to be easy for me because it's not. It's going to be *fucking brutal* but it's what is best for Colton." He shoves up from the his seat and walks over to the railing, hands spread out supporting himself as he leans into them. "Until you came along it was the only thing he cared about. The only thing that kept him fucking sane." He blows out a biting breath. "It's the only thing he knows." He turns back around to face me, eyes hidden behind aviators. "So yes, he needs to get his ass on the track and I'll be his biggest fucking cheerleader, but don't let that fool you into thinking my heart's not going to be racing every goddamn minute he's out there."

My eyes follow him as he paces to one end of the patio to let his agitation abate and then back toward me before grabbing his bottle and turning the end up, downing the remainder of his beer.

"Racing's about eighty percent mental and twenty percent skill, Rylee. We've got to get his head back in the game, thinking he's ready, then he'll be ready."

I see the logic behind his reasoning, but it doesn't mean I'm not scared to death.

I lift my face up to catch the last rays of sun before they dissipate and sink into the horizon. I hum along to *Collide* playing softly on the outdoor speakers as my mind wanders to Beckett and our conversation, to how I'm going to feel watching Colton get behind the wheel again and if he'll fear it as much as I do.

"Hey, what are you doing out here all by yourself?" Colton's rasp pulls at me on every level, and I open my eyes to find him looking down at me from my comfortable spot on the chaise. Warmth spreads through me when I see the pillow crease in the side of his cheek, and

I can't help but wonder what he was like as a little boy.

"Did you have a good nap?" I scoot over as he sits down beside me, but I purposefully don't move too far so I can snuggle up closer to him.

He wraps his arms around me and pulls me in. "Yeah, I was out." He laughs pressing a kiss to the top of my head. "But no more headache so all is good.

"I can't imagine why you'd have any type of pain with the amount of beer you two put away."

"Smart ass."

"I'd rather be a smart ass than a dumb ass."

"Aren't we feisty tonight?" he says as he tickles my rib cage. "You know what feisty does to me, baby, and I sure as fuck could use it right now."

I squirm out of his grasp. "Nice try, but we most likely only have a couple more days and then I'll be any kind of feisty you want me to be," I say with a raise of my eyebrows as his fingers ease up and smooth down my back.

"Don't promise shit like that to a man as desperate as I am, if you're not going to deliver, sweetheart."

"Oh, no worries, Ace," I say, snuggling back into him, "I'll deliver truckloads of feisty as long as I know you'll be okay."

Colton doesn't say anything, rather he makes a non-committal sound in response. We settle into a comfortable silence for a while, and I welcome it because this is the first time in the past few days where there isn't that inexplicable tension vibrating between us. As the sun sinks and the ocean waves sigh into the oncoming night, my mind begins to wander back to my conversation with Becks. And being me, I have to ask, have to know Colton's thoughts about racing again.

"Can I ask you a question?"

"Mmm-hmm," he murmurs into the crown of my head.

I hesitate at first, not wanting to bring up any thoughts if they're not there already, but ask anyway. "Are you scared to get back on the track? To race again?" The words rush out and I wonder if he can hear the underlying trepidation in my tone.

His hand pauses momentarily on its trek up my spine before it continues, and I know I've touched on something he's not completely comfortable talking about or admitting to. He sighs out into the silence I've given him. "It's hard for me to explain," he says before shifting so that we're side by side, our eyes meeting. He shakes his head subtly and continues. "It's like I fear it and I need it all at the same time. That's the only way I can put it."

I can sense his unease so I do what I do best, I try to soothe him. "You've figured it out with me."

Confusion flickers in his eyes. "What do you mean?"

I had no intention of taking the conversation here, making him feel uncomfortable in talking about the "us" that was there before the crash. The "us" he *raced* and doesn't remember. I reach out and rest my hand on the side of his stubbled jaw and make sure I have his attention before I speak. "You feared and yet needed me ..." My voice fades.

He draws in a breath as emotions flicker through his eyes. His lips purse momentarily. The silence mixed with the intensity in his eyes unnerves me. I can hear the hitch of his breath, the sound of the ocean, the pound of my heart in my ears, and yet silence from him. He looks away and I prepare myself, for what I'm not sure. But when he looks back at me, a slow, shy smile curls up one corner of his mouth, and he nods his head in acceptance. "You're right, I do need you."

Parts way down deep sag in relief that he's finally acknowledging our connection. Accepting it. And I don't care that he isn't telling me he races me, because this, the fact that he needs me, is more than I could ever have hoped for.

He brings a hand up gently to cup the side of my face and brushes his thumb over my bottom lip. He leans in and whispers his lips over mine tenderly before kissing the top of my nose. When he pulls back I see the wicked grin on his face. "Now it's my turn."

"Your turn?" I ask as his fingers play over the buttons of my top.

"Yep. It's question and answer time, Ryles, and it's your turn in the hot seat."

"I'd like a turn in your hot seat," I say back to him, earning the lightning fast grin that pulls on every hormone in my body like a magnet.

"Watch it, sweetheart, because I'm a walking case of blue balls that wants nothing more then to be buried in that finish line between your thighs." As he speaks, he leans forward, close enough to kiss but doesn't grant me one. Talk about sweet torture. When he speaks next, his breath feathers over my lips. "It's best not to test my restraint."

Every part of my body angles into him—wanting, needing, daring him—but he proves he still has control when he chuckles out a pained laugh. "My turn. Why haven't you seen the boys yet?"

Of all of the questions he could have asked me, I had not expected this one. I must look a little shell-shocked because he's right. I do desperately want to see the boys, but I don't know how to see them without bringing the circus with me. The circus that their already fragile lives don't need and can't handle.

"You need me more right now," I tell him, not wanting to give him the exact reason, so that he doesn't have something besides recovering to worry about.

"That's bullshit, Ry. I'm a big boy. I can be left alone for the night. Nothing is going to happen to me."

But what if it does? What if you need me and no one is here and something horrible happens? "Yeah ... I just," I trail off, needing to say it and at the same time not wanting to offend him. "I don't want your world to collide with theirs. They don't need cameras in their faces telling everyone they're orphans—that no one wanted them—or any of the fallout I'm sure would come with it."

"Ry, look at me," he says as he lifts my chin up to meet his eyes.

"You and me? I don't ever want it—me, the craziness around my life, the press, whatever—to come between you and the boys. They are what's important, and I understand that more than most."

Between telling me he needs me and then this declaration, I swear I could have just won the lottery and it wouldn't matter because those two things just made me the richest person in the world. *He really gets me.* Gets that my boys make me who I am and that in order to be with me, he needs to love them. Beckett says I'm Colton's lifeline, but I think he just proved it goes both ways.

I swallow back the lump of tears in my throat as he continues staring at me, to make sure I hear what he's saying. I murmur in agreement, my voice robbed of emotion. "I'll figure something out," he says, leaning in to brush a kiss to my lips. "I'll make sure you get to see the boys soon without interference, okay?"

I nod my head and then curl myself into him as my mind whirls with numerous questions when one jumps out at me. "My turn," I say, wanting and fearing the answer to the question.

"Mmm-hmm."

"That first night," I pause, undecided about how to ask the question. I decide to dive in head first and hope I'm in the deep end. "What were you doing with Bailey in the alcove before you found me?"

Colton barks a laugh followed by a curse, and I think he's a little surprised by my question. "You really want to know?"

Do I? Now I'm not so sure. I nod my head and close my eyes in preparation for the explanation to come.

"I walked backstage to take a call from Becks." He laughs. "Shit, the minute I hung up she was on me like a pit viper. She had my jacket stripped, the front of her dress unzipped, and her mouth on mine faster than …" He fades off as I try not to react to the words, but I know he feels my body tense because he presses a kiss into the top of my head in reassurance. "Believe me, Rylee, it was not what it sounds like."

"Really? Since when does the infamous ladies' man, Colton

Donavan, turn down a willing woman?" I can't hide the sarcasm in my voice. Even though I asked the question, it still hurts to hear the answer. "Besides, I thought you like women taking control."

He laughs again. "There's no need to be jealous, sweetheart ... even though it's kind of hot that you are." I poke him with my finger, content that he's trying to soften the blow of the truth, and instead of pulling away, he just holds on to me tighter. "And I've only ever let one woman take control because she's the only one that's ever mattered."

I scrunch up my nose as my heart sighs at the comment, but my head questions whether he is just trying to exercise self-preservation. Cynicism wins. "Hmpf." I puff out. "I do believe I heard *sweet Jesus* come out of your mouth and not *get off me*."

I feel Colton's body shudder as he laughs in that full bodied way I love. "Think of it more like being eaten alive by a piranha with dull teeth." I can't help the laugh that bubbles up from his comment, and I just shake my head. "No seriously," he says. "The minute I was able to come up for air, that was the first thing that came out of my mouth because the woman kisses like a fucking bulldog." I can't stop laughing now, my jealousy easing toward relief. "And the funniest part was at that moment my mom called to see how things were going and unknowingly rescued me from her claws."

"You mean from her voodoo pussy?"

"Fuck no," he chuckles. "You, baby—you're my voodoo pussy. Bailey? She's more like a piranha pussy."

We laugh a bit more as his analogies get funnier and funnier and then he says, "Okay, so..." he trails a finger down the bare skin of my arm leaving tiny sparks of electricity in its wake "...*Ace?*"

I was waiting for the question, and I just pull back from him and shake my head. "You're going to waste your next question on that? You're going to be so disappointed." I twist my lips and look at him. "Don't you want to know something else?"

"Quit stalling, Thomas!" His fingers dig into my ribs, and I squirm trying to evade them.

"Stop," I tell him as I keep wriggling. "Okay, okay!" I put my hands up and he stops right before I shove his shoulders. "Tyrant!" He tickles me one more time for good measure and then grunts as I try to explain. "Haddie tends to have a ridiculous penchant for rebellious bad boys." I stop mid-sentence as he raises his eyebrows at me.

"Talk about the pot calling the kettle black, huh?" I can see him trying to keep the smile off of his face.

"I told you that night at the carnival that I *don't do* bad boys."

"Oh, baby, you most definitely did me."

I don't even fight the laugh that comes out because the cocky, mischievous grin is back on his face, lighting up his eyes, and solidifying the theft of my heart. "I sure did, but you were most definitely the exception to the rule," I tell him with a smirk.

"As you were mine," he says, and I think back to how easy it seems for him to say these things now when a month ago I never thought it would be a possibility. He leans forward and brushes his lips against mine, his tongue delving between them to taste and tantalize. I groan, unsatisfied, when he pulls away. "Now give me answers, woman. Ace?" he says with the raise of his eyebrows.

"Okay, okay," I relent, although I'm still very distracted by how close Colton's lips are to mine and how much I crave just one more taste even though my lips are still warm from his. "Like I said, Haddie goes for tattooed men destined to break her heart. Some are good for her, most are not. Max and I used to always laugh at the revolving door of rebels that surrounded her. In college she dated this guy named Stone." I just nod when Colton shakes his head, making sure he heard me correctly.

"Yes, Stone was in fact his name. Anyway, the guy was a jerk but Haddie was madly in lust with him. One night he stood her up for his boys, and as we sat with a bottle of tequila and a bag of Hershey kisses, I told her he was a "real ace in the hole" she'd picked this time. One thing led to another shot, and then another shot." I laugh at the memory from all those years ago. "And the more we drank, we decided to make ace stand for something ... we thought we were hilarious with our guesses and once we decided on the perfect one for Stone, we couldn't stop giggling. Later that night after he'd been out on the town with his buddies, he showed up at the door and when Haddie answered it, she said "Hey, Ace!" and the nickname stuck. He thought she was telling him he was an ace in the sack when she was really telling him he was an *arrogant, conceited egomaniac.*" Colton's eyes meet mine when I finally give him what he wants to know. "And from there on out, every time she dated a guy who was like Stone, we called him Ace."

He just stares at me for a second before nodding his head subtly. "Hmpf," is all he says after a beat, his expression stoic and unexpressive. I worry my bottom lip between my teeth as I wait, and then a slow, lazy grin curls up one corner of his mouth. "It's still *a chance encounter* to me, but I guess I earned that title the first night we met."

I snort. "Umm, yeah, you can say that again."

"Don't kick an injured man when he's down." He pouts in mock sadness, and I lean in and brush my lips against his.

"You poor thing," I croon.

"Yep, and just because you feel sorry for me, you're going to let me ask another question. What other memory am I forgetting that you're not telling me?"

I swear my heart skips and lodges in my throat. I try to not falter. Try not to show the break in my figurative stride, which would most definitely let him know that I know something he doesn't. "Nice try, Ace," I tease, swallowing hard and figuring distraction is key at this point.

I lower my lips and kiss little pecks down his neck and chest and then instantly know my next question. I probably shouldn't ask it—know it's a no-go area and I really intend to ask about the knock four times on the hood of the car thing—but the question is out of my mouth before I can stop it. "What do your tattoos mean?" I feel his chest hitch momentarily as I look up and meet his eyes. "I mean, I know what the symbols represent … but what is their meaning to you?"

He stares at me, tumult in his eyes and uncertainty in his grimace. "Ry … " My name is an exhale on his lips as he tries to find the words to express the warring emotions dancing at a rapid pace through his irises.

"Why'd you get them?" I ask, thinking maybe I'll switch gears, anything to get rid of the fear flickering in them.

"I figured I was scarred permanently on the inside—live with it every day, a constant reminder that never goes away—I might as well scar myself on the outside too." He shifts his eyes away from mine with a deep breath and looks out toward the ocean. "Show everyone that sometimes what you think is a perfect package is filled with nothing but damaged goods, scarred and irreparable." His voice breaks on the last word and with it so does a little piece of my heart. His words are like acid eating at my soul.

I can't stand the sadness that overtakes him so I take the reins. I want him to see that whatever the tattoos represent, it doesn't matter. Show him that only he could take what he deems an invisible disfigurement and make it visibly, beautiful art. Explain to him that the scars inside and out are meaningless because it's the man that wears them—*owns them*—who is important. Is the man I've fallen in love with.

And I'm not sure how to show him this, so I move on instinct, touching his arm so he raises it up. I very slowly lean forward and press my lips to the uppermost one, the Celtic symbol representing *adversity*. I feel his chest vibrate beneath my lips as he tries to control the rush of emotion swamping him when I move ever so slowly down to the next one: *acceptance*.

The notion that anyone should ever have to scar themselves permanently to accept horrors I can't even fathom hits me hard. I leave my lips pressed against the artistic reminder and close my eyes so he doesn't see the tears pooling in them. So he doesn't mistake them for pity. But then I realize I want him to see them. I want him to know that his pain is my pain. His shame is my shame. His adversity is my adversity. His struggle is my struggle.

That he no longer has to battle it alone, body and soul stained in silent shame.

As I lift my lips from the symbol of *acceptance* and move it down to *healing*, I look up at him through my tear blurred eyes. His eyes lock on to mine and I try to pour everything in myself into our visual conversation.

I accept you, I tell him.

All of you.

The broken parts.

The bent parts.

The ones filled with shame.

The cracks where hope seeps through.

The little boy cowering in fear and the grown man still suffocating in his shadow.

The demons that haunt.

Your will to survive.

And your spirit that fights.

Every single part of you is what I love.

What I accept.

What I want to help heal.

I swear neither of us breathe in this silent exchange, but I can feel walls crumbling down around the heart that beats just beneath my lips. Gates that once protected are now forced apart from the rays of hope, love, and the trust breaking through. Walls collapsing to let someone else in for the first time.

The absolute impact of the moment causes the tears to fall over and trail down my cheek. The salt on my lips, his scent in my nose, and the thunder of his heart breaks me apart and puts me back together in a magnitude of ways.

He squeezes his eyes shut, fighting the tears, and before he opens them, he's reaching down and pulling me up so we're at eye level. I can see the muscles in his jaw tic and see the fight over how to verbalize it in his eyes. We sit like this a moment as I allow him the space he needs.

"I ..." he starts out and then his voices fades, lowering his eyes for a beat before raising them back up to mine. "I'm not ready to talk about it yet. It's just too much and as much as it's clear in my head—in my soul and my nightmares—saying it out loud when I never have, is just ..."

My heart splinters for the man I love. Fucking shatters into the tiniest shards possible from the memories that just put that lost, apologetic, shameful look in his beautiful eyes. I reach out and cup his jaw in my hands trying to smooth away the pain etched in the magnificent lines of the face.

"Shh, it's okay, Colton. You don't need to explain anything." I lean in and press a kiss to the tip of his nose as he does to me and then rest my forehead against his. "Just know I'm here for you if you ever want to."

He exhales out a shaky sigh and pulls me tighter against him, trying to make me feel secure and safe when I should be doing that for him. "I know," he murmurs into the darkening night. "I know."

And it's not lost on me that he let me kiss all of his tattoos—express love for all of the symbols of his life—except for the one denoting vengeance.

Chapter Sixteen

COLTON

"**M**OTHERFUCKER!"

Where the hell am I? I jerk awake and sit up. My heart's racing, head's pounding, and I'm out of breath. Sweat beads on my skin as I try to wrap my head around the jumbled images floating, then crashing through my dreams. Memories that vanish like goddamn ghosts the minute I wake up and leave nothing but an acrid taste in my mouth.

Yeah, the two us—nightmares and me—we're tight. Thick as motherfucking thieves.

I glance at the clock. It's only seven-thirty in the morning, and I need a drink already—screw that—*a whole damn fifth* to deal with these dreams that are going to be the death of me. Talk about motherfucking irony. Memories of a crash I can't remember are going to kill me trying to remember them.

Can you say fucked up with a capital F?

I laugh out loud only to be answered by the thumping of Baxter's tail against his cushion on the floor beside me. I pat the bed for him to jump up on it, and after a bit of petting, I wrestle him to lie down, laughing at his wildly licking tongue.

I lie back on my pillow and close my eyes trying to remember what I was dreaming about, what empty spaces in my mind I can try and fill. Absolutely fucking nothing.

Sweet Jesus! Throw me a goddamn bone here.

Baxter groans beside me. I open my eyes and look over at him, expecting puppy dog eyes begging for attention. Nope. Not in the slightest. I can't help but laugh.

Fucking Baxter. Man's best friend and shit and also comedic relief when needed most.

"Seriously, dude? If I could lick myself like that, I wouldn't need a woman." My words don't even make him hesitate as he finishes cleaning himself. After a beat Baxter stops and looks at me, head angled, handy tongue hanging out the side of his mouth. "Don't give me that smug look, you bastard. You might think you're top dog now with all that flexibility and shit, but, dude, you'd hold out too for Ry's pussy. Fucking grade A voodoo, Bax." I reach out and scratch the top of his head and laugh again with a shake of my head.

Am I that damn desperate that I'm talking to my dog about sex? And the doc says my head's not screwed up? Shit, I think he's taken one too many right turns on an oval track.

Baxter stands and jumps off the bed. "I get it, use me and then leave me," I say to him, and Rylee's words to me the first night we met resurface. *Fuck 'em and chuck 'em.* Fucking Rylee. Pure class, gorgeous with a defiant mouth and feisty attitude. How the hell did we get from there to here?

I swear to God life is a fucking series of moments. Some unexpected. Most not. And very few inconsequential. Hell if I would have ever expected a stolen kiss to lead to this. Rylee and me.

Motherfucking checkered flags and shit.

Blowing out a breath as the headache starts, I roll over on the bed to grab my pain meds from the nightstand. It feels like my head explodes with a bright burst of white—a flash of memories from the drivers' meeting hits me like a fucking sledgehammer—and then disappears before I can hold on to more than a tenth of what flickered.

"Goddamnit!" I shove up and out of the bed, the dizziness not as bad as yesterday. As the day before yesterday. I feel restless as I try to force myself to remember, to make my jacked up head recall all that I'd just glimpsed. I pace, my mind drawing nothing but blanks. I'm frustrated, feeling confined, unsettled.

More fucked up than not.

I don't feel like me anymore. And I need that right now more than anything. To be me. To be in control. To be on top of my game.

To still be Colton *fucking* Donavan.

"Aaarrrrgggghh!" I shout because *fucking* is most definitely what I need right now. What will help me find the fucking me I need to be again. I may be pacing in front of my bedroom window, but my dick is hard as a rock and my balls are so fucking blue I'm gonna turn into goddamn Papa Smurf if the doc doesn't clear me soon.

Pleasure to bury the pain, *my ass*. When you can't have the pleasure, what the hell do you do with the pain?

And fuck me if it's not the worst—sweetest—torture sleeping next to the only woman I've ever ached for. I can't take another damn day of this. Even though it aches like a bitch, just the thought of her has me reaching down to palm my dick, make sure it didn't shrivel up and fall off from lack of damn use.

Yep, still there.

And then my hand trembles. Shakes so that my fingers can't even hold my own dick anymore.

Motherfuck, cocksuck! I'm shaking with frustration right now. At me, at Jameson for crashing into me, at the damn world in general! This confinement is suffocating me. Making me lose my shit! I'm going fucking crazy!

I pick up the pillow next to me on the couch and chuck it at the wall of glass in front of me before flopping down into a chair. "Shit!" Squeezing my eyes shut, I suddenly feel like images zoom and collide at a rapid pace slamming against the front of my mind. The bright flash of white returns with a vengeance, crippling and freezing me at the same fucking time.

Go, go, go. C'mon, one-three. C'mon, baby. Go, go, go.

Too fast.

Fuck!

Spiderman. Batman. Superman. Ironman.

I jolt my eyes open as memories lost to me rush back in high definition color.

My stomach tumbles to my feet as the forgotten feelings hit me. Fear strangles me as I try to piece the crash together from the Swiss-cheese sized holes still in my memory.

The anxiety attack hits me at full force and I can't shake it. Dizziness. Vertigo. Nausea. Fear. All four mix like a Long Island Iced Tea I'd kill to gulp down right now as my body trembles with the tiny bits of knowledge my memory has chosen to return.

I feel like I'm on a roller coaster, mid free fall as I struggle to draw in a damn breath.

Suck it up, Donavan. Quit being such a pussy! Fuck me because all I want right now is Rylee. And I can't have her. So I rock myself back and forth like a goddamn puss to prevent myself from calling her on her first full day back with the boys.

But hell if I don't need her, especially because I get it now ... get her now. Understand the claustrophobia that cripples her, because right now I can't even function. All I can fucking do is lie flat on the floor with the edges of my vision blurring, the room spinning, and my head pounding.

And in a moment of lucidity amidst the strangling panic, my mind acknowledges that if I didn't feel like myself before, then I most definitely hate this pussified version of myself—falling to pieces, lying on the floor like a little bitch because of a few memories.

I close my eyes as my mind swims in a goddamned fog.

... If it's in the cards ...

More memories graze my mind, but I can't reach them or see

them long enough to hold on to the fuckers.

... Your superheroes finally came ...

I push the memories back, push them down into the blackness. I'm so useless right now. As much as I need to remember, I'm not sure if I can handle them. I've always been a balls-to-the-wall kind of guy, but right now I need motherfucking baby steps. Crawl before you walk and all that shit.

I close my eyes to try and make the room stop the fucking Tilt-A-Whirl it's become.

Thwack!

And another flash of a memory hits me. Five minutes ago I couldn't remember shit and now I can't forget. Screw being broken or bent, I'm a motherfucking scrap yard of parts right now.

Breathe, Donavan. Fucking breathe.

Thwack!

I'm alive. Whole. Present.

Thwack!

I take in a couple of deep breaths, sweat staining the carpet as it pours off of me. I struggle to sit up, to piece together the parts of me scattered all over the damn place to no avail, because it's gonna take a whole hell of a lot more than a torch to weld me back the fuck together.

And it hits me like a motherfucking freight train what I need to do right now. I'm on the move. If I were more coherent, I'd laugh at my naked ass crawling across the floor to reach the television's remote, at how low I've stooped.

But I don't give a flying fuck because I'm so goddamn desperate.

To find myself again.

To control the one fear I can control.

To confront the memories and take their power away.

To not be a fucking victim.

Ever.

Again.

I reach the remote with more effort than it usually takes me to run my typical five miles, and I've only crawled ten feet. I'm weak right now in so many ways I can't even count them. I'm out of breath and the jackhammer is back to work in my head. I finally reach my bed and I push myself on my ass so I can prop my back against the footboard.

Because it's time I face one of the two fears that dominate my dreams.

I aim the remote at the television, push the button, and it sparks to life. It takes me a minute to focus, my eyes have trouble making my double vision merge. My fingers are like Jell-O, and it takes me a few tries to hit the right buttons, to find the recording on the DVR.

It takes every ounce of everything I have to watch my car sling-shot into the smoke.

To not look away as Jameson's car slams into mine. Lighting the short fuse on a fireworks display.

To remember to fucking breathe as it—the car, me—flies through the smoke-filled air.

To not cringe at the sickening sound and sight of me hitting the catch fence.

To watch the car shred to pieces.

Disintegrate around me.

Barrel roll like throwing a fucking Hot Wheels down the stairs.

And the only time I allow myself to look away is when I throw up.

Chapter Seventeen

EXPECTATION VIBRATES AND CONTENTMENT FLOWS through me as I drive the sun drenched highway back to Colton's house, back to what I've been calling home for the past week. A silent tiptoe within a monumental step of our relationship.

It's just out of necessity. Not because he wants me to stay with him for an unspecified period of time. Right?

My heart is lighter after spending my first twenty-four hour shift in over three weeks with the boys. I can't help but smile, recalling Colton's self-sacrifice to get me out of the house and to the boys without a paparazzi entourage. As I was behind the wheel of the Range Rover and its heavily tinted windows, Colton opened the gate on his driveway and walked right out into the media frenzy, drawing all of the attention on himself. And as the vultures descended, I drove out the other side and left without anybody tailing me.

Anticipation is not inconsequential. The phrase dances through my mind, a parade of possibilities rain from the four words Colton texted me earlier. And when I tried to call him to ask what he meant, the phone went to voicemail and another text was sent in response. **No questions. I'm in control now. See you after work**.

And the simple notion that after being with him basically non-stop for three weeks and now I'm not allowed to talk to him—that in itself has created serious anticipation. But the question stands, what exactly am I supposed to be anticipating? As much as my body has already decided, vibrating at what it knows to be the answer, my mind is trying to prepare me for something else. I'm afraid that if I think he's really been cleared by the doctor, and he hasn't, I'll be so frenzied with need and overwhelmed with desire that I'll take what I want—am desperate to have—even though it's not safe for him.

I can't help but smile in satisfaction as I think of what tonight just might bring, on the heels of a great shift with the *other* men in my life. I felt like a rock star walking into The House from the warm and loving reception I received from the boys. I missed them so much and it was such a comforting sound to hear Ricky and Kyle bickering over who is the best baseball player, to hear the sweet sound of Zander's voice in its sporadic but steady bouts, to listen to Shane rattle on about Sophia and Colton getting better so he can teach him how to drive. There were hugs and affirmations that Colton really is okay and all of the headlines in the papers saying otherwise were not true.

I turn up the radio when *What I Needed* comes on and start singing aloud, the lyrics bolstering my good mood, if that's even possible. I look over my shoulder and change lanes, noticing the dark blue sedan for the third time. Maybe I didn't escape the paparazzi after all. Or maybe it's one of Sammy's guys just making sure I get home okay. Regardless, I have a slightly unnerving feeling.

I start to get paranoid and reach for my phone to call Colton and ask him if he had Sammy put a security detail on me. I reach across to the passenger seat and my hand hits all of the homemade gifts the boys made for Colton. It's then I realize that when I loaded my stuff into the back of the car, I set my phone down, and forgot to pick it back up.

I glance in my mirror again and try to shake the feeling away that eats at me, that makes me worry when I see the car still a few lengths back, and force myself to concentrate on the road. I tell myself it's just a desperate photographer. Not a big deal. This is Colton's territory, something he's completely used to but not me. I blow out an audible breath as I make my way through the beachside community and onto Broadbeach Road.

I shouldn't be surprised that the paparazzi still obstruct the street outside of Colton's gates. I shouldn't cringe at having to navigate the street as they descend upon me when they notice I'm driving his car. I shouldn't check my rearview mirror again as I push the button for the gates to open and see the sedan park itself against the curb. I should notice that the person in the car never gets out—never claims his camera to take the shot he's been following me for—but driving with camera flashes exploding around me, it's hard to concentrate on anything else.

I breathe out a shaky breath as the gates shut behind me and park the Rover. I exit the car, my hands a little jittery and my head wondering how anyone gets used to the absolute chaos from the frenzied media as I hear them still calling my name from over the wall. I look up to where Sammy stands just inside the gate and accept the nod he gives me. I start to ask if he's added a man on me but I suddenly remember Colton's text.

Anticipation is not inconsequential.

Everything in my body clenches and coils, my nerves are already frenzied and aching for the man inside the house in front of me. I open the back of the car and grab my purse, figuring I'll leave everything else and get it later. I move quickly to the front door, have the key in the lock, and the door open in seconds. When I close the door the cacophony outside is silenced, and I lean back against the wood, my shoulders sagging at the literal and figurative notion that I've just shut out the world and am now in my little slice of Heaven.

I'm now with Colton.

"Tough day?"

I almost jump out of my skin. Colton steps out of the shadowed alcove, and it takes everything I have to remember to breathe as he leans against the wall behind him. My eyes greedily scrape over every defined edge—every inch of pure maleness—of his body, covered only in a pair of red board shorts hanging low on his hips. My gaze roams up his chest and over inked reminders to take in the lopsided ghost of a smile, but it's when our eyes lock that I catch the spark right before the dynamite detonates.

And from one breath to the next, predicated by a carnal groan, he is on me—body crashing into mine, pressing me against the door, mouth doing so much more than kissing. He's taking, claiming, branding me with unfettered need and reckless abandon. I immediately reach up and fist the hair at the back of his neck while one of his hands does the same to me, the other is on my hip, his desperate fingers digging into my willing flesh. My breasts pillow and pebble against the firmness of his chest, the warmth of his skin adding heat to the blaze building inside of me.

An inferno of need rises inside me that I don't think will ever be sated.

We move in a series of fervent reactions, his hand holds my curls hostage so my mouth is at the mercy of his dexterous lips. So his tongue may delve and tantalize and taste like a man savoring his last meal, like a man saying fuck off to his restraint and accepting gluttony as a welcome sin.

My hands graze down the blades of his shoulders as he gasps—so grateful to have the chance to feel again—before he hikes my leg up and over his hip. I moan, the change in position allowing his rock hard erection to be perfectly placed against my aching core. I throw my head back against the door as the muted friction swamps me, and Colton takes advantage of my newly exposed neck. His mouth is on the tender flesh in the beat of a heart, his tongue sliding against nerves, bringing them to life and then simultaneously singeing them with desire.

My fingers grab onto flexing biceps as his hands make quick work of the button on my jeans. I wiggle my hips when his hands slide between the fabric and my anticipatory flesh. I step out of them as his fingers roam, feathering over my swollen folds to tempt but not take. His other hand palms my backside, a barrier between me and the door, and presses me further into him.

Need swells to unfathomable heights as the parasitic strains of desperation consume every part of my body.

"Colton," I groan, wanting—no needing—him to complete our connection. My hands grope his torso and tear apart the Velcro on his board shorts. I hear the hiss of his breath as my hands find and encircle his tortured length. His whole body tenses at the feel of my skin on his.

"Ry …" He pants my name as I slide my hand up and down him. His hands find their way beneath my top, stripping it off me and making fast work of my bra clasp. "Rylee," he says between gritted teeth. He's so overwhelmed with the sensations ricocheting through him that he stops kissing me, stops moving his hands over my flesh, and braces them against the door on either side of my head. He presses his forehead against mine as he vibrates with the need coursing through him, his breath coming out in short, sharp breaths against my lips.

He says something so quietly I can't hear it underneath the heavy breathing filling the otherwise silent room. I move my hands again, enjoying the feeling of him trembling against me. "Stop," he says quietly against my lips, and this time I hear him. I instantly stop and move back to look at him, fearing that his head is hurting. And I am immediately unnerved by the sight of his eyes squeezed shut.

He draws in a pained breath and opens his eyes slowly to meet mine, as his fingers gently knead my ass. "I'm fucking desperate to bury myself—feel, lose, find myself—in you, Ry …" he says, the strain in his neck visible and his desperation audible. "You deserve soft and slow, baby, but all I'm going to be able to give you is hard and fast because it's been so fucking long since I've had you."

My God the man is so damn sexy, his admission such a turn on, that I don't think he realizes I don't care about soft and slow. My body is strung so tight—emotions, nerves, willpower—that a single touch from him will undoubtedly break me, shatter me into a million fucking pieces of pleasure that oddly will make me whole again.

I angle my head up to him, lean in, and brush my lips to his. I hear his pained intake of breath, feel the tension in his lips as I pull gently on his bottom one from between my teeth. When I pull back, I meet his lust-laden eyes.

"I want you," I whisper to him, one hand wrapped around his iron length and the other fisted tight in the hair at his nape, so he can feel the intensity of my desire. "Any way I can have you. Hard, fast, soft, slow, standing, sitting—it doesn't matter so long as you're the one buried in me."

He stares at me for a beat, disbelief warring with the need raging in his eyes. I can see him try to rein it in, can feel him tremble with need, and know the instant his resolve crumbles. His mouth meets mine—bruising lips and melding tongues—as he takes, tastes, and tempts as only he can. Strong hands map the lines of my torso, thumbs brushing the underside of my breasts already heavy with need, before descending back down the curve of my hips.

If I thought the seeds of desire planted before had bloomed, I have never been more wrong because right now—*right now*—I'm a garden of nee.

He grows even harder in my hand as I rub my thumb over the moisture at his crest and am rewarded with a groan from deep in his throat. My other hand scratches up the skin of his back as my lips brand his with just as much fervor. In an instant, Colton has his hands on my hips, lifting me up and pressing my back against the door. My legs try to wrap around his waist but he holds me up, suspended so the one connection I want the most isn't made, so the steeled length of him against my thighs is a torturous tease to my begging apex.

He sucks in a breath as I reach between my legs and grip him, wanting to control the man who is uncontrollable. Needing him in the worst way. The best way. In any way.

His eyes flicker with some undecipherable emotion, but I'm so pent up, so preoccupied with what's going to happen in the next few moments I don't even give a second thought to what it is.

I release him momentarily and reach between my legs to wet my fingers with the pool of moisture within before encircling his crest and coating it, preparing him physically and showing him figuratively what he does to me, and what exactly I want from him. And my little demonstration weakens all of his restraint.

His fingers dig into my hips and lift me up a little higher as I line him up before he pulls me back down and onto him. We both cry out as our connection is made. As my wet heat stretches past its limits to accommodate his invasion.

And it feels like it's been so long since he's filled me, my body has forgotten the pleasurable burn his presence can evoke. "My God," I breathe as my body takes him in. "I'm so tight," I tell him, chalking it up to the fact that it's been over three weeks since we've been intimate.

"No, baby," Colton says, mirth dancing in his eyes as he stills his hips so I can adjust. "I'm just that big."

The laughter fills my mind but never makes it to my lips before I see a flash of his cocky grin and then his mouth is on mine again. But this time as his kiss claims mine, his hips begin to move, hands begin to guide, and his cock begins to stroke over every attuned inch within my nerve-laden walls. He is in complete control of our movements, our motions, our escalation of sensations.

I lift my head up from its leaning position against the door and take in the sight of him. His own eyes are closed, lips slightly parted, hair mussed from my hands, and shoulder muscles rippling as he moves us in rhythmic motion.

My broken man is now in pure dominant mode, and every nerve in my body screams to be taken. To be made his. To be the one he proves his virility to.

"Fuuuccckkk you feel good," he tells me as he pushes me up and then plunges back into me as my muscles clench and nerves are paid the attention they most definitely have been craving.

"Colton," I pant, my fingers digging into the tops of his shoulders as he drives me higher and higher. Sensation spirals—little shock waves of pleasure preparing me for him to shake the earth beneath my feet—and warmth starts to spread like a wildfire through my core. He drives back in again as my thighs tighten around him, my fingernails score lines, and my mouth seeks his with a frenzied need.

It only takes a few more seconds before the pleasure ratchets into an explosion of white in the abyss of darkness that has consumed me. And I am instantly lost to a world beyond our connection. It's just him and me—sensation overwhelming and breath robbed— as I drown in the liquid heat and lose myself to the feeling, his name a repeated pant from my lips.

Within moments, Colton's cry breaks through my pleasure induced coma at the same time his hips convulse wildly beneath mine, finding his own release. He rocks back and forth in me a few times trying to draw out the moment, his breath ragged and chest gleaming with our combined sweat.

His body sags against mine as he buries his face into the crook of my neck. My arms wrap around him from my position atop his pelvis and pressed against the door. I absorb the moment—the rapid rise and fall of his chest, the warmth of his breath against my neck, the unmistakable scent of sex—and understand without a doubt that I'd move Heaven and earth for this man without a second thought.

Colton adjusts his grip on my hips, and I slowly lower my feet to the ground; although my head is still figuratively in the clouds. He slips out of me and yet our connection is not lost because he gathers me in his arms, skin to skin, as if he doesn't want to let me go just yet.

And I'm okay with that because I don't think I'll ever be able to let him go either.

"Fuck, I needed that," he sighs with a slight chuckle and all I can give him is a noncommittal answer because frankly I'm still riding my own high.

We fall silent for a few moments, lost in the moment, enjoying the comforting feel of just being together.

"I can't believe you didn't tell me," he says, breaking the silence and shakes his head back and forth before pulling back so he can look at the questioning look on my face.

"Tell you?" I'm confused.

A ghost of a smirk graces his mouth as he brings one hand up to cup the side of my face, his thumb brushing ever so softly over my lips still swollen from his kisses. "What I said to you before I got in the car ..."

My inhaling breath dies and my heart skips a beat, lodging itself in my throat from the words on his lips and the emotion in his eyes. I want to ask him to say it, to tell me the words himself, because hell yes I know what he said, but I want to hear that he remembers those words and still feels the meaning behind them.

I try to control the hitch in my breath and wavering in my voice but I have to ask. "What do you mean?" I'm a horrible liar and I know he can see right through my feigned confusion.

He chuckles a quiet laugh and leans in to brush a tender kiss against my lips and then the tip of my nose before leaning back so he can look into my eyes. He darts his tongue out to wet his lips and says, "*I race you, Ryles.*"

My heart melts and my soul sighs at hearing him repeat those words I've used like glue to bind the broken pieces the crash created. Even though the words bring me peace, I can hear nerves shake his voice, can sense the anxiety in the bottom lip he worries between his teeth. And now I'm starting to get nervous. Did he say the words and now doesn't feel the same way he did then? I know it's a ridiculous thought, considering what happened between us moments ago, but the one thing I've learned about Colton is that he is anything but predictable.

"Yeah," I sigh, meeting the temerity in his eyes. "Those words ... are you saying them now because you've reclaimed the memory or because you still mean them?" *There.* I've laid it out on the table, given him the option to say it's the former and not the latter—an *out* in case he no longer *races* me. In case the accident has changed how he feels and this—us, me and him—have reverted back to a *just casual* status.

Colton angles his head and studies me a moment, eyes beseeching but lips motionless. The silence stretches as I wait for the answer, as I wait to see if he'll rip me apart or be the soothing balm to my healing heart.

"Ry ... don't you know I never forget a single moment when I race ... *on or off* the track?" It takes a moment for the words to register, for the words and what they mean to sink in. That he remembers and that he still feels the same way. And the funny thing is now that I know—now that all of this worry can go away and we can move forward—I'm frozen in place.

We're naked, leaning against a door that a hundred or so reporters are on the other side of, the man I *race* has just told me that he races me back, and yet all I can do is stare at him as my soul realizes the hope filling it, is finding its permanent home.

Colton leans in so his mouth is a whisper from mine, hands framing my face as he looks into the depths of my soul. "I race you, Rylee," he says to me, mistaking my silence as not understanding his prior statement. Little does he realize I'm so head over heels in love with him, right here, right now—body naked and heart bared—that I'm robbed of the ability to speak. So instead I accept the brush of his lips over mine in a kiss that's soft and reverent before he rests his forehead against mine. "Don't you know?" he asks. "You're my motherfucking checkered flag."

I can feel his lips curve up in a smile as they brush against mine, and I let the laughter that bubbles up fall free. It feels so good to suddenly have that thorn removed from my side.

To know the man I love, loves me in return.

To know he's caught my free-falling heart.

Colton's hands start the descent back down the line of my spine—the tremor of his right hand so slight now I barely notice it—and then back up as I feel him start to harden again against my lower belly.

"I take it you've been cleared from the doc?" I ask, my sated body already thrumming with newfound desire.

"Yeah I did, but after my day," he says, kissing my forehead and pulling me back into the comfort of his arms, "it didn't fucking matter if I got the okay or not, I was taking what was mine."

"What was yours, huh?" I tease him despite the words warming my heart.

"Yep."

And then the words he said before register and have me pulling back to search for an answer. "What was wrong with your day?"

I see something cloud his eyes momentarily before he pushes it away. "Don't worry about me," he says, and I'm immediately concerned.

"What else happened, Colton? Was there something you remembered—something that—"

"No," he says, quieting me with a press of his lips against mine. "I only remembered what was important. Some voids are still there." Ever the master of deflection, he continues, "It seems I've been neglecting you as of late."

So whatever is bugging him, he doesn't want to talk about. Okay … well, then on the heels of the past twenty minutes, I will most definitely give him the unasked for space and not push. "*Neglecting me?*"

"Yes, not treating you properly," he says as he slaps my butt; the sting it leaves has nothing on the shock waves that ripple through the hypersensitive flesh between my thighs. "You've been taking care of me—of everyone else but yourself as usual—and I haven't properly taken care of you."

"I do believe you did just take care of me … *and quite properly,*" I tease, wiggling my naked body up against his and earning the hum that comes from deep within his throat. "If that's considered not taking care of me—neglecting me—Ace, *then please...*" I nip at the skin on the underside of his jaw "...neglect me some more."

"My God, woman, you test a man's restraint," he groans as his hands run down my spine and clasp together against my lower back. "But, that was just a minor sidetrack to—"

"*Minor* is not what I'd call it," I quip with a raise of my eyes and another wiggle of my hips that causes him to laugh out loud. "I'll take one of your sidetracks any day."

"Bet your ass you will," he teases with a quick squeeze of my hips, "but as I was saying, it's time I treated you to a proper night out rather than gross hospital food and keeping me occupied while I lie in bed." When I just quirk a suggestive eyebrow at the occupy in bed part, he just shakes his head at me and that grin I love lights up his face. He leans in and kisses me softly, murmuring his next words against my own lips. "There'll be plenty of time for you to occupy me in bed later because right now—tonight—I'm taking you to a movie premier."

His words catch me by complete surprise. "Wh-what?" I look at him with incredulity on my face and lips parted in shock. He just grins at me with a cat-that-ate-the-canary look because he's surprised me.

A little thrill of excitement shoots through me at the thought of experiencing something new with Colton—making new memories— but at the same time that means I'll have to share him with *them*. The *paparazzi* who sit outside the gate and will no doubt be at the event with their intrusive questions and in-your-face cameras. And it also means we have to step outside of this world, away from our cozy little realm where we can make sweet, lazy love whenever and wherever we want.

I know which one I prefer.

His sarcastic comment to Becks from days earlier chooses right now to hit my ears and take hold. The words are out of my mouth before I can filter them. "I thought once you got the okay, nothing was going to come between you and me but a change of sheets for a *long, fucking time.*" I repeat his own words back to him.

Colton's eyes instantly darken with lust and spark with mischief as his mouth twists, his mind figuring out which option he'd prefer.

"Well," he says with a laugh, "I did in fact say that." He traces a finger lazily down my cheek, to my neckline, and then down between my breasts. I can't help the breath I suck in, the pebbling of my nipples, or the swelling of my heart. "And you know me, Ryles, always a man of my word ... so how exactly am I going to keep you naked with the exception of a sheet and at the same time attend a premier I've already committed to? Hmm ... decisions," he whispers as he leans down and traces the curve of my neck with the tip of his tongue. "What shall we do?"

I open my mouth to answer but all I can do is try and breathe when his teeth tug playfully on my earlobe. "I guess the world's about to learn how damn sexy you look wrapped in a sheet."

My eyes snap open to meet his as shock kicks my libido down a notch. Within a second Colton and his devilish grin have picked my naked self up and placed me over his shoulder.

"No!" I shriek as he starts toward the stairs. "Put me down!"

"The media's going to have a field day with this one," he taunts as I swat his ass, but he carries on. "Well one way to look at it, it's not going to take you long to pick out what to wear."

"You've lost your marbles!" I shout, my comment earning me another smack on my bare ass perched so seamlessly over his shoulder.

"My loss is your gain, sweetheart!" He chuckles as he climbs the last step up the stairs.

"Gain, *my ass!*" I mutter under my breath, and he belts out another laugh.

"Oh really," he says, angling his head to the side and placing a chaste kiss on my hip beside his face. "I didn't know you liked to play *that way,* but I'm sure we could explore that avenue when the time's right."

My mouth gapes open and I sputter a nervous laugh as Colton stops and slowly slides my body down every firm inch of his until my feet touch the floor. The impish gleam in his eye causes me to wonder if that's yet another something Colton might be into that's never crossed my mind before. I'm so lost in my momentary thoughts and the quiet calculation in his eyes that I miss the fact he's set me down on the private, second story terrace.

And when I realize it—when I notice my surroundings—I'm shocked once again … but this surprise is one that melts my heart.

"Oh, Colton!" The words fall out of my mouth as I take in all of the preparations around me. A portable movie screen has been set up on the far end of the patio and the chaise lounges have been arranged in theater style seating, draped in several layers of none other than sheets. A smile spreads over my face and warmth permeates my soul as I take in the little touches, little things that let me know he cares: a bowl of Hershey's kisses, a bottle of wine, funnels of cotton candy, lighted candles sprinkled everywhere, and clouds of pillows to lie back on.

I can't help the tears that well in my eyes nor do I care when one slips over and slides silently down my cheek. The thoughtfulness that went into everything that sits beautifully in front of me leaves me at a loss for words. I turn back to face him and just shake my head at what I see … because if what's behind me robs my words, the beauty inside and out of the man before me steals my heart. He stands there naked— unshaven, hair mussed and, not including the shaved patch, in desperate need of a haircut, and a look in his eyes that reinforces the words he said to me downstairs.

"Thank you," I tell him with a broken breath. "This is the sweetest thing …" My voice drifts off as he takes a step toward me and brings his hands up to cup my cheeks and angle my head up so I can meet his eyes. "The best kind of night out. A movie with my Ace and sheets *… nothing between us but sheets.*"

He smiles that shy smile that undoes me and leans in for a whisper of a kiss before pulling back. "That's exactly right, Ry. Nothing between us but sheets. *Nothing between us ever again but a set of sheets.*"

His words stagger me, move me, complete me, and all I can do is step forward and press my lips to his—feel his heart against me, the scrape of his unshaven jaw against my chin, see the love in his eyes—and say, "*Nothing but sheets.*"

Chapter Eighteen

THE HEAT OF THE MORNING sun warms my skin, chased by the cool blow of the ocean's breeze. The stereo we forgot to turn off lastnight plays Matt Nathanson's voice just barely audible above the noise of the surf. I snuggle in closer to Colton, so content with the unexpected turn our lives have taken when we more or less crashed into one another that I swear my heart hurts from the enormity of it all. With the second chances we've both been given—that we're both slowly accepting—that a year ago we could have never imagined.

I squint my eyes, thankful for the trellis above that blocks the sun from where we fell asleep last night on the bed of chaise lounges. I don't even bother to suppress the sigh of a more than satisfied woman as I reminisce making slow, sweet love to him under a blanket of stars and in a bed made of possibilities.

I recall rising over him, sinking down onto him, and watching the unguarded emotion flow through his eyes. How the soft and slow with Colton is just as mind blowing as the hard and fast. How a man used to showing no emotion—used to guarding his heart at all costs—is slowly opening up, moving each brick one at a time, allowing the key to turn in the lock.

I smile softly as I lift my head and look at all the reminders of last night. How sweet the gesture was from a man who swears he doesn't subscribe to the notion of romance, when everything around us screams just the opposite. What man calls in a favor from his dad to get a copy of his not-released-yet but soon-to-be-blockbuster movie so he can have an uninterrupted date night with his girlfriend? And even though I came to find out he had Quinlan's help, it was all his idea … the little touches here and there, because it's the little things that mean so much more to me than the extravagant ones.

I raise my head up from where it rests on his chest and watch him sleep, let my love for him warm the parts of me the breeze has cooled. "I can feel you watching me," he says groggily with a curl of his lip even though his eyes remain closed.

"Mmm-hmm." I can't help the smile on my face.

"Whose idea was it to sleep out here? It's too damn bright." He shifts, eyes still closed, but brings the arm that rests behind his head down to pull me closer to him.

"I believe the words were, 'Your voodoo pussy has worked its magic and stolen mine. I have no energy to move,'" I repeat, not hiding the smug look on my face or the pride in my voice.

"Nope, definitely not my words," he says before cracking open an eye and looking over to me, that salacious smirk I love displayed proudly. "I've got magic in spades, baby, it must have been some other guy your voodoo sucked the life from."

I fight back the urge to laugh because that gravelly morning voice and those sleepy eyes are the perfect combination of sexy, making it extremely hard to feign nonchalance. "Yeah, you're right. Remember, I don't do bad boys such as yourself." I shrug. "It was that clean-shaven guy I see on the side. The one who gives me what you can't," I taunt as I lift the sheet resting over our hips and peek under it, my eyes roaming greedily over his impressive morning hard-on. My muscles, slightly sore from last night, immediately clench in welcome anticipation of more to come. I close my eyes to hide the desire I'm sure clouds them and make a satisfied moan.

"See something you like? Something he can't give you?" I love the playful tone in his voice.

I make sure my voice is even when I speak because all of this bantering foreplay is making me crave what is beneath my fingertips.

"No worries." I force the words out as I look up from beneath my eyelashes to find his eyes dancing with humor. "*This woman* is more than satisfied. No need to experience your magic when that man can drive his stick down the homestretch like you wouldn't believe."

Within a heartbeat Colton has flipped me on my back and hovers over me, weight resting on one elbow, and his other hand cuffing my wrists above my head. His face is inches from mine, smirk locked in place, and eyebrows raised in challenge. "I believe my words the other day were a *long, fucking time*," he says, pressing his erection at my apex. "There's the *long*, sweetheart, now we just need to fulfill the *fucking time* part of it."

I start to belt out a laugh but it ends in a pleasurable moan as he sinks into my willing body. I'm not fully ready for his entrance, and although this would normally hurt, it doesn't. Instead it adds the perfect amount of friction to awaken every nerve possible, including any he might have missed last night.

"Sweet fucking Jesus, you feel like Heaven woman," he murmurs into my ear as his hips pull out and slide back forward, his one hand still pinning my hands above me. In an oddly intimate action, he lowers his face and rests it just beneath the curve of my neck so each time he withdraws and sinks back into me, the scrape of his stubble and the warmth of his breath teases my skin. And maybe it's because of his face being so closely positioned by my ear or just that we are so in tune with one another again, but there's something about the sounds he makes that are such a turn on. Grunts turn into moaning sighs, audible satisfaction.

I try to move my arms but his grip holds me still. "Colton," I pant as my body starts to quicken, warmth spreading, the desire coiling so tight I'm waiting for it to spring free. "Let me touch you."

"Hmm?" he murmurs, the vibration of his mouth against my

neck rolling through me. He moves again, grinding his hips in a circular motion, cock hitting hidden nerves, before he pulls back out and angles up so he rubs against my clit adding a pleasurable friction that has me forgetting all thoughts about needing my hands to be released. He chuckles, knowing exactly what he's just done. "That feel good?"

"God yes!" I moan as he does it again, my thighs starting to tense and my skin becoming flushed as the tidal wave of sensation surges in preparation for its final assault on my body.

"I know I'm good, baby, but God might get a little jealous if you start comparing us."

The playful tone, the lazy lovemaking, because this is making love for us—he may call it racing, but this ... murmured words, utter acceptance, complete knowledge of the other's body, comfort—is most definitely him showing me how he loves me.

I can't help the carefree laugh that falls from my mouth any more than I can help the arch of my back and the angling of my hips on his next thrust in his slow, skillful rhythm. "Well ... be prepared to get jealous in turn," I taunt, causing him to lift his head from his position on my neck and scrape his whiskers purposefully across my bare nipple causing unfettered need to mainline straight to where he is manipulating so expertly between my thighs. He raises his eyebrows at me in amusement, trying to figure out what exactly I mean as his hips rotate again within me, and I'm lost.

To the moment.

To him.

To the orgasm singlehandedly ripping through my body and drowning me in its overwhelming sensations.

To the, "Oh God, oh God, oh God!" that falls from my lips as wave after wave surges through me.

And I succumb to the haze of my desire but I hear him chuckle when he realizes just why I thought he might be jealous. My body is still pulsing around him, still coming, when he leans down into my ear, his morning rasp adding a soft tickle to the violent sensations reverberating through me. "You may be calling his name now, sweetheart, but in a minute you're going to be thanking me," he says as he nips my shoulder with his teeth before my hands are released and the warmth of his body leaves mine.

I'm so lost in riding out my climax that the warmth of his mouth on my already sensitive flesh has me calling out his name, hands fisting in the hair on his head positioned between my legs, tongue sliding along the length of my seam. "Colton!" I cry as his tongue licks into me, drawing out the intensity of my orgasm, prolonging the free fall of ecstasy. "Colton!" I say again, starting to squirm my hips against his mouth as the pleasure becomes almost too much to bear.

He licks his tongue back up again and this time keeps going, drawing a line of open mouth kisses and licks up my belly, chest, and neck to my mouth so when his tongue pushes between my lips, I can taste my own arousal. His mouth on mine absorbs my gasped moan as he enters me once again and begins to chase his own orgasm.

When he pulls back from my mouth and sits back on his knees, holding my legs apart as he starts to move within me, he grants me that lightning flash grin I can never resist. "I told you, it would be my name you were calling in the end."

I start to say something but he grips my hips and rears back and thrusts into me. The start of a punishing rhythm that has my hands gripping the sheets and his name becomes a pant on my lips as he takes us to the edge together.

"What'd Becks want?" I ask Colton as I walk into his office and lean my backside on the desk to face him. If it weren't for my positioning, I would have missed the uncertainty flicker through his eyes before he grimaces.

"Is it a bad one?" I ask of the headache I can tell he's trying to hide.

"Nah, not too bad. They're getting fewer and farther between," he says falling silent as he unbends the paperclip in his hand with fierce concentration.

"Becks?" I prompt, sensing that something is wrong.

"He uh, asked if I wanted to reserve some time at the track since they book out far in advance. To make sure I had some time if I wanted it." He averts his eyes and focuses on the paperclip he's unfolding with his fingers. "He thinks I should get back in the car."

Fucking Beckett!

I want to scream at the top of my lungs but settle for chastising him silently. Okay. I've gotten my unfounded anger out at him for doing what I agree is right, but it still doesn't mean I like it … at all. I'd feel a whole hell of a lot better if I had a punching bag too because I'm still terrified by the thought of Colton suited up and behind the wheel, but the question is, is Colton?

"What are your thoughts on it? Are you ready?"

He sighs and leans back in his chair, lacing his fingers behind his head and looking up to the ceiling. "Nah," he says finally, drawing the word out, stalling for time for his explanation. "Yesterday I—" he stops mid-thought and shakes his head. "Doesn't matter … My hand's still too fucked up to grip the wheel," he says. And I know it's a bull-shit lie since he had no problem holding me up so he could have his way with me against the front door yesterday, but I know saying it out loud would be akin to kicking a man when he's down; not only would I know he's scared, but I'd also be proving he's lying.

But his aborted explanation that he didn't complete, mixed with his comment yesterday about it being a rough day, collide together not so subtly in my mind. I move without asking and sit across his lap and nestle into him. He blows out a resigned breath before unlacing his fingers and closing his arms around me.

"What happened yesterday?" I ask after a moment. I can feel his body pause momentarily, and I kiss his bare chest beneath my lips as a silent sign of support.

"I watched the replay."

He doesn't need to say anything further. I know perfectly well what *replay* he's referring to because I still can't bring myself to watch it. "And how did you handle it?"

His body vibrates with an unsettled energy, and when he starts to shift beneath me, I can tell that he needs to release some of it. I move off his lap and when he rises and walks to the window, I sink back into the leather, still warm from his body.

Colton shoves a hand through his hair, tension evident in the bare muscles of his back as he looks out the window to the beach down below. He forces out a laugh. "Well, if you call a grown man crawling around on the fucking floor naked while he dry heaves from the goddamn panic attack after every single fucking feeling from the crash hits him like a sucker punch," he says, voice thick with sarcasm, "then shit, if that's considered handling it? Then fuck yeah … I'd say I aced that motherfucking test." He rolls his shoulders and walks out of the office without a backward glance. I exhale the breath I'm holding when I hear the door to the patio slide open and then shut behind him.

I let some time pass, lost in my thoughts, my heart hurting for Colton's obvious struggle between needing and fearing racing, and I stand up to go find him.

I walk out onto the patio and hear the splash of water before I see his long, lean figure slicing through the top of the water with graceful fluidity. He covers the distance of the pool quickly, reaches the end and does some kind of underwater flip and resurfaces before heading the other way.

I sit cross-legged on the edge of the pool and admire his natural athleticism—the rippling of muscles, his complete control over his body—and wonder if this absolute attraction I have for him has any limitations.

After a bit, he does his underwater turn at the edge farthest from me and instead of immediately starting his stroke again, he flips over on his back and floats, his momentum causing him to drift toward where I'm sitting. He looks so peaceful now, despite his chest expanding from his exertion, and I wish I could see this type of serenity in his features more often.

His torso rises from the water as he lowers his feet to the bottom and scrubs his hands over his face. When he removes them, he looks up, startled to see me sitting there watching him, and the most breathtaking smile spreads across his lips. He scrunches his nose up, reminding me of what he'd look like as a little boy, and any of my concern over his state of mind vanishes.

He walks over to where I sit, eyes locked on mine. "I'm sorry, Ryles." He shakes his head with a sigh. "It's hard for me to admit I'm scared to get back in the car."

His admission shocks the hell out of me. I reach out and run a thumb over his cheek, never more in love with him than right now. "That's okay. I'm scared too."

He reaches out to my hips and pulls me closer toward him so he can kiss me. A brush of his lips and the scent of chlorinated water on his skin is all I need to feel right with him again. He starts to say something and then stops. "What?" I ask softly.

He clears his throat, licks his lips, and averts his eyes to the beach beyond. "When I get back in the car ... will—will you be there?"

"Of course!" The words are out of my mouth and my arms are wrapped around his wet body instantly, a physical emphasis to my words. I feel his chest shudder and hear the hitch in his breath as he squeezes me tighter. I bring my fingers up and tease his hair with my nails as his face remains nuzzled under my neck.

I love you. The words are in my head, and I have to stop them from coming out of my mouth because the intensity of what I feel for him is indescribable. Unconditional love.

The distant sound of the doorbell ringing from inside the house has us pulling back from one another. I look at him confused. "It's probably one of the security guys," he says as I rise and he swims towards the steps.

"I'll get it," I tell him as I walk in the house, pulling my now wet shirt away from my body, glad I opted for the red tank top instead of the white one.

My hand is turning the knob, pulling on the slab of wood, when I hear Colton's voice from outside tell me to *"Wait!"* but it's too late. The door's swinging open and unbeknownst to me, one of my worst nightmares is standing opposite me.

All I can do is sag my shoulders at the sight. Long legs, blonde hair, and a condescending smirk is all I catch before she starts to walk past me and then stops, angling her head over her shoulder to look back at me. "You can run along now, little girl. Playtime is over because Colton doesn't need you anymore. He's in good hands now. Momma's here."

My jaw drops open, her audacity renders me speechless. Before I can find my words, she breezes into the house like she owns the place, leaving me in the wake of her overpowering perfume.

"Colton?" I shout out at him the same time he walks into the foyer, the towel he's using to dry his hair drops to the ground.

Several emotions flicker through his eyes, the most prevalent one being annoyance, but his face shows absolutely nothing.

And with Colton, when his face is that cold and devoid of emotion, it means a storm is brewing just beneath.

"What the fuck are you doing *here*, Tawny?" The ice in his voice stops me in my tracks but doesn't even faze her.

"Colt, baby," she says completely unaffected by the bite in his words. "We need to talk. I know it's been a while and—"

"I'm not in the mood for your melodramatic bullshit so cut the crap." Colton takes a step farther into the room. "You know you're not welcome here, Tawny. If I wanted you here before, I would've invited you myself."

I shrink back at the venom lacing his voice, but at the same time, I'm pissed. Pissed that she just waltzed in here—a home where I'm the only woman he's ever brought—like she deserves to be here.

"Testy, testy," she scolds playfully, unfazed by his complete disinterest. "I was so concerned about you and how you're doing and if you've gotten your memory back yet that—"

"I don't give a flying fuck about your concern! You have two seconds. Start talking or I'm throwing your ass out." Colton takes another step toward her and I can see his grinding jaw and his complete callous disregard for her.

"Just because you're pissed your recovery is going so slow—that you can't remember *important* things—doesn't mean you get to take it out on me." Tawny lets out a condescending laugh and turns slightly to look over at me with disbelief in her eyes as if she's saying *"Really? He's picked you over me?"* before she says, "I'm sure this is amusing to you being his nursemaid and all, doll, but you're no longer needed."

I'm off the wall in an instant, a ball of anger flying at her, but Colton beats me to the punch. Rage emanates off of him in palpable waves as he grips her bicep. "Time to go!" he growls out as he starts to direct her toward the door. "You don't come into my house and disrespect, Ry—"

"I'm pregnant."

The words that float out of her mouth die in the sudden silence of the room, and yet I can see them vibrating within Colton. His body stops, fingers flex on her arm, and teeth grind. It takes a beat for him to catch his stride again, pulling her toward the front door.

"Good for you. Congrats." He bites out, sarcasm dripping from his words. "Nice knowing ya." He starts to open the front door as she yanks her arm free.

"It's yours."

Colton's hand stills on the doorknob as my heart twists at the words coming from her lips. I'm watching this unfold—all of it right before my eyes—but I feel like a complete outsider, a hundred miles away. I watch his head sag down between his shoulders for a beat, notice his hands clench in fists at his sides, see the fury rage in his eyes as he turns ever so slowly around. His eyes dart over and hold mine for a beat, and what I see knocks the wind out of me. It's not the rage they glisten with—no—it's the disbelief laced apology he's offering up to me. The apology that tells me deep down he fears her words are true. Lead drops into my stomach as the mask he's let slip is reapplied, and he turns to direct his anger toward Tawny.

"You and I both know that's not possible, Tawny." He takes a step forward and I can see every ounce of restraint he has—how he's trying so hard to not pick her up and physically throw her out. His eyes dart from her face to her stomach and then back up again.

"What?" she gasps, shock laced with hurt in her voice. "You don't remember?" She holds a hand to her mouth, tears welling in her eyes. "Colton you and I … the night of Davis' birthday party … you don't remember that?"

My stomach wrenches because if I thought she might be acting—playing the part to get him back—she just stole the show with the hurt look on her face and desperation in her voice.

Oh my God. Oh my God. It's my only coherent thought because my entire body trembles with every imaginable emotion possible.

"No," Colton says, shaking his head back and forth, and the look on his face—the one that says if he keeps repeating no over and over this will all just be a nightmare—kills me. Tears into parts deep inside of me opening me up, preparing me for the onslaught of hurt to come.

"It's the only possibility," she says quietly, placing her hand over her midsection where I can see the slight bump now that her shirt is smoothed down. "I'm five months, baby."

I have to fight the bile that rises in my throat as my faith falters. I have to force myself to breathe. To focus. To realize that this isn't about me. That this is about Colton's worst nightmare coming true on the heels of a truly magical night between us. But it's hard not to.

All my mind can focus on is dates—days past—as her words sink their claws into me. *Five months, five months, five months,* I repeat over and over because time is so much easier to focus on than the world that's just been shifted beneath my feet. When my mind can formulate coherent thoughts again, I realize it's been a little shy of five months since we met. Fuck, *it's possible.*

I tell myself she's lying. That she's trying to dig her hooks into Colton—catch the prize she wants more than anything—by pulling the *I'm pregnant* card. The oldest one in the book. But the evidence is there in her swollen belly and the terrified look on Colton's face says it's a possibility—that he's reaching deep within the locked vault of memories and trying to find the one she's telling him about. Fear flickers across his face, embeds itself in those eyes of his that all of a sudden refuse to look at me.

And no matter how much I want to, I can't look away. It's like if I keep staring at him, he's going to look up at me and give me that smile he gave me moments ago in the pool and she'll just disappear.

But it never comes.

He stands in the middle of us, motionless, lost in thoughts I can only imagine. The playful man I love from last night is nonexistent. I can see the cogs in his head turning, notice the wince of pain that I'm sure is from another headache hitting him … but if he's completely frozen, then I'm fucking paralyzed.

Tawny's eyes flicker over and assess me with complete disregard, before looking back at Colton, a soft smile on her face. "You drove me home from Davis' house, asked to come in … we had sex, Colton. The first time we were drunk … desperate to be with each other again and didn't use a condom."

And if her dagger isn't already breaking skin and pushing into my heart, she has to add the notion that they were together multiple times to twist it a little deeper.

"Before … when we dated before..." he clears his throat "...you used to be religious about taking your pill." I don't recognize his voice, and I've been on the receiving end of Colton's wrath, but right now the absolute contempt in his tone sends shivers up my spine.

"I wasn't on the pill," she says softly with an unapologetic shrug as she takes a step toward him, the possible mother of his child. The gentle intimacy in her tone causes tears to spring in my eyes. She reaches out to touch Colton's arm and he yanks it out of her reach.

His reaction and the unfettered panic in his eyes causes the reality of this all to begin to seep through my denial, the possibility that this isn't a ploy to merely get him back.

I sag against the wall behind me, my ghosts and inadequacies as a woman threatening to rear their ugly head. I place a hand on my abdomen to stifle the pang I feel in my useless womb. The one that will forever remain empty. The one that can't give him the only thing *she can.* I feel the beginnings of a panic attack—breath laboring, heart racing, eyes unable to focus—as I wonder if the man who professes to never want kids just might change his mind when faced with the possibility of one. It happens all the time. And if it does, then where does that leave us? Leave me? The woman who can't give him that.

"No!" It falls from my lips in response to my silent thoughts.

Colton whips around to look at me quickly, distress etched in his features at my unexpected words. And then she snorts out in disregard and adds gasoline to Colton's fire.

"Get out!" He shouts so loudly I jump, and for a moment, because he's facing me, I fear that he's speaking to me. I force a swallow, his eyes flicking over me before he turns his back to me and points toward Tawny and then the door. "Get. The. Fuck. Out!"

"*Colty* ..."

"Don't you ever call me that!" he yells, grated steel in his voice as he raises his eyes to look toward where she's not moved an inch. "*No one gets to call me that*! Do you think you're special? Do you think you can just waltz in here and tell me you're five fucking months pregnant? That I'd care? Why are you telling me now, huh? Because it's too late for me to have a say in anything, so you think you've trapped me? Found your golden fucking ticket?" He begins to pace, lacing his fingers behind his head and blowing out a loud breath. "I'm not Willy fucking Wonka, sweetheart. Go find yourself another sugar daddy."

"You don't believe me?"

Colton whirls around in a flash, his gaze meeting mine and the void in his expressionless eyes startles me. Dead eyes look at me momentarily before he breaks our connection and strides back across the room to where Tawny still stands. "You're goddamn right I don't believe you. Quit the crap and get the fuck out with your bullshit lies." He's inches from her face, eyes glaring, and posture threatening.

"But I still love—"

"You don't get to love me!" he bellows, fist slamming down on the sideboard next to him, vases rattling and noise resonating in the otherwise quiet of the house. Tawny lets out a sob and Colton remains completely unaffected by her outburst of emotion. "You don't get to love me," he repeats again so quietly that I can hear his pain beneath it, feel the desperation roll off of him in waves.

He reaches up and rubs his hands over his face. He looks out the window for a moment toward the tranquility of the ocean as I watch the storm rage inside of him. I'm rocked in the turbulence of his emotions without a lifeline to hold on to. When he looks back at Tawny, I can see so many emotions behind his slipping mask that I'm unsure which one he is going to grab and hold onto.

"I want a paternity test."

Tawny gasps, her hand resting protectively over her belly, but when I look back up to her face, I watch the transformation happen. I see the damsel in distress morph into the vindictive vixen. "This baby is yours, Colton. I don't sleep around."

Colton snorts a laugh with a shake of his head. "Yeah, you're a regular patron fuckin' saint." He stalks to the front door and turns back to look at her. "Go tell it to some other gullible son of a bitch who cares. My lawyer will be in touch."

"You're gonna have to come at me with something a hell of a

lot bigger than threatening me with your attorney to get out of this one," she says, straightening her spine. "Get your checkbook ready and your ego prepared for some serious damage, *sweetheart!*"

"Did you actually think you could just waltz in here, drop your bullshit bomb, and I'd take your word for it? Write you off with a hefty check or marry you and ride off into the motherfucking sunset?" His voice thunders. "It's. Not. Mine!"

Tawny shrugs her shoulders and a smarmy expression transforms her features. "The press is going to have a field day with how I spin this one … a nice juicy scandal to sink their teeth into."

She starts to walk toward the front door and just when I think I might be able to take a breath, Colton's palm slams against the door, the sound assaulting the dead silence of the room. He turns and gets back within inches of her face, his voice trembling with rage. "Newsflash, *sweetheart*, you better hit me with something stronger than that threat if you think the press scares me. Two can play that game," he says opening the door. "Make sure you tell them all the juicy details because I sure as fuck won't hold back. It's amazing how quick a promising career can be dashed in this town when rumors hit the papers about what a demanding diva one can be. No one wants to work with a fucking bitch, and you definitely fit that bill. Now get the fuck out."

Tawny walks up to him, stares at him, although he refuses to meet her eyes, and then walks out the front door that shuts with a resounding slam behind her. Colton immediately grabs one of the vases on the sideboard he'd hit moments earlier and throws it against the wall. The shattering sound of glass followed by tinkling as it bounces off the tiled floor is such a contrast to the heaviness of the moment. Not getting the release he needed, he places his hand on the sideboard and braces his weight against it.

I step forward from the shadows of the foyer, still not sure what to do when he looks up and locks his eyes with mine. I try to get a read his emotions but I can't—his guard is back up and locked in place. The knowledge of how much work it's going to take to break that wall back down causes a little piece of me to die, to die and fall to rest beside the piece that broke off the day the doctor told me it'd be nothing short of a miracle for me to get pregnant again.

The emptiness of my womb hits me again as I walk toward him. He watches me, jaw ticking, body tense. "Colton ... I—"

"Rylee," he warns, "back the fuck off!"

"What if it's true? What if you guys really did and you don't remember?" It's the only coherent thought I can verbalize, my mind spinning with *what-ifs* and *never-going-to-bes*.

"*Why?*" He turns to face me, and I swallow nervously. "So you can play house?" He takes a step toward me and the look in his eyes has me cringing. "Because you want a baby so bad that you can taste it? Would do anything to have one? Take one that might or might not be mine so you can sink your hooks in me too? Get the best of both worlds, huh? A hefty sum and a baby—every woman's fucking dream." His words whip out and slap me, rip apart the part of me that knows I would do anything to have the chance to have a baby. "It's not true!" His voice thunders at me. "It's not true," he says again in too calm of a voice.

I'm stuck in place—wanting to run, wanting to stay, hurting for me, devastated for him—at a crossroads of uncertainty, and all I want to do is curl into a ball and shut the world out. Shut Colton out, and Tawny out, and the ache that will never go away, to feel a baby move within me. To create something out of love with someone I love. Bile threatens at the thought, and I cover my mouth as I gag audibly to prevent myself from puking.

"Yeah, the thought of me being a dad makes me want to puke too." He sneers at me, so much more than contempt lacing his voice. And that's not why I'm going to be sick, but I can't tell him that because I'm too busy trying not to be. "*Between the sheets.*" He belts out a patronizing laugh, looking up at the ceiling before looking back at me. "How fucking ironic is it when it's between the sheets with someone else that's causing this little dilemma, huh, Ryles? How's that phrase working for ya now?"

"Fuck you." I say it more to myself than to him, a quiet voice laced with hurt. I've had it. He can be upset. His horrible past can be dredging through his mind, but that doesn't give him the right to be a fucking asshole and take his shit out on me.

He turns to look at me, a picture of fury against the tranquility behind him. "Exactly." He spits out. "*Fuck me.*"

And with those parting words, Colton yanks open the door to the deck. I don't call out to him—don't care to—and watch him jog down the stairs to the beach with a whistle beckoning Baxter.

Chapter Nineteen

THE LONGER I SIT AND wait for him to come back the more nervous I become.

And more pissed.

I'm nervous because besides his swim earlier, Colton hasn't exercised since being cleared ... and he was only cleared yesterday. I know his anger will push him to run harder, faster, longer, and that only unnerves me because how much can the healing vessels in his brain withstand? It's been almost an hour since he left, how much is too much?

And I'm pissed that after everything he said to me, I even care.

I shake my head, the words he said to me rattling around as I look down the stretch of beach. I get his anger, the inherent need to lash out over his rather fragile hold on his preconceptions, but I thought we were past that. Thought that after everything we've been through in our short time together that I'd proven otherwise to him. Proven that I am not like *other women*. That I need him. That I will never manipulate him to get what I want like so many other women in his life have. That I will not abandon him. And I so desperately want to leave right now—escape the argument and further hurt I fear will happen upon his return—but I can't. More than ever I need to prove to him right now that I'm not going to run when he needs me the most, even if the thought of him having a child with someone else is killing me now.

I swallow the bile that wants to resurface again, and this time I can't hold it down. I run to the bathroom and upset the contents of my stomach. I take a moment to compose myself, talk myself down from the ledge I want to leap from because this is too much for me. So many things are happening in such a short amount of time that my mind wants to shut off.

But if it's true, what does that mean? To him as a person and us as a couple and to me as the woman who can't ever give him that? And especially given to him by *her*? My stomach revolts at the thought again, and all I can do is drop my forehead on the lid of the toilet, squeeze my eyes close, and shut out images of an adorable little boy with inky hair, emerald eyes, and a mischievous smile. A little boy I'll never be able to give him.

But she can. And if that's the case, how in the fuck am I going to be able to handle it? Love the man but not the baby that's his because I'm not the mother—simply because he's part Tawny—now what kind of horrible person would that make me? And I know that's not true, know I could never not love a child because of circumstances he has no control over, but at the same time, there would be that constant devastating reminder of what someone else can give him that I can't.

The ultimate gift.

Unconditional love and innocence.

I wipe away the tears I didn't even realize were falling when I hear the distant bark of Baxter and make my way out onto the deck. The harmless beast of a dog clears the top of the stairs coming up from the beach and plops down exhausted on the deck with a groan. I take a deep breath and prepare myself for Colton's arrival, unsure which version of him I will be facing.

Within moments he appears, hair dripping with sweat, cheeks red, and chest heaving from the exertion. I want to ask how he's feeling, where his head is, but I think better of it. I'll let him set the tone of this conversation.

He looks up and I see the shock flicker across his features when he sees me. He stands, hands propped on his hips, and just stares at me for a beat. "Why the fuck are you still here?"

So that's how this is going to be.

I thought I had calmed down, hoped that he had with his run, but obviously we're both still bound with a barbed wire ball of hurt. We're both still hell-bent on proving our points. The question is how is he going to handle what I have to say? Is he going to lash out again? Rip me apart for a second time? Or is he going to realize that despite Tawny's bombshell, our figurative race doesn't stop? That we can withstand the collateral damage?

"You don't get to run anymore, Colton." I hope my words— words he'd used with me before—will hit their target and sink in.

He stops mid-stride beside my chair but keeps his head angled down to avoid looking at me. "You don't fucking own me, Ry. You don't get to tell me what I can or can't do any more than Tawny can." His voice is a whisper but his words sucker punch me.

"Non-negotiable, *remember*?" I warn him with challenge I don't feel reflected in my eyes. He just stands there impatiently, muscles tense, and I feel compelled to continue. To either stop or start the fight brewing between us. "You're right." I shake my head. "I don't own you ... nor do I want to. But when you're in a relationship, you don't get to hurt someone because you're hurting and then bail. There are consequences, there are—"

"I told you, Rylee ..." He turns to face me now, his eyes still averted, but the tone of his voice—one of pure disgust—has me rising to my feet. "I do as I damn well please. It's best you *remember* that."

"Colton ..." It's all I can manage, feeling like I've been knocked back a few steps by his sudden assertion, his sudden need to grab his life that he feels is spiraling out of control. But he doesn't get it. It's not just *his* life anymore. It's my life too! This is about the man I love and the possibilities I feel. This is killing me just as much as it is him, but he's too wrapped up in his own head to see differently. I force a swallow as I try to find the words to tell him this, to show him we're both hurting, not just him. But I'm too slow. He beats me to the punch.

"You tell me we're in a relationship, Rylee ... Are you sure it's what you want because this is how my life goes," he shouts, his body moving restlessly with all of his negative energy. "The *charmed* life of Colton fuckin' Donavan. For every up there's a motherfucking free fall down. For every good there's a goddamn bad." He takes a step toward me, trying to antagonize me and push my buttons. I dig my nails in my palms to remind myself to let him get it off of his chest. To let him blame everyone in the world if need be, so he can calm down, realize this is not the end of his world, despite it feeling like it is for me. "Are you ready for that kind of *spin* on the track of my life?" He finishes, the sarcasm dripping from his words as he steps within a few feet of me. I can feel the anger vibrate off of him, can sense his desperation at which straw to grab and hold onto to get me to react. I force a swallow and shake my head.

"Okay," I say, drawing the word out, buying time as I try to think of what to say. "What is the good and the bad then?"

"The good?" he asks, his eyes widening as sweat drips down his torso. "The good is I'm alive, Rylee. I'm fucking alive!" He shouts, thumping his chest with his fist. I cringe as his voice rings in my ears. He mistakes my reaction and feeds off of it. "What? Did you think I was actually going to say *you*?" I tell myself not to cry, tell myself that's not the answer I was hoping for, but who am I kidding? Did I really think that in the midst of all of this he'd hold onto me as his strength? His reason? I can hope, but for a man so used to relying on himself, I shouldn't be surprised.

"You think you can waltz in here and play house, nurse me back to health, and all my troubles—all my fucking demons—are going to disappear? I guess Tawny just proved that theory wrong, huh?" He laughs a patronizing chuckle that eats tiny holes in what resolve

I still have left. "The perfect fucking world you think exists, sure as fuck doesn't. You can't make lemonade with a lemon that's rotting from the inside out."

And I'm not sure which hurts more, the acid eating at my stomach, his anger hitting my ears, or the ache squeezing my heart. The aftershock left by Tawny turns into a full-blown earthquake of disbelief and pain as my thoughts spin out of control and slam headfirst into the wall just like Colton did. But this time the collateral damage is too much to handle as it all comes crashing down around me. My stomach heaves again as I try to grasp on to something, anything, to give me an iota of hope.

I need air.

I can't breathe.

I need to get away from all of this.

I take a few steps backwards, needing to escape, and stumble against the railing. I fight the need to throw up again, my hands squeezing the wood beneath my fingers as I try to steady myself.

"You don't get to run anymore, Rylee, *we're in a relationship.* Aren't those your rules?" His mocking voice is closer than I expect and something about the way he says them, the intimacy laced with sarcasm, sets me off.

I whirl around. "I'm not running, Colton! I'm hurting! Fucking falling apart because I don't know what to say or how to respond to you!" I scream. "I'm fucking pissed that I'm angry at you for being so goddamn callous because *you're right*! I would give anything to have a baby. *Anything*! But I can't and the thought that someone can give you the one fucking thing that I can't is tearing me apart."

I bring my hands up to my head and just hold them there for a moment as I try to stop crying, as I try to collect the thoughts I need to say. I lift my head and meet his eyes again. "But you know what? Even if I could, I would never use or manipulate you to get one. I am not fucking Tawny, and I am not the poor excuse of life your mother was." Tears stream down my face and I look at him, standing there stunned by my outburst through my blurred vision.

He starts to say something, and I raise a hand to stop him, needing to finish what I have to say. "No, Colton, I'm not running and I'm not leaving you, but I don't know what to do. *I have no fucking clue!* Do I stay here and let you rip me apart more? I'm dying inside, Colton. Can't you see that?" I wipe the tears from my eyes and shake my head, needing some kind of reaction from him. "Or do I just leave? Give us a couple of days to fix the shit that's fucked up in our own heads? So I don't resent you for getting a choice when I don't. So you realize I'm not like every other woman who's ever used you."

I take a step toward him, the man I love, and I wish I could do something—anything—to ease the turmoil inside of him, but know that I can't. I can sense he's at a breaking point just like I am, that being faced with the possibility of a child is more than even he—a man who has survived so much—can bear, but I'm at a loss how to help when I'm filled with turmoil too.

The muscle in his jaw pulses as I watch him struggle to remain in control over his emotions, his anger, his need for release and wish I could do something more for him because if my heart is breaking, then I can't imagine what his is doing. And the only thing I think I can do is give us some space … let us calm down … figure ourselves out so we can be good again.

Find us again.

I take another step toward him and he finally raises his eyes to meet mine so I can read what he's feeling. And maybe it's the fact that we really know each other now, have broken down each other's walls, because regardless of how hard he's trying to mask his emotions I can read every single one of them flickering through his eyes. Fear, anger, confusion, shame, concern, uncertainty. The truth is there—what I knew would be—he's pushing me, daring me to run to prove to him I am in fact what he perceives all other women to be. And at the same time, I see remorse swimming there, and a small part of me sighs at the sight, gives me something to hold on to.

He takes a step toward me so we stand close but don't touch. I can see the emotion flickering across his face, how his muscles tense as he tries to contain everything I see in his eyes. I fear if I touch him, we'll both break and right now one of us needs to be strong.

It has to be me.

"Look at me, Colton," I tell him, waiting for his eyes to find mine again. "It's me, the one who races you. The one who'll fight tooth and nail for you. The one who will do anything—anything—to make that hurt in your eyes and the pain in your soul disappear … make Tawny's accusation go away … *but I can't*. I can't be anything to you until you stop pushing me away." I step closer, wanting to reach out and touch him and erase the pain in his eyes. "*Because all I want to do is help*. I can handle you being an asshole. I can handle you taking your shit out on me … but it's not going to fix things. It's not going to make Tawny or the baby or anything else go away." I choke on the tears that fill my throat. "I just don't know what to do."

"*Rylee* …" It's the first time he's spoken and the desperation in the way he says my name with such anguish sends chills up my spine. "My head's pretty fucked up right now." I force a swallow down my throat and nod my head so he knows I hear him. He closes his eyes for a beat and sighs aloud. "Look I—I … I need some time to get it straight … so I don't push you farther away … I just …"

I bite my lower lip, not sure if I'm upset that he's telling me to go or relieved, and nod my head. He reaches out to touch me and I step back, afraid if he does, I won't be able to walk away. "Okay," I tell him, my voice barely audible as I take a step backwards. "I'll talk to you in a couple of days."

And I can't look at him again, both our pain right now is so palpable for different reasons, so I turn and head toward the house.

"Rylee," he says my name again—no one can say it like he does—and my body stops instantly. I know he feels like I do—uncertain, unresolved, wanting me to stay and wanting me to go—so I just keep my back to him and nod my head.

"*I know.*" *I know* he's sorry—for hurting me, for loving me and that I'm being put through this, for Tawny, for the uncertainty, for my own insecurities when it comes to what I can't give him … so many things I know he's sorry for … and the biggest one is that he's sorry for letting me walk away right now because he can't find it in him to ask me to stay.

Chapter Twenty

"I'M SO PROUD OF YOU, buddy." I look into Zander's eyes and fight my own tears. I want him to see the depth of feelings I have for him and for what he just did. For giving the district attorney all they needed to press formal charges against a man that's disappeared like the wind. To sit at a table full of scary grown-ups and explain, in a voice you just found again, how your father murdered your mother—how he attacked her from behind, stabbed her repeatedly and then waited for her to die while you hid behind the couch because you were supposed to be in bed. Now that, is a courageous kid. I squeeze him tight in my arms, more for me than for him, and wish I could take away the memory from him.

"How'd you get so brave?" I ask him.

I don't expect an answer, but when he responds it stops me in my tracks.

"The superheroes helped me," he says with a shrug. I force a swallow down my throat burning with so much emotion I can't speak. I look into the eyes of a little boy that I love with all my heart, and I can't help but see pieces of the grown man who owns it too. My heart twists for both, and even though I am filled with such an incredible sense of pride, it's tinged with a bit of sadness because I know Colton would want to know what Zander did today. The imaginary barriers he vaulted over that most adults could never fathom.

But I can't tell him.

It's been four days since I left his house.

Four days without speaking.

Four days for him, for us to get our individual shit together.

And four days of absolute chaos for me in more ways than one: The House, my emotions, the media frenzy over a possible baby, missing Colton.

I tell Zander I'll put his beloved stuffed dog in his bedroom and tell him to go play tag with the rest of the boys. Go be a kid, play, laugh, and forget the images that haunt him—if that's even possible.

I go through the motions of getting dinner together, while the familiar and comforting sounds of the boys outside help me cope.

I miss Colton. We've been together every day for over a month and I'm used to his presence, his smile, the sound of his voice. I'm hurt he hasn't called but at the same time I don't expect him to. Other than texting to make sure I'd gotten home okay and the song *I Am Human*, I haven't heard from him. He has a lot to figure out, a lot to come to terms with. And *God yes,* I want to be there by his side, helping him figure it all out, but it's not my situation to figure out. Plain and simple.

I can't count how many times I've picked up the phone to call him—to hear his voice, to see how he's doing, to just say hi—but I can't. I know better than anyone that until Colton lets me back in to his barricaded heart, a call won't do any good.

I frost the cake I'd made earlier as a little reward for Zander's bravery today, when my phone rings. I look over at the screen and push ignore. It's an unknown number and most likely a journalist wanting to pay me handsomely for my side of Tawny's story. She's told the press that I am the mistress who broke up her, the pregnant victim, and the love of her life … Colton.

The only blessing is that the paparazzi have not discovered The House yet. But I know it's not long until they do, and I'm still trying to figure out *what do I do then*?

And for some reason, the story Tawny's painted makes me laugh. I don't believe the inside scoop on Page Six that says she and Colton have rekindled their love affair. I was in Colton's house. I know how much he despises her and everything she represents. That's not why I'm sad.

I just miss him. Everything about *him*.

The funny thing is, this time around, I'm not worried he's going to turn to another. We've passed that hurdle and quite frankly adding another woman to the mix would just complicate his life further. No, it's not him turning to another woman I worry about, it's him not turning to me.

Voices break through my thoughts as I cut the potatoes up for dinner. I catch Connor saying, "The douche bag's here again."

"We could always egg him." That one was Shane.

What in the heck are they talking about?

"Hey, guys?" I call out to them as I wipe my hands off and head out to the living room. "Who's here again?"

Shane tilts his head toward our front window. "That guy," he says, pointing. "He thinks he's so incognito parked over there."

"Like we can't see him," Connor interjects. "And don't know he's a *photographer*. Camera's a dead giveaway, dude."

I'm immediately pulling the curtains back, looking down the street. Before I even spot the car, I know what I'm going to see. The dark blue sedan is parked a couple of houses down partially hidden by another car. I had completely forgotten about it.

At least this lone paparazzo is greedy and keeping my whereabouts quiet so he can get all the monetary gain for himself. For that I can be grateful. But it also means that if he's figured it out, others will soon follow wanting to get the scoop from the home-wrecker I am purported to be.

Fuck! I knew The House's anonymity was too good to be true.

"C'mon guys. Time to—"

"That's so cool that you're gonna be famous!" Connor says as he starts walking down the hall.

I start to correct him when Shane does it for me, with a playful shove to his shoulder. "No she's not, dickweed! Colton's the one who's famous. Don't you know anything?"

"Hey! Clean it up!" I shout after them.

"Thanks for picking me up."

"Not a problem," Haddie says as she guns the motor when the light turns green. "It was kind of fun teasing the photographers, although I don't think any of them believed me when I said you were hiding away inside the house."

I groan. It's taken a while to get used to photographers milling about the house, but now I fear that the few I'm used to will turn into a whole yard full. "Dare I ask?"

Haddie looks over at me and just flashes her devil-may-care grin. "Nope, you may not because we're not thinking about it … or Colton … or me … absofuckinglutely nothing of any significance."

"We're not?" I look over at her and can't help but smile, can't help but be happy she was available to pick me up from work to try and keep the vultures at bay.

"Nope!" she says as the tires squeal on a turn. "We're gonna find a dark corner and drown our sorrows, and then we're going to find a wicked hot beat to dance to until we can't remember shit!"

I laugh with her, the idea sounding like Heaven. A moment to escape from the thoughts constantly running through my head and the heaviness in my heart. "What's going on with you? What sorrows are you drowning?" And for a minute I'm sad we've been so busy over the past few weeks that I don't know the answer to the question, when before I would never have had to ask.

She shrugs and is unusually quiet for a beat before she speaks. "Just some stuff with Lexy." I'm about to ask what she's talking about, because she and her sister are so close, but she beats me to the punch. "We're not talking about anything that needs to be talked about, remember?"

"Sounds good!" I tell her as music springs to life in the car and we both start singing along.

I set my glass down with a clink, realizing my lips are a little bit numb. No, make that a *lot* numb. I watch Haddie smirk at the man across the bar and then turn her focus back on me, her smirk spreading into a full out grin. "He looks kinda like Stone," she says with a shrug, and I'm glad my drink is empty or else I would have spit it out.

I don't know why it's so funny, because it really isn't, but my head starts playing connect the dots with memories. Stone makes me think of Ace and Ace makes me think of Colton and the thought of Colton just makes me *want* … him. Everything about him.

"Uh-uh-uh," Haddie says realizing what I'm thinking about. "Another round," she says to the bartender. "Don't think about him. You promised, Ry. No boys. No sadness. No penis perturbance allowed."

"You're right," I tell her with a laugh, hoping she believes me even though I know I'm not being very convincing. "No penis perturbance allowed." The waiter slides new glasses in front of us. "Thank you," I murmur as I concentrate on stirring the ice with my straw instead of thinking of Colton and wondering what he's doing, where his head is at. And I fail miserably. "I told him about Stone the other day."

I'm surprised Haddie can hear me. My voice is so soft, but I know she does because she slaps her hand on the bar. "I knew you couldn't do it!" she shouts, garnering the attention of the people around us.

"I knew that no matter how much you've had to drink we'd end up there."

"I'm sorry," I tell her, twisting my lips. "I really am." I focus back on my drink, upset over letting my friend down.

"Hey," she says, rubbing a hand up my arm. "I can't imagine … I'm sorry … I was just trying to shake the dick dominance and embrace our inner slut for a bit." I arch an eyebrow at her smirk and just shake my head.

"Inner slut embraced," I say, resting my head on her shoulder but not really feeling like it.

"So have you talked to him?" She asks.

"I thought we weren't talking about dick dominating, penis perturbing men named Colton or *Stone*." I snicker.

"Well," she draws the word out. "Yours is damn hard not to talk about when he looks like that with his sexy swagger, come-fuck-me eyes, and all around holy hotness. Shit, the only reason to kick a man like him out of bed would be to fuck him on the floor."

I start laughing, really laughing until all of a sudden the laughter has tears welling in my eyes and causes my lower lip to tremble. I hiccup back the sob and I immediately curse the alcohol—it has to be the alcohol's fault—that I am suddenly sad and missing him like crazy.

Get a grip, Thomas! It's been one frickin' week. Man up. My internal pep talk fails because one day or ten days, it doesn't matter. I miss him like crazy. Whatever the opposite of pussy whipped is, I've got it bad.

"And she finally lets it out," Haddie says, putting her arm around my shoulders and pulling me into her side.

"Shut up!" I tell her but don't mean it.

I mean I'm sitting in a bar on a Friday night with my best friend and I should be having a great time, but all I can think about is Colton. Is he okay? Has he taken the paternity test yet? Is he going to call me? Why hasn't he called me? Is he thinking about me like I am him?

"So I'm gonna throw this out there because we both know that even though we're sitting here together, Colton is figuratively between us. And as much as the idea might excite him …"

I finally give her the laugh she's been working for. "Ugh! I hate this."

"Then why don't you call him?"

And therein lies the million dollar question.

"This whole thing with Tawny fucked him up. It's dredging up shit from his past and as much as I want to be there—to call him—I won't take the brunt of it. I called Becks to check on him, make sure he's okay." I shrug. "He said he did and that Colton's still kind of fucked up. I want to talk to him," I admit as she smooths a hand up my arm, "but I need to give him the space he asked for. He'll call me when he gets his shit together."

"Hmm, I wonder where I've heard that phrase before?" she teases and I just shrug.

"A very wise woman said it, I believe."

"Very wise indeed," she laughs, rolling her eyes and clinking her glass to mine. "And being as I am *that* woman, may I offer you another tidbit of advice?"

"A Haddie-ism?"

"Yes, a Haddie-ism. I like that term." She nods her head in approval as she takes another sip of her drink and smiles again at the guy across the bar. "I asked you once before if you thought Colton was worth it … and now that you have more time invested in it, do you still feel that way? Do you see the possibility of a future with him?"

"I love him, Had." The answer is off of my tongue in a split second. No hesitation, no doubt, complete conviction.

She stares at me a second and I can tell that beneath the surface she is gauging my reaction, trying to figure out the whole picture and a little surprised at my *all in* response. "Do you love him because he's the first guy since Max or because he's the one you choose? Not because you want to fix him, because we both know you like the damaged souls, but because you choose *the him* he is now and *the him* he'll be five years from now?"

I don't answer her, not because I don't know the answer, but because I can't form the words over the lump that's strangling them in my throat. And she can see my answer, knows the person I am enough to know how I feel.

"And if the baby is his?"

I find my voice. "Geez … you're really hitting with the hard questions tonight. I thought tonight was supposed to be thinking about absofuckinglutely nothing? I thought there was a Haddie-ism in here somewhere?" And it's not like I haven't asked myself these questions, but hearing her say them makes it all seem so real.

Because sometimes baggage can be a powerful thing and love just isn't enough to overcome it.

"I'm getting there," she says, pushing my drink toward me. "But this is important because my bestie is hurting so take a drink and answer the question."

I take a sip and can't fight my resigned smile. "It's not if the baby's his that's the problem … it's his reaction that scares me." And for the first time, I'm actually admitting aloud what I fear the most. "What if he is the father and he can't handle it? How can I love a man that can't love his own child regardless of who the mother is? Writing a check to buy her off and acting as if a child doesn't exist? What if that's the option he chooses? How could I spend the night in the bed of a man who writes his own child off and then go to work in a houseful of boys who had the very same thing happened to them? What kind of hypocrite would that make me?"

And there. *It's out there.* My biggest fear, I'm in love with a man that will walk away from his own child. That I'll have to walk away from the man I love because he can't face his own demons, can't accept the fact that he can be the man his child would need him to be. Compromising choices, preferences, and wants to be in a relationship are one thing, compromising who you are—the things ingrained in you, your beliefs, and your morals—are non-negotiable.

I sigh and just shake my head. "What happens then, Haddie? What if that's the choice he makes?"

"Well..." she reaches out and squeezes my hand "...there are no answers yet so it's a moot point right now. Secondly, you have to give him the benefit of the doubt … he was shocked, upset, pissed off the other day when she blindsided him … but he's a good person. Look how he is with the boys."

"I know, but you weren't there. You didn't see how he reacted when—"

"You know what I say?" she says, cutting me off and raising the two shots of tequila that have been sitting untouched on the bar in front of us. I look at her, trying to figure out why all of a sudden she wants to toast mid-heart to heart talk, but I raise my shot glass. "I say, never look down on a man unless he's between your legs."

I choke on the simple breath of air I'm drawing in. I should be used to her by now, I really should, but she continually surprises me and makes me love her that much more. When I stop laughing I look up at her. "One for luck …"

"And one for courage," she finishes as we toss the alcohol back.

I welcome the burn, welcome the here and now with my best friend, and when I wrap my head around what the hell she's just said, I look over at her out of the corner of my eye. "Unless he's between your legs, huh? Is that an old family adage? One passed down from generation to generation?"

"Yep," she says, twisting her lips, fighting the smile I know that's coming. "Never disturb a man when he's eating at the Y."

"Haddie," I laugh. "Seriously?"

"I can keep going all night long, sister!" She clinks her glass with mine again, my cheeks hurting from smiling so hard. "And here's another one. When your best friend is sad? It's your job to get her shit-faced and go dancing."

"Well," I say, sliding off of the barstool and taking a minute to let the room stop spinning, "I think that's a fucking perfect idea!"

Haddie squares up our tab and calls for a cab as we clumsily walk to the front door. And I talk myself out of making her take me to Colton's house because right now, I just really want Colton—in the best way, in the worst way—in all ways.

"C'mon, we're good to go. Three hours in a bar is way too long," she says as she puts her arm around me and helps me walk respectably to the exit.

And as we clear the bar's door, the darkened night sky explodes into an electrifying barrage of blinding camera flashes and shouts.

"How does it feel being known as the home wrecker?"

"Don't you have any remorse coming between Colton and Tawny?"

"Isn't it hypocritical that you tried to make Colton abandon his baby when that's what you do for a living?"

And they keep coming at me. One after another after another. I feel trapped as Haddie tries to guide me through the congestion of cameras and microphones and flashes and contempt.

I guess the press has found me.

Chapter Twenty-One

COLTON

"YOU'RE FUCKING KIDDING ME, RIGHT?" I fight the urge to smash something. That urge driving my every emotion, the one that makes me crave the sound of destruction. The sound of my fucking life imploding.

My mind pushes out the images flashing through it from the past couple of days.

Blood draws and DNA markers and goddamn paternity tests.

Tawny and her bullshit lies and crocodile tears the fucking vultures are eating up like fresh meat.

Visiting with Jack and Jim and getting so sick of looking at my life through the bottom of an empty glass, I just choose to drink straight from the goddamn bottle.

And then there is Rylee.

Motherfucking Rylee.

Little pieces of her everywhere. Sheets that still smell like her. A ponytail holder on the bathroom counter. The cans of her beloved Diet Coke lined perfectly in the refrigerator. Her Kindle on the nightstand. The strands of her hair on my shirt. Evidence that her perfection exists. Evidence that something so good—so pure—actually can want someone like me—tainted and fucked up with a capital F.

I want, need, hate that I want, hate that I need her so damn bad, but I can't do it. I can't pull her into this rainstorm of bullshit surrounding me, don't want her to deal with the fucked up me that even I hate until I can wrap my head around everything. Until I can control the emotions that are ruling my actions.

Until I get a negative on the DNA match.

My mom was fucking right. Fucking right and she only knew me for eight of my thirty two years … if that doesn't say something, I'm not sure what else does. I can't be loved. If someone loves me—if I let someone in too much—my own demons will start in on them too. Work their way through the cracks in me and find a way to ruin them.

"Colton, are you there?"

I pull myself from my thoughts—the same goddamn ones that have been running like a hamster on the wheel through the shit in my head over the past week. "Yeah," I reply to my publicist. "I'm here, Chase." I push the rags on the table in front of me away, but it doesn't matter if I throw them in the trash or set a match to the fuckers because the image of Rylee coming out of that bar is still burned in my brain. Shocked eyes, parted lips, and an all-around look of being overwhelmed from the maelstrom that hit her when she left.

And it fucking kills me! Rips me apart that my bullshit—being with me—caused that look on her face. The fear in her eyes. All I want to do is be the one with her, my arm around her, but I'm not. I can't because I don't have the words or actions to make it better. To make it go away. To protect her.

"This is fucking bullshit and you know it."

I hear my publicist sigh on the other end of the line. She knows I'm pissed, knows no matter what she says I'm not going to be happy unless she tells me to find the bastards that are harassing Ry, and let loose my need to destroy. "Colton, in light of Tawny's accusations, it's best that you do nothing. If you react, your public image—"

"I don't give two fucks about my public image!"

"Oh believe me, I know," she sighs. "But if you react the press eats it up and then the longer they hang around to see you screw up or lose it. That means the longer they hang around Rylee …"

Fuck all if she's not right. But shit, what I wouldn't give to walk outside the gates and give them my two cents worth. "One of these days, Chase," I tell her.

"I know, I know."

I toss my phone on the couch across from me and scrub my hands over my face, before sinking back in the couch and closing my eyes. What the hell am I going to do? And since when do I give a shit?

What the hell happened to me? I went from not giving a fuck about anything or anyone to missing Rylee and wanting to see the boys. Strings and shit. *Fuck me.*

A voice thanking my housekeeper, Grace, brings me back to the present from the unicorns and rainbow shit that doesn't belong in my thoughts. Crap that's associated with pussies and whipped assholes. Shit that has no place in my head mixed with the other poison living there.

I wait a second. I know he's there, watching me, trying to figure out my current state of mind, but doesn't say anything. I crack open an eye and see him leaning against the doorjamb, arms folded across his chest and concern filling his eyes.

"You just gonna stand there and watch me or are you going to come in and pass judgment on me face-to-face?"

He stares at me a beat more and I swear to God I hate this feeling. I hate knowing that along with every other fucking person on the long and distinguished list, I am letting him down too. "No judgment, son," he says as he makes his way into the room and sits on the couch across from me.

I can't bring my eyes to meet his and thank Christ for Grace or this place would be a disaster, and he'd really know how much this whole Tawny situation has screwed me up. I draw in a deep breath wishing I had a beer right now. Might as well get this party started, right? "Lay it on me, Dad, because I sure as shit know you're not here to just say hi."

He sits silent for a bit longer and I can't fucking stand it. I finally look at him. He meets my gaze, gray eyes contemplating what to say as he twists his lips in thought. "Well, I can honestly say I stopped by to see how you were doing in the midst of all of this," he says, waving his hand in the air with indifference, "but it's pretty obvious since you're in such a shitty mood." He leans back in the chair and props his feet up on the coffee table and just stares. *Shit, he's making himself comfortable.* "You gonna talk, son, or are we going to sit and stare at each other all night? Because I've got all the time in the world." He looks at his watch and then back up to me.

I don't want to talk about this shit. I don't want to talk about babies and gold digging women and little boys I miss and a woman I can't stop thinking about. "Fuck, I don't know."

"You're gonna have to give me more than that, Colton."

"Like what? That I fucked up? Is that what you want to hear?" I goad him to react. And it feels good to push someone for a change. Everyone else has been walking around me, treating me with kid gloves this past week afraid of my temper snapping, so it feels good even if I'm going to feel like shit later for doing it to my dad. "You want me to tell you I fucked Tawny and now I'm getting what I deserve because I dumped her like a hot coal and now she's coming after me saying she's pregnant? That I don't want a kid—*will not have a kid*—with her or anyone else? *Ever.* Because I refuse to let someone use a child as a pawn to get what they want from me. Because how the hell can someone like me be a father to a kid when I'm just as fucked up now as I was when you found me?"

I shove up off of the couch and start pacing the room. I'm annoyed with him that he hasn't taken the bait—hasn't pushed back and given me the fight I'm itching for—and is just sitting there with that look of complete acceptance and understanding. Pacification. I want him to tell me he hates me, that he's disappointed in me, that I deserve all that I'm getting right now because that is so much fucking easier for me to hold on to and believe than the opposite.

"And what does Rylee think of all of this?"

I stop and turn to look at him. *What?* I didn't expect that to come out of his mouth. "What do you mean?"

"I asked, what does Rylee think about all of this?" He leans forward, elbows on his knees, eyes questioning me beneath arched brows.

"Hell if I know." I grunt and my dad shakes his head. *God, I hate having to explain myself.* But it's my dad. My end game superhero, how can I not? "She was here when Tawny dropped the bomb. We got in a fight because I was taking everything out on her, being an inconsiderate ass. Bitching about a baby I don't want when she can't have one. I was in stellar form," I tell him with a roll of my eyes. "We agreed to a few days apart to get our heads straight again. Get my shit together."

"And you haven't talked to her since?"

"What is this, Dad? Twenty fucking questions? Does it look like I have my shit figured out yet?" I snort out a derisive laugh. One step forward and then fucking twenty steps backwards. "Is Tawny still pregnant? Have the test results come back yet? Yes, and a *big fucking no* … So no, I haven't called her back yet. Chalk it up to just another thing for you to hold against me."

He just stares at me. "Is that what I'm doing? Holding your shit against you? Because it looks like you're doing a damn fine job of it yourself, son. So let me ask you the question you should be asking yourself: Why haven't you pulled your head out of your ass and called her?"

I blow out a loud breath. Fuckin' A. "I don't want to go there right now, Dad." *Just go away.* Let me down the next bottle of Jack while the clock ticks for the doctors to take their sweet ass time to decide if I've just fucked up the life of an unborn child. Because if the kid's mine, shit, he's already starting off with a tainted soul and that—that's something I can't have on my conscience."

"Well I do want to go there, so pull up a chair to your own pity party, Colton, because I'm not leaving until we finish talking. Understood?"

My mouth falls open, and I'm transported back to fifteen years ago and my one night in custody for drag racing. To that moment in time when he picked me up, raked me over the proverbial mother-fucking coals, and told me how it was going to be from there on out. Damn. I've got chest hair and houses and shit now, but he can still make me feel like a teenager.

Anger flashes through me. I don't need a fucking shrink right now, I need a negative blood test. And Rylee wrapped around me with a soft sigh falling from her lips as I sink into her. The ultimate pleasure to bury all of this bullshit pain.

"So," he says, pulling me back to him instead of thoughts of her. "You're seriously going to let her go without a fight? Let her walk out of your life because of *Tawny*?"

"She's not walking away!" I shout at him, upset that he would even think she would. *Would she?*

He just quirks an eyebrow. "Exactly." My eyes snap up to meet his. "So quit treating her like she did. She's not your mother."

I want to scream at him that I sure as shit know she's not. To not even put her in the same sentence as my mother, but instead I play with the seam on the couch as I search for the answer I think he wants to hear. That I'm trying to convince myself is the truth. "She doesn't deserve this ... the shit that comes with me. My past ... now my possible fucking future."

He makes a hum in his throat, and I hate it because I can't figure out what it means. "Isn't that up to her to decide, Colton? I mean you're making decisions for her ... shouldn't she get a say?"

Shut up, I want to tell him. Don't remind me what she deserves because I already know. I already fucking know! And I know because I *can't give it to her*. I thought I could ... thought I might be able to and now with this, I know I can't. It's reinforced all of the things *she* said

… all of the things I'll never be able to cleanse from my damned soul.

"You say she's not going to leave you when things get tough, son, but your actions are telling me something completely different. And yet you didn't see her fighting for you every damn day you lay in that hospital bed. Every damn day. Never leaving. So that leads me to believe this little dilemma you have here isn't about her at all."

Every part of me revolts against the words he says. The words that said by anyone else would have me ready to rage, but respect has me holding back from yelling at the man who's words are hitting a little too close to home.

"*It's about you.*" The quiet resolve in his voice floats out in the room and slaps me in the face. Taunts me to take the bait, and I can't hold back anymore.

And I don't want to do *this* any more than I want to spend another night without Rylee in my bed. Looking too close causes dead ghosts to float to the goddamn surface, and I don't have any more room for ghosts because my closet's already full of fucking skeletons.

But the match is lit, gasoline thrown. Fire inside fucking ignited and all of the frustration and uncertainty and loneliness from the past week comes to a head, explodes inside of me. I wear a hole in the goddamn floor pacing as I try to fight it, try to rein it in, but it's no use.

"Look at me, Dad!" I shout at him while he perches on the couch. I hold my hands out to my side, and I hate myself for the break in my voice, hate myself for the unanticipated show of weakness. "Look what *she* did to me!" And I don't have to explain who *she* is because the contempt dripping from my voice explains enough.

I stand there arms out, blood pumping, temper raging, and he just sits there, calm as can fucking be and smirks—fucking smirks— at me. "*I am, son.* I look at you every day and think what an incredible person you are."

His words knock the wind out of my sails. I yell at him and he comes back at me with *that*? What kind of game is he playing? Fuck up Colton's head more than normal? Shit, I hear the words but don't let them sink in. They're not true. Can't be. Incredible and damaged don't go together.

Incredible can't be used to describe a person who tells the man molesting him that you love him, whether the words are forced or not.

"That's not fucking possible," I mutter into the silence of the room as vile memories revive my anger, isolate my soul. I can't even meet his eyes because he might see just how messed up I really am. "That's not possible," I repeat to myself, more emphatically this time. "You're my dad. You have to say that."

"No, I don't. And technically, I'm not your dad, so I don't have to say anything." Now that stops me dead in my tracks ... brings me back to being a scared kid afraid to be sent back. He's never said anything like this to me before, and now I'm fucking freaked out about the direction this conversation has taken. He stands and walks toward me, eyes locked on mine. "You're wrong. I didn't have to stop and sit with you on the doorstep. I didn't have to take you to the hospital, adopt you, love you ..." he continues feeding into every childhood insecurity I've ever had. I force myself to swallow. Make myself keep my eyes locked on his because all of a sudden I'm scared shitless to hear what he has to say. The truths he's going to admit. "... but you know what, Colton? Even at eight years old, scared and starving, *I knew*—I knew right then the amazing person you were, that you were this incredible human being I couldn't resist. Don't you walk away from me!" His voice thunders and shocks the hell out of me. From calm and reassuring to angry in an instant.

I stop in my tracks, my need to escape this conversation that's causing so much shit to churn and revolt within me begging me to keep walking right on out the door to the beach below. But I don't. I can't. I've walked away from every fucking thing in my life, but I can't walk away from the one person who didn't walk away from me. My head hangs, my fists clench in anticipation of the words he's going to say.

"I've waited almost twenty years to have this conversation with you, Colton." His voice is calmer now, steadier, and it freaks me out more than when he rages. "I know you want to run away, walk out the fucking door and escape to your beloved beach, but you're not going to. I'm not letting you take the chickenshit way out.

"Chickenshit?" I bellow, turning around to face him with years of pent up rage. Years of wondering what he really thinks of me coming to a head. "You call what I went through the chickenshit way out?" And the smirk on his face is back, and even though I know he's just goading me, trying to provoke me so I take the bait and get it all out, I still take it. "How dare you stand there and act like even though you took me in, it was easy for me. That *life* was easy for me!" I shout, my body vibrating with the anger taking hold, the resentment imploding. "How can you tell me I'm this incredible person when for twenty four years you've told me a million goddamn times that you love me—*LOVE ME*—and not once have I *ever* said it back to you. Not fucking once! And you're telling me you're okay with that? How can I not think I'm fucked up when you've given me everything and I've given you absolutely nothing in return? I can't even give you three goddamn words!" When the last words leave my lips I come back to myself and realize I'm inches from my dad, my body shaking with the anger that's eaten me whole for a lifetime as tiny flecks of it are being chipped away from my hardened fucking heart.

I take a step back and in a flash, he's right back in my face. "Nothing? Nothing, Colton?" His voice shouts out into the room. "You gave me *everything*, son. Hope and pride and the goddamn unexpected. You taught me that fear is okay. That sometimes you have to let those you love chase the fucking wind on a whim because it's the only way they can free themselves from the nightmares within. It was you, Colton, who taught me what it was to be a man … because it's easy to be a man when the world's handed to you on a silver platter, but when you're handed the shit sandwich you were dealt, and then you turn into the man you are before me? Now that, son, that's the definition of being a man."

No, no, no, I want to scream at him to try and drown out the sounds I can't believe. I try to cover my ears like a little kid because it's too much. All of it—the words, the fear, the fucking hope that I just might in fact be a little bent and not completely broken—is just too much. But he's not having any of it, and it takes every ounce of control I have to not take a swing at him as he pulls my hands from my ears.

"Uh-uh." He grunts with the effort it takes. "I'm not leaving until I've said what I came to say—what I've pussyfooted around saying to you for way too long—and now I realize how wrong I was as a parent not to force you to hear this sooner. So the more you fight me, the longer this is going to take so I suggest you let me finish, son, 'cause like I said before, I've got all the time in the world."

I just stare at him, lost in two warring bodies: a little boy desperately begging for approval and a grown man unable to believe it once he's been given it. "But it's not poss—"

"No buts, son. None," he says, turning me around so he's not touching me from behind knowing I can't handle that still all these years later, so he can look into my eyes … so I can't hide from the absolute honesty in his. "Not a single day since I met you have I ever regretted my choice to choose you. Not when you rebelled or fought me or drag raced down the street or stole change off of the counter …"

My body jolts from the comment—the little boy in me devastated I've been caught—even though he's not angry.

"… Did you think I didn't know about the jar of change and box of food you hid beneath your bed … the stash you kept in case you thought we were going to not want you anymore and kick you out on the streets? You didn't notice all the change I suddenly left everywhere? I left it out on purpose because I didn't regret a single moment. Not when you pushed every limit and broke every rule possible, because the adrenaline of the defiance was so much easier to feel than the shit she let them do to you."

My breath stops at his words. My fucking world spins black and acid erupts like lava in my stomach. Reality spirals at the thought that my biggest fear has come true ... *he knows.* The horrors, my weakness, the vile things, the professed love, the stains on my spirit.

I can't bring my eyes to meet his, can't push the shame far enough down to speak. I feel his hand on my shoulder as I try to revert back to focusing on the numbing blur of my past and escape the memories tattooed in my mind—on my fucking body—but I can't. Rylee has made me feel—broken that goddamn barrier—and now I can't help but do anything but.

"And while we're clearing the air," he says, his voice taking on a much softer tone, his hand squeezing my shoulder. "*I know, Colton. I'm your dad, I know.*"

The fucking floor drops out beneath me, and I try to pull my shoulder out of his grip but he doesn't let me, won't let me turn my back on him to hide the tears burning my eyes like ice picks. Tears that reinforce the fact that I'm a pussy who hasn't handled anything at all.

And as much as I want him to shut the hell up ... to leave me the fuck alone ... he continues "You don't need to say a word to me. You don't need to cross that imaginary line in your head that makes you fear an admission will make everyone leave you, will prove you to be less of a man, will make you the pawn she wanted you to be ..."

He pauses and it takes every ounce of everything inside of me to try and meet his eyes. And I do for a split second before the door to the patio, the sand beneath my feet, and the burn of oxygen in my lungs as my feet pound down the beach calls to me like heroin to an addict. Escape. Run. Flee. But I'm fucking frozen in place, secrets and lies swirling and colliding with the truth. The truth he knows but I still can't bring myself to utter after twenty-four years of absolute silence.

"So don't speak right now, just listen. I know she let *them* do things to you that are vile and repulsive and make me sick." My stomach pitches and rolls, my breath shuddering at hearing it aloud. "... Things no one should *ever* have to endure ... but you know what, Colton? *That doesn't make it your fault.* It doesn't mean you deserved it, that you let it happen."

I slide down the wall behind me until I am sitting on the floor like a little kid … but his words, my dad's words … have brought me back there.

Have scared me.

Changed me.

Messed with my head so memories start pushing through the wormholes in my fucked up heart and soul.

I need to be alone.

I need Jack or Jim.

I need Rylee.

I need to forget. Again.

"Dad?" My voice is shaky. The sound of a little bitch asking for permission and shit, right now, isn't that what I am? On the damn floor once again about to throw the fuck up, body shaking, head racing as my stomach revolts?

He's sitting on the floor beside me like he used to do when I was little, his hand on my knee, his patience calming me some. "Yeah, son?" His voice is so soft, so tentative, I can tell he's afraid he's pushed me too far. That he's broken me more when I've already been fucking shattered and held together with scotch tape for way too long.

"I need—I need to be alone now."

I hear him draw in a breath, feel his resigned acceptance, and his unending love. And I need him to go. Now. Before I lose it.

"Okay," he says softly, "but you're wrong. You may have never said the words aloud—may have never told me you loved me—but I've always known because you have. It's in your eyes, how your smile lights up when you see me, the fact that you'd share your beloved Snickers bars with me without asking." He chuckles at the memories. "How you would let me hold your hand and let me help you chant your superheroes as you lay in bed so you could fall asleep. So words, no, Colton … but you told me every day in some way or another." He's silent for a moment as a part of me allows the fact to sink in that he knows. That all the worry I've had over all of these years that he didn't know how much I felt didn't matter. *He knew.*

"I know your worst fear is having a child …"

The elation that lifted me is choked by fear with his words. This is all just too much—too much, too fast when for so long I've been able to hide from it. "Please don't," I plead, squeezing my eyes shut.

"Okay … I've thrown a lot of shit at you, but it was time you heard it. And I'm sorry I probably messed with your head more than you needed me to, but, son, only you can fix that now—deal with it now that all of the cards are on the table. But I have to tell you, you're not your mother. DNA doesn't make you a monster like her … just as if you were to have a child, your demons won't be transferred to that new life."

My fists clench and teeth grind at the last words—words that feed off the worst of my fears—the urge to break something returning. To drown the pain that's back with a vengeance. I know he's pushed me to the breaking point. I can hear his quiet sigh through the screams of every ounce of my being.

He stands slowly and I tell myself to look at him. To show him that I've heard him, but I can't make myself do it. I feel his hand on the top of my head, like I'm a little boy again, and his uncertain voice whispers, "I love you, Colton."

The words fill my fucking head but I can't get them past the fear lodged in my throat. Past the memories of the chant I used to say that was followed by the brutality and unspeakable pain. As much as I want to tell him—feel the need to tell him—I still can't.

See, perfect example, I want to tell him, to demonstrate how fucked up I am. He just bared his self to me and I can't give him a god-damn response because *she* stole it from me. And he thinks I could be a parent? She made my heart black and my core rotten. There's no way in hell I could pass that on to someone else if there were the remote chance it could happen.

I hear the door shut and I just remain on the floor. The outside light fades. Jack calls to me, tempts me, allows me to drown myself in his comfort, no glass needed.

Confusion fucking swamps me. Drags me under.

I need to clear my fucking head.

I need to figure my shit out.

Only then can I call Ry. And God *I want to call her.* My finger hovering over the damn Call button. Hovering there for well over an hour.

Call.

Call End.

Call.

Call End.

Shit!

I squeeze my eyes shut, head fuzzy from however much I've drank. And I start to laugh at what I've been reduced to. Me and the floor are becoming best fucking friends. Fuckin' A.

It's not hard to go up when you're already at rock bottom. Time to ride the damn elevator. I start laughing. I know there's only one other way to clear my head—my only other fucking high besides Rylee— that will help keep the demons at bay for a bit. And as much as I need Rylee right now, I need to do this first to get my shit figured out. My right hand trembles as I go to push Call, and when I do, I'm scared out of my goddamn mind, but it's time.

Head straight.

Then Rylee.

Motherfucking baby steps.

"Hey, douche bag. I didn't realize you knew my phone number it's been so damn long since you've called me."

Such a fucking old lady. God, I love this guy.

"Get me in the fucking car, Becks."

His laughter stops in an instant, the silence assuring me he's heard me, heard the words I know he's been waiting to hear since I got the all clear.

"What's going on, Wood? *You sure?*"

What's with everyone questioning me tonight? "I said get me in the goddamn car!"

"Okay," he drawls out in his slow cadence. "Where's your head at?"

"Seriously? First you push me to get in the fucker and now you're questioning the fact that I want to? What are you, my goddamn wet nurse?"

He chuckles. "Well, I do like my nipples played with, but shit, Wood, I kinda think you touching them would give me a reverse boner."

I can't stop the laugh that comes. Fucking Beckett. Always a bucket of laughs. "Quit screwing with me. Can you get me on the track or not?"

"Can you get the slur out of your voice and put down Jack, because that's a dead giveaway your head is still screwed up … so I'll repeat my question again. Where's your head at?"

"All over the fucking place!" I shout at him, failing miserably to not sound drunk "Goddamn it, Becks! *That's why I need the track.* I need to clear the shit from it to help fix me."

There's silence on the line, and I bite my tongue because I know if I push he'll hang up on me. "The track's not going to fix that fucked up head of yours, but I think a certain wavy haired hottie could do that for you."

"Drop it, Becks." I bite the words out, not in the mood for another shrink session.

"Not on your life, fucker. Baby. No baby. You really gonna push the best thing you got going for you out the damn door?"

And session number two begins.

"Fuck you."

"No thanks. You're not my type."

His condescending tone pisses me off. "Stay the hell out of it!"

"Oh! So you are going to let her go? Isn't that a song or some shit?

Well, since you're gonna let her go, I guess I'll give her a run then."

Motherfucker. Are my buttons that easy to push tonight? "If you're smart, you'll shut the hell up. I know you're pushing me … trying to get me to call her."

"Wow! He does listen. Now that's a news fucking flash."

I'm done. "Quit fucking around, do your job, and get me on the goddamn track, Beckett."

"Be at the track at ten tomorrow morning."

"What?"

"It's about time. I've had it reserved for the past week waiting for your ass to get with it."

"Hmpf." He had me pegged.

"You won't show." He laughs.

"Fuck off."

"You wish."

Chapter Twenty-Two

I BLOW OUT A BREATH and roll my shoulders, welcoming the burn as I stretch my warm and thoroughly tired muscles. I desperately needed this run—the escape into our backyard and through the gate of the neighbor behind us so I could get away undetected from the persistent press.

I look up from my stretch and something across the street catches my eye. I'm immediately on guard when I see the dark blue sedan across the street with the man leaning against it, camera in hand with a telephoto lens blocking his face. Something about him strikes me as familiar, and I can't put my finger on it … but I know my little piece of freedom—by secret passage—has been compromised.

The thought pisses me off and although I've yet to engage with any press, my feet have a life of their own and start walking toward him. My mind running the verbal lashing I'm about to give him over and over in my head. He watches my approach, the shutter clicking at rapid fire pace, the camera still blocking his face. I'm just about to start my spiel when I'm about fifty feet away and my phone rings in my hand.

Even after many days of no contact, my pulse still races at the sound, hoping it's Colton but knowing it's not before I even look at it. But I'm taken back a bit when I look at the screen and see Beckett's name. I stop immediately and fumble with my phone, worried that something's happened.

"Becks?"

"Hey, Ry." That's all he says and falls silent. *Oh shit*. Dread drops like a lead weight through me.

"Beckett, what's wrong with Colton?" I can't stop the worry that weighs heavy in my voice. The silence stretches and my mind runs as I glance at the photographer momentarily before turning my back and hurrying home.

"I just wanted you to know that Colton's on his way to the track right now."

I'm standing outside in the open, but I suddenly find it hard to draw in a breath of air. "What?" I'm surprised he can even hear me, my voice is so soft. Images flash through my head like a slideshow: the crash, the mangled metal, a broken Colton unresponsive in the hospital bed.

"I know you two ... the whole baby thing and he hasn't called you." He sighs. "I had to call you and let you know ... thought you'd want to know." I can tell he's conflicted over breaking his best friend's trust and doing what he thinks Colton needs the most.

"Thanks." It's the only thing I can manage as my emotions spiral out of control.

"Not really sure you mean that, Ry, but I thought I should call."

Silence stretches between us and I know he's just as worried as I am. "Is he ready, Becks? Are you pushing him?" I can't hold back the contempt that laces my question.

He breathes out and chuckles at something. "Nobody pushes Colton, Ry, but Colton. You know that."

"I know, but why now? What's the urgency?"

"Because this is what he needs to do ..." Beckett's voice fades as he finds his next words. I push open the gate and scramble over the little fence separating the neighbor's yard and mine. "First of all, he needs to prove he's just as good as before. Secondly, this is how Colton deals when there's too much going on in his head and he can't shut it all off, and thirdly …"

I don't hear what Beckett says next because I'm too busy remembering our night before the race, our conversation, and the words fall from my mouth as I'm thinking aloud. "The blur."

"*The what?*"

It's when Beckett speaks that I realize I have in fact said it out loud and his voice shocks me from my thoughts. "Nothing," I say. "What's the third reason?"

"Never mind."

"You've already said more than you should, why stop now?"

There is an uncomfortable silence and he starts and stops for a moment. "It's nothing really. I was just going to say that in the past he's turned to one of three things when he gets like this. I'm sorry—I shouldn't have—"

"It's okay. I get it—get him. In the past he turned to women or alcohol or the track when life got to be too much, right?" Becks remains silent and there's my answer. "Well, I guess I should be lucky there was an opening at the track, right?"

Beckett belts out a laugh, and I can tell he's relieved. "God, he doesn't deserve you, Rylee." His words bring a smile to my face despite the worry eating at my insides. "I just hope you both realize how much he needs you."

Tears prick my eyes. "Thank you for calling, Becks. I'm on my way."

I'm thankful that traffic is light as I speed to the track in Fontana, and that the security at the parking lot prevent the press from following me into the facility. I park the car on the infield and freeze as I hear the crank try to start the car. The engine roars to life, its sound echoing against the grandstands and vibrating in my chest.

I don't know how I'm going to do this. How I'm going to be able to watch Colton, belted in and flying around the track, when all I can see in my head is the smoke and feel the fear? But I promised him I would be there the day he climbed back behind the wheel. Little did I know I'd get a call to collect on that promise when everything was unsettled between us.

But I can't not be here. Because I keep my promises. And because I can't stand the thought of him being out there without knowing he's okay. Yes, we've not spoken and are confused and hurt, but that doesn't mean I can turn my feelings off.

The motor revving again pulls me from my thoughts. My trepidation and the need to be there for him, for me, for my sanity, pushes me to put one foot in front of another. Davis meets me at the outskirts of pit row and nods as I take the hand he offers in greeting, before leading me to where Colton's crew is working.

I stop when I see the car, the curve of Colton's helmet in the capsule behind the wheel, Beckett's body bent over him, tightening his belts as only Colton will let him do. I force my throat to swallow but realize there is nothing to ingest because my mouth is filled with cotton. I find myself going to worry the ring I no longer wear, out of nervous habit, and have to make do with clasping my hands.

Davis leads me up the flight of stairs to the observation tower above, much like the one I sat in while I watched Colton spiral out of control. Each step up reminds me of *that* day—the sound, the smell, the churning of my stomach, the absolute terror—each riser is another memory of the moments after the car hit the catch fence. My body wants to turn and flee, but my heart tells me I have to be here. I can't quit on him when he needs me the most.

The pitch of the engine changes and I don't have to turn and look at it to know he's driving slowly down pit row toward the banked asphalt of the track. I stand in the tower, a few members of the crew focused on gauges reading the car's electronics, but in the mere seconds

I stand there, I can sense the nervous energy, can feel that they are as anxious about Colton being in the car as I am.

I hear footsteps on the stairs behind me and know it must be Becks. Before I even have a chance to say anything to him, the sound of the car's motor eases, and we both look toward it at the end of the vacant pit row. After a moment, the engine's rumble revs again and the car moves slowly onto the track.

Beckett looks over to me quickly and hands me a headset. The look in his eyes tells me that he's just as on edge and uneasy about this as I am, and a small part of me is relieved by this. He leans in close before I situate the headphones on my ears and says, "He doesn't know you're here."

I just nod at him, eyes telling him thank you, lips telling him, "I think that's for the best."

He motions toward a chair at the front of the tower, but I just shake my head resolutely. There is no way in hell I can sit down right now. Nervous energy assaults my senses, and I shift back and forth on my feet while my soul remains anchored solid from my fear.

The engine purrs gently into the back end of turn one, and I twist so my eyes can track Colton, although I want to scream for him to stop, to get out, to come back to me. The car starts to accelerate into turn two.

"That's it, Wood. Nice and easy," Becks says to him in a gentle coaxing voice. All I hear on the open mic is the cadence of the engine and Colton's harsh breathing, but no response from him. I bite my lip and glance over at Beckett, not liking the fact that he's not speaking. I can only imagine what is running through Colton's head.

"Goddammit, Becks!" It's the first time I've heard his voice in over a week and the sound in it—the fear woven through the anger—has me holding tight onto the ear pieces. "This car is shit! I thought you checked everything. It's—"

"Nothing's wrong with the car, Colton." The evenness of Becks' voice comes through loud and clear, and Beckett glances over to another crew member and subtly shakes his head no at something.

"*Bullshit!* It's shuddering like a bitch and is gonna come apart once I open her up." The vibration that's normally in his voice from the force of the motor isn't there, he's not even going fast enough out of turn two to affect him.

"It's a new car. I checked every inch of it."

"You don't know what the fuck you're talking about, Beckett! Goddammit!" he yells out into the car as it comes to a stop on the backstretch between turns two and three, frustration resonating over the radio.

"It's a different car. No one's on the track to hit you. Just take it nice and easy."

There is no response. Nothing but the distant hum of an idling motor that I'm sure will die soon and then they'll need to get a crank start out on the track to get it going again. More time for Colton to sit and think and remember and relive the crash that is incapacitating him.

And as time stretches, my concern for the man I love has my own anxiety escalating. Even though we're all here supporting him, I know he's over there feeling all alone, isolated in a metal casket on wheels. My heart lodges in my throat as the panic and helplessness I feel starts to strangle me.

Beckett paces back and forth, his hands shoving through his hair, uncertain how to coax his best friend off of the ledge when he's not listening already. I shift again—Colton's ragged breathing the only sound on the radio—and I can't take it anymore.

I walk up to Beckett. "Get everyone off the radios." He looks at me and tries to figure out what I'm doing. "Get them off," I say, desperation tingeing the urgency in my request.

"Radios off everyone," Beckett orders immediately as I move to the mic on the counter at the front of the box. I sit down in the seat and wait for the nod from Beckett once he realizes what I'm doing.

I fumble with the buttons on the mic and Davis leans over and pushes down on the one I need. "Colton?" My voice is shaky but I know he hears me because I hear the hitch in his breath when he does.

"Rylee?" It's my name—a single word—but the break in his voice and the vulnerability in the way he says it causes tears to well in my eyes. He sounds like one of my boys right now when they wake from a terrifying dream, and I wish I could run out onto the track so that I can hold and reassure him. But I can't, so I do the next closest thing.

"Talk to me. Tell me what's going through your head. No one's on the radio but you and me." Silence stretches for a bit as my palms become sweaty with nerves and I fret that I'm not going to be able to help him through this.

"Ry," he sighs in defeat, and I'm about to jump back on the mic when he continues. "I can't … I don't think I can …" His voice fades as I'm sure memories of the accident assault him, as they do me.

"You can do this," I say with more resolve than I feel. "This is California, Colton, not Florida. There's no traffic. No rookie drivers to make stupid mistakes. No smoke you can't see through. No wreck to drive into. It's just you and me, Colton. You and me." I pause a moment and when he doesn't respond, I say the one thing circling in my mind. "Nothing but sheets."

I hear the sliver of a laugh, and I'm relieved that I got through to him. Used a good memory to break through the crippling fear. But when he speaks I can still hear the trepidation in his tone. "I just …" He stops and sighs, vulnerability a hard thing for a man to accept, especially in the face of a crew who idolizes and respects him.

"You can do this, Colton. We can do this together, okay? I'm right here. I'm not going anywhere." I give him a few seconds to let my words sink in. "Are your hands on the wheel?"

"Mmm-hmm … but my right hand—"

"Is perfectly okay. I've seen you use it," I tell him, hoping to ease some of the tension. "Is your foot on the pedal?"

"Ry?" His voice wavers again.

"Pedal. Yes or no?" I know right now he needs me to take the reins and be the strong one, and for him, I'll do anything.

"Yes ..."

"Okay, clear your head. It's just you and the track, Ace. You can do this. You need this. It's your freedom, remember?" I hear the engine rev once or twice, and I see relief mixed with pride in Beckett's eye before I focus back on Colton. "You know this like the back of your hand ... push down on the gas. Flick the paddle and press down." The engine's pitch purrs a little higher and I continue. "Okay ... see? You've got this. You don't have to go fast. It's a new car, it's going to feel different. Becks will be pissed if you burn up the engine anyway so take it slow."

I turn to watch the car with bated breath as Colton starts slowly into turn three. He's nowhere near even practice speeds, but he's going and that's all that matters. We're facing our fear of him getting back into the car again together. I just never figured it would be me coaxing him to drive that would lessen my own.

The motor guns again, the reverberation hitting my chest as he nears turn four and I hear him cuss. "You okay?" There is nothing but silence around me and the roar of the approaching engine. "Talk to me, Colton. I'm right here."

"My hands won't stop shaking." I don't respond because I'm holding my breath as he picks up the pace and enters into turn one. "Becks is gonna be pissed because my head's fucked up."

I glance over at Becks again and see the smile flash on his face, and I know he's listening in, making sure his best friend is okay. "It's okay ... watching you out there? Mine is fucked up too ... but you're ready, you can do this."

"Aren't we a fucking pair?" He snorts into the radio and I can sense a little of his anxiety and fear dissipating with each passing second. I see the guys around me relax some as they notice the smile widen on Beckett's face.

"We are indeed," I laugh before releasing an exhale in relief. God, I love you, I want to say, but refrain. The rumble increases down the backstretch and I can't fight the grin on my face at the sound of success. "Hey, Ace, can I bring the guys back on?"

"Yeah," he says followed quickly by, "Ry … I …"

My heart swells at the emotion in his voice. I can hear the apology, feel the absolute sincerity behind it. "I know, Colton. Me too."

I fight the tears of happiness that well up, and when I look up at Beckett he has a soft smile on his face. He shakes his head ever so subtly and mouths the word *lifeline* to me.

Chapter Twenty-Three

THE CAR ENTERS THE PITS and rolls to a stop. Beckett's at its side in an instant while I fidget behind the wall, wanting to see Colton face to face to make sure he's okay. He removes the steering wheel and hands it to Becks before unbuckling his helmet. Becks helps him unfasten it from the HANS device, and when he pulls it from his head, removing the balaclava with it, the crew erupts into a roar of cheers.

Chills dance at the celebratory sounds as Becks helps him out of the car. I step over the wall with the rest of the crew, unable to stay at a distance any longer because now Colton stands there hot, sweaty, and oh my God sexy. Pride tinged with desire spears through me at the sight of him.

Attending to the car is forgotten as his crew pats him on the shoulders and welcomes him back. Beckett just looks at him with a shit-eating grin on his handsome face. "I'm proud of you, dude, but fuck, *your lap times sucked.*"

Colton laughs again, slinging an arm around his friend. "I can always count on you to knock me down a few pegs." He goes to say something else and then stops when he sees me.

I have a déjà vu moment, Colton standing amidst the whirling chaos of his crew, eyes locked on mine, sexy-as-sin grin wide on his lips. Time stops again as the world falls away and we stare at each other.

I know there are so many things we need to talk about—need to figure out from the last time we spoke—but at the same time I need this connection with him. Need the carnal physicality between the two of us that hits me like a shock wave as it crosses the distance between us and crashes into me before we can figure the rest out.

And I know he feels it too because within a beat Colton strides toward me with purpose. Within an instant of reaching me, my legs are wrapped around his waist and our mouths are on one another's with a frenzied need. My hands grip his shoulders. One of his grabs my backside while the other grips my neck, holding my mouth to his, so he can take everything I am offering, and then some.

"God, I fucking missed you," he growls into my mouth between kisses. And without preamble we are on the move. His powerful legs stride beneath me, and strong arms hold me secure while his lips bruise mine in unbidden possession.

Noise filters back. Hoots and hollers of the crew ring through the empty stadium as Colton makes no apologies for walking away without a second thought. Someone shouts "Get a room!" and I am so overwhelmed, so desperate to sate the desire unfurling within and shocking through my system that I answer before Colton can.

"Who needs a room?" I say before my lips crash back against his, hands fisting in his hair, hips grinding into his as his erection rubs against me with every step.

Laughter rings out followed by catcalls, but they're only background noise to the freight train of desire bearing down on us. "Hurry," I tell him in between desperate kisses.

"Fuck," he mutters as he tries to find an open door at my back without wanting to take his mouth from mine.

"Oh, you better plan on it," I reply as I pull back so he can find the handle. He belts out a laugh as my tongue glides to his neck, the taste of salt on my tongue, the vibration of his laughter beneath my lips.

We're on the move again, up a set of stairs in a darkened corridor, and I have no clue where we are. I hold on for the ride, laughter bubbling up, relief flowing through me as my body tenses with the anticipation of what's to come.

We're suddenly bathed in a muted light, and I turn my head and blink my eyes to take in our surroundings. We are in one of the luxury boxes on pit row: plush couches, a concessions bar on one side, a table spanning the length of the wall of tinted windows that looks down on the track, where his crew is tinkering with his car.

That's all I have time to take in because Colton's lips find mine again, his mouth a toxic concoction of need and lust. My legs fall from his hips, feet dropping to the ground, as we move toward the counter in a clumsy choreography of steps. We reach the lip of the counter, and I lean my hips back against it, as Colton's hands roam down my torso, before I feel bare hands beneath my shirt on my ribcage.

And I'm not sure if it's the heightened arousal from the adrenaline of the race track, or our reconciliation, but I feel like I can't get enough of him—his touch, his taste, the sound in the back of his throat, my name on his lips. I reach up and unfasten the Velcro against his throat so I can pull his zipper. And even this small action pains me because I have to pull away from his lips. But the minute I yank the zipper down, my mouth meets his again. Our hands unfasten, arms pull out of our sleeves, fingers shove down my shorts and underwear, clothes thrown haphazardly to the floor, our mouths never leaving one another's.

"Ry," he says between kisses, one hand gripping my hair tightly while the other tests my readiness for his entrance. Foreplay isn't an option right now. We're so pent up, so desperate to right the wrongs of our last conversation that without speaking, we both know we need this connection. Talking will come later. Cuddling and niceties later. Right now desire consumes, passion overwhelms, and love takes hold. "Fuck, I need you right now."

"Take me." Two simple words. They're out of my mouth without a second thought, but within a second of saying them, Colton has me flipped over, hands braced on the counter, his hands gripping my hips, his throbbing cock lined up at my entrance from behind. He rests the crest in between my folds and then slides it up and back causing my body to tense and a moan to fall from between my lips.

And there's something about this moment, about Colton on the precipice of taking me without asking, that has every part of me aching for release, begging for more of his touch. "Please. Now," I pant as my sex quivers with need, body so in tune to his every action that my body automatically responds, opens, invites.

I rear back and try to take him on my own, trying to demonstrate the need spearing and spiraling throughout my every nerve, robbing my rationality, and making my senses crave more. "*Behave!*" He chuckles out a laugh of pure male appreciation as one hand fists in my mane of hair as his other lands smartly on the left side of my ass. The sting shocks my head back but has nothing on the assault of sensation that occurs as he enters me in one slick, earth-shattering thrust. I can't help the hitched breath followed by a soft sigh that falls from my mouth as sensation ripples and my walls convulse around him.

He pulls on my hair, angling my head back, so when he leans forward his lips are at my ear. "That is the sexiest fucking sound in the world," he growls before his lips find my bare shoulder, stubbled beard tickling the usually forgotten erogenous zone of my back. His teeth nip my shoulder followed by the press of his lips as his hips grind into me, and I moan in pure rapture as the scrape of his beard moves down my spine.

And now it's my turn to enjoy the sounds he makes as we start to move in rhythm with each other. Goose bumps appear despite the heat spreading through my body. One hand grips the flesh on my hip, controlling each pleasure inducing drive in and subsequent withdrawal tantalizing every single nerve. My body quickens, overtaken by the animalistic nature of his hold on my hair and my body.

"Oh God!" I pant, needing, wanting, not being able to take any more all at the same time. My hands start to slide on the surface of the counter as they dampen with sweat.

"Fuuuuccckkk!" he grates out, his desire to control his tempo apparent in his voice. And call it a challenge, or me just channeling the inner vixen he's helped me find, but I want to break that control. I want to push him harder, faster—to take with reckless abandon—because my God, the guttural sound in his throat, the fullness as he seats himself to the hilt when he thrusts into me, the clockwise motion of his hips as he moves within me pushes me harder, faster, than I've ever known. Makes me want to bring him an ounce of the pleasure that his body gives me.

I reach a hand down between my legs, fingers sliding over the temptation to caress my own clit, and instead grab a hold of his balls as he grinds his hips into me again. Fingers caress, nails tease, and hands cradle as he pulls back tighter on my hair. I can hear the sounds he's making, know he's clenching his jaw, that he's riding that razor-thin edge of being controlled versus relinquishing to the carnal nature of the act. To take for himself without thought. And it eggs me on, tempts me to push him harder, force him over that edge that much quicker, because fuck if he's not driving me there in the process.

I get lost in the feeling, the sounds of his body smacking against mine, the feel of his hand possessing my hip, the fall of my name from his lips and without realizing it, I'm there, teetering on my own razor thin edge. I crash into the endless free fall of bliss as my climax overwhelms me, my body an inferno of warring sensations.

"Colton!" I cry, over and over as he slows his pace, sliding his tongue up the plain of my back to help draw out my orgasm.

I can feel my muscles pulse around him still within me, moving slowly, and then a feral cry fills the air as he can't hold back anymore. His hips thrust a few more times before his arms suddenly wrap around my torso and hold my weight as he pulls me to a standing position, his front still to my back.

In an unexpected move of tenderness in complete contrast to the thorough dominance of my body, he squeezes me back into him and buries his face into the curve of my neck. We stand like this for some time, absorbing each other, accepting the silent apologies.

Chapter Twenty-Four

THE SILENCE DESCENDS AROUND US as we pull our clothes back on. Now that we've had our way with each other physically—now that our bodies are no longer connected—my mind worries about how we're going to connect verbally.

Because we can't leave things as is. And we can't ignore them. Hopefully the miserably lonely time apart has helped us so we can move forward.

But even if we can, where exactly do we go from here?

I steal a glance over at him as he zips up his fire suit and looks through the tinted window at the crew below, and I just can't get a read on him. I pull my shirt over my head and lick my lips as I try to figure out how to start this conversation.

"We need to talk," I say softly as if I'm afraid to disturb the blanket of silence smothering the room.

"I'm putting the Palisades house up for sale." He speaks the words quietly, never once looking my way, and I'm so focused on him and his lack of emotion, it takes a moment for his words to sink in.

Whoa! What? So that's how we're going to play this? Classic avoidance?

Even though he's not looking at me, I know he's aware of me so I try to visibly hide the shock from the words he's just hit me with, as well as the ones he hasn't said.

"Colton?" I say, his name like a question—one that asks so many different things. Are we going to address this? Are we going to ignore this? Why are you selling the house?

"I don't use it ..." he answers my unasked question, sliding a glance over at me, before he looks back at his guys down below. And the way he says it, almost apologetically, makes me feel like this is something he's doing to tell me he's sorry for everything that's happening—Tawny, a possible baby, the space he needs.

When I don't respond and just watch him patiently, he turns and faces me. Our eyes lock and we stare at each other for a moment, asking unanswered questions without words.

"I don't need it anymore," he explains as he watches me for a reaction.

And as much as there is unresolved drama between us, what he's just said tells me he's really in this for the long haul. That even with everything thrown at us over the past week that might turn his world upside down, he's selling the one place I'd vowed never to return to. That I mean enough to him that he's willing to get rid of a place signifying his old way of life full of stipulations and mitigations.

"Oh ..." It's all I can manage to say because I'm at a loss for words, so we just continue to stare at each other in this room that still smells like sex. I can see him thinking, trying to figure out what to say—how to go from here—so I begin. "What's on your mind, Colton?"

"Just thinking," he says, pursing his lips and running a hand through his hair, "about how I didn't realize how much I needed to hear your voice today out on the track until you came through the headset."

The gentle sigh of satisfaction comes from every part of me, warming me inside and out, as it weaves its way around the hold he has on my heart. And the old me would have rolled my eyes at his comment and said he's trying to get on my good side, but the old me didn't need and miss Colton as much as I do now, didn't know all he had to offer.

"All you had to do was call me," I say softly, reaching a hand out and placing it on top of his beside me. "I promised you I'd be here your first day back."

He emits a self-deprecating chuckle with a shake of his head. "And say what? I've been an asshole—haven't called at all—but I need you on the track with me today?" The sarcasm is thick in his voice.

I squeeze his hand. "It's a start," I tell him, my voice trailing off. "We agreed to figure our shit out, get our heads straight, but I would've been here in a heartbeat if you'd called me."

He sighs, angling his head out toward the track beyond. "I'm sorry for what I said to you … the things I accused you of … I was an ass." Emotion causes his voice to waver, which makes what he's saying that much more endearing.

I don't want to ruin the moment, but I have to let him know. "You hurt me. I know you were upset and lashing out at the person nearest to you … but *you hurt me* when I was already torn apart. We struggle day to day with our pasts, and then something like this happens and … I …" I can't find the right words to say it, so I just don't finish my thought.

Colton steps toward me and reaches out to grab my hand, pulling me gently toward him so the only barrier between us is our clothes. "I know." He draws in a shaky breath before he continues. "I've never done this before, Ry. I'm trying to figure it out as I go and fuck, I know the excuses are getting old and pretty soon aren't going to be excusable, but … fuckin' A, I'm trying." He shrugs.

I nod at him, words escaping me because he's doing something he's never been good at: communicating. And they may seem like baby steps to him, but they gain us massive ground in our relationship.

He leans forward and brushes an unexpected kiss on my lips before murmuring, "C'mere." He leans his butt against the ledge behind him the same time he pulls me into him so we stand with my back to his front, his legs surrounding mine. I lean my head against his chest and feel stupidly content as he brings his arms around me and holds me tight. He rests his chin on my shoulder. "Thank you for today. No one's ever done something like that for me before."

His words kind of surprise me but after a minute I understand his line of thinking and need to correct it. "Becks, your family, they do it all the time. You just don't allow yourself to see or accept it."

"Yeah, but they're family, they have to." He pauses and even though I can't see the look in his eyes, I can sense his mind working as I wonder what exactly he classifies me as. "And you? You're my fucking checkered flag." I angle my head to the side just enough so I can see a diminutive smile spread on his lips as a full-fledged one lights up mine. "It's a little hard to get used to the idea when I've never done this before. I have to get used to you being there for me and needing you, and fuck if that doesn't knock me back a few pit stop steps sometimes because it scares the ever-loving shit out of me."

Holy shit! I'm stunned to silence once again by his attempt to explain the trepidation I'm sure is tickling the outer edges of his psyche. I put my hands over his arms that are locked around me and squeeze them in a silent acknowledgment of the growth he is trying to show.

"I'm not going to run, Colton," I say, my voice resolute. "I haven't yet, but you *really* hurt me. I know you're going through a lot of shit, but hell if you aren't a lot to take in. I'm going to need a pit stop sometimes too. I mean, between you, the limelight, the women still wanting you and hating me, the possibility of ..." I can't finish the thought, can't force the word *baby* from my lips or rid the sudden acrid taste from my mouth.

"*Hello elephant in the fucking room.*" He lets out an audible sigh, and his jaw tenses on my shoulder.

I don't want to ruin the moment—the heart-to-heart we need to have more of—but since I unexpectedly brought it up, I'd rather address it and get it over with. "What's going on with ... that?" I close my eyes and grit my teeth as I await the answer.

"I don't care what she says about what I supposedly did or didn't do that I can't fucking remember. I know it's not mine, Rylee."

The simplicity of his statement and the vigor with which he delivers it causes my hope to soar. And then to fall. If he got the results back, then why didn't he call me? "You got the test results back already?" I say cautiously, trying to hide my wariness.

"No." He shakes his head as the hope I have falls completely. "I took the test two days ago. Results will come any day now. But I know … I know it's not mine." And from the sound of his voice, I can't tell who he's trying to convince more: himself or me.

"How do you know, Colton, if you can't remember?" I say loudly, frustrated and needing this to just be over, needing more emotion from him than what I'm getting. I take a deep breath and try to calm myself. "I mean even if you and Tawny did..." I stop, unable to finish the thought "...she said you didn't use a condom." My voice is so quiet when I speak, hating that we even have to have this discussion. Hating that once again our moment of contentment is ruined by the outside world and the consequences of our pasts.

"You're the only person, Ry … the only woman I've ever not used a condom with. I don't care if you think I slept with her, but I know, Rylee … I know I would have used a condom." I can hear the pleading in his voice for me to believe him. For me to understand an iota of the fear he's feeling at the prospect of a child. When I don't respond he pushes back away from me and starts to pace back and forth on the deck. The calm of five minutes ago is now replaced with pure agitation, a caged animal needing to escape its confines.

"It's not mine!" he says, raising his voice. "There's no fucking way it can be mine!"

"But what if it is?" I reiterate with full knowledge of the fire I'm lighting.

"It's not," he shouts. "Fuck! All I know is that I don't know fucking anything! I hate the goddamn media following you and fucking harassing you. I hate the look on your face right now that says you're going to fucking lose it if it is my baby even though you tell me you won't. I hate fucking Tawny and everything she represents. The bull-shit lies she's fucking spewing about you that Chase says I can't re-spond to because they'll only hound you more. I hate that once again I'm fucking hurting you … that I'm going to fuck this up because my past is what it is … " He closes his eyes and rolls his shoulders as he tries to rein in his anger.

This is the kind of fighting I can handle. Him venting, me lis-tening, and then hopefully a little bit of the pain in his eyes and the weight on his shoulders will be eased, even if just for a bit.

"You've got enough on your plate. You don't need to worry about me." I tell him this and yet I love the fact that he's upset by the fallout affecting me.

"I don't?" he says with incredulity. "It's my fucking job to look out for you, and I can't even do that right now because everything's so fucked up!"

"Colton—"

"I swear to God, your life gets turned upside down by me and you're more worried about me and the boys than yourself." He walks toward me with a shake of his head. He points to me and I look at him with confusion. "You are most definitely the fucking saint I don't deserve."

"Every sinner needs a saint to balance them out," I say with a smirk.

He laughs softly and reaches out to cup my cheeks in his hands. And even though we've already had each other, my body vibrates instantly at his nearness, at wanting him, at needing him. His eyes lock on mine, hints of what he wants to do to me dancing behind the fringe of lashes.

"God, I fucking race you." The emphatic words on his lips are followed by a lopsided smirk and a shake of his head, as if he's still comprehending the depths of his emotions.

How many more times can my heart fall harder for this man? Because there it is again, the unpredictability of Colton that makes what he says just that much more poignant. Every part of my body shivers at his words.

It's useless to try and fight the moisture pooling in my eyes because those words mean so much more than just "racing" to me. They mean he's trying, he's apologizing for the times when he's going to fuck up. And for a man previously closed off from everyone, he's handing me the key to the lock, and giving me an all-access pass.

I reach my free hand out and cup the back of his neck, pulling him into me because a man this magnificent, inside and out, is just too irresistible. I kiss him tenderly, licking my tongue between his lips so it dances intimately with his. No urgency, just soft, gentle acceptance. It's only been minutes since our last kiss but it already feels like a lifetime. As the kiss ends, he rests his forehead against mine and I say, "I race you too."

I can feel his smile spread against my lips, and in this moment, I know he actually gets it. He actually accepts the fact that I love him and it's such a figurative ray of light from this dark angel of mine that I grasp onto it, silently vowing to always remember how I feel right here, right now.

We may not have everything figured out, may not know what the future's going to hold, but at least I know we're in this race together.

"C'mon," he says, pulling on my hand. "Let's get out of here."

We head toward the garage area where the guys are working on the car. As we enter, Beckett shakes his head and smirks at us. I avert my gaze quickly, so very aware that every guy in the garage knows exactly what we were just doing. The walk of shame is one thing, but when you have an audience that knows you're doing it, well … that's a lot more embarrassing.

Colton laughs beside me and squeezes my fingers laced with his. "What's so funny?" I mumble, still keeping my eyes trained on the ground.

"You're cute when you blush," he teases. "I prefer the pink parts elsewhere on you more though."

My mouth shocks open and before I can even recover, his mouth is on mine. The clang of tools surround us and yet all I hear is the beat of my heart. The kiss is merely a tease of what we did earlier, but when he pulls back after kissing the tip of my nose, a smirk curls up one corner of his mouth.

"What was that for?" Like I even care what the answer is. He can do that to me anytime, anywhere.

"You know me, sweetheart. If they're gonna stare, you might as well give them something good to stare at, right? Besides, if it wasn't clear enough earlier, I want everyone in here knowing you're mine."

My heart swells at his words before the sarcasm is off my tongue. "Staking a claim are we?"

"Baby, claim's already been made," he says, stopping to look at me with a smirk. "No doubt about that."

I roll my eyes and laugh at him as I keep walking. "C'mon, Ace," I say over my shoulder, "can't you keep up?"

I feel his hand smack my butt. "You sure as hell know I can keep anything up," he says, wrapping an arm around my shoulders and leaning down so his mouth is near my ear. "My dick, you pressed against the door, my stamina, and any other thing that can be considered up … but those are the most important ones, don't you think?" He chuckles as I shake my head and make a sound of amusement.

We sort out the fact that Sammy is going to take my car home for me and then Colton leads me to a covered parking area where Sex sits. I can't deny that the sight of the sexy-as-sin car brings back a rush of more than memorable memories that put a smirk on my face. From my locked gaze on the hood, I stare over to Colton where a lascivious grin meets mine. He raises his eyebrows, mischief dancing in his eyes, his tongue darting out to wet his bottom lip as he opens the door for me.

"Nice choice of car today," I tell him as I slide into the opulent interior.

"This reminds me of you, and I needed you here today," he says before shutting my door so I can't respond. And maybe it's best that I can't, because his simple statement means so very much to me.

Baby steps.

Within seconds we're on the freeway with the sounds of the Dave Matthews Band floating around us, the purr of the motor cocooning us, and the frenzied media following us. Colton looks in the rear view mirror before looking over at me from behind his sunglasses. "You buckled in?" he asks and all of a sudden my stomach twists in knots, fearing what's going to happen next.

I don't even have a chance to respond before the car surges forward, the motor revving, Colton laughing as the car flies faster than the press chasing us can go. I feel a surge of adrenaline and for a split second I can understand the pull of his addiction, but then I look up as he weaves in and out of traffic, and my heart lodges in my throat as the world beyond blurs.

Chapter Twenty-Five

I SQUARE UP THE DOCUMENTS on the kitchen counter. I'm satisfied with the transcription of Zander's deposition to bring formal charges against his father. I tuck them in the manila folder and realize I've lost track of time; the clock reads seven-forty and the boys have to be at the field by eight. Oh crap! I need to finish getting the stuff together for their games. I rise from the table and start filling sport bottles and putting them on the counter next to bags of sunflower seeds. I strain to hear the commotion in the bedrooms and can tell that Jackson has the boys on task and almost ready to leave.

"Hey, Ry?"

"Yeah?" I look up to see Jackson leaning his shoulder against the wall with concern in his eyes.

"Zander and Scoot are still asleep." He pauses for a minute and then continues. "Were you awake when Shane came in last night?"

I look at him, trying to figure out why he's asking. "Yes. I was reading in my room. Why?"

"Did you physically see him? Talk to him?"

Now alarm bells sound in my head, and I stop what I'm doing and turn to face him. "Uh-uh. I called out his name and he said goodnight and went to his room. You're scaring me, Jax, what's going on?"

"Well, it looks like Shane tied one on last night. He's passed out in his bed, his room reeks of beer, and by the looks of the bathroom he was reliving the night backwards into the toilet." He has a half-smirk on his face, and I know it's not appropriate but I have to stifle a laugh that Shane did something so normal for his age.

And then the responsible part of me takes over. I bite my lip and look at Jax. "We knew this would happen someday ... shit, do you want me to deal with him or do you want to?"

"We'll be out in the van, Jax!" Ricky yells.

"Kay!" he responds before looking back to me. "I can stay here with Zand, Scoot, and Shane if you want to take baseball today?"

"No, that's cool," I tell him as he grabs the bottles. "We'll meet you at the field later to watch the games. I can handle Shane."

"You sure?"

"Positive."

Jax says goodbye and as he closes the door I don't feel so sure anymore. I sit down on one of the barstools and contemplate how exactly to handle a hungover sixteen year old. He's the oldest and the first of the lot to go through this, so I'm kind of lost. Of course I was too scared to drink in high school—always the consummate good girl—so I'm on foreign ground here.

My phone rings and I look down, a smile immediately lights up my face when I see it's Colton. "Good morning," I say as warmth fills my heart. The past few days have been good between us despite the underlying tension we've blatantly been ignoring over the impending paternity test results. Colton's been excited that he'll be returning to the office next week, wanting to be there to oversee the new adjustments to the safety device they're working on. I laughed and told him I thought it was funny that he'd returned to the track before the office, but he just said with a smirk that the track was a necessity and the office not so much.

"Hey ... this bed is awfully lonely without you in it." His sleepy morning rasp pulls at me and his words seduce me when I have no business being seduced.

"Believe me, I'd much rather be there with you—"

235

"Then get here as quick as you can, baby, because time's wasting. I have a long list of things to do today," he says, humor edging the suggestive tone of his voice. And I love this about him—about us—that just his voice can help ease the stress of my morning.

"What is it you have to do today?"

"You on the couch, you on the counter, you against the wall, you just about any place imaginable …" His voice drifts off as the parts of my body still asleep suddenly snap awake.

I groan into the phone. "You have no idea how tempting that sounds because today's already turned to shit."

"Why? What happened?" he asks concerned.

"Shane had his first experience with alcohol and from what Jax says, it doesn't sound like it was a good one."

Colton belts out a laugh. "He got shit-faced? Attaboy, Shane!"

"Colton! I'm trying to raise respectable boys here!" And the minute the words are out of my mouth I realize what an old-fashioned prude I sound like, but it's true.

"Are you telling me I'm not respectable, Ryles?"

I smirk because I can picture the impish grin on his face right now. "Well, you do in fact do dirty things to me …" I tease, my body tensing and the ache in my lower belly pulsing at the thought of our last little sexcapade on the stairs of the Malibu house the day before last.

His chuckle is seductive yet naughty. "Oh, baby, dirtying you up is what I do best, but I'm talking about everyone else. I got drunk with the best of them in high school, and I turned out all right."

"That's debatable," I tease. "So you're saying it's no big deal? To let him off the hook without any repercussions?"

"No, that's not what I'm saying. I just think it's a good sign that he's out being a typical sixteen-year-old kid. Not that it's good or bad, just typical. And as long as it's a one time deal—that he's not drinking to escape his past—then good for him."

In a sense I agree with Colton, but at the same time I know I need to address it with Shane, need to tell him it's not okay and it can't happen again, even though I know it will. "So how, man-that-used-to-be-a-reckless-teenager, should I handle this best?"

"I'm still reckless, Ry," he says with amusement in his voice. "That, my dear, will never change. Jax needs to deal with him because he's not going to listen to you."

"I beg to differ." I don't want the boys to not want to talk to me or listen to me because I'm one of the few female counselors in the house.

"Don't get your panties in a bunch, Thomas," he says with a laugh. "I'm not saying you can't handle it. I'm just saying that he's going to listen better if it comes from a man."

"Well, Jax, is at baseball so it has to be me."

"You're at the house alone?" I can hear the concern fill his voice immediately, and smile at his sudden need to watch out for me, protect me. It's quite cute.

"Colton." I sigh. "There are fifty photographers out front. I'm perfectly fine."

"Exactly. Fifty photographers that have no fucking business being there except to harass you and the boys. Fucking Christ!" He barks out to himself. "I'm so sick of my goddamn bullshit being on your doorstep."

"Really, it's not a—"

"I'll be there in thirty minutes," he says and the line clicks dead.

Okay. So he's coming to deal with the press, which will do no good, and I still have to figure out how to deal with Shane.

Fuck!

"You can play for another hour or so, Scooter, and then we have to head to the field, okay?"

"Yep!" he yells to me as he hustles down the hallway toward the family room where I'm sure Saturday morning cartoons will be in full swing momentarily.

I continue down the hall and stop when I pass Zander and Aiden's room. Zander's on the bed, blanket wrapped around his shoulders, precious stuffed dog grasped to his chest, and he is rocking back and forth with his eyes closed. I angle my head, take a step into the room, and watch him for a moment so I can figure out if he's dreaming or awake. When I step closer, I hear the quiet keening within his chest and then I move on instinct.

"Hey, Zander, you okay, buddy?" I ask gently, as I lower myself ever so slowly onto the mattress next to him.

He just continues rocking but lifts his head up to look at me, tears staining his face and utter heartbreak reflected in his eyes. Because no matter how much time passes, the memories will always be there burrowing their tentacles of destruction as deep as they can so he will never be able to forget. He might be able to move on at some point, but he will never forget.

"I want my mommy," he whimpers, and if my heart could shatter into a million pieces, it would for this little boy, who I love more than anything.

I ever so slowly pull him into my lap and wrap my arms around him, nestling his head under my neck so he doesn't see the tears I'm crying for him, his lost innocence, the part of him he'll forever ache for—his mother.

"I know, buddy," I tell him as I rock him. "I know. She'd be here if she could. She never would have left you if the angels hadn't needed her."

"But—but I need her too …" He sniffs and there is nothing I can say to that. Nothing. So I press a kiss to his head and just hold him tighter, trying to let my love for him ease some of the heaviness in his heart, but know it will never be enough.

We sit there for a bit, him drawing comfort and solace from me as much as I am from him. He calms down some as minutes tick by, my hand smoothing over his hair and back as I try to figure out something to make him smile. "Hey, bud? Colton's on his way over."

I feel his body jerk to attention as red-rimmed eyes look up at me. "Really?"

And as if on cue, I hear commotion outside the front of the house. Even with the windows and blinds shut I can hear the purr of an engine, the clicks of the camera shutters, and the questions being called out.

"Yep, in fact I think he just got here."

Grateful for Colton's timing and the instant spark it puts in Zander's eyes, we rise and head toward the front of the house. I make sure the boys are in the family room so when I open the front door, they're out of the camera lens' way.

Colton pushes into the narrow opening of the doorway with a muttered curse as the door shuts behind him. He looks at me, lines of frustration etched in his face, and a brown grocery bag propped under his arm. He smiles. "Hey."

"Hiya, Ace," I say, stepping toward him to give him a kiss hello but his body stiffens. I immediately step away realizing one of the boys is behind me. Colton is always so aware of them and cautions kissing me in their presence, even a peck on the lips, because he knows how overprotective they are, and he never wants to upset that balance.

"Just kiss her and get it over with!" Scooter's exasperated voice behind me has Colton and me bursting out laughing as I turn to face him, a smile plastered on my lips.

I feel Colton's free hand on my lower back as he steps beside me and squats down in front of Scooter. "It's okay?" he asks the little boy whose eyes have just become the size of saucers. "I mean, it's not really polite to walk into another man's house and kiss his girl ... but since you're one of the men in the house, I guess I could kiss her if you tell me it's okay."

Scooter's mouth falls lax at Colton's comment and his spine stiffens with pride. "Really?" The excitement in his voice has me putting a hand over my heart. "Yeah ... it's okay. As long as you don't make her sad."

"Deal." Colton sticks his hand out, and they shake on it. My heart overflows with love, and I have to fight back the tears welling in my eyes for the second time today, but this time they're from the pride I feel for two of the men in my life.

"Well then," Colton says as he stands and looks at me, "the man of the house says I can kiss you."

My smile widens as Colton leans in and pecks my lips in a brotherly fashion. "Eeeewwww gross!" Scooter says, wiping his mouth off with the back of his hand and turning to run into the family room to tell Zander.

Colton looks over his shoulder to make sure Scooter is gone and when he turns back his lips find mine without a second thought. It's a brief kiss, but man does it pack a punch, more than reinforcing that he's the drug I can't live without. "Wow!" I say as he pulls back.

"He said I could do it." He just smirks and shrugs. "Where's our drunk skunk at?"

"Still asleep," I tell him as I look down at the brown bag under his arm. "What's that?"

Colton just grins. "A little something to make sure that he remembers this morning for a long time. Hair of the dog and all that."

"Colton," I warn as I notice the shape of the bag looks a little too similar to a six pack. "I can't give him beer! I'll get fired," I shout at him in a hushed tone.

He has the gall to just stand there and chuckle. "Exactly. That's why I am." And with that, Colton strides down the hallway to my right into Shane's room. Colton's words earlier that Shane won't listen to me has me walking down the hallway to see what he's going to do.

Colton pulls the blinds up, and bright light floods the room, before he looks over to his dresser, a huge smile spreading on his face.

Within seconds, the pair of speakers that Shane's iPod is plugged into blare to life with a base thumping beat. Shane springs out of bed instantly, shouting and covering his ears and does a double take when he sees who is standing in front of his bed, arms crossed over his chest and eyebrows raised.

They stare at each other for a moment before Shane grabs the pillow and pulls it over his head to stop the sound and block the bright light. "Stop it!" he yells. Colton laughs and walks over to the iPod and flicks it off. "Thank you!" Shane's muffled voice says from beneath the pillow.

"Uh-uh," Colton says to him as he bounces on the bed beside him and pulls the pillows from his hands as Shane then uses his arms to cover his eyes. "By the smell of your room and the look on your face, I'd say you tied one on nice and hard last night. That right, bud?" He laughs, an amused borderline sinister laugh, when Shane doesn't respond. "Is your head pounding? The room spinning? Your eyes hurt? Does your stomach feel like you want to throw up but there's nothing there?"

"Shut up," Shane groans as he tries to pull the covers over his head, and Colton just yanks them back down.

"Nope. You wanna hang with the big boys—get plastered like they do—then it's time to wake up and take it like a man." From my vantage point in the hallway I watch Colton prop his back against the wall and get comfortable before he digs into the brown paper bag. I hear the crack of the beer can opening and Shane immediately sits up in bed, and looks at Colton like he's lost it.

"Are you fucking crazy?" Shane croaks in a panicked voice.

"Yep," Colton says as he looks over at Shane and grins. He takes a sip of the beer and then holds it out to Shane. "Sure as hell am. Drink up, son."

"No way!" Shane says as he backs away from the can like it's on fire. "You can't give me a beer!"

Colton raises his eyebrows. "I believe I just did. Now quit using that as an excuse. You were grown up enough to chug it down last night, right? So it's time to remind you just why you liked it so much." Colton shoves the beer back at him. "C'mon, take a drink. I dare you."

"What the—"

"Drink!" Colton pressures him. "What? You're cool enough to drink with your friends but not me?"

"It's going to make me puke!"

"Now you're catching on!" Colton says with a smirk as he reaches with his free hand back into the bag and grabs another beer. "I've got five more here for ya when you finish this one."

Shane's eyes grow huge and his face pales when Colton's words hit him. "No way! I'm going to throw up."

"*Good,*" Colton says as he gets in close to Shane's face. "Drink this," he says. "I want you to remember just how good it tastes coming back up the second time around. The next time your buddies push you to drink or you want to drink to look cool for the ladies ... I want you to remember how fucking cool you look bent over the toilet throwing this back up because I guarantee you from experience, it's not a pretty sight." Colton backs away from him and returns to his position against the wall, a smug smile on his face. He leans his head back but angles his eyes over to watch Shane. "You sure you don't want this beer? Don't want to remember what it tastes like?"

Shane shakes his head, a little shocked at the verbal lashing his idol just gave him, as am I.

When Colton speaks next, his voice is eerily calm. "Now that I've got your attention, a few ground rules, shall we?" He doesn't wait for Shane to respond. "How'd you get home last night, Shane?"

The question surprises me, just as it does Shane. "Davey brought me home."

"Did Davey drink last night too?" The quiet calm in Colton's voice has Shane averting his gaze, which makes my heart sink.

"He had a few." I can hear the shame in Shane's voice; he knows it was wrong.

"Eeeehhh! Wrong answer!" Colton says as he turns his head to look at him again. "You wanna be stupid and get drunk? That's one thing I can get. You want to step in a car and let someone else drive you who's drunk—because let's face it you were shit-faced so how do you know how many Davey had—that's something I won't tolerate! You have way too many people who love you in this house. *Care about you, Shane*—Ry, the boys, *me*—we don't want something to happen to you. So let me rephrase the question, okay? I'm not going to ask you if you're going to get drunk again because then you'll have to lie to me. Here's my question: Are you going to get in a car with another person who's been drinking?"

Shane swallows loudly and shakes his head no. When Colton just stares at him, he says aloud, "No."

"Good! Now we're getting somewhere ..." Colton says, pounding his hand against the wall loudly that has Shane jumping and grabbing his head, while Colton belts out a laugh. "You sure you don't want this beer?" He offers again to a frantic shake of Shane's head. "I love a smart kid so listen up, I don't care how the fuck you get home, call me if you have to, but don't do it again. Last thing ... *why*?"

Shane's eyes lift up to meet his. "What do you mean *why*?"

Colton stares at him long and hard and it drives me crazy that I'm not close enough to see the unspoken words pass between them. "To be cool? To impress a girl? To cover the pain from your mom? You don't have to tell me, Shane, but the answer is very important. It's something you need to answer for yourself." I see Shane's head lower and I suck in a breath with concern. Shane shifts and leans against the wall like Colton, legs crossed out in front of them, arms crossed over their chests, and heads angled up at the ceiling. The sight of them together like this is priceless, and I know this is one moment that will forever be etched in my memory.

Colton blows out a breath and when he starts speaking, his voice is so soft that I strain to hear him. "When I was little I had some bad shit happen to me. *Really bad shit*. And no matter what I did, or how good I was, or how hard I tried … nothing mattered … nothing stopped it. No one helped. So in my seven year old brain, it was my fault and even some days now, I still think that way. But the worst part was living with the pain and guilt from it." He sighs and turns his head from the ceiling and waits for Shane to do the same so they're looking at one another. "Shit, I started drinking when I was a helluva lot younger than you, Shane … and I drank because it hurt so fucking much. And after some stupid stunts and some situations I was lucky enough to walk away from, my dad sat me down and asked me the same question I just asked you. Said the same things I said to you. But then he asked, 'Why drink to cover it up because hurting is feeling and feeling is living, and isn't it good to be alive?'" Colton shakes his head. "And you know what? Some days I thought it was bullshit, that I would never be able to spend a single day without thinking about it or hurting from it or feeling guilty about it … and fuck, those days? I wanted to drink. At fifteen Shane, I wanted to drink to deal with it … but my dad would sit me down and repeat those words to me. And you know what? He was right. It took time. Lots of time. And it never, ever goes away … but I'm so glad I chose to feel over being numb. So glad I chose living over being dead."

I don't realize that I have tears sliding down my cheeks like Shane does until Colton reaches out and hooks an arm around his neck and pulls him close. He gives him a quick, but gruff man-hug that causes a sob to shake through Shane's body. Colton presses an uncharacteristic kiss to the top of his head and murmurs again, "Remember, hurting is feeling and feeling is living, and isn't it good to be alive?"

My heart is in my throat, my breath robbed, and any hope I ever had of walking away from this beautiful disaster of a man is completely stolen from me forever.

The damaged man helping the broken child.

He releases Shane from the hug and I can immediately sense they are both uncomfortable with their show of emotion. Colton shoves off of the bed and laughs when he offers Shane the beer again and he pushes it away. He gathers the bag with the rest of them and starts to walk toward the door but turns back. "Hey, Shane? You stink, dude. Take a shower and get dressed, we've got some baseball to go watch."

Colton walks out of the door and stops to stare at me, so many emotions swimming in his eyes as he sees the tears staining my cheeks. I say the only thing I can. "Thank you," I mouth. He nods as if he doesn't trust himself to speak and walks down the hall.

Chapter Twenty-Six

COLTON

"**Y**OU'VE GOT THEM NOW, JAX?" I ask as I watch Scooter buy some sugary crap from the snack bar with the cash I gave him. Shane refused. Fucker's still green in the face. He won't be eating anything for a while, unless he wants it to come back up.

Ah, sweet memories of being a teenager and getting lit like a goddamn Christmas tree. I can't help but feel sorry for him, but hell if it's not kind of funny watching this rite of passage.

Jax adjusts his baseball cap, sets his bat down and walks over to me. "Yeah, I got 'em." He reaches out to me and we shake hands. "Thanks for …" He lifts his chin over in Shane's direction.

"No prob." I laugh. "He had nothing on my first dance with the bottom of the bottle, but I talked to him."

"Thanks. Did Ry change her mind? Is she not coming?"

"No," I shake my head as I watch Ricky take a swing and rip the ball out of the infield during his batting practice. I whistle so he knows I saw him and he has the cutestdamn grin on his face when he looks at me. I know more than anyone that acknowledgment in any form goes a long way. "She is. I guess Zander had a rough morning so she didn't want him paraded around in front of the press. So I brought the boys, hoping they'd follow me."

Fucking vultures. I look out toward the parking lot by the Range Rover and see them all standing there, cameras slung around their necks, long range lenses pointing at me; hoping to catch … fuck if I know what at a kids' little league game. But shit, they maintain their distance and don't bombard me when I'm with the kids, and I'm a little shocked. Since when do they have any goddamn manners? It's not like I'm going to be doing anything exciting behind the bleachers and creating any more unfounded illegitimate children. "Anyway…" I shrug "…it seems to have worked."

Jax laughs as he looks at the mob of them in the parking lot. "Ya think? Craziness, man, to live with that all the time. Do you ever get used to it?"

"Can a car drive without wheels?" Stupidest fucking question ever but it's Jax. Dude's cool. Looks out for Ry.

"True," he says with a nod.

I make a bit more small talk with him before I head out to give the parasitic shitbags by my car the close up pictures that'll land them some money. That will hopefully keep them at bay for another goddamn day.

They hit me with their cameras as I walk by, and it takes everything I have not to throw a punch because hell if it wouldn't feel good to just let loose and have at 'em. Fucking Chase. Her words stop me only because it will harm Ry if I pull the reckless bad boy gone crazy that they're pushing for with their bullshit questions about her being a home wrecker.

Motherfucking promises. Fuck them all to hell. This is why I never make them. Never did before Rylee anyway. Who'd have thought the day would come that I'd be pussy whipped and okay with it.

Add another layer of ice to Hell because it's become colder than the arctic circle with the shit she's changing in me.

I told her I was trying to be a better man. Well, fuck me. Little did I know we were going to get thrown into this shit storm that was gonna pull us every which way like a motherfucking tug-of-war.

I've been good so far. Haven't picked up my phone and ripped Tawny apart for this bullshit charade she's pulling, for throwing Rylee to the damn wolves to try and hurt me. But I know if I do it's just going to prove that she's gotten to me. And to her, that's winning half the battle.

"So when's the wedding, Colton?"

"Does Tawny know you're with Rylee today?"

"Have you picked out names for your son yet?

Another cameraman jostles me from the side, and I whirl on him, fists clenched, jaw grinding. "Back the fuck off, man!"

Rylee. Rylee. *My fucking Rylee.* I have to repeat it over and over to help me ignore their bullshit lies and prevent myself from losing my shit.

At least the guy backs off so I can open the door to the car. Thank God for expensive ass cars because the minute I slam the door shut the sound silences and the tinted windows make it hard for the cameras to get their shot of me about to go apeshit. As much as I need to sit here and calm the fuck down, there's no way I can with the circus surrounding me.

I rev the engine and hope they get the clue and back off so I don't run them over. One more rev of the engine and the slight movement backwards has them all running off to get in their cars so they can chase me.

Fucking Christ.

Have drama, please follow. If I put stupid-ass bumper stickers on my car, that's what it would say.

I check for kids and rev the engine once more before I quickly leave the lot. I get clear of the craziness when I lose most of the cars at a red light I fly through on the tail end of a yellow. I finally breathe a sigh of relief, can have a minute of peace humming along to *Best of You* on the radio, and then I look down at my phone.

And the air I just got back gets sucker punched right out of me. My foot falters on the gas like a fucking rookie driver from the text displayed on the screen.

Sealed envelope sitting on my desk. Results are back. Call me.

My entire body freezes—lungs, heart, throat, everything. I stare straight ahead, my knuckles turn white as I grip the steering wheel, trying to get a grip on the onslaught of emotions burying me alive.

I force myself to breathe, to blink, to think. The minute my head's commands to my body click, I swerve across the lane causing horns to blare. I pull into the closest driveway I see, a strip mall parking lot, and slam on the brakes.

I pick up my phone to call my lawyer but put it back down as I squeeze my eyes shut and try to get a handle on the nerves suddenly shooting through me. *This is it.* The answer on the other end of the line is going to be either my biggest fuck up or my greatest relief.

The certainty I felt before that this couldn't be true, doesn't feel so goddamn certain anymore. I blow out a breath, pound a fist on the console, grab a figurative hold of my balls, and pick up the phone.

Each ring destroys me. It's like waiting for the chair to be kicked out from beneath my feet with a noose looped harmlessly around my neck.

"Donavan."

It takes me a minute to respond. "Hey, CJ." My voice sounds so foreign, like a little kid waiting for his punishment to be decided.

"You ready?"

"Fucking Christ, tell me already, will you?" I bark.

He chuckles as I hear the paper tear. Easy for him to laugh right now when my heart's hammering, head is pounding, and foot is bouncing on the floorboard. And then I hear CJ exhale.

"You're good."

There's no way I heard him right. "*What?*"

"She lied. The baby's not yours."

I pump my fist out into the air and shout. I squeeze my head in both of my hands as the adrenaline hits me at full force, hands tremble and tears well. I can't even process a thought. I know CJ is talking but I can't hear him because my heart is pounding in my ears from the adrenaline hitting me like it does at the start of a race. I raise a hand to run it through my hair but stop midair to pound on the steering wheel before scrubbing at my face because I'm so overwhelmed ... so inundated with fucking relief I can't keep a single thought straight, except for one.

It's not mine.

I didn't fuck up a poor soul's life by tainting it with my blood.

By being born to a manipulative bitch like Tawny.

"You okay, Wood?"

It takes me a minute to swallow and find my voice. "Yeah," I sigh. "Better than okay. Thanks."

"I'll have Chase issue a press release for—"

"I'll cover that," I tell him, wanting nothing more to than to feed the vultures a taste of crow and get their fucking obtrusive cameras out of our lives for a bit. Let Rylee adjust to my crazy-ass life while we find our footing.

There I go again. Thinking about finding our footing and the future and shit with her. My fucking kryptonite.

Motherfucker.

And it hits me.

Rylee.

I need to tell her.

"Thanks again, CJ, I gotta call—I gotta go."

I hang up and immediately start to dial Rylee but my hands are shaking so badly from the adrenaline racing through my blood, I stop for a second.

And then I realize I want to end this once and for all before I talk to Ry. I want to call her with the slate clean so I can tell her this is all behind us. Baby, Tawny, lies—everything is over and fucking done with.

I take a deep breath as I dial the number that used to be so familiar but now just makes my blood boil.

"Colton?" I like the fact she's surprised, that I've caught her off guard.

Time to play ball.

"Tawny." My voice is flat, unemotional. I don't say anything else. I want her to squirm. I want her to wonder if I know or not. She's ballsy enough to lie to my face, let's see if she's gonna keep up the charade or lay her cards on the table.

Because fuck if the paternity test isn't my ace in the hole.

"Hi," she says so softly that I can't really figure out if she's being timid or trying to sound seductive.

Either one has my stomach churning.

I chew my cheek, trying to figure out where I want to go with this conversation because as much as I want to make her suffer, I just want her gone. Sayonara, adios, the whole fucking goodbye. She clears her throat and I know the silence is killing her.

Good.

"Colton," she says my name again, and I have to bite my tongue, let her suffer. "Did you need something? I—I'm surprised to hear from you …"

"Really? Surprised?" The sarcasm drips from my voice like fucking motor oil. "Now why would that be?"

She starts to stutter out words but none of them get past the first syllable. "Save it Tawn. Just tell me one thing. *Why*?"

When the hell did she get like this? When did she go from my college sweetheart to the conniving, manipulative bitch on the other end of the line? What the fuck did I miss?

"Why?" she asks, drawing the word out. We've been friends for so long, I can tell she's fishing. She's looking for a clue so she can take it and twist it and manipulate it into whatever I'm going to say that suits her best.

And I'm done. The innocent routine ended a long time ago when it comes to her and her goddamn lies. At least I recognize it now. After what she did to Ry? And now tried to do to me?

Batter up, sweetheart.

"Yeah, why?" I bite out. "Because you fucking lied through those perfect white teeth of yours? Used my accident to—"

"Colton I didn't try to—"

"Shut up, Tawny! I don't care about your goddamn pathetic excuses! " I shout at her because I'm on a roll and fuck if it doesn't feel good to let it out. Release all of the anger and the fear and the uncertainty that's ruled my life over the past few weeks. Left me a goddamn disoriented mess just like driving blindly into the smoke after a crash to hope I come out the other side of its oppressive fucking haze. "You didn't try to what?"

My anger's eating me raw. I need to move. Need to expel some of it so I shove open the door of the Rover and start pacing back and forth, shoving my free hand through my hair as my feet hit the ground beneath me.

"You didn't try to use my accident—*my fucked up head*—as a means to get what you wanted? Tell me I slept with you when I didn't? Trap me into being the daddy for your illegitimate kid? *How fucked up is that*? What kind of piece of shit does that, Tawn? Huh? Can you answer me why the woman I used to know—*was my friend* once upon a fucked up time—had to stoop so damn low that you used a kid to try and get me back?"

There's not enough asphalt in this parking lot right now to help me abate the fury in my veins, because the more I think about it—about what she was trying to do to me—the stronger my rage grows.

Goddamn right she's quiet, I tell myself, when she doesn't respond to a single thing I've said. All I hear are whimpering cries on the other end of the line.

"To think I used to care about you. Fucking unbelievable, T." I shake my head and swallow a huge gulp of air. "Is this how you treat the people you claim to love? Use a kid to manipulate? To deceive to get love?"

"You got back the results." It's not a question, just a soft statement that's eerily calm.

And she knows.

"Yeah, I got them back." The quiet steel in my voice should have her running for cover.

"You fucked with me once, Tawn. I dealt with it as gently as possible since our families are connected." I lean my back against the Rover and just keep shaking my head, my pulse racing, and breath panting out in shallow breaths. "But you obviously don't care about that because you just majorly screwed with me again. Tried to ruin me with the one thing you know would fuck me up more than anything else. So I suggest you listen closely because I'm only going to say this once. I'm done with you. Don't contact me. You sure as fuck better not contact Ry. And family functions?" I laugh and it sure as shit isn't because I'm feeling happy. "I suggest you have the stomach flu or some other reason not to attend. Got it? You were my friend and now you're just ... nothing."

"Please listen," she pleads and her voice—the voice that used to mean something—does absolutely nothing to me. At all. "Don't be so cold—"

"Cold?" I shout at her, my body vibrating with anger. "Cold? Cold? Get ready for the polar fucking ice cap because we're done. You're dead to me, Tawny. Nothing else left to say." And I hang up the phone despite the sob I hear coming through the other end. I turn and brace my hands on the side of my car as I process everything. As I try to comprehend how a childhood friend could do that to me.

And I realize it doesn't really fucking matter. The *whys*, the *what fors*. Any of it.

Because I have Ry now.

Holy shit. I'm so wrapped up in my head and what I just did, that I forgot the whole reason I did it.

Rylee.

I get in the car as I fumble with the phone in my hand, and it takes me a second to bring her up from my recent calls list. The phone rings but I'm mpatient. "C'mon, Ry!" I pound the steering wheel with my fist as the ringing filters through the speakers of the car.

"Hey!" She laughs.

The sound. *My fucking God*, that carefree sound in her voice grabs a hold of my damn heart and just squeezes it so tight I feel like I can't breathe. It's like all of a sudden all of the bullshit is gone with Tawny and the crash, and even though I can't take a breath, I feel like I can breathe for the first time in a long ass time. Is this what it's supposed to feel like? Fucking clarity and shit?

I start to speak and I can't. What the hell? It's like I want to say everything to her at once and yet I can't think of how to start. I start laughing, like batshit crazy laughing, because I'm the middle of some shitty strip mall and it hits me now?

"You okay?" she asks in that sexy tone of hers.

"Yeah," I choke out through my laughter. "I just—"

The giggle comes through the speaker loud and clear and I just stop talking. It's Zander's and it's the first time I've ever heard it. The sound cuts me open like a filet knife. I swear to God I couldn't be any more of a chick right now with my emotions all over the fucking place.

"Go get your glove in the backyard and we'll get going, okay?" I hear him agree through the line. "Sorry, you were going to tell me what was so funny."

And I start to talk, begin to tell her about the test results when I hear a sound that is so horrifying it reaches into my chest and tears into my hardened heart. "What the fuck is that?" I can't say it quickly enough because despite the high-pitched scream that sounds like a wounded animal fighting for his life, I can still hear Rylee moving through the phone line.

My stomach churns at the sound and her goddamn silence. "Ry? Tell me what's going on. Ry?"

"No, no, no, no!" she says and there's something in her voice—fear, disbelief, and shock mixed with defiance—that has shivers dancing up my spine and has me immediately starting the car and throwing it into gear.

"Goddammit, Ry! Talk to me. What the fuck is wrong?" I yell into the phone, panic overtaking me, but all I hear is her heavy breathing. And then whimpering. "Rylee!"

"You can't have him!" she says in an eerily calm voice, which sounds far away and has me cutting off some poor schmuck in the lane next to me.

"Who's there, Ry? *Tell me, baby, please,*" I plead, fear like I've only ever known in my youth tasting like bile in my mouth. Fear in my every fucking nerve. I struggle with deciding whether to hang up and call 9-1-1, but that would mean I'd have to hang up on her—not hear her, not know she's okay.

"You fucking bitch!" is all I hear before she cries out in pain and the phone goes dead.

"No!" I scream and smash my hand into the steering wheel. My eyes blur as I try to push the numbers on my phone, but my fingers are shaking so damn bad that I can't even manage 9-1-1 until after the third try.

"9-1-1. What's your emergency?" The disembodied voice answers.

"Please help them. They're screaming and … they're screaming!" I plead with her.

"Who's screaming, sir?"

"Rylee and Zand…" I can't fucking think straight; ice floods my veins and my only thought is I need to get to them so I don't even realize I'm not making any goddamn sense. "Please, someone is there and—"

"Sir, what's your name? What's the address?"

"Co-Colton," I stutter out when I realize I don't even know the address. Just the street. "Switzerland Avenue."

Oh fuck. Oh fuck. *Hang on, baby. Hang on.* I'm coming. It's all I repeat in my head—over and over—as my body shakes.

"What's the address sir?"

"I don't fucking know!" I shout at the 9-1-1 operator. "The one with all the goddamn paparazzi out front. There's no one else in the house but her and a little boy. *Please!* Quickly."

And when I look up from ending the call, I have to slam on the brakes as I hit fucking road construction.

"Fuck!" I yell, laying in on my horn like it's my lifeline.

Rylee.

She's my only thought.

Rylee.

Please God, no.

Chapter Twenty-Seven

"SPIDERMAN. BATMAN. SUPERMAN. IRONMAN. SPIDERMAN. Batman ..." Zander repeats it over and over as he sits balled up in a corner behind me in the backyard. It's the only thing I can hear over the buzzing in my head right now from the force of the punch. Zander's hands are over his ears and he rocks back and forth as he chants, withdrawing into himself. Into the world he wants to exist, where there are no bad men wielding guns or fathers holding knives cutting their wives apart.

The problem is that in Zander's world, they are one in the same.

I notice all of this in the split second after I'm punched in the face, my body flinging and twisting from the impact to see my sweet boy shrinking into himself. Time stands still then begins to move in slow motion. The pain in my cheek and eye does nothing to abate the fear in my heart as I look up to meet the eyes of the man that's been a constant presence in my life over the past few weeks. His hat and dark glasses have been knocked off and it hits me.

I know this man.

I've seen him before.

He's the man who gave me the creeps in the Target parking lot. He's the man from the dark blue sedan parked outside of The House and my house, following me. Without his hat and sunglasses I can see Zander in him. I know why he seemed so familiar in the parking lot that day. He has the same color eyes, the same features; his hair is longer and a bit darker, but the resemblance is unmistakable.

My eyes skim over the matte black metal of the pistol he has pointed at me and then to his eyes—dark pools of unemotional blackness—that are flickering back and forth from me to Zander and his incessant chanting of superheroes in the background.

"What did you do to him?" he shouts at me angling the gun over to Zander and then back to me. "Why's he doing that? Answer me!"

Stay calm, Rylee. Stay calm, Rylee.

"He—he's scared." *You did this to him,* I want to scream at him. *You did this, you useless piece of murdering sack of shit,* but all I do is repeat myself, trying to hide my fear and keep myself from stuttering. I try to focus on the pounding of my heart, counting the beats thumping in my ears to keep me calm. I can feel the rivulets of sweat trickle between my shoulder blades and breasts. I can smell the fear and my stomach revolts, knowing it's mine that I smell—mixed with his.

And I hold onto that thought.

That he's scared too.

Think, Ry. Think. I need to keep him calm but protect Zander, and I have no clue how to do that. The unfettered fear I feel is scattering my thoughts, robbing me of coherency. Of what in the hell I should do, because I know he's murdered before. Murdered the mother of his child, his wife no less.

What's going to stop him from murdering me?

He has nothing to lose.

And that more than anything scares the shit out of me.

I force a swallow, my eyes flicking all over the backyard. I see his camera and fake press pass on the ground by the gate. I see my cell phone in the edge of the grass, where it scattered when he hit me, and I immediately think of Colton.

I instantly grab on to the hope that he heard me, knows we're in trouble, will call for help—because if he didn't, I have no chance at protecting Zander against this madman. Of protecting myself.

My tears sting, and the swelling in my eye from where he ambushed me, hurts like a bitch. My hands are shaking and my breath hitches in fear, while the increased volume of Zander's chant is adding a heightened level of stress to the whole situation.

It's the only sound I can hear in the early morning silence—the chants of a little boy knowing he has no hope left. And with each passing moment, the whispered words get louder and louder as if he's trying to drown out the sound of his dad's voice.

"Wh—what do you want?" I finally ask over Zander's voice, sensing his grasp on reality is long gone. And I don't know how to rationalize with a crazy person.

He steps toward me, his eyes running down the length of my body, and even though my nerves are already on high alert, the look in his dead eyes when he scrapes them back up causes new ones to hum. Warning bells go off and my stomach squeezes violently—so much so that I have to fight the nausea that threatens.

He reaches the gun out, and I freeze as he runs the tip of it up and down the side of my cheek. The cold of the steel, the hard reality of the metal on my flesh and what it represents, causes the blood in my veins to turn to ice.

"You're a pretty little thing aren't you, *Rylee*." The way he says my name, as if he's fucking it with his tongue, has me gagging. In an instant he has my cheeks squeezed tightly in his hands, his face inches from mine. Tears start streaming down my face. I want to be tough. I want to tell him to fuck off and die. I want to scream for Zander to run and get help. I want to plead with God, *with anyone*, for help. I want to tell Colton I love him. But I can't because none of that is possible right now. My knees are shaking, my teeth are trying to chatter inside of his grip. Everything I am—my future, my possibilities, my next breath—is at this man's whim.

He comes in closer so I can feel his breath feather over my lips as his fingers dig deeper into the sides of my cheeks, and I can't help the cry of fear that falls from my lips. "The question is, *Rylee* ... exactly how far would you go to protect one of *your boys*?"

"*Fuck you*." The garbled words are out of my mouth before I can stop them, anger removing the filter between my head and mouth. And before I can blink, his fist slams into my abdomen, and I'm propelled backwards. I land with a thud against the concrete patio, my shoulders and head hitting the wood fence behind me.

The terror consuming my body overshadows pain from the blow. I've landed near Zander so I scramble as quickly as I can over to his side and pull him into me, trying to protect him in any way I can. I know he's behind me, can feel the heavy presence of the gun I know is pointed at me, but I rock Zander.

"It's okay, Zand. He's not going to hurt you. I'm not going to let him hurt you," I tell him in a hushed voice, but Zander doesn't stop rocking, doesn't stop chanting, and I'm so petrified right now I start chanting for the superheroes with him as we sit in a backyard built on hope and what I fear will soon be marred with violence.

"I've come to take my son." If I thought his voice was cold before, his tone now matches the steel of his gun.

"No," I tell him, the waver in my voice betraying the confidence of what I want to say.

"Who the fuck do you think you're dealing with?" he growls, pointing the gun into my back, its hard nose digging deep between my shoulder blades. "It's time to step away from my son."

I squeeze my hands into fists to quit their shaking so Zander doesn't know how scared I am. I don't want his father to realize it either. I force a swallow as Zander's sobs start racking through his body, and if I didn't already know, I know now with such clarity—with a cold sweat breaking over my skin and fear in my heart—that I can't let his father take him. That I'll protect him with everything I have because no one else could before.

The muzzle in my back digs deeper, and I bite back a yelp of pain as tears freely flow down my cheeks. I begin to worry my bottom lip between my teeth, because in a moment I'm going to stand up. And when I turn around I have to show him I'm not scared of him. I have to put on the performance of a lifetime in order to save this little boy.

"Now!" he shouts at me, my body jumping as his voice cuts through the constant hum of Zander's chanting.

I lean my mouth down by Zander's ear and try to still him as he rocks, hoping that my words get to him—break through the world he's transported his mind to—in order to save himself from the fear and memories of his father.

"Zander, listen to me," I tell him. "I'm not going to let him take you. I promise. The superheroes are coming. They're coming okay? I'm gonna stand now but when I say Batman I want you to run as fast as you can into the house okay? *Batman*."

I just finish my words when I feel the gun leave my shoulder blades but feel his boot connect with my left side. I groan in pain as I absorb the impact, tensing my arms around Zander as we push harder into the fence we're cornered against.

"Get the fuck up, *Rylee*."

"Batman, okay?" I say again, gritting my teeth as I breathe through the pain and force myself to rise on wobbly legs. I take a deep breath and turn to face him.

"You're a tough cookie!" He sneers at me. "I *like* my women tough."

I swallow the bile rising in my throat and force evenness in my tone that I hope I can maintain. "I'm not letting you take him."

He laughs out loud, raises his face up to the sky, before looking back at me, and I wonder if I just missed my one chance to tell Zander to go. To run. My heart twists at the thought. "Now, I really don't think you're in the position to be telling me what exactly I *can and cannot* be doing. Right?"

My head races for things to say. Ways to calm down the nerves I can see are starting to overtake him with each passing second. But all the same, I need this time. The longer I have, the more likely help might be coming. "There's a yard full of press out front. How are you going to leave with him?"

He laughs again and I know the sound will haunt my dreams for the rest of my life. "That's where you're wrong. They all left with your hotshot boyfriend and followed him." He steps closer and raises the gun to my face. "It's just you, and me, and Z-man over there. So what do you have to say to that, huh?"

I swear all of the blood in my body drains to my feet because I have to struggle to remain focused on standing as the dizziness assaults me. After a moment, I manage to steady myself, to see through the blackness clouding my vision, and try to figure out what to do next.

The only thought I can come up with is to distract him somehow, lunge for the weapon, and scream at Zander to run.

But how?

When?

We stand for what seems like forever—a silent standoff where it's more than evident who holds all the power in this forced relationship. As time stretches I see his hands starting to shake, his facial muscles twitching, and the sweat beading, all while the sound of Zander's escalating chants continue to add more pressure to the unstable situation.

"Shut him the fuck up!" he screams at me as his eyes flicker all over the yard like a trapped animal unsure of its next move.

I startle when I hear a noise behind Zander's dad. My heart leaps in my chest as the next door neighbor's dog barks viciously through the fence. Zander's father twists at the sound, the gun moving with him. I act on instinct, not allowing myself to think of the consequences.

"BATMAN!" I scream at the same time I lunge at Zander's father. I collide into him, the harsh impact of my athletic frame against his knocks all thoughts from my head, except for one, I hope Zander heard me. That I got through to him and he's running to save himself because I just sealed my fate if I'm not successful.

The sound is deafening.

The crack of the gun going off.

The jerk of his body from its recoil.

My scream, a primal sound I hear but don't even recognize as my own. Then it stops. The wind is knocked out of me as we slam to the ground. I'm momentarily stunned—my body, my mind, my heart— as I land on top of him, before I try to struggle to get away. I have to get the gun, I have to make sure Zander is gone.

I push up off the vile man beneath me, still struggling. My only thought is *get the gun, get the gun, get the gun*, and my hands slip in the slickness beneath me. I shove backwards as panic and pain radiate through me. I land with a thud on my ass, the force jolting all the way up my spine and snapping my mind out of the shock it's in.

I lose focus on the man, as I look at the blood on my trembling hands. I take in the blood covering my T-shirt with Ricky's team's mascot printed on the front. My mind scrambles to think, frantically searches its recesses for what I'm supposed to be doing because the sight—so much blood—is making me dizzy.

I'm confused.

I'm scared.

Dizzy.

My world goes black.

Chapter Twenty-Eight

"**P**LEASE, BABY, PLEASE WAKE UP."

Colton? My head is foggy as I hear his voice and smell him near. I try to figure out what exactly is going on. My eyelids feel so heavy, but I can't open them just yet.

"Sir, you need to let me examine—"

"I'm not going fucking anywhere!"

It's so warm and cozy here in the darkness—so safe—but why is Colton … Then it all hits me like a tidal wave of overwhelming emotions. I start to fight to sit up. "Zander!" His name is barely a croak as I struggle against arms, hands, not sure what else is holding me down.

"Shh, shh, shh! It's okay, Ry. It's okay."

Colton.

My whole body sags momentarily. Colton is here. My eyes open, tears already welling in them, and the first sight I see is him. My ace. A shining light in all of this darkness. His eyes meet mine, the lines around his deep with concern and a forced smile on those devastating lips of his. "You're okay, baby."

I blink rapidly as everything else comes into focus, the flurry of activity around us in the backyard—policemen, medics. "Zander. Gun. Dad." My mind is reeling and I can't get the thoughts into words fast enough, my eyes flitting back and forth, focusing on a group of men hunched over something to the side of me.

I keep repeating the words until Colton leans down and presses a kiss to my mouth. I taste salt on his lips and my mind tries to grasp why he's been crying. When he pulls back, his smile is a little less shaky. "There's my girl," he says softly, his hands smoothing over my hair, my cheeks, my face. "You're okay, Ry. Zander's okay, Ry." He leans his forehead against mine.

"But there was blood—"

"Not yours," he says, his lips curving into a relieved smile against mine. "Not yours," he repeats. "You were ridiculously stupid and I'm so angry at you for it, but you went for the gun and the police took their shot. His blood, baby. It was his blood. He's dead."

I suck in a breath. Relief I didn't realize I hadn't released yet rushes out of my lungs. And the tears come now—hard, ragged, body shaking sobs that release everything. He helps me sit up and pulls my body into his so I'm sitting sideways across his lap, his arms hold me so tight, supporting me, ensuring my safety. He buries his nose in the side of my neck as we cling to one another.

"Zander's safe. He's inside. Jax is keeping the boys away so they don't know—don't see—what happened. He called Avery to come be with Zander. His therapist is on the way to come help him if he needs it," he tells me, knowing all of the worries I'd have and assuaging them with every word he speaks. "Are you—where do you hurt?"

"Sir, can we please—"

"Not yet!" Colton snaps at the voice at my back. "Not just yet," he says so softly I can barely hear him before he pulls me in tighter, breathing me in. I'm completely alert now, can see the activity around Zander's father's body. I think I understand the risk I took until I feel Colton's body shake beneath mine, shudder as he holds in the quiet sobs racking his body.

I'm lost. I don't know what to do for this strong man silently coming undone. I start to move so I can shift and turn into him, and he just squeezes me that much tighter. "*Please*," he pleads in a gruff voice, "I don't want to fucking let go yet. Just a minute longer."

So I let him.

I let him hold me in this backyard, on a plot of grass where violence tried to rob Zander of hope for the last time.

Colton closes the car door for me and climbs into his side of the Range Rover before starting it. He pulls out of the police barricades and past the flashing lights of the awaiting media as we leave The House. Three very long hours have passed. Three hours of questions and retelling everything I could remember about the backyard exchange. About telling Zander to run on "Batman." The constant looks from Colton sitting in the corner as I refused medical assistance or a check-up at the hospital. His growing anger as I replayed Zander's father's comments and physical attacks. Signing statements and having photographs taken of the bruises on my body as evidence. I field phone calls from Haddie and my parents to reassure them that I'm okay, that I'll call them later to explain more.

Three hours of feeling helpless to comfort my boys, wanting to tell them I was okay. The therapist thought it was best they didn't see me with my bruised eye and swollen cheek, because it might dredge up their own histories. As much as it hurt not to see them—show them I'm okay—I kissed Zander and held onto him as long as I could while I repeated my praise over and over to him that this time he didn't hide behind a couch. This time he helped save someone. I know I'm not his mom, but to ease the guilt and assuage the feeling of helplessness in his traumatized psyche was huge.

We merge onto the freeway and besides Rob Thomas' voice ironically singing *Unwell* through the speakers, the car is silent. Colton doesn't say a word despite his hands gripping the steering wheel so tight his knuckles are white. I can sense his anger, can feel it vibrating in waves off of him, and the only reason I can think of that he's mad is because I've put myself in danger.

I lean my head back on the seat and close my eyes but have to open them immediately because all I see are *his* eyes, all I feel is the cold steel pressed against my cheek, all I hear is Zander chanting over and over.

I want to ease the tension between Colton and me, because right now I just really need him. I don't need him closed off in Colton-I'm-pissed-off-land. I need his arms wrapped around me, the warmth of his breath on my neck, the security I always feel when I'm with him.

"He did what you told him to do." My voice is so soft I'm not sure he hears me tell him the one thing I didn't tell the police officers. The one thing I felt would violate a part of the trust Colton had instilled in me. After a few minutes, I hear him blow out a sigh and see him glance over at me. So I continue. "When I went outside, Zander had curled up in a ball and all I could hear the whole time we were out there was him calling to your superheroes."

I yelp as Colton swerves abruptly across two lanes, car horns blaring, and slams the car into park on the side of the freeway. I don't even have a chance to catch my breath or for my seat belt to unlock before he is out of the car and stalking toward the shoulder of the road to my side of the car. I dart my eyes back and forth trying to figure out what in the hell is going on. Is something wrong with the car? I watch him as he passes my door and paces to the end of the Rover and back up past the front. He keeps walking for about ten feet, and with his back to me I hear him yell something at the top of his lungs in a feral rage I've never heard from him before.

If I'd thought about getting out of the car, I know for sure I'm not now. I can see the tension in his shoulders as they rise and fall with his labored breaths. His hands are fisted as if he's ready to fight, him against the world.

I watch him, can't take my eyes off of him, as I try to figure out what's going on inside his head. After some time, he turns back and walks to my car door and yanks it open. I turn instinctively toward him as I take in his grinding teeth, the strain in his neck, and then my eyes lock onto his. We stare at each other and I'm trying to read what his eyes are saying, but it's such a contradiction to his posture that I must be wrong. I see his jaw muscle pulse as his hand reaches out toward my cheek and then pulls back. I angle my head in question, my bottom lip trembling because I'm just on overload from everything today. I notice his eyes flicker down to my mouth, take in my vulnerability, and within an instant I'm crushed against his chest, one arm spanning my back, one hand holding the back of my head as he clutches me to him in a hug teeming with absolute desperation.

My tears fall onto his shirt as we cling to each other. "I've never felt so helpless in my entire life," he tells me, voice weighed down with emotion as he squeezes me tighter. "I'm so angry right now and I don't know how to handle it." I can hear the growl of his rage simmering just beneath the surface.

"It's over now, Colton. We're okay—"

"He had his goddamn hands on you!" he yells as he pushes away from me and walks a few feet before spinning around and shoving his hands through his hair. He just stares at me, his eyes pleading for forgiveness that isn't for him to ask because he didn't do anything wrong. "He put his hands on you and I wasn't there! I didn't protect you, and that's my fucking job, Rylee! To protect you! To take care of you! And I couldn't! Fucking couldn't!" He looks down at the gravel on the side of the road and the anguish in his voice kills me, rips me to shreds, because there was nothing he could have done, but I know telling him that is useless.

When he looks back up, I see the tears glisten in his eyes as he stares at me. "I fought the officer at the barricade. They put me in the back of a car to calm me down because I was going in the house with or without them. I heard you on the phone, Rylee, heard your voice and it just kept replaying over and over in my head and I couldn't get to you." He shakes his head as a single heartbreaking tear slides down his face. "I couldn't get to you." His voice breaks and I shift to get out of the car, and he just holds up his hand for me to stop, to let him finish.

"The gun went off," he says, and I can see him fight to hold back the emotions overtaking him, "and I thought … I thought it was you. And those few moments waiting and then seeing Zander run out of the front of the house screaming and waiting to see you and you didn't come … fucking Christ, Ry, I lost it. Fucking lost it." He takes a step closer to me, dashing away a tear with the back of his hand. I force a swallow over the emotion swelling in my throat.

"I made sure Zander was okay before I pushed into the house. I had to get to you, see you, touch you … and I came into the family room and you were both on your backs on the grass. You both had blood all over your chests. And neither of you were moving." He steps between the V of my legs, making the physical connection I so desperately need, and cradles my cheek in his hand.

"I thought I'd lost you. I was so fucking petrified, Ry. And then I got to you and fell to my knees to hold you, to help you, to … I don't know what the fuck I was going to do with you, but I had to touch you. *And you were okay.*" His voice breaks again as he leans in and rests his forehead against mine. "You were okay," he repeats before pressing his lips to mine and holding them there as his shoulders shake and tears fall down his cheeks until I taste the salt of them mixed between our lips.

"I'm right here, Colton. I'm okay," I reassure him as we press our foreheads together, our hands holding the back of each other's necks as the outside world whizzes past us at eighty miles per hour, but it's just him and me.

Feeling like we're the only two people in the world.

Accepting that the emotions we're feeling are only getting stronger with the passage of time.

Coping with the notion that we won't always be able to save the other.

Loving one another like we never thought possible.

We turn down Broadbeach Road, our hands linked between us, and drive into a media frenzy bigger than I have ever seen. Colton blows out a loud breath. Our emotions have been put through the ringer, and I fear how much more Colton can take before he snaps.

And I pray this unruly crowd isn't going to be the straw that breaks the camel's back because, frankly, I just can't take any more.

I bow my head and put my hand up to shield the swollen side of my face from the constant flashes and thumps on the car for us to look up. Within minutes Colton drives slowly forward and we edge into the opening gates as Sammy and the two other security guys on duty step forward to prevent the press from entering the property. We park and within moments Colton is opening my door, the sudden roar from the media over the gates hits me like a tidal wave.

He helps me out of the car, and I wince in pain as my body starts to stiffen from everything it has been put through. Colton notices my grimace and before I can object, he has me cradled in his arms and is walking us toward the front door. I lay my head under his neck, feel the vibration in his throat as he says, "Sammy," and nods his head in acknowledgment at him.

And then he stops dead in his tracks. I'm not sure what's he's heard or what sets him off, but he unexpectedly turns and is walking toward the gates at the front of the driveway. "Open the fucking gates, Sammy!" he barks as we near them, and I immediately shrink into Colton as confusion and uncertainty fills me.

I hear the clank of metal as the motors start moving, hear the reporters become even more frenzied at the sight of the gates opening, and then I hear them go absolutely ballistic when they see the two of us standing there. My heart is pounding and I have no idea what in the hell he is doing. We stand there for a moment, him holding me, me burying my face into his neck, the incessant questions ringing out one after another, and the camera flashes so bright I can see them through my closed eyelids.

Colton angles his face down and places his mouth close to my ear, and even though there is all this outside noise, I can hear him clear as day. "This is something I should have done when this first started. I'm sorry." He presses a chaste kiss to my cheek. "I'm gonna put you down now, okay?"

I try to figure out what he's referring to, but I just nod my head. *What is he doing?*

He lowers me to the ground. "You okay?" he asks as he looks in my eyes like we are the only two people standing here. When I nod he gets that little smirk on his face, and before I can read it his lips are on mine in a soul-devouring, heart thumping, thigh-clenching-together kiss that leaves no questions about who Colton's heart and emotions belong to. His lips claim me, tasting like a needy man starving. And I am so lost in him, to him—just as needy for him—that I don't hear the people around us, the clicks of the cameras, because regardless of the outside world, it always comes back to us.

He breaks the kiss with a gasp from me and gives me that smirk again. "If they're gonna stare, Ryles." And shrugs his shoulders un-apologetically as I mentally finish the phrase he said to me in Vegas *… we might as well put on a good show.*

"Did you all get a good picture?" he shouts to the crowd around us, and I look over at him confused. "Now this is what you can print with your goddamn picture. Rylee isn't the home wrecker folks. Tawny is. Just like Tawny is a fucking liar." He glances over at me as I stand there with my mouth agape over his comment. "Yep," he shouts. "Paternity test is negative. So your story? Isn't really a story anymore!"

It takes a minute for the meaning of his words to sink in and I just stare at him as he looks at me with the hugest grin on his face, and shakes his head as he pulls me under his arm and tucks me against him. "Wha—why—how?" I stutter as so many emotions flicker through me at a rapid pace, the most prominent one: relief.

"Chase is going to kill me for that one," he mutters to himself with a smirk on his face that I don't quite understand. Before I can ask, Colton turns us around and starts walking back through the gates as questions are yelled out about what happened today at The House. He ignores them and waits for the gates to shut before turning and looking at me. "That's what I was calling to tell you ... and then everything happened."

I just stare at him. I can see the burden that's been heavy in his eyes is gone—has probably been gone all day—but then again I've been a little preoccupied. I nod my head, unable to speak as he takes my hand and raises it to his lips.

And it hits me harder than ever before.

We can do this. All of the obstacles between us have been removed in one way or another. It's just this selfless girl and this healing boy and we can really make this work.

He looks at me as tears well in my eyes, and I step into his arms and don't let go, because I'm exactly where I want to be.

Exactly where I belong.

Home.

Chapter Twenty-Nine

"ARE YOU SURE YOU'RE OKAY?"

It's only the hundredth time he's asked me, but a part of me smiles silently at how well he's taking care of me. The day had just gotten longer and longer as I assured an adamant Haddie I was okay and that she didn't need to fly home from her job in San Francisco to physically see I was all right, and that I'd call her again in the morning. Next it was my parents and the same reassurances, and then the boys … checking in on Zander and wishing I was there to speak to him face to face as well as talk to the rest of the boys. Colton cut me off after that, telling the rest of the people who called—his parents, Quinlan, Beckett, Teddy—that I needed rest and I'd call them in the morning.

"I'm fine. I'm not feeling too well but I think it's because I'm exhausted. My stomach is upset. I should've eaten more food before I took the pain meds. And now they're making me super sleepy …"

He sits up in bed. "Do you want me to go get you something to eat?"

"No," I tell him, pulling his arm so he lies back down. I look over at him. "*Hold me?*"

He instantly shifts and gingerly places his arms around me, pulling me into him so our bodies fit against each other. "Okay?" he murmurs into the crown of my head.

"Mmm-hmm," I say, snuggling in as close as my sore body will allow because the pain is a little more bearable with his arms holding me tight.

We sit there for a bit, our breathing slowly evening out. I'm just on the cusp of sleep when he murmurs, "I race you, Ry. I really, really race you."

Every part of me sighs at those words, at the admission I know is hard for him. I press a kiss to my favorite place beneath his jawline. "I race you too, Colton."

More than you'll ever realize.

The cramps in my stomach wake me up.

I lie in the pitch black, moonless night as the little, continuous stabs of pain combined with the sweat coating my skin, and the dizziness in my head, tell me I need to get to the bathroom quickly before I throw up. I slide out of Colton's loosened grip on me, trying to be quick but also trying not to disturb him. He mumbles something softly, and I still momentarily before he rolls onto his back and quiets down.

My head's fuzzy as I stand, and I'm super groggy from the pain medication. Talk about feeling like I'm walking through water. I laugh because the floor even feels kind of wet and I know it's just my drug laden brain. I run my hand along the wall to help steady myself and guide me through the dark room so I don't accidentally bump something and wake up Colton.

My God, I'm going to be sick! I feel the huge rugs covering the bathroom floor beneath my feet and almost moan out in pain mixed with relief knowing the toilet is so close. I slip some as I hit the tile and curse Baxter and the damn water bowl he always drips from. I shut the bathroom door and flick on the light, the sudden brightness hurting my eyes so I squeeze them shut as the dizziness hits me at full force. I bend over, hand on the toilet rim, stomach tensing and ready to puke, but all I feel is the room spinning. My stomach revolts, the dry heave hitting me over and over. My stomach is tensing so forcefully I feel wetness run down my legs.

And I start laughing, feeling so pathetic that I'm puking so hard I've just peed myself, but my mind is so sluggish, so slow to piece my thoughts together that instead of figuring out what to do next, I sink down on my knees. I slide on the slick marbled floor coated with urine, but my stomach hurts so badly and my head's so dizzy I don't really care. All I can think of is how pathetic I must look right now. How there is no way in hell I'm going to call Colton for help.

And I'm so tired—so sleepy—and afraid I'm going to throw up again, I decide to lay my head atop my hands on the rim of the toilet and just rest my eyes for a minute.

My head starts to slide off of the toilet, and I don't know how much time has passed but the falling motion jerks me awake. I'm immediately assaulted with such a wave of heat through my body followed up by an absolute chill that I force myself to stop a minute and take a deep breath.

Something's not right.

I feel it immediately, even though my mind is trying to snap my thoughts together, line them up so that they're coherent. And I just can't. Nothing's making sense to me. My head is heavy and my arms feel like a million pounds. I try to call out to Colton for help, not caring anymore if I'll be embarrassed about sitting in a pool of piss. Something's just not right. I put my hand on the wainscot to help support myself so I can stand up and open the door so he'll hear me call his name, but my hand slips. And when I can open my eyes, when I can focus, my handprint is smeared in blood down the wall.

Hmm.

I kind of laugh as delirium takes over. As I look down to see that

I'm not sitting in urine.

No.

But why is the floor covered in blood?

"Colton!" I call, but I'm so weak I know my voice isn't loud enough.

I'm floating and it's so warm and I'm so tired. I close my eyes and smile because I see Colton's face.

So handsome.

All mine.

I feel sleep start to pull on me—my mind, my body, my soul—and I let its lethargic fingers begin to win the tug-of-war.

And right before it takes me, I understand the why, *but not the how.*

Oh, Colton.

I'm sorry, Colton.

Darkness threatens to pull me under its clutches.

Please don't hate me.

I have nothing left to resist its smothering blackness.

I love you.

Spiderman. Batm—

Chapter Thirty

COLTON

THE SOUND OF THE GUNSHOT startles me awake. I spring up in bed and have to catch my breath as I tell myself it's all over. Just a goddamn nightmare. The fucking bastard is dead and got what he deserved. Zander is fine. Rylee is fine.

But something's off. Still not right.

"Say something I'm giving up on you ..." I jolt from the panic I feel from hearing the lyrics as they pass through the overhead speakers. *Shit.* I forgot to turn them off last night. Is that what scared the hell out of me? I scrub my hands over my face trying to snap me from my sleep-induced haze.

That had to have been it.

"... I'm sorry that I couldn't get to you ..."

I reach for the control on the nightstand to shut the music off. And then I hear it again, the sound that I'm sure was what woke me up. "Bax?" I call out into the room as I realize Ry's side of the bed is empty. He whimpers again. "Fuckin' A, Bax! You really have to take a piss now?" I say to him as I place my feet on the floor and stand, waiting for a second to steady myself and thank God this is getting easier because I'm sick of feeling like an eighty-year-old man every time I stand.

I immediately look out toward the top of the stairs to see if any lights are on downstairs and the hairs on the back of my neck stand up when it's dark as fuck. Baxter whimpers again. "Relax, dude. I'm coming!" I take a few steps toward the bathroom and feel a bit of relief when I see the sliver of light around the closed door to the toilet room. *Jesus, Donavan, chill the fuck out, she's fine.* No need to go smothering her and shit just because I'm still freaked out.

Baxter whimpers again and I realize he's in the bathroom too. What the hell? The dog's licked his balls one too many times and is going crazy. "Leave her alone, Bax! She doesn't feel good. I'll take you out." I walk into the bathroom, knowing he's not going to come with me unless I grab his collar. I yell a hushed curse trying to get him to obey but he doesn't move. I'm beat and not in the mood to deal with his stubborn ass. I slip on the water on the floor and my temper ignites. "Quit drinking the goddamn water and you won't have to go to the bathroom in the middle of the fucking night!" I take another step and slip and I'm pissed. I've had it right now and am having trouble keeping my cool.

Baxter whimpers again at the bathroom door and when I reach it, I rap my knuckle against it. "You okay, Ry?" Silence. *What the fuck?* "Ry? You okay?"

It's a split second of time between my last word and the door flinging open but I swear to God it feels like a lifetime. So many thoughts—a fucking million of them fly through my mind, like at the start of a race—but the one I always block out, the one that I never let control me, owns every goddamn part of me now.

Fear.

My mind tries to process what I see, but I can't comprehend it because the only thing I can focus on is the blood. So much blood, and sitting in the middle of it, shoulders slumped against the wall, eyes closed and face so pale it almost matches the light marble behind it, is Rylee. My mind stutters trying to grasp the sight but not processing it all at once.

And then time snaps forward and starts moving way too fucking fast.

"No!" I don't even realize it's my voice screaming, don't even feel the blood coat my knees as I drop to them and grab her. "Rylee! Rylee!" I'm shouting her name, trying to jostle her the fuck awake, but her head just hangs to the side.

"Oh God! Oh God!" I repeat it over and over as I pull her into my arms, cradle her as I jolt her shoulders back and forth to try to wake her up. And then I freeze—I fucking freeze the one time in my life I need to move the most. I'm paralyzed as I reach my hand up and stop before it presses to the little curve beneath her chin, so afraid that when I press my two fingers down there isn't going to be a beat to meet them.

God, she's so beautiful. The thought flickers and fades like my courage.

Baxter's wet nose in my back snaps me to, and I suck in a breath I didn't even know I was holding. I get a little better grip on my reality—my fucking sanity—and it's not very strong but at least it's there. I press down and let out a shout in relief when I feel the weak pulse of her heart.

All I want to do is bury my face in her neck and hold her, tell her it's going to be okay, but I know the thirty seconds I've wasted sitting here have been more than too much.

I tell myself that I need to think, that I need to concentrate, but my thoughts are so fucking scattered I can't focus on just one.

Call 9-1-1.

Carry her downstairs.

So much goddamn blood.

I can't lose her.

"Stay with me, baby. Please, stay with me." I plead and beg but I don't know what else I can do. I'm lost, scared, fucking beside myself.

My mind whirls out of control with what I need to do and what's most important … but the one thing I know more than anything else is I can't leave her. But I have to. I pull her out of the small room housing the toilet, my feet slipping on the blood all over the floor, and the sight of it smearing—dark marring the light floor—as I drag her to the rug causes new panic to arise.

I lay her gently down. "Phone. I'll be right back." I tell her before I run, slipping again to the nightstand where my phone is. It's ringing in my ear as I reach her and immediately bring my fingers to her neck as it rings again.

"9-1-1—"

"5462 Broadbeach Road. Hurry! Please—"

"Sir, I need to—"

"There's fucking blood everywhere and I'm not sure—"

"Sir, calm down, we—"

"Calm down?" I scream at the lady. "I need help! Please hurry!" I drop the phone. I need to get her downstairs. Need to get her closer to where the ambulance can get to her faster.

I pick her up, cradle her, and I can't help the sob that overtakes me as I run as fast as I can through my bedroom to the stairs and down them. Panic laced with confusion and mind-numbing fear runs through me. "Sammy!" I'm screaming. I'm a madman, and I don't fucking care because all I can see is her blood coating the bathroom. All I can think of is being a little kid and that damn doll Quin used to have—Raggedy Ann or some shit like that—how her head and arms and legs lolled to the side regardless of how she held her. How she'd cry when I'd tease her over and over that her doll was dead.

And all I keep thinking of is that fucking doll because that's what Rylee looks like right now. Her head hangs back over my bicep completely lifeless, and her arms and legs dangle.

"Oh God!" I sob as I hit the bottom of the stairs, the image of that doll stuck in my head. "Sammy!" I scream again, worried that I told him to go home last night like usual, rather than sleep in the guest room because the press were so out of control.

"Colton, what's wrong?" He runs around the corner and I see his eyes widen as he sees me carrying her. He freezes and for the odd moment I think how mad Rylee would be at me right now for letting him see her like this—in just a tank top and panties—and I hear her voice chastising me. And the sound of her voice in my head is my undoing. I drop to my knees with her.

"I need help, Sammy. Call 9-1-1 back. Call my dad. Help me! Help her?" I plead with him as I sink my face into her neck, rocking her, telling her to hold on, that it's going to be okay, that she's going to be okay.

I know Sammy's on the phone, can hear him talking, but my shocked brain can't process anything other than the fact that I need to fix her. That she can't leave me. *That she's broken.*

"Colton! Colton!" Sammy's voice pulls me from my hypnotic panic. I look up at him, the phone held up to one ear as I'm sure he's getting instructions from the 9-1-1 operator, and am not even sure if I speak or not. "Where's she bleeding from?"

"*What?*"

"Look at me!" he shouts, snapping me somewhat out of my fog. "Where is she bleeding from? We need to try and stop the bleeding."

Holy shit! What is wrong with me? I open my mouth to speak, to tell him, and I realize that I'm so panicked I have no fucking clue.

Sammy's eyes lock on mine as if to tell me I can do this, that she needs me, and he's able to break through my slow motion mental state. I immediately lay her down—as much as it kills me to because I feel like she's so cold that I need to keep her warm. I start running my hands over her body, and I start shaking I'm so mad at myself for not thinking of this, so scared at what I'm going to find.

I cry out in fear as I realize blood is still running down her legs, and I can't even begin to process why. "Her accident. Something from her accident," I tell Sammy as I lift her shirt up her abdomen to show him the scars that mar her skin as if that will explain it. And then I grab her and pull her onto me again—her cold body against my warm skin—as Sammy starts talking again to whomever's on the other end of the phone.

"Hang tight, sweetheart. Help's coming," I tell her as I rock her, knowing that there is no way I can stop the bleeding—hers or my heart's.

I hold her tight and I swear I feel her move. I scream out her name to try and help her come back to me. "Rylee! Rylee! Please, baby, please." But there's nothing. Fucking nothing. And when I sob in despair her body shudders again, and I realize it's me moving her. It's my body shaking and begging and pleading that's moving her.

"Oh God!" I cry out. "Not her. Please not her. You've taken every-thing good from me," I scream into an empty house to a God I don't really believe exists any more right now. "*You can't have her,*" I yell at him, holding onto the only thing I can because everything else I hold true is slipping through my fingers. I bury my face in her neck, the sobs ruining me as my warm breath heats up her skin cooling beneath my lips. "*You ... can't ... have ... her.*"

"Colton!" A hand jolts my shoulder and I snap out of my trance, unsure of how much time has passed, but I see them now. The medics and the flashing lights swirling on my walls through the open front door. And I know they need to take her from me to help her, but I'm so fucking scared right now I don't want to let her go.

She needs me right now but I damn well know I need her more.

"Please, please don't take her from me," I croak as they lift her from my arms and I'm not sure who I'm talking to, the paramedics or God.

"How long, Sammy?" I shove up from the chair, nerves gnawing at me and my legs not able to eat up enough ground to make them go the fuck away.

"Only thirty minutes. You gotta give them time."

I know everyone in this waiting room is staring at me, watching the man with blood all over his clothes pace back and forth like a caged animal. I'm antsy. Restless. Fucking terrified. I need to know where she is, what's wrong with her. I sit back down, my knee jostling like a goddamn junkie needing a fix and realize that I am. I need my fix. I need my Ryles.

I thought I lost her today only to know I didn't, and then when I think she's safe—protected in my arms as we fall asleep—she's ripped the fuck away from me. I'm so goddamn confused. So fucking angry. So ... I don't even know what I am anymore because I just want someone to come out from behind those automatic doors and tell me she's going to be okay. That all the blood looked a hundred times worse than it really was.

But no one is coming. No one is giving me answers.

I want to scream, want to punch something, want to sprint ten fucking miles—anything to get rid of this fucking ache in my chest and churning in my stomach. I feel like I'm going crazy. I want time to speed the fuck up or slow the fuck down, whichever is best for her, as long as I can see her soon, hold her soon.

I get out my phone, needing to feel a connection to her. Something. Anything. I start to type her a text, express to her in the way she understands best how I feel.

I finish, hit send, and hold on to the thought that she'll get this when she wakes up—because she has to wake up—and know exactly how I feel in this moment.

"Colton!"

It's the voice that's always been able to fix things for me and this time he can't. And because of that ... when I hear his voice call out to me, I fucking lose it. I don't stand to greet him, don't even lift my head to look at him because I'm so overtaken by everything that I can't function. I drop my head in my hands and start sobbing like a damn baby.

I don't care that there are people here. I don't care that I'm a grown-ass man and that men don't cry. I don't care about anything but the fact that I can't fix her right now. *That my endgame superhero can't fix her right now.* My shoulders shake and my chest hurts and my eyes burn as I feel his arm slide around me and pull me into his chest as best he can and try and comfort me when I know it's not going to do a goddamn fucking thing for her. It's not going to erase the images of her lifeless Raggedy Ann body and pale lips that are staining my mind.

Humpty fuckin' Dumpty.

I'm so upset I can't even speak. And if I could, I don't even know if I could put words to my thoughts. And he knows me so damn well he doesn't even say a word. He just holds me against him as I expel everything I can't express otherwise.

We sit in silence for some time. Even when my tears are gone, he keeps his arms wrapped around my shoulders as I lean forward with my head hanging in my hands.

His only words are, "I've got you, son. I've got you." He repeats them over and over, the only thing he can say.

I squeeze my eyes shut, trying to rid my mind of everything but it's not working. All I can think of is that my demons have finally won. They've taken the purest thing I've ever had in my life and are stealing her fucking light.

Her spark.

What have I done?

I hear shoes squeak on the floor and stop in front of me, and I am so scared of what the person has to say that I just keep my head down and my eyes closed. I stay in my dark world, hoping I have the control to keep it from claiming her too.

"Are you the father?" I hear the soft, southern accent ask the question, and I feel my dad shift and assume he's nodding to her, ready to listen to the news for me, bear the brunt of the burden for his son.

"Are you the father?" The voice asks again, and I move my hands off of my face and look over at my dad, needing him to do this for me, needing him to be in charge right now so I can close my eyes and be the helpless little kid I feel like. When I look over, my dad is looking straight at me—meets my eyes and holds them—and for the first time in my life I can't read what the hell they're saying to me.

And they don't waver. They just look at me like when I was in little league and afraid to go up to the plate because Tommy-I always-hit-the-batter-Williams was on the mound, and I was scared to get beaned with the ball. He looks at me like he did way the fuck back then—gray eyes full of encouragement telling me that *I can do this*—I can face my fear.

My entire body breaks out in a cold sweat as I realize what that look is trying to tell me, what she's trying to ask me. I swallow loudly as the buzzing in my head assaults me, then leaves me shaken to the core, as I angle my head up to look at the patient brown eyes of the woman in front of me.

"Are you the father?" she asks again with a somber pull to her lips as if she's smiling to abate the words that she's about to tell me.

I just stare at her, unable to speak as every emotion I thought I'd just emptied out of myself while my dad held me comes flooding back into me with a fucking vengeance. I sit stunned, speechless, scared. My dad's hand squeezes my shoulder, urging me on.

"Rylee?" I ask her, because I have to be mistaken. She has to be mistaken.

"Are you the baby's father?" she asks softly as she sits down next to me and places her hand on my knee and squeezes. And all I can focus on right now is my hands, my fucking fingers, the cuticles still caked with dried blood. My hands start to tremble as my eyes can't move away from the sight of Rylee's blood still staining me.

My baby's blood staining me.

I raise my head, tear my eyes away from the symbol of life cracked and dead on my hands, and hope and fear for things I'm now not sure of all at the same fucking time.

"Yeah," I say barely above a whisper. I swallow over the gravel scraping my throat. "Yes." My dad squeezes my shoulder again as I look over at her brown eyes as mine beg for a yes and no at the same time.

She starts out slowly, like I'm a two year old. "Rylee is still being tended to," she says, and I want to shake her and ask what the fuck does *tended to* mean. My knee starts jogging up and down again as I wait for her to finish, jaw grinding, hands squeezing together. "She suffered from either a placental abruption or a complete previa and—"

"Stop!" I say, not understanding a word she's saying, and I just look at her like a goddamn deer in the headlights.

"The vessels attaching her to the baby severed somehow—they're trying to determine everything right now—but she lost a lot of blood. She's getting transfusions now to help with—"

"Is she awake?" My mind can't process what she just said. I hear baby, blood, transfusion. "I didn't hear you say she's going to be okay, because I need to hear you say she's going to be fucking okay!" I shout at her as everything in my life comes crashing down around me, like I'm back in the goddamn race car, but this time I'm not sure what parts I'm going to be able to piece back together … and that more than anything scares the fuck out of me.

"Yes," she says softly, that soothing voice of hers makes me want to shake her like an Etch A Sketch until I get a little more assurance. Until I erase what's there and create the perfect fucking picture that I want. "We've given her some meds to help with the pain of the D & C, and once she gets some more blood transfused, she should be in a lot better state, physically."

I have no clue what she just said, but I cling onto the words I understand: she's going to be okay. I hang my head back into my hands and push my heels into my eyes so I don't cry, because any relief I feel isn't real until I can see her, touch her, feel her.

She squeezes my knee again and speaks. "I'm so sorry. The baby didn't make it."

I don't know what I expected her to say because my heart knew the truth even though my head hadn't quite grasped it yet. But her words stop the world spinning beneath my feet and I can't breathe, can't draw in any air. I shove myself to my feet and stagger a few feet one way and then turn to go the other way, completely overwhelmed by the buzzing in my ears.

"Colton!" I hear my dad, but I just shake my head and bend over as I try to catch my breath. I bring my hands to my head as if holding it is going to stop the turmoil bashing around inside of it. "*Colton.*"

I push my hands out in front of me gesturing for him to back off. "I need a fucking pit stop!" I say to him as I see my hands again—the blood of something I created that was a part of Rylee and me—saint and sinner—on my hands.

Untouched innocence.

And I feel it happen, feel something shatter inside of me—the hold the demons have held over my soul for the last twenty-something-years—just like the mirror in that goddamn dive bar the night Rylee told me she loved me. Two moments in time where the one thing I never wanted to happen, happens and yet … I can't help but feel, can't help but wonder why hints of possibilities creep into my mind when I knew then and know now this just can't be. This is something I never, ever wanted. And yet everything I've ever known has changed somehow.

And I don't know what this means just yet.

Only how it feels: different, liberated, incomplete—fucking terrifying.

My stomach turns and my throat clogs with so many emotions, so many feelings that I can't even begin to process this new reality. All I can do to keep from losing my sanity is focus on the one thing I know that can be helped right now.

Rylee.

I can't catch my breath and my heart's pounding like a fucking freight train, but all I can think of is Rylee. All I want, all I need, is Rylee.

"Colton." It's my dad's hands on my shoulders again—the hands that have held me in my darkest hours—trying to help me break away from this smothering darkness trying to pull me back into its clutches. "Talk to me, son. What's going through your head?"

Are you fucking kidding me? I want to scream at him because I really don't know what else to do with the fear consuming me but lash out at the person closest to me. Fear that is so very different than ever before but still all the same. So I just shake my head as I look up at the brown-eyed lady trying to figure out what to do, what to feel, what to say.

"Does she know?" I don't even recognize my own voice. The break in it, the tone of it, the complete disbelief owning it.

"The doctor's spoken to her, yes," she says with a shake of her head, and I realize in that moment Rylee is dealing with this all by herself, taking this all in … *alone.* The baby she'd give anything for— was told she would never have—she actually had.

And lost.

Again.

How did she take it? What is this going to do to her?

What is this going to do to us?

Everything is spiraling out of control, and I just need it to be in control. Need the ground to stop fucking moving beneath me. Know the only thing that can right my world again is her. I need the feel of her skin beneath my fingers to assuage all of this chaos rioting through me.

Rylee.

"I need to see her."

"She's resting right now but you can go sit with her if you'd like," she says as she stands.

I just nod and suck in my breath as she starts to walk down the corridor. My dad's hand is still on my shoulder, and his silent show of support remains until we walk farther down the hallway to the door of her room.

"I'll be just outside, if you need me. I'll wait for Becks," my dad says, and I just nod because the lump in my throat is so huge that I can't breathe. I walk through the doorway and stop dead in my tracks.

Rylee.

It's the only word I can hold on to as my mind tries to process *everything.*

Rylee. She looks so small, so pale, so much like a little girl lost in a bed of white sheets. When I walk to her side I have to remind myself to breathe because all I want to do is touch her, but when I reach out I'm so scared that if I do, she's going to break. Fucking shatter. And I'll never get her back.

But I can't help it because if I thought I felt helpless sitting in the back of the police cruiser, then I feel completely useless now. Because I can't fix this. Can't charge in and save the damn day, but this ... I just don't know what to do next, what to say, where to go from here.

And it's fucking ripping me to shreds.

I stand and look at her, take all of her in—from her pale bee-stung lips, to the soft-as-sin skin that I know smells like vanilla, especially in the spot beneath her ear; and I know this feisty woman full of her smart-mouthed defiance and non-negotiables, *owns* me.

Fucking owns me.

Every goddamn part of me. In our short time together she's broken down walls I never even knew I'd spent a lifetime building. And now without these walls, I'm fucking helpless without her, because when you feel nothing for so long—when you choose to be numb—and then learn to feel again, you can't turn it off. You can't make it stop. All I know right now, looking at her absolute beauty inside and out, is that I need her more than anything. I need her to help me navigate through this foreign fucking territory before I drown in the knowledge that I did this to her.

I'm the reason she's going to have to make a choice, one I'm not even sure I want her to make any more.

I sink into the seat beside her bed and give in to my one and only weakness now, the need to touch her. I gently place her limp hand between both of mine, and even though she's asleep and doesn't know I'm touching her, I still feel it—still feel that spark when we connect.

I love you.

The words flicker through my mind, and I gasp as every part of me revolts at the words I think, but not the feelings I feel. I focus on the fucking disconnect, on shoving those words that only represent hurt out, because I can't have them taint this moment right now. I can't have thoughts of him mixed with thoughts of her.

I try to find my breath again as the tears well and my lips press against the palm of her hand. My heart pounds and my head knows she just might have scaled that final fucking steel wall, opened it up like Pandora's box so all the evil locked forever within, could take flight and exit my soul with just one thing left.

Fucking hope.

The question is, what the hell am I hoping for now?

Chapter Thirty-One

My HEAD IS FOGGY AND I'm so very tired. I just want to sink back into this warmth. *Ah, that's so nice.*

And then it hits me. The blood, the dizziness, the pain, the rectangular tiles on the ceiling as the stretcher rushes down the hallway, once again foreshadowing the doctor's words I never expected to hear again. I open my eyes, hoping to be at home and hoping this is just a bad dream, but then I see the machines and feel the cold drip of the IV. I feel the pain in my abdomen and the stiff salt where tears have stained my cheeks.

The tears I'd sobbed when I heard the words confirming what I'd already known. And even though I'd felt the life slipping out of me, it was still heartbreaking when the doctor confirmed it. I screamed and raged, told her she was mistaken—wrong—because even though she was bringing my body back to life, her words were stopping my heart. And then hands held me down as I fought the reality, the pain, the devastation until the needle was pressed into my IV and darkness claimed me once again.

I keep my eyes closed, trying to feel past the emptiness echoing around inside of me, trying to push through the haze of disbelief, the unending grief I can't even comprehend. Trying to silence the imaginary cries I hear now but couldn't hear last night as my baby died.

A tear trickles down my cheek. I'm so lost to everything I feel, so

I focus on every single feeling as it makes the slow descent because I feel just the same.

Alone. Fading. Running away without any certainty but the unknown.

"And she's back with us now," a voice to my right says, and I look over to a lady with kind eyes in a white coat—the same lady that broke the news to me earlier. "You've been out for a while now."

I manage a weak smile, my only apology for my reaction, because the one person I wanted to see, the one person I need more than anyone isn't here.

And I'm devastated.

Does he know about the life we'd created? Part him, part me. Could he not handle it so he left? The panic starts to strangle me right away. The tears start to well as I shake my head, unable to speak. How is it possible that God would be so cruel to do this to me twice in my life—lose my baby and the man I love?

I can't do this. I can't do this again.

The words keep running through my mind, the scalpel of grief cutting deeper, pressing harder, as I try to feel anything but the unending pain, the incomparable emptiness owning every part of me. I grasp for anything to hold on to except for the handfuls of razorblades I keep coming up with.

"I know, sweetie," she says, rubbing her hand over my arm. "I'm so very sorry." I try to control my emotions over the baby and Colton—two things I can't control—and two things I now know I've lost. My chest hurts as I draw in breaths that aren't coming fast enough. As I try to swallow over the emotion that's holding my air hostage. And then I think it'd be easier if I choke. Then I'd be able to slip away, creep back under that cloak of darkness, and be numb again. Have hope again. Be bent and not broken again.

"Rylee?" she says in that questioning way to see if I'm okay or if I'm going to freak out on her like I did when she told me about the miscarriage.

But I just shake my head at her because there's nothing I can say. I focus on my hands clasped in my lap and I try to get a hold of myself, try to get used to the loneliness again, the emptiness.

When I've finally calmed down some, she smiles. "I'm Dr. Andrews. I told you that before but understandably you probably don't remember. How are you feeling?"

I shrug, the discomfort in my empty womb is no match for the deep ache in my heart. "I'm sure you have questions, should we start or do you want to wait for Colton to come back first?"

He didn't leave me? I gasp in a huge breath of air as the lump in my throat loosens, lets air in, and her words help the slice of the proverbial scalpel hurt a little less. She just angles her head and looks at me with sadness, and I feel like she's telling me something without telling me. *But what? Colton's reaction to the news?* I'm so scared of facing him, of having to speak to him about this on the heels of knowing how he reacted with Tawny's bombshell, but at the same time a flicker of relief shudders through me that he's still here. "He's here?" I ask, my voice barely audible.

"He just left for the first time since you've been here," she explains, sensing my fears. "He's been beside himself and his father was finally able to get him to go stretch his legs for a minute."

The words fill me with such a sense of relief, shivers dancing over my arms as it hits me that he didn't leave me. *He didn't leave me.* Silly really to even think he would, but we've been overloaded with so many things lately and every person has a breaking point.

And mine passed a long time ago.

I finally find my voice and look back up to meet her eyes. "Now is fine." I have so many questions that need explanations. So many answers that I fear Colton is not going to want to hear. "I'm trying to process everything still." I swallow as I bite back the tears again. "What...?"

"...happened?" she finishes for me when I don't continue.

"I was told I could never get pregnant, that the scarring was so ..."

I'm so shaken, mentally and physically, that I can't finish my thoughts. They hit my mind like rapid fire so I can't focus on one for more than a few minutes.

"First off, let me say that I spoke to your OB and reviewed your files and yes, the chance of you being able to carry a fetus, conceive even, was extremely slim." She shrugs, "But sometimes the human body is resilient … miracles can happen, nature prevails."

I smile softly, although I know it doesn't reach my eyes. How was I carrying a life—my baby, a piece of Colton—and I didn't know it? *Didn't feel it?*

"How did I not know? I mean how far along was I? Why did I miscarry? Was it my fault, something I did or was the baby—*my baby*—never going to make it full term anyway?" The questions come out one after another, running together, because I'm crying now, tears coursing down my face as I wear the vest of guilt over the miscarriage. She just lets me get all of my questions out as she stands there patiently, compassion filling her eyes. "Was this a one-time thing, or is there a possibility that this can happen again? I'm just so overwhelmed," I admit, my breath hitching. "And I don't know … I just don't know what to believe anymore. My head's swimming …"

"That's understandable, Rylee. You've been through a lot," she says, shifting her position, and when she does he's right there leaning against the doorjamb, hands shoved in his pockets, shirt stained with blood—my blood, the baby's … *our baby's blood*—and if I thought the floodgates had burst before, they completely disintegrate at the sight of him.

He's at my side in an instant, face etched with pain and eyes a war of unfathomable emotions. He reaches out to comfort me and hesitates when he sees my gaze flicker down and focus through my tear blurred vision on the stains of his shirt. Within a flash, he has his jacket off and his shirt over his head, throwing them into the chair before wrapping his arms around me, pulling me into him.

The ugly tears start now. Huge, ragged, hitching sobs that rack through my body as he holds onto me—completely at a loss for what to do to make it better—and lets me cry. His hands move up and down my back as he whispers hushed words that don't really break through my haze of disbelieved grief.

And there are so many things I feel all at once that I can't pick a single one out to hold onto. I'm confused, scared, devastated, hollow, shocked, safe, and I feel like so many things have been forever altered.

For me.

Between us.

Hopes, dreams, wants, that were ripped away from me and pre-determined by a fate that I never got a say in. And the tears continue to fall as I realize what I've lost again. What hopes might just be a possibility I never expected to be able to get back.

And all the while Colton laces my tear stained face with kisses, over and over, trying to replace the pain with compassion, grief with love. He leans his head back and his eyes fuse with mine. We sit there for a moment, eyes saying so many things and lips saying nothing. But the worst part is, besides utter relief, I can't get a read on what his are telling me.

The only thing I know for sure is that he's just as lost and confused as I am, but deep down, I fear he feels this way for the exact opposite reason I do.

"Hey," he says softly as a soft smile tugs up the corner of his mouth. I can feel his hands tremble slightly. "You scared the shit out of me, Ryles."

"Sorry. Are you okay?" My voice sounds sleepy, sluggish.

Colton looks down and shakes his head with a stilted laugh. "You're the one in the hospital bed and you ask me if I'm okay?" When he looks up I see the tears welling in his eyes. "Rylee, I …" He stops and blows out a breath, his voice swamped with emotion.

And before he can say anything further there is a knock on the door jamb. It's Dr. Andrews asking if it's okay for her to return. Neither of us even realized she had left because we were so absorbed in one another.

"Are you ready for your answers?"

I nod at her, hesitant and yet needing to know. Colton releases me momentarily—the loss of his touch startling to me—as he puts his arms through his sweatshirt. He comes back to take my hand in his as she walks back over to the side of the bed and sighs. "Well, unfortunately nothing I can tell you is concrete because we only had the aftermath of everything to try and piece together. Now that you're a little more coherent than when we first met, do you mind telling me what you remember?"

My head feels like I'm swimming underwater but I go through everything I remember, up to sitting on the bathroom floor and then nothing until I was here. She nods and makes some notes on her iPad. "You're very lucky Colton found you when he did. You'd lost quite a lot of blood and by the time you reached us you were going into hypovolemic shock."

There are so many questions I want to ask her ... so many unknowns my mind is still processing. I glance over at Colton andhesitate to ask the question I want answered the most because of everything we went through with Tawny. So I opt for another one that's been nagging at my mind.

"How far along was I?" My voice is soft and Colton holds my hand tight. The idea that I'd ever even get to ask those words strikes me to the core. I was carrying a baby. *A baby.* My chin quivers as I try desperately not to cry again.

"We're guessing around twelve to fourteen weeks," she says, and I squeeze my eyes shut trying to comprehend what she's telling me. Colton's fingers tense around mine, and I hear him exhale a controlled but uneven breath. She waits a beat to let everything sink in before continuing. "From what we can tell, you either experienced a placental abruption or a complete previa where the vessels burst."

"And what does that mean?"

"By the time you were admitted, the bleeding was so extensive and so far advanced we can only guess as to the cause. We are assuming it was a previa because we rarely see an abruption this early on in a pregnancy unless there is some sort of violent trauma to the abdomen and ..."

She keeps talking but I don't hear another word, and neither does Colton, because he's off of my bed in an instant, legs pacing, body vibrating with negative energy, and anger etched in the lines of his face.

And it's so much easier for me to focus on him and the explosion of emotions on his face than my own. My overwhelmed brain thinks that by looking at him, I don't have to face how I feel. I don't have to wonder if I pushed Zander's dad a little too hard, a little too much, and I am the reason this all happened.

Dr. Andrews looks at him and then back at me, concern in her eyes, as I relay the events of the day. Each time I mention Zander's father hitting me, I can physically see Colton's agitation increase. I don't know what this is doing to Colton, not sure where exactly his head is or how much more he can take, and I'm afraid of so many things because I know how I feel.

"That very well could have been the cause—the trigger of everything—that led to the miscarriage," she says after a few seconds.

I squeeze my eyes shut momentarily and force a swallow down as Colton barks out a curse under his breath, his body still restless, his hands clenching into fists. And I study him, trying to read the emotions flickering through his eyes before he stops and looks at me. "I need a fucking minute," he says before turning and barreling out of the doorway.

Tears return and I know I'm an emotional mess, know that I'm not thinking clearly when the notion flickers through my mind that Colton's mad at me for being pregnant, not because the loss of our child. I immediately push the thought away—hate myself for even thinking it—but on the heels of the past few weeks and everything we've been through, I can't help it. And then that thought causes so many more to spiral out of control that I have to tell myself to get a grip. That Colton cares about me, wouldn't walk away from me because of something like this. I force myself to focus on answers and not the unknown.

And without another thought, the next question is off of my tongue and hanging in the air still vibrating with Colton's anger. "Is it possible for … can I get pregnant again? Would I be able to carry to term?"

She looks at me, sympathy flashing over her stoic face, a sigh on her lips, and tears welling in her eyes. "Possible?" She repeats the word back to me and closes her eyes for a moment as she gently shakes her head back and forth. She reaches out and grabs my hands in hers and just stares at me for a moment. "This wasn't supposed to be possible, Rylee." Her voice breaks, my grief and disbelief obviously affecting her.

"I'd hope fate wouldn't be cruel enough to do this to you two times and not give you another chance." She quickly dashes away a tear that falls and sniffles. "Sometimes hope is the most powerful medicine of all."

I can feel him before I even open my eyes, know he is sitting beside me. The man who waits for no one is waiting patiently for me. My body sighs softly into the thought and then my heart wrings at the thought of a little boy lost forever to me—dark hair, green eyes, freckled nose, mischievous grin—and when I open my eyes, the same eyes in my imagination meet mine.

But his eyes look tired, battle weary, and concerned. He leans forward and takes the hand I'm reaching out.

"Hey," I croak as I shift from the discomfort in my abdomen.

"Hey," he says softly, scooting forward to the edge of his seat, and I notice his shirt has been replaced with a pair of hospital scrubs. "How are you feeling?" He presses a kiss to my hand as my tears well again. "No." He rises, sitting his hip on the edge of my bed. "Please don't cry, baby," he says as he pulls me against his chest and wraps his arms around me.

I shake my head, feelings running a rampant race of highs and lows through me. Devastated at the loss of a child—a chance that I might not ever get again despite the dash of possibility this whole situation presented—and at the same time guilty feeling relief because if I had been pregnant, where would that leave Colton and me?

"I'm okay," I tell him, pressing a kiss to the underside of his jaw, drawing strength from the steady pulse beating beneath my lips, before leaning back on my propped up pillows so I can look at him. I blow out a breath to get my hair out of my face, not wanting to use my hand and break our connection.

The look in his eyes is so intense, jaw muscle clenching, lips strained with emotion, that I look down at our joined hands to mentally prepare myself for the things I need to say to him but fear his responses. I take a deep breath and begin. "We need to talk about this." My voice is barely a whisper as I raise my eyes back up to meet his.

He shakes his head, a surefire sign of the argument that's about to fall from his lips. "No." He squeezes my hand. "The only thing that matters is that you're okay."

"Colton …" I just say his name but I know he can hear my pleading in it.

"No, Ry!" He shoves up off the bed and paces the small space beside it, making me think of him on the side of the freeway yesterday, overwhelmed with guilt. Was it just yesterday? It feels like a lifetime has passed since then. "You don't get it, do you?" he shouts at me, making me cringe from the vehemence in his voice. "I found you," he says, his eyes angled to the ground, the break in his voice nearly destroying me. "There was blood everywhere." He looks up and meets my eyes. "Everywhere … and you …you were lying in the middle of it, covered in it." He walks to the edge of my bed and grabs both of my hands. "I thought I'd lost you. For the second time in one fucking day!"

In an instant, his hand is holding the back of my neck tightly and he's pressing his lips possessively against mine. I can taste the raw and palpable angst and need on his tongue before he pulls back and rests his forehead against mine, hand still tight on the back of my neck while his other one comes up and cups the side of my cheek.

"Give me a minute," he whispers, his breath feathering over my lips. "Let me have this okay? I just need this … you … right now. To hold you like this because I've been going out of my fucking mind waiting for you to wake up. Waiting for you to come the fuck back to me because, Ry, now that you're here, now that you're in my life … become a part of me, I can't fucking breathe without knowing you're all right. That you're coming back to me."

"I'll always come back to you." The words are out of my mouth before I can think, because when the heart wants to speak it does so without premeditation. I hear him breathe in a shaky breath, feel his fingers flex on my neck, and know how hard the man who's never needed anybody is desperately trying to figure out what to do now that the one thing he's never wanted he suddenly can't do without.

We sit like this for a moment, and as he leans back to press a kiss on the tip of my nose, I hear the commotion before I see her barrel into the room. "Christ on a crutch, woman! Do you enjoy giving me heart attacks?" Haddie is through the door and at my side in an instant. "Get your hands off of her, Donavan, and let me at her," she says, and I can feel Colton's lips form into a smile as he presses them against my cheek. Within seconds I am engulfed in the whirlwind that is Haddie, held tight as we both start crying. "Let me look at you!" she says, leaning back, smiling through the tears. "You look like shit but are still beautiful as ever. You okay?" The sincerity in her voice makes the tears well again, and I have to bite my lip to prevent them from falling. I nod and Haddie looks up and over my bed, and meets Colton's eyes. They hold each other's gaze for a few moments, emotion swimming in both of their eyes. "Thank you," she tells him softly, and I close my eyes for a moment as the enormity of everything hits me.

"No tears, okay?" Her hand's squeezing mine and I nod my head before I open my eyes.

"Yeah." I blow out a breath and look over to meet Colton's eyes. There's something there I can't latch onto, but we've both been through so much in the past few days it's probably emotional overload.

We sit for some time. Each moment that passes, Colton becomes more withdrawn, and I can tell Haddie notices it too but she just keeps chatting away as if we aren't in a hospital room and I'm not mourning the loss of a baby. And it's okay that she is, because as usual, she knows just what I need.

She's in the middle of telling me that she's spoken to my parents and they're on their way up from San Diego when her phone receives a text. She looks at it and then looks over at Colton. "Becks is down in the parking lot and wants you to come show him where to go."

He gives her an odd look but nods, kissing me on the forehead and smiling softly at me. "I'll be right back, okay?"

I smile back at him and watch as he walks out the door before looking over at Haddie.

"You want to tell me what the fuck is going on here?" I laugh, expecting nothing less than her frankness. "I mean shit." She blows out a breath. "I told you to have reckless sex with him, clear the cobwebs and shit. You couldn't be any more Jerry Springer if you tried. Getting knocked up, wrestling a gun-wielding man, and miscarrying a baby you didn't even know you were carrying."

The tears come now—tears of laughter—because anyone else listening to this conversation would think Haddie is being callous, but I know deep down she is dealing with her sudden anxiety the only way she knows how—with sarcasm, and then some. And for me, it's my own personal therapy because it's what I've clung to the past two years on the really rough nights after Max's accident.

She's laughing with me too but her laughter is chased by tears as she looks at me and continues. "I mean who knew the man had sperm with super powers that could just swoop on in, rescue and repair a broken womb like a damn superhero?"

I choke out a cough, startled by what she's just said because I've never told her about Colton and his superheroes, never wanting to betray his trust. And she never notices, she just keeps going. "From now on, every time I see a Superman logo, I'm going to think it stands for Colton and his super sperm. Breaking through eggs and taking names."

I laugh with her, all the while silently smiling softly at her words and looking toward the doorway, wanting him—needing him—to come back in the worst way.

"How's he doing?" she asks after her laughter tinged tears slowly abate.

I shrug. "He's not really addressing the—the baby." I struggle even saying the word and squeeze my eyes shut to try and push the tears back. She squeezes my hand. "He won't say it but he blames himself. I know he thinks that if he hadn't left me at the house alone then Zander's dad wouldn't have been there. Wouldn't have hit me. I wouldn't have ..." And it's silly really that I can't say the words—miscarriage or lose the baby—because after all this time, you'd think my lips would be used to saying them. But each time I think it ... say it, I feel like it's the first time.

She nods her head and looks at me before looking down at our joined hands. I wait for her to speak, one of her Haddie-isms to fall from her mouth and make me laugh, but when she looks up, tears are welling in her eyes. "You scared the shit out of me, Ry. When he called me ... if you could have heard what he sounded like ... it left no doubt in my mind how he feels about you."

And of course my eyes tear up because she is, so she stands and shifts to sit on the bed next to me, pulling me into her arms and holding on tight—the same position we'd spent hours in after I lost Max and our baby. At least this time, the burden weighing down on my heart is a little lighter.

Chapter Thirty-Two

I FEEL LIKE I'M IN a parade as Colton pushes my wheelchair toward the hospital's exit. I don't need the wheelchair but my nurse says it's hospital policy. My mom is chatting quietly with Haddie and my dad is listening with a half smile on his face because even he isn't immune to Haddie's charm. Becks is pulling the Range Rover up front for Colton while Sammy stands at the entrance to the hospital, wary of any press who luckily have not caught wind of the story. Yet.

Colton is quiet as he pushes me, but then again he has been for the better part of the last two days. If it were anyone else I'd chalk his withdrawal up to the unexpected meeting with my parents. I mean, meeting your significant other's parents is a huge step in any relationship, let alone someone like Colton who has a nonexistent history with this kind of thing. Add to that meeting your girlfriend's parents after she miscarried a baby she never knew existed.

But not Colton—no—it's something different. And as much as I love my parents for rushing up here, Haddie and her nonstop humor, Becks with his unexpected wit, and every other person who has stopped by to wish me well, all I want is to be alone with Colton. When it's just the two of us he won't be able to hide from me and ignore whatever is on his mind. The silence is slowly smothering us, and I need us to be able to breathe. I need us to be able to yell and scream and cry and be angry—get it all out—without the eyes of our families watching to make sure we don't crack.

Because we need to crack. We need to break. Only then can we pick up each other's pieces and make each other whole again.

I glance behind me and steal a quick glance at Colton and his sedate expression. I can't help but wonder what if Zander's dad hadn't happened? What if I was still pregnant? Where would we be then?

Don't focus on that, I tell myself, even though it's all I can think of—me being pregnant. It feels like such a real possibility, tangible even, that it's constantly flickering through my mind. Colton stops the wheelchair as we exit the doors of the hospital and walks around the front of me. His eyes meet mine, a softness to the intensity that I've noticed there over the past few days. A smile creeps over his lips. Could I ever walk away from this man because I want a child and he doesn't? Would I be willing to leave the one man I know I can't live without for the one thing I once thought I'd do anything to have?

No. The answer is that simple. This man—damaged, beautiful, work-in-progress man—is just too much of everything I need to ever walk away from.

Colton leans in, pressing a soft kiss to my lips as guilt flickers through me for even thinking such thoughts. "You doing okay?"

I reach up and place my hand softly on the side of his cheek and smile with a subtle nod of my head. "Yeah, you?"

The grin lights up his face because he knows I'm referring to the looks we've both seen my dad giving him as he figures out if this man is good enough for his little girl. "Nothing I can't handle," he says with a wink and a shake of his head as he stands up, eyes still locked on mine, smile still warming my heart. "Do you doubt my abilities?"

"No, that's one thing I most definitely do not." I laugh and stop when he tilts his head to the side and stares at me. "What?"

"It's just good to see you smile," he says softly before his eyes cloud and he averts his attention to something over my shoulder. When he looks back his eyes are clear and his expression is gentler. "You ready to blow this joint?"

Colton holds one elbow and my mom the other, as I stand, both remaining there to make sure I'm stable, which is unnecessary. "I'm fine, really," I tell them.

My mom wraps her arms around me and holds me against her a little longer than normal. "If you want us to we can stay in town an extra day. Make sure you're nice and comfy before we head back home."

"She's not going home." I swear, everyone's heads whip over to look at Colton, including mine. Despite all eyes on him, his are only on me. "You're staying with me. No questions."

And with that decree, Colton walks around a smirking Beckett, a satisfied Haddie, and my stunned parents. He closes the back of the Rover and walks over to my parents. "You're more than welcome to come and stay at my place. I have plenty of room." He raises his eyebrows at them, welcoming any argument that might come.

"No. That's fine," my dad says, reaching out to take the hand Colton has extended. "I'm trusting that you'll take good care of her."

And it's as simple as that. The unspoken bond from father to the man his daughter loves passes between the two of them. Man to man. Protector to protector. Colton holds my father's hand firm and nods his head in acceptance of the trust just bestowed to him. Colton is now responsible—in *man-speak*—for me. They hold each other's eyes and hands a moment longer. Emotions lodge in my throat as I slide my eyes over to my mom who is watching the exchange, a tear in her eye as well.

We both watch them for a moment before my mom helps me get in the car. She straps the belt across my lap and then looks at me, holding my cheeks in both of her hands. "You told me once that you weren't sure what was between you and Colton." She moves an errant curl from my ponytail off of my face. "The man is head over heels in love with you, honey." She smiles softly and nods her head when I automatically start to speak and downplay it. "I'm your mom, it's obvious to me, Ry. Men never see it, accept it, want it, until they trip and fall face first into it. You're lucky to get the chance twice in your life, to have a man willing to trip on purpose, to take that bottomless step. Even when he messes this up—" She holds her hand up when I start to defend him and just rolls her eyes before continuing. "Let's face it, he's a man, he's going to mess this up … have some patience because he loves you just as much as you love him. The words he can't speak are written all over that handsome face of his."

I just nod, my bottom lip worrying between my teeth to prevent the endless stream of tears from starting again. "I know." My voice is so quiet, happiness and sadness overwhelm me.

She reaches down and squeezes my hands where they're clasped in my lap. "If a baby's meant to be, Ry, it will happen. I know it doesn't make you feel better to hear me say it, but in the middle of the night when you're sad, you'll be able to hear my voice telling you. Remember, life isn't about how you survive the storm, but rather how you dance in the rain." She leans in and presses a kiss to my cheek. "I love you."

"I love you too, Mom," I reach out and wrap my arms around her, her words of wisdom dancing in my head. "Thank you."

Goodbyes are said quickly with everyone else since the car is in the loading zone. Beckett is last to say goodbye. He reaches into the car and gives me a quick hug while Colton talks to Sammy about something outside of the car. He starts to close the car door and then stops a moment and looks at me with a shake of his head. "That life-line thing goes both ways, you know? Use it. Use him. He won't break if you do … but you just might if you don't."

"Thanks, Becks. You're a really good friend to him."

"Asshole's more like it!" Colton says, sliding into the seat beside me. "He'd be an even better friend if he got his hand off of my girl and let me take her the fuck home."

"Speaking of our mild-mannered friend," Becks says with a laugh, squeezing my hand. "I love you too, Wood!"

"Ditto, dude!" Colton laughs as he pushes the button on the dash and the engine roars to life.

"Keep him in line," Becks says with a wink to me and a shake of his head before he shuts the door.

We pull out of the parking lot, both of us falling into a comfortable silence as we drive. I'm anxious to get home, sleep in my own bed with Colton's reassuring warmth against me. I close my eyes and lean my head back, my mind racing over every chaotic event that's happened in the last few weeks. I sigh into the silence and Colton switches the radio on before reaching over to hold my hand.

Sarah Bareillis' voice floats through the air, and I can't help but hum softly and smile at the poignancy of the lyrics. I know Colton hears the words too because he squeezes my hand, and when I open my eyes to look over at him, I'm startled by the sight in front of me.

"Colton, what…?"

"I know you're still sore, but I wanted to bring you somewhere that made you happy."

"You make me happy," I say, locking eyes with him to reinforce my words before looking out at the stretch of beach beyond us.

"I'm prepared this time around." He smiles shyly at me. "I have blankets, jackets, and some food if you'd like to go sit a while in the sun with me."

Tears well in my eyes again and I start laughing. "Yes. I'm sorry," I say in reference to the tears I'm wiping away. "I'm an emotional mess. Pregnancy hormones and …" My voice fades, realizing I've touched on the taboo topic we've yet to discuss. The uncomfortable silence settles between us. Colton grips the steering wheel tight and blows out a loud breath before climbing out of the car without another word.

He opens the back door, and collects some things, and then helps me out of the Rover. "Easy," he says as I slide gingerly off of the seat.

"I'm okay."

We link hands and walk a ways down the beach in silence. There are people here today, unlike the last time we were here months ago— our first official date. The fact that he thought to bring me to a place I find solace in makes my heart happy.

"This okay?" he asks as he lets go of my hand and lays a blanket out onto the sand. He sets a brown paper bag down and then puts his hands on my hips as I start to sit down.

"I'm not going to break," I say softly to him even though I love the feeling of his hands on me—strength, comfort, and security—all three things given with their simple placement.

He sits down behind me, frames my legs with his, and pulls me back against his chest, leaving his arms wrapped tight around me. He lowers his mouth and chin to the curve of my neck and sighs. "I know you're not going to break, Ry, but you came damn close. I know you're strong and independent and used to doing things all by yourself, but please just let me take care of you right now, okay? I need ... I need you to let me do this." He ends his words with a kiss pressed to my skin but never moves his mouth, he just keeps it there so I can feel the warmth of his breath and the chafe of his stubble.

"Okay," I murmur, a deep sigh on my lips and a twinge in my abdomen reminding me that we need to talk. I tilt my chin toward the sun and close my eyes, welcoming the warmth because I still feel the cold inside of me.

"Just say it," he tells me, exasperation lacing his voice. "I can feel you tensing up, pretending your mind isn't going a million miles a minute with whatever it is you want to ask me. You're not going to relax like you need to until you say it." He chuckles, his chest vibrating against my back, but I can sense he's not too thrilled.

I close my eyes a moment, not wanting to ruin the peace between us but at the same time needing to address the underlying tension. "We need to talk about ... the baby ..." I finally manage and am proud of myself that my voice didn't waver like it has over the past few days every time I try to bring this up. "You're not talking to me and I don't know what you're thinking ... what you're feeling? And I need to know ..."

"Why?" The single word snaps out, a knee jerk reaction I'm sure since I can't see his face, but can feel his body tense up. "Why does it matter?" he finally asks again with a little more control in his voice.

Because that's what you do when you're in a relationship, I want to tell him but exhale softly instead. "Colton, something major happened to us ... to me at least—"

"To us," he corrects, and his comment throws me for a moment. It's the first time he's really acknowledged the baby we lost. Something we created together that linked us together indefinitely.

"... to us. But I don't know how you feel. I know my world has been rocked and I'm reeling with everything. I just ... You're here and going through this with me, but at the same time I feel like you're closing yourself off, not talking to me." I sigh, knowing I'm rambling but not sure how to break through to him. I give it one last try. "You tell me you need me to let you take care of me. I understand that. Can you understand that I need you to talk to me? That you can't shut me out right now? The last thing I need to be right now is worried about where we stand."

I force myself to stop rambling because I can hear the desperation in my voice, and he still hasn't responded, so now we're surrounded by an awkward silence. Colton starts to pull away from me, and I immediately prepare myself for the emptiness of him distancing himself when I need him the most. Then I feel his nose nuzzle into the back of my hair and just breathe me in. I close my eyes as chills dance over my skin because I know he's not going to push me away, but rather is taking his Colton way of taking a minute to gather his thoughts.

"Rylee..." he sighs my name in that way that makes me hold my breath because there's so much emotion packed in it. He rests his forehead against the back of my head as his hands squeeze my arms. "I can't talk about *it*. I just can't." And the way he says *it* tells me that he's referring to the baby. "I can only deal with one thing at a fucking time, and right now I'm still trying to wrap my head around the fact that I almost lost you."

He rocks his forehead back and forth against my head. "I'm not used to feeling, Ry. I'm used to being numb ... running the first time shit gets too real. And you, us, this …" He sighs "… it's as fucking real as real can get. I feel like I've been sucker punched by what happened when I was just getting used to the new fucking normal. I'm shaken up. I don't know which goddamn way is up, but I'm dealing with it the best way I know how right now. And that means dealing with getting the image of you looking like a lifeless Raggedy Ann doll out of my head."

His words reach into the depths of my soul and give me back the tiny pieces of hope I lost with the miscarriage and the fears that ate at me from his silence. So he doesn't want to—can't—deal with the baby, at least he's told me. And as much as I want and need to speak to him about it, reassure him that he's what I need and everything else can be figured out later, I keep quiet and let him deal with what happened to me.

I shift between his legs so I'm sitting sideways in his lap, my legs resting over the top of one of his. I need to see his face, need to show him I'm okay. I look into his eyes brimming with confusion and reach a hand up to rest on his cheek with a soft smile on my lips. "I'm okay, Colton. You saved me." I lean in and brush a tender kiss on his lips that I can't seem to ever get enough of. "Thank you for saving me."

"I think I should thank you." He subtly shakes his head. "You're the one who's saving me."

His words rob all thoughts from my head except for the words I can't tell him. *I love you.* I love you more than you'll ever know or I'll ever be able to express. Doesn't he realize the only way I could possibly save him was because he finally let me in? When is he going to accept that he is worth saving? Our eyes are locked onto one another's as unspoken words are exchanged. I'm surprised by the tears pooling in the corners of his eyes and the shuddered inhale of his breath.

"We're fine, Ry. I just need a minor pit stop to work through all the crap in my head I'm not used to, okay? I'm not asking for space or time apart, just a little patience as I try to figure it all out."

I nod my head, bottom lip between my teeth because I can't

speak—physically can't speak—because he's just rendered me speech-less. He gets my biggest fear and wants to assuage it before my mind can over-think and over-analyze everything, as I typically do.

We sit for a bit, the silence settling around us into an easy comfort. "You hungry?" he asks after a while. I just shrug, enjoying my head nuzzled under his chin and his arms wrapped around me. "The first time we came here, you threw me for a loop."

"Why?" My voice is sleepy and content. There is nowhere else I'd rather be right now.

I can feel his shoulders shrug against me. "I don't know. I was expecting you to get pissed that I brought you to a beach and fed you salami and cheese and wine out of Dixie cups." He chuckles. "Little did I know you were going to rock my fucking world."

Warmth floods through me. Images flicker through my mind of sitting here months ago with this achingly handsome man, wondering what in the hell he saw in me. And I get it now. He saw the pieces of me that could make a whole. Accepted the jagged edges that needed to be healed, because he too had the same thing. And here we sit again, in parts and pieces, needing to be put back together. But this time we have each other to lean on, to look to for help.

"God you were cocky as hell but I just couldn't resist you, *Ace*."

"Oh, baby, I've still got all of the arrogance and definitely a whole lot of cock."

I roll my eyes and giggle. "My God!" I can't stop laughing as he presses a kiss to the top of my head. "The man has arrogance in spades."

"Nope," he says. "Just in aces."

"Lame!" I say, enjoying the lighthearted banter between us and leaning back to look at his face. "Seriously? That's all you can give me? You can't come up with anything better than that?"

"Oh, Ry." He smirks at me, a salacious look in his eyes, as he leans in and presses a quick kiss to my lips. "No worries about the coming or the getting it up part because you'd be hard pressed to find any man that can give a fucking better than I can."

Before I can even respond, his lips are on mine, his hands winding around my back, and our hearts entwining in a way I never thought possible.

We've loved.

We've lost.

And now we're just finding our footing again. Us again. And it's never felt so good to lose myself in someone so I can find myself again.

"You sure you're okay?"

I feel his weight on the bed as he sits down next to me, his cologne momentarily masking the antiseptic smell the cleaning crew left behind. "Mmm-hmm. I'm just tired," I tell him as I roll on my side so I can look at him. "Thank you for this afternoon," I say, thinking about our time on the beach. Our conversation, our food from the deli reminiscent of our first date, and of the silence between us that isn't so lonely or pained any more. "Are you okay?" I ask the same question back to him.

He pets Baxter on the head and leans down to press a tender kiss to my lips, and it's not lost on me that he never answers the question. "I'm gonna go do some work for a bit," he says as he rises from the bed. "You sure you'll be okay?"

"I'm fine, Colton. I'm just going to go to sleep." I squeeze his hand as he turns to walk out of the bedroom. "Hey, do you know where my phone is so I can let Haddie know I'm all right?"

He walks over to the dresser and brings it to me, pressing another kiss to my forehead and then my nose before walking out of the room. I watch him leave knowing the sight of him will never get old. I will never take it for granted since it has taken so much work for us to get to this point.

I power on my phone, surprised it has any battery left since it's been here since the night everything happened. It turns on and I shake my head at the endless texts of well-wishes. I read a few about the ground breaking ceremony we have coming up to commemorate the new project beginning. And then my last text completely throws me.

Knocks the wind out of me, and steals my heart.

It's from Colton and I don't think words from him have ever been so honest or the depths of his despair so raw.

I'm lost here. You're somewhere in this damn hospital and I need to talk to you. Fucking touch you. Something to you because I'm scared as fuck … so I'm going to tell you the way I know you'll hear me. *Broken* **by Lifehouse.**

And the tears come now. They fall freely down my face and I don't try to stop them or hide them because no one is here to see them now. And because they are tears of joy.

He loves me.

Chapter Thirty-Three

COLTON

"Y**OU GOING TO SIT OUT** here and drown your sorrows all night like a whiny little bitch or what?"

The voice coming from the pitch black night scares the shit out of me. "Jesus Christ, Becks!" I bark as I turn to see him walking down the side of the house. "What the fuck, dude? You ever heard of the front door?"

"Yeah, well, you ever heard of answering your cell phone? Besides, knocking's for friends and I'm fucking family so quit your bitching."

"I've been in the hospital more than enough over the past two months, a heart attack's not part of my fucking game plan." I take a long tug on the beer, my head finally becoming fuzzy enough that when I think of Rylee, the image of her cold, covered in fucking blood, and unresponsive isn't what comes to mind first.

"Well, what is part of the game plan then?" he asks as he opens the beer he's pulled out of the fridge, that smirk on his face telling me he has a point and *fuck me*, I don't need any more points or advice or fucking anything right now.

"Really, make yourself at home," I tell him. "Steal my beer."

"Nah, just borrowing it," he says as he plops down in the chair beside me and we sit in silence, trying to gauge the other's mood. "We didn't get a chance to talk much at the hospital."

"Yeah? Well, I had more important things on my mind than shooting the shit with you." And fuck if I'm not being an asshole. I needed him there too, but I'm not real comfortable with where he's going with this. I feel a Becks' dress down coming. *Shit!*

"She asleep?" he asks, lifting his chin up toward the second story.

"It's past midnight, what do you think?"

"Don't be such an asshole. Look, you've been handed a lot of shit to deal with and—"

"Butt the fuck out, Becks. Let me just drink my goddamn beer in peace." I toss my empty bottle toward the trash can and fucking miss. I must be drunker than I thought. Fuckin' A.

"No can do, brother." He sighs as I mutter *asshole* under my breath which garners a drawn out chuckle from him. "You've fucked this up one too many times so I'm here to help."

"Don't let the door hit you in the ass on the way out, *sweetheart*." I just want to be left alone. Me, my beer, my dog, and my fucking peace.

"Nice try but you're stuck with me. Kind of like herpes, only better."

What? "Dude, did you just actually compare yourself to fucking herpes?" I lean my head back and look at the stars in the sky before angling it over to stare at him and shake my head. "Because at least with herpes, my dick gets serviced first. With you, it's more like being bent without any lube."

He laughs that laugh of his that tugs a smile up at the corner of my mouth. The stubborn fucker is getting to me when all I want is to be left alone.

"Well at least it's nice to know you'll let me in somehow," he says, winking and staring at me until I can't take it. I let out the laugh I've been holding in.

"You're a sick fuck, you know that?" I say, uncapping another bottle of beer.

"You wouldn't want me any other way."

"Mmm-hmm," I say as I down half of the bottle letting the night's silence settle around us. As much as I want to be left alone—to deal with the jacked up shit in my head that's telling me a decision's going to have to come sooner than later—it's nice that Becks is here, even if he's a pain in my ass. I drum my thumbs to Seether playing through the speakersas he gives me a couple of minutes before he starts playing shrink to the fucking poisonous shit in my head.

"Remember that girl, Roxy Tomlin?" he asks finally, throwing me for a loop.

"*Hoover*?" I laugh, curious as to why he's bringing up the blow job queen from our past. The one who sucked Becks off just to get to me. And normally, I'd be shoving that shit out the door with a stunt like that, but after he'd bragged she gave the best head he'd ever had, I took advantage of the more than willing offer.

"Yeah, fucking Hoover. The suction that never stopped." He laughs with me, shaking his head at the memory. "Still pretty goddamn high on the ranking scale in my book."

"No fucking Rylee, but yeah." I shrug. "She was decent."

"Decent?" he barks out. "I swear to God, the woman had no gag reflex."

"Maybe that's 'cause you're not big enough to reach the back of her throat." I quirk my eyebrows as I finish another beer. He wants to come to my house and mess with my head, I sure as fuck am going to mess with his.

"Fuck off, Wood."

His bottle cap hits me in the chest as I sit back and smirk. "I've had much better offers, my friend, but thanks anyway." My head's spinning trying to figure out where the hell he's going with this line of thinking, but hell if I can figure it out.

"I ran into her the other day." His calm cadence makes me to turn my head and look at him.

"*And ...?*"

"Shocked the shit out of me is what she did."

"Why's that?" I pretend to be interested but he's losing me. I glance up at the bedroom window behind me where the light's still off, and even though I'm way beyond the road to drunk, I like knowing Ry's up there. I try to focus back on Becks but why the hell do I care about the easy piece we both had way back when with a head so screwed up it rivaled mine?

"I barely recognized her. Still gorgeous as sin. Filled out in all the right places now."

Yeah, yeah, get to your fucking point, Beckett.

"And she had three kids in tow."

"Look, dude, I know there's some kind of six degrees of Kevin Bacon happening here right now, but I'm not fucking following you so just spit out your goddamn point." Then it hits me. *Oh shit!* "They're not your kids are they, Becks?"

"Jesus Christ, Donavan, you're drunker than I thought." He chokes out a cough before raising his hand in the air and pointing to himself. "King of double bag before you stab, right here!"

"And who taught you that, douche bag?"

"Apparently not you since you obviously didn't practice what you fucking preach."

His unexpected words cause a twinge in my gut that I hate. The same damn twinge I get every time I think of Rylee lying there on the goddamn floor all by herself, for who knows how long, and every time I think of the small piece of me dying inside of her. I gulp down the beer, pushing the thoughts from my head and force myself to breathe.

"Where the hell are you going with this, Daniels, because I'm drunk, have no fucking patience, and kind of think you're trying to push my buttons to get me to react to whatever point you're taking your sweet ass time getting to. So just fucking get to it."

"Remember that one night we all got plastered at Jimmy's bonfire?"

"Beckett!" I growl at him because my tolerance ran out like five goddamn minutes ago.

"Chill out, shut the hell up, and listen." I snap my head over to look at him because I'm in no fucking mood. "We were wasted and she started talking about the shit that had happened to her—bad shit—you remember?" I give him a measured nod, still not following the fucking road map he's lost himself on, but recall the story of abuse in all forms. A conversation I took no part in. "And she said she never wanted kids, that life's too messed up and she didn't want them to go through the shit she did. And now she has three kids, is married, and seems genuinely happy."

"The fucking point?" I growl at him

"Quit being so goddamn stubborn, Donavan, and connect the fucking dots, will you?"

"I'm not a fucking constellation. Your dots aren't drawing a picture so help me the fuck out."

"You look like the Little Dipper to me." He smirks.

I pick up the pillow next to me and chuck it at him. "Fuck off! Big Dipper's more like it." I take a long tug on my beer. Shit, it's empty. They're disappearing faster than I can count them. Usually I'd just crash right here, but fuck Ry's up there. No way I'm sleeping without her next to me. I sigh, Becks' words running circles in my head, hinting at his point but never really landing on the damn bull's-eye. "Seriously, Becks, what are you trying to tell me here? Just spit it out."

"Things change, dude! Life changes. Priorities change. Pre-fuck-ing-conceived notions change. You have to adjust and change with them or your ass gets left behind." He shoves up out of his chair and walks to the railing and looks out into the blackness beyond. When he turns back around, he is dead serious. "We've been best friends for what? Almost twenty years. I love ya, man. I never interfere with the shit you've got going on ... which woman's warming the sheets, but fuckin' A, Wood ..."

I'm not liking where this conversation is going. Deflection is my only thought. "I thought you told me I needed to fuck a B instead," I say, trying to add some humor to this serious conversation, and fuck all if I can follow how we went from Hoover Tomlin to Becks sticking his goddamn nose where it doesn't belong.

He laughs—has the balls to fucking mock me—before walking over to me and shaking his head at me. "You don't get it, do you? Fuck the A or the B, you have the *whole goddamn alphabet* upstairs and she's asleep in your bed right now, but the only letter that can fuck this up is U!" he shouts at me.

What the fuck? He's taking her side? I swear to God, Ry's worked her voodoo pussy magic on him and he's never even had it before. Talk about super powers and shit.

"Becks? How am I going to screw this up? She's here isn't she? I want her here, brought her here, so what the hell else do you want from me? And how does Hoover factor into this shit?"

"Jesus fucking Christ!" he swears as he paces in front of me and takes a long pull on his beer. "She's here for now! She's here until you start thinking too damn much about how, now that she might be able to have a baby, she just might not want you anymore because you've never wanted one. Until you start pushing her the fuck away and trying to hurt her so she makes the decision for you so you don't have to make it for yourself. But things change, Colton! Look at Roxy 'Hoover' Tomlin. She never wanted kids because of the shit that happened to her as a kid and now her kids? They're her whole goddamn world!"

"Fuck. You." The ice in my voice rivals the chill of the polar ice cap.

"No, fuck you, Colton! You sat in that goddamn hospital room when she needed you the most and sure as hell you were there … but fluffing pillows doesn't fix the shit that's hurting inside of her. Or in you. I sat there and plain as day watched you start to pull away from her."

"I'm warning you, Becks!" I say, standing up, fists clenched, fury racing through my veins. His words hit a little too close to home. A little too close to a truth I always said I never wanted—would never tolerate—but now all of a sudden I can't get out of my mind. Ideas of a life I never even thought could exist for me. But how is that even fucking possible? The broken merry-go-round in my head keeps whirling, but all I can think about is shutting Becks up because he's right about me pulling away. About me not being there for her when she needed me most. So right my stomach is a motherfucking mess.

"Truth hurt, dude? You want to throw a punch at me? Take the truth you don't want to face out on me?"

I grit my teeth and throw my bottle into the can and watch it shatter into a million fucking pieces. And once again I'm back here—broken glass, broken mind, and fucked up all around. He pushes my shoulder from behind, egging me on, and I take the goddamn bait so quick it's not even a thought. I whirl around, arm cocked back, fists clenched, and a fucking freight train of anger tears through me.

And Becks just stands there, eyes locked on mine, chin raised in that *fuck you* position daring me to take a shot. "What's your problem, hotshot? Not so tough now, are ya?"

My body hums, vibrates with every fucking ounce of emotion I've held in over the past week, but all I can do is stare at him, wanting so desperately to expel the guilt eating at every goddamn piece of me.

Guilt that all of this happened because of me—not stepping up to be a man, leaving her alone with Zander, not getting to The House quick enough, not getting to the bathroom quick enough. The guilt clings to so many fucking things inside of me—the poison and the hope— that the only thing I want to do is drink another beer, numb myself, and push it away.

"You wanna fight? How 'bout you save it? How about you fight for what fucking matters? Because she," he says, pointing up to the bedroom window and lowering his voice to a quiet steel, "she's worth the fight, dude. Worth every goddamn fear eating at you. Every piece of it, Colton—A to motherfucking Z." He steps into me and jabs a finger into my chest. "Time to deal with your past, because Rylee?"

He points up to the room again and then back at me. "She's your goddamn future. It's fight or flight time, man. Let's just hope you're the man I've always thought you were."

My whole body tenses at his words, and I'm so pissed at myself that I don't immediately tell him he's full of bullshit. I'm so mother-fucking angry that for a moment—just a flicker of a moment—fear consumes me so I think of flight.

Think of flight when she's done nothing but prove she's a fight-er—a gorgeous, defiant, scrappy brawler when it comes to what's hers—while I fucking hesitated. My teeth are gritted so goddamn hard I swear my molars are going to break, and I turn my back to him and walk over to the railing and cuss out into the darkness that rivals the black I feel in my soul right now.

I don't deserve her. Sinner and saint. My caution to her mother-fucking checkered flag. And as much as I know this—as much as my chest hurts with each breath because of this—she's the only thing I see. The only one I want. *My fucking Rylee.*

"Cat got your tongue, Colt?" he taunts from behind me. "Are you that stupid you're going to walk away because she got pregnant? Be-cause of some shit that hap—"

And I'm done.

Temper snapped.

Gas added to my fucking fire.

"You have no fucking clue about what happened!" I yell at him, my voice breaking as I turn to face him. "Not a clue!"

Beckett's in my face in five strides. "You're right! I don't have a fucking clue!" He grabs my shoulders so I can't turn away from him, and as hard as I try I can't shrug them off of me. "But, Colton, *brother,* I've watched you struggle for years with whatever the fuck that bitch of a mother did to you as a kid, but *that's not you anymore.* You're not that kid. *Never again.* And, dude, Rylee accepts that. Accepts you. *Fucking loves you.* Figure out how to accept it and the rest will figure itself out." He reaches out and cuffs the side of my face with a hand before stepping back and shaking his head. "It's time to man the fuck up and realize you love her too, before it's too goddamn late and you lose the one person who's made you whole again. Figure out how to deal with your past so you don't lose your fucking future."

And with that the fucker nods his head and walks toward the house as if he didn't just mess with me. He stops as he opens the door and turns back to face me. "When we were younger I didn't get it, but what your dad used to tell you about hurting is feeling and some shit like that?" I just nod. "Yeah, I think you need to remember that now."

He turns back around and disappears into the house, leaving me all alone with nothing but an empty night and haunting memories.

Hurting is feeling and feeling is living, and isn't it good to be alive? My dad's mantra passes through my mind as I walk into my room and see Ry asleep.

Fuck me.

She still takes my breath away. Still makes me want and need and ache like no one ever has. And shit I still want to corrupt her—that part will never go away. I laugh at my fucked up mind, but I know deep down corruption doesn't matter anymore. Because she's what matters now.

Rylee. Motherfucking checkered flags and shit.

I walk toward the bed knowing I could sit and stare at her for hours. Dark curls fanned across my pillow, tank top covering those perfect fucking tits and riding up on her abdomen so the moonlight shows the scars of her past. The scars that robbed her of a future she thought was impossible, until three days ago.

I rub my hand down my side as I watch her, slide it over my inked scars that remind me of a future I never imagined was a possibility—

until three days ago, and my fingers linger over the last one—uncolored and empty. The one thing left I have to figure out before I know for sure if I can do what my head and heart agree on.

Because baggage can be a powerful thing. It can contain you. Prevent you from moving on. Kill you. And sometimes feelings aren't enough to break its hold. To allow you to move on. But right as rain, standing here, watching her chest rise and fall, it's time my 747—baggage and all—takes fucking flight.

Because I chose fight.

My breath catches in my throat as I come to the realization that I want this. I fucking want her. In my life—day, night, now, later—and the thought staggers me. Breaks and mends me. Tames the un-fucking-tamable. Fuckin'A.

I shake my head and laugh softly. I guess I should say *A to fucking Z*. And I can't resist anymore. I sink down softly into the bed next to her and push away images of what happened the last night we lay there together.

I give into the necessity coursing through me like the adrenaline I crave. I reach out and pull her in tight against me. When I do, she rolls over in my arms so her face is nestled under my chin, her arms pressed between our chests, and the heat of her breath tickling my skin as she murmurs, "I love you, Colton."

It's so soft I almost don't hear it. So quiet and sluggish that I realize she's still asleep but it doesn't matter, my breath stops. My pulse races and my heart constricts. I open my mouth but then close it to swallow because I feel like I just ate a mouthful of cotton. I do the only thing I possibly can. I press a kiss to the top of her head.

I want to blame it on the alcohol. And I want to think that someday it might be possible to actually say those words without feeling like I'm opening old wounds just to re-infect them.

I want to have hope that normal might just be a possibility for me. That this woman curled up beside me really is my cure.

So I settle for the only words that will come, the ones I know she knows matters.

"I race you, Ry." I press a kiss to her shoulder. "Night, baby."

Chapter Thirty-Four

"THE CEREMONY STARTS AT FOUR. You'll be there right?"

"Yes, Mother! We'll be there." Shane calls out to me as he heads out the front door with a huge grin on his face, a little swagger in his step, and car keys rattling around in his hand.

"I fear we're creating a monster." I laugh as I look over at Colton, who has one shoulder leaned against the wall and is staring at me with a quiet intensity. I notice the dark circles still under his eyes that have been there for the last few weeks, and it saddens me he's having nightmares again and isn't talking to me about them. Then again he isn't really talking to me at all about anything, other than work or the boys or the ribbon cutting ceremony later today to kick off the project. And it's weird. It's not as if anything is off between us, actually it's the opposite. He's more attentive and physical than ever before, but it feels like this is his way to make up for the fact we still haven't talked about the miscarriage.

He asked for space and I've given it to him, not talking about the loss or how I'm feeling, how I'm coping. I even went so far as to not tell him about my follow-up appointment yesterday.

I get that we're both dealing with this in our own ways. His way is to wall himself off, figure it out alone, when mine is to hold on a little tighter, need him a little more. The momentary distance between us

I can handle—I know it's temporary—but at the same time, it's killing me to know he's hurting. To be hurting myself when I need him and can't ask for any more from him. Needing the connection that's always been a constant between us.

To give him the space he asked for, when all I want to do is fix.

Late at night when I wake from dreams filled with car crashes and floors filled with blood, I watch him sleep and my mind wanders to those deep, dark thoughts that I can hide from in broad daylight. I wonder if he's not addressing or dealing with the miscarriage because he's worried that maybe a baby is what I want now. That maybe we're doomed because he never will.

But if I can't talk to him, if he changes the subject any time I try to bring it up, I can't tell him otherwise.

And yes, while thoughts of a baby have crossed my mind, I can't hang my hat on the idea. I can't let myself think that I'll be granted that post-accident miraculous chance more than once in my lifetime. Hope like that can ruin you if it's all you're holding on to.

But what if I'm hanging on to the hope that he'll talk to me—come back to me—rather than slowly slip away through my fingers? Won't that hope ruin me too? Becks has told me to sit tight, that Colton's figuring out his shit as much as he can tell from their years of friendship, but to not let him pull too far away. How in the hell am I supposed to know exactly how far is too far?

I need him to need me as much as I need him while I go through the emotions of losing a piece of something that was uniquely ours … and the fact that he doesn't, kills me. Yes, his arms are wrapped around me at night while we sleep, but his mind is elsewhere. Lost perhaps in his endless texts and hushed conversations as of late. The ones that unnerve me, despite knowing deep down, he's not cheating on me.

But he's hiding something, dealing with something, and it's without me when I need him to help me deal with this.

I try to tell myself it's the lack of our physical connection that's making me read into everything way too much. Over analyzing everything. While I lie in his arms every night, pulled tight against his chest exactly where I long to be, we've yet to make love since coming back from the hospital. We kiss and when I try to deepen it, move my hands down his body and entice him to want me like I crave him, he'll cuff my wrists and tell me to wait until I feel better, despite me telling him I'm not hurt and that I'm perfectly fine. That I want to feel him in me, connecting with me, taking me again.

The rejection stings something fierce because I know Colton—know the virile, physicality he needs when he's hurting—so why isn't he taking it, taking me, if he's in the pain I see rampant in his eyes?

I shake myself from my thoughts and focus on the emerald eyes locked onto mine. The man I love. The man I fear like hell is slipping away from me.

"A monster? No," he says with a shake of his head and a smile tilting up the left corner of his mouth so his dimple deepens. "A teenager on the loose? Most definitely."

I smile at him as he closes the distance between us, free to touch me since the rest of the boys are at baseball practice and will meet us at the ribbon cutting afterward. "You okay?" I ask him, probably for the umpteenth time in the past week.

"Yeah, I'm fine. You?"

"Mmm-hmm." And so goes our usual thrice daily conversation—at least. Our affirmation that everything is all right even though everything feels so very different. "Colton ..." My voice fades as I lose the courage to ask him more.

He senses my hesitation and reaches out to cup the side of my face, his thumb rubbing gently over my cheek. I close my eyes and absorb the resonance of his touch because it's so much more than just skin to skin. It vibrates through me and delves into every fiber of my being, seeping into places unknown and forever stamping them with his presence, ruining me for anyone else ever again with invisible tattoos.

When I open my eyes, his are front and center in my line of sight. "Hey, quit worrying. Everything's going to be okay. We're okay." He swallows and lowers his eyes before bringing them back up to mine. "I'm just trying to figure out my shit so it doesn't affect us."

"But—" My question is cut off when his lips meet mine. It's a soft sigh of a kiss that he slowly deepens when he slips his tongue between my lips to dance in a slow entanglement with mine. I taste need laced with desire, but all my head can think about is why won't he act on it?

I move my hands up so my fingers can twist in the hair curling over his collar and tell my mind to shut up, tell it to quiet down so I can enjoy this moment, enjoy him. I feel the tears well as the tenderness behind his touch overwhelms me. As if I'm fragile and will break.

I'm not sure if he can feel the shudder of my breath as I try to rein in my emotions, but he places one more soft kiss to my lips and then to my nose, that almost breaks my floodgates, before pulling back to look at me. Hands frame the side of my face and eyes search mine. "Don't cry," he whispers before leaning in and pressing another kiss to my forehead. "Please don't cry," he murmurs.

"I just … " I sigh, words escaping me on how to express what I feel and need and want from him without pushing him too hard.

"I know, baby. I know. Me too." He presses a kiss to my lips that causes another tear to slide down my cheek. "Me too."

The crowd is clapping as I finish my speech and step down from the podium, my eyes sweeping over the audience. I see Shane sitting next to Jackson, clapping like the rest of the boys, but I don't see Colton.

I scramble to come up with a valid excuse for why the biggest sponsor of the project is going to be AWOL at the ribbon-cutting ceremony and press photo session, taking place in less than ten minutes.

Where in the hell is he? He would never purposefully miss something for the boys or the project he was so instrumental in making a reality. I look down at my phone as I head toward Shane to ask him where Colton is and there is nothing. No missed call, no text, no anything.

The clapping subsides as Teddy takes the podium again to wind the press conference down. "Shane!" I whisper loudly as I motion him over to me. "Shane!"

Jax nudges him so that he stands and walks toward me. I turn my back and start walking away from the crowd, assuming he's following me. We turn a corner so we're away from the press and I force myself to take a breath.

"Where's Colton?" I ask without trying to sound like I'm anxious.

"Well," he says, shuffling his feet before looking back up to meet my eyes. "When we were on our way here, he got a phone call from someone named Kelly and he made me pull over to the side of the road so he could get out and talk to her privately."

My heart skips and lodges in my throat despite telling myself that there has to be a perfectly logical explanation for this. Telling myself and convincing myself are two very different things though.

"Are you okay?" he asks me, blue eyes looking over my face and meeting my eyes.

I mentally chastise myself and have to remember that Shane is no longer a twelve year old but rather a teenager on the verge of manhood who notices things. "Yeah, I'm good, fine, just surprised he's not here. That's all."

"Well he got back in the car and told the lady he'd call her back in a couple of minutes because he had to get us here on time. We parked right before the speeches started and he told me to head on in and he'd be right there. He got out and watched me sit next to Jax and I saw him talking on the phone as he waved goodbye to me. Why? Is something wrong, Ry?"

"No. Not at all. I just missed his call," I lie to Shane, and most likely myself, to soften the blow. "I wanted to see if he told you when he'd be back because I'd hate for him to miss the ribbon cutting ceremony."

"Yeah, well I'm sure something pretty important came up for him to not be here. He knows how much it means to you and stuff," he says, twisting his lips, trying to comfort me in that awkward prepubescent way that makes my heart swell with pride.

"It must have been very important." I smile at him. "You guys mean the world to him." I put my arm around his shoulder and start walking back toward the crowd, hoping he misses what I'm not saying, that maybe I don't mean the world to him anymore.

We make it back in time for the ribbon cutting ceremony, and I can't stop my eyes from frantically searching the crowd for him. My mind repeats Shane's words over and over. *It must be something very important.* Something huge, but the question is what?

And then of course doubt creeps in and nibbles at my resolve. Did something come up with Tawny? With his family? But if it had, he would have called me, texted me, something, right?

By the time the ceremony is over and I've said goodbye to the boys, my nerves are frayed. I've gone from concerned, to pissed, to uneasy, to angry, and as I speed up Pacific Coast Highway toward Broadbeach Road—his voicemail answering every time I hit dial—I'm sick to my stomach with worry.

By the time I reach the gates and pull into an empty driveway, I'm a freaking mess. I unlock and fling open the front door, his name a shout of my lips. But before I even make it past the kitchen, I know he's not home. It's not just the frantically excited Baxter that tells me but also the eerie silence in the house.

I open the sliding glass door to let Baxter out as a new thought hits me. What if something happened to his head? What if he's injured somewhere and needs help and no one knows?

I run back to the kitchen counter and dial Haddie.

"Hey!"

"Has Colton called the house?"

"No, what's wrong?" Concern floods Haddie's voice but I don't have time to go into details.

"I'll explain later. Thanks." I hang up on her while she's still talking, telling myself I'll apologize later while the phone's already ringing for the next person.

"Rylee!"

"Becks, where's Colton?"

"No clue, why?"

I hear a female giggle in the background and I don't even give a second thought about interrupting whatever it is I'm interrupting. "He didn't show up at the ceremony. Shane said he got a call and that's the last anyone's seen of him."

I hear Becks tell the woman to be quiet. "He didn't show?" Apprehension laces his voice as I hear shuffling on the other end of the line.

"No. Who's Kelly?"

"Who?" he asks before the line goes silent for a moment. "I have no clue, Ry."

His silence makes me question his honesty and the scattered thoughts in my mind reach my mouth. "I don't give a fuck about man code and all that, Beckett, so if you know—I don't care if it's going to hurt me—you have to tell me because I'm worried fucking sick and ... and ..." I'm rambling frantically and I force myself to stop because I'm starting to get hysterical and I really have no reason to be, except for the intuition that tells me something isn't right.

"Calm down. Take a breath. Okay?" I squeeze my eyes shut and get a grip. "Last I talked to him he was taking Shane out driving and then heading to the ceremony. You know—"

"Why is he not answering his phone then?"

"Ry, he's got a lot of shit he's sorting through, maybe he just ..." He fades out, not sure what to say to me. I hear him blow out a loud breath as I walk over to shut the door Baxter's just come in through.

The house phone on the counter starts ringing and the caller ID says Quinlan. Something's going on and the sight of her name tells me that I'm right to be worried.

"Q's calling. Gotta go," I tell him, switching the phone as I hear him tell me to call him back.

"Is he okay?" My words come out in a rush of air as I answer her call, anxiety causing acid to churn in my stomach.

"That's what I was calling to ask you." The concern in her voice rivals mine.

"What? How did you know something's wrong?" *I'm confused.* I thought she knew what was going on.

"I was in class all day and had my phone off. I just turned it back on and he left a message." I'm afraid to ask her what that message said. "He sounded upset. He rambled saying that he needed to talk to someone because his head was all fucked up. *That he knows.* But he didn't say what that meant."

Lead drops through my soul as I try to connect puzzle pieces that don't belong together.

"Did something happen, Ry? Is it because of the miscarriage? I've just ... I've never heard him sound like that before."

Thoughts flicker and fade in my mind as I try to figure out what could have happened to Colton. And I'm already on the move and racing upstairs as my brain starts grasping at the possibilities of where he could be. "Q, I think I know where he is. I'll call you when I know for sure."

I toss the phone on the bed as I rush into the bathroom stripping my business suit off, leaving a trail of clothes as I go. Within minutes I've changed into my exercise clothes and am lacing up my shoes as fast as I can. I grab my phone and am down the stairs, out the doors leading to the deck, and racing down to the beach below.

I break out in a full sprint toward the place Colton took me on that first fateful night here, his happy place, where he goes to think. The more I think of it, the more confident I am that this is where he is. He's probably sitting on his rock watching the sun sinking into the sea and coming to terms with everything that's happened.

But why did he not take Baxter? Where is his car? I push the doubts away, convincing myself that he's just there contemplating things, but uncertainty starts to grow with every pounding step.

But I know when I round the bend I'm not going to find him here. And as I come to the clearing, I already have my phone dialed and ringing.

"Did you find him?" I can tell Becks is freaked, and I feel bad for making him feel that way, but I'm worried.

"No. I thought I did but ..." I have to stop to catch my breath because my lungs are burning from my sprint down the beach.

"Ry, what's going on?"

"He called Quin and said he *knows* and his head is fucked up." I pant out. "So I ran to his place on the beach but he's not here. You know him better than anyone ... where does he go when he needs to clear his head besides here?"

"You."

"What?"

"He goes to you." The honesty in his voice resonates through the phone line.

My legs stop moving at his words. They strike deep and make my heart twist with love and worry. Tears spring in my eyes as I realize how desperately I miss him in this moment—the him I'd only gotten back weeks ago to be taken away again by God's cruel twist of fate with the miscarriage. I swallow the lump in my throat and it takes me a minute to find my voice. "Before me, Becks ..."

"The track."

"That's where he's gotta be." I start running back toward the house. "I'm headed there now."

"Do you want me to—"

"I have to do this, Becks. It's gotta be me." I've never spoken truer words because deep down I know he needs me. I don't know why,

I just know he does.

"I'll text you how to get in the facility, okay?"

"Thanks."

Chapter Thirty-Five

I T FEELS LIKE IT'S TAKEN me forever to reach the speedway because of the traffic on the freeway. I pull off the exit in Fontana, my heart lodged in my throat and my hope up in the air as I wonder what I'll be walking into when I find him.

Panic strikes when I pull through the gates of the complex because it's pitch black except for a few random parking lot lights. I drive around the side of the facility toward the infield tunnel, and I breathe out a huge sigh of relief when I see Colton's Range Rover.

So he's here, but now what am I going to do?

I pull up beside it, the darkness of the empty speedway seeming ominous. I put my car in park and shriek when I hear a knock on the passenger side window. My heart is hammering, but when I see Sammy's face in the window I tell myself to breathe and get out of the car.

The concern in his eyes has me even more worried. "Please just tell me he's okay, Sammy." I can see him struggling about speaking to me, and betraying his boss and his friend.

"He needs you." That's all he says—the only thing he needs to.

"Where is he?" I ask, although I'm already following him through a darkened entrance underneath the massive grandstands. We reach a gap between the bleachers and I realize I'm in the middle of the grandstands, looking out on an eerily empty race track. I meet Sammy's eyes through the darkness, and he signals over my left shoulder.

I turn around instantly.

And I see him.

There is a single light on in a section of the grandstands and just in its fringes I see a lone shadow sitting in the darkness. My feet move without thinking and start climbing the stairs, one by one, to him. I can't see his face in the darkness, but I know his eyes are on me, can feel the weight of his stare. I reach the row of bleachers he's sitting on and I start walking toward him, anxious and calm all at the same time.

I try to think of what to say, but my thoughts are so jumbled with worry I can't focus. But once I'm able to see his shadowed face, everything vanishes but heart wrenching, unconditional love.

His posture says it all. He sits leaned over, elbows on his knees, shoulders sagging, and face stained with tears. And his eyes—the ones always so intense but dancing with mischief or mirth—are filled with absolute despair. They lock onto mine, begging, pleading, asking so much of me, but I'm not sure how to respond.

When I finally reach him, his grief crashes into me like a tidal wave. Before I can say a single thing, he strangles out a sob the same time he reaches out and pulls me into him. He buries his face into the curve of my neck and just hangs on like I'm his lifeline, the only thing keeping him from slipping under and drowning. I wrap my arms around him and cling to him trying to give him what he needs.

Because there is nothing more unsettling than watching a strong, confident man come completely undone.

My mind races as his muffled sobs fill the silence and the trembling of his body ricochets through mine. What happened to reduce my arrogant rogue to this distraught man? He continues to hold on as I shush him and rock subtly back and forth—anything I can to quiet the storm that's obviously raging inside of him.

"I'm here. I'm here." It's the only thing I can say to him as he releases all of the tumultuous emotion. And so I hold him in the dark, in a place where he made his dreams come true, hoping that just maybe he's coming to terms—stopping and facing head on—the demons he usually uses this track to outrun.

Time passes. The sounds of traffic on the highway beyond the empty parking lot lessen and the moon moves slowly across the sky. And yet Colton still holds on, still draws whatever he needs from me while I revel in the fact that he still needs me when I thought he didn't anymore. My mind jockeys back and forth from memories of a shower bench and him clinging to me then like he is now. Of what could figuratively knock this man of mine to his knees. So I just hold him now like I did then, my fingers playing in his hair for comfort until his tears slowly subside and the tension in his body abates.

I don't know what to say, what to think, so I just say the first thing that comes to my mind. "Are you okay? Do you want to talk about it?"

He loosens his grip and presses the palms of his hands into my back, pulling me tighter against him, if that's even possible, while drawing in a shaky breath. He's scaring me, not in a bad way but in the sense that something huge had to have happened to draw this kind of reaction out of him.

He leans back and squeezes his eyes shut before I have a chance to look into them, scrubbing his hands over his face before blowing out a loud breath. He hangs his head back down and shakes it, and I hate that I can't see his face right now.

"I did ..." He blows out another breath and I reach out and place a hand on his knee. He just nods his head as if he's talking to himself and then his body tenses up again before he speaks. "I did what you said I should do."

What? I try to figure out what exactly I told him to do.

"I did what you said and now ... now my head is just so fucked up over it. I'm a goddamn mess."

The raw grief breaking his voice has me sitting beside him and waiting for him to look up into my eyes. "What did you do?"

He reaches out and grabs my hand, lacing our fingers together and squeezing tightly. "*I found my mom.*"

The breath catches in my throat because when I made that comment, never in a million years, would I have thought he'd actually do it. And now I don't know what to say, because I'm the catalyst for all of this pain.

"Colton …" It's all I can say, all I can offer besides lifting our hands and pressing a kiss to the back of his.

"Kelly called me while I was … Oh fuck! I missed the ceremony. I stood you up." And I can tell by the absolute disbelief in his voice that he really, truly forgot.

"No, no, no," I shush him, trying to tell him that it doesn't matter. That only facing his fears is what matters. "It's okay." I squeeze our hands again.

"I'm so sorry, Ry … I just … I can't even fucking think straight right now." He breaks his eyes from mine and averts them in shame as he uses his other hand to wipe the tears from his cheeks. "You know…" he shakes his head as he looks out at the darkened track in front of us "…it's kind of funny that this is the place I come to forget everything and tonight it's the first place I thought to go in order to come to terms with it all."

I follow his eyes and look out at the track, taking in the enormity of it all—the track and his actions. We sit in silence as the importance behind his words hit me. He's trying to face things, to move on, to begin to heal. And I've never been more proud of him.

"I asked my dad a couple of months ago if he knew what had happened to *her*. He got me in touch with a PI—Kelly is his name—that he'd hired when I was younger who kept tabs on her for ten years to make sure she didn't come back for me." His voice is even, flat, such a contrast to the hiccupping despair from moments ago, and yet I can feel the extremity of the emotion vibrating just beneath the surface. "He called me today. He found her." He looks over at me, and the forlorn look in his eyes—a lost little boy trying to find his way—undoes me, breaks the hold on the emotion I'm trying to hold in so I can be strong for him.

Be the rock while he crumbles.

My first tear falls as I reach out and place my hand on his cheek, a simple touch that relays so very much about what I think, how I feel, what I know he needs from me. I lean in, his jaw clenching beneath my palm, his eyes fused with mine, and place a feather soft kiss to his lips. "I'm so proud of you." I whisper the words to him. I don't ask him about what he found or who she is. I focus on him, on the now, because I know his head is desperately trying to reconcile the past while trying to figure out the future. So I focus on the here, the now, and hope he understands that I'll be here for every single step of the way if he lets me.

We sit like this, the silence reinforcing the reassurance of my touch and the understanding behind my kiss. And for once, the silence is comforting, accepting of his tortured soul.

He works a swallow in his throat and blinks his eyes rapidly as if he too is trying to understand everything, and yet he has so many more pieces of the puzzle than I do, so I sit and wait patiently for him to continue. He breaks our eye contact and leans back, eyes drawn back to the track.

"My mom is dead," he says the words without any emotion, and even though they float out into the night, I can sense them suffocating him. I stare at him, take in his moonlit profile against the night sky, and I choose to say nothing, to let him lead this conversation.

Restless, he shoves up out of his seat and paces to the end of the aisle and then stops, his figure haloed by the single light beyond him. "She never changed. I guess I shouldn't have expected to find anything different," he says so quietly, but I can still hear every single inflection in his tone, every break in his voice. He turns to face me and walks a few feet toward me and stops.

"I'm … I'm—my head is such a fucking mess right now I just …" He scrubs his hands over his face and through his hair before emitting a self-deprecating laugh that sends shivers up my spine. "I don't even have any positive memories of her. None. Eight years of my fucking life and I don't remember a single thing that makes me smile."

I know he's struggling and I so desperately want to cross the distance between us and touch him, hold him, comfort him, but I know he needs to get this out. Needs to rid himself of his self-proclaimed poison eating his soul.

"My mom was a drugged out whore. Lived by the sword and died by the sword ..." The spite in his voice, the pain, is so powerful and raw I can't help the tears that well in my eyes or the shudder in my breath as I inhale. "Yep," he says, that laugh falling out of his mouth again. "A druggie. She wasn't discriminate though. She'd take anything to get that rush because it was what was important. Fucking more important than her little boy sitting scared as fuck in the corner." He rolls his shoulder and clears his throat as if he's trying to choke back the emotion. "So I just don't get it ..." His voice fades and I try to follow what he is saying but I can't.

"Don't get what, Colton?"

"I don't get why I fucking care that she's dead!" he shouts, his voice echoing through the empty stadium. "Why does it bug me? Why am I fucking upset over it? Why does it make me feel anything other than relief?" His voice cracks again, his words ricocheting off the concrete.

My stomach knots up over the fact that he's hurting because I can't do a goddamn thing about it. I can't fix or mend or resolve, so I reassure. "She was your mom, Colton. It's normal to be upset because deep down I'm sure in her own way she loved you—"

"Loved me?" he screams, startling me with the sudden change from confused grief to unfettered rage. "Loved me?" he yells again, walking toward me and pounding on his chest with his words before walking five feet and stopping. "Do you want to know what love was to her? Love was trading her six year old son for fucking drugs, Rylee!"

"Love was letting her drug dealing pimp rape her son, *fuck her little boy while he had to repeat out loud how much he loved it, loved him*, so she could get her next fucking fix! Treat him worse than a fucking dog so she could score enough drugs to ensure her next high! It was knowing the fucker is giving her the smallest fucking quantities possible because he can't wait to come back and do it all over again. Love was sitting on the other side of the closed bedroom door and hearing her little boy scream in the worst motherfucking pain as he's ripped apart physically and emotionally and not doing a goddamn thing to stop it because she's so fucking selfish."

He cringes at the words, his body strung so tight I fear his next words will snap the tension, relieve the boy but break the man within. I look at him, my own heart shattering, my own faith dissolved imagining the horror his small body endured, and I force myself to stem the physical revulsion his words evoke because I fear he'll think it's for him, not the monsters who abused him.

I can hear him struggling to catch his breath, can see him physically revolt against his own words with a forceful swallow. When he starts speaking again, his voice is more controlled but the eerily quiet tone chills my skin.

"Love was snapping her little boy's arm in half because he bit the man raping him so hard that now he won't give up her next fucking speedball. Love was telling her son he wants it, deserves it, that no one will ever love him if they know. Oh and to seal the deal, it was telling her son that the superheroes he calls to while being violated—ruined—*yeah those,* they're never fucking coming to save him. Never!" He's shouting into the night, tears coursing down both of our faces, and his shoulders are shuddering with the relief of being unburdened from the weight he's carried for over twenty-five years.

"So if that's love?" He laughs darkly again, "...then yeah, my first eight fucking years of my life, I was loved like you wouldn't fucking believe." He walks up to me, and even through the darkness I can feel the anger, the despair, the grief that's running rampant through his body. He looks down for a beat, and I watch the tears falling from his face darken the white concrete below. He shakes his head once more, and when he looks up, the resignation in his eyes, the shame that edges it, devastates me. "So when I ask why I'm confused about how I can feel anything other than hatred to know she's dead? That's why, Rylee," he says so quietly I strain to hear him.

I don't know what to say. Don't know what to do, because every single part of me has just shattered and crashed down around me. I've heard it all in my job, but to hear it from a grown man broken, lost, forlorn, burdened with the weight of shame over an entire lifetime, a man I would give my heart and soul to if I knew it would take away the pain and memories, leaves me at a complete loss.

And in the split second it takes me to think all of this, it hits Colton what he's just said. The adrenaline from his confession abates. His shoulders begin to shake and his legs give out as he crumbles to the bench behind him. In the heartbeat of time it takes me to get to him, he is sobbing into his hands. Heart wrenching, soul cleansing sobs that rack through his entire body as, "Oh my God!" falls from his lips over and over again.

I wrap my arms around him feeling completely helpless but not wanting to let go, never wanting to let go. "It's okay, Colton. It's okay," I repeat over and over in between his repeated words, my tears falling onto his shoulders as I hold tight letting him know that no matter how far he falls, I'll catch him.

I'll always catch him.

I try to hold back the sobs racking through my body but it's no use. There's nothing left for me to do but feel with him, grieve with him, mourn with him. And so we sit like this in the dark, me holding onto him, and him letting go in a place that's always brought him peace.

I just pray that this time the peace will find some permanence in his scarred soul.

Our tears subside but he just keeps his head in his hands, eyes squeezed tight, and so many emotions stripping him straight to the core. I want him to take the lead here, need him to let me know how to help him so I just sit quietly.

"I've never ... I've never said those words out loud before," he says, voice hoarse from crying and eyes focused on his fidgeting fingers. "I've never told anyone," he whispers. "I guess I thought that if I said it, then ... I don't know what I thought would happen."

"Colton," I say his name as I try to figure out what to say next. I need to see his eyes, need for him to see mine. "Colton, look at me please," I say as gently as possible, and he just shakes his head back and forth like a little kid afraid of getting in trouble.

I allow him time, allow him to hide in the silence and darkness of the night, my thoughts consumed with pain for this man I love so very dearly. I close my eyes, trying to process it all, when I hear him whisper the one line I'd never expect in this moment.

"*Spiderman. Batman. Superman. Ironman.*"

And it hits me like a ton of bricks. What he's trying to tell me with the simple, whispered statement. My heart falls and my head screams. "No, no, no, no!"

I drop to my knees in front of him, reaching out my hands to the side of his face and direct it up so that his eyes can meet mine. And I cringe when he flinches at my touch. He's petrified to take this first step toward healing. Scared of what I think of him now that I know his secrets. Worried about what kind of man I perceive him to be, because in his eyes, he allowed this to happen to him. He's ashamed I'll judge him based on the scars that still rule his mind, body, and soul.

And he couldn't be any further from the truth.

I sit and wait patiently, my fingers trembling on his cheeks for some time until green eyes flicker up and look at me with a pain I can't imagine reflected in them.

"There are so many things I want and need to say to you right now ... so many things," I say, allowing my voice to tremble, my tears to fall, and goose bumps to blanket my entire body, "that I want to say to the little boy that you were and to the incredible man you are." He forces a swallow as his muscle in his jaw tics, trying to rein back the tears pooling in his eyes. I see fear mixed with disbelief in them.

And I also see hope. It's just beneath the surface waiting for the chance to feel safe, to feel protected, to feel loved for it to spring to life, but it's there.

I am in awe of the vulnerability he is entrusting me with, because I can't imagine how hard it is to open yourself up when all you've ever known is pain. I rub my thumb over his cheek and bottom lip as he stares at me, and I find the words I need to convey the truth he needs to hear.

"Colton Donavan, this is not your fault. If you hear one thing I tell you, please let it be this. You've carried this around with you for so long and I need you to hear me tell you that nothing you did as a child, or as a man, deserved what happened to you." His eyes widen and he turns his body some, opens up his protective posture, and I'm hoping it's a reflection of how he feels with me. That he's listening, understanding, *hearing*. Because there are so many things I've wanted to say to him for so long about things I'd assumed, and now I know. Now I can express them.

"You have nothing to be ashamed of, *then, now, or ever*. I am in awe of your strength." He starts to argue with me and I just put a finger to his lips to quiet him before I repeat what I was saying. "I am in awe of your strength to keep this bottled up for all this time and not self-destruct. You are not damaged or fucked up or hopeless, but rather resilient and brave and honorable." My voice breaks with the last word, and I can feel his chin quiver beneath my hand because my words are so hard to hear after thinking the opposite for so very long, but he keeps his eyes on mine. And that alone signals that he's opening himself up to the notion of healing.

"You came from a place of unfathomable pain and yet you … you're this incredible light who has helped to heal me, has helped to heal my boys." I shake my head trying to find the words to relay how I feel. So he understands there is so much light in him when all he's seen for so long is darkness.

"Ry," he sighs, and I can see him struggling with accepting the truth in my words.

"No, Colton. It's true, baby. I can't imagine how hard it was to ask your dad for the help to find your mother. I can't imagine how you felt taking that call today. I can't fathom how hard it was for you to just confess the secret that has weighed so heavy on your soul for so very long ... but please know this, your secret is safe with me."

He sniffles back a sob, his eyes blinking rapidly, his expression pained, and I lean forward and press a soft kiss to his lips—a touch of physicality to reassure the both of us. I press a kiss to his nose and then rest my forehead against his, trying to take a moment to absorb all of this.

"Thank you for trusting enough to share with me," I whisper to him, my words feathering over his lips. And he doesn't respond, but I don't need him to. We sit like this, forehead to forehead, accepting and comforting each other and the boundaries that have been crossed.

I don't expect him to share any more, so when he starts to speak, I'm startled. "Growing up I didn't know how to deal with it all, how to cope." The absolute shame in his voice washes over me, my mind reeling from the loneliness he must have endured as a teenager. I rub my thumb back and forth over his cheek so that he knows I'm here, knows I'm listening. He sighs softly, his breath heating my lips as he finishes his confession.

"I tried quickly to prove that I wasn't damned to Hell even though he did those things to me. I ran through the gamut of girls in high school to prove to myself otherwise. It made me feel good—to be wanted and desired by females—because it took that fear away ... but then it also became my way of coping ... my mechanism. *Pleasure to bury the pain.*"

I whisper it the same time he does. The line he said to me in the Florida hotel room that stuck with me, ate at me, because I wanted to understand why he felt that way. And I get it now. I get the sleeping around. The fuck 'em and chuck 'em. All of them a way to prove to himself that he was not scarred by his past. A way to place a temporary Band-Aid over the open wounds that never healed.

I squeeze my eyes shut, my mind and heart aching for this man, when his voice interrupts the silence.

"I don't remember everything, but I remember that he used to come up to me from behind. That's why ..." his voice so soft it trails off, answering a question I asked the night of the charity gala.

"Okay," I tell him so he knows I hear him, knows I understand why he was robbed of the ability to accept such an innocent touch.

"The superheroes," he continues, his stark honesty stealing my breath. "Even as a kid, I had to hold on to something to try and escape the pain, the shame, the fear, so I would call to them to try and cope. To have some kind of hope to hold on to."

I taste the salt on my lips. I assume it's from my own tears but I can't be sure because I can't tell where he ends and I begin. And we don't move, remaining forehead to forehead, and I wonder if it's easier for him to sit like this—eyes shut, hearts pounding, souls reaching— to get it all out. So he doesn't have to see the despair, pain, and compassion in my eyes. But even though his eyes are closed I can still feel the chains that have bound his soul for so long begin to break free. I can feel his walls starting to crumble. I can feel hope take flight out of this place in the dark. Just him and me in a place where he can now chase his dreams without his past closing in on him.

I angle my head down and press a kiss to his lips. I feel them tremble beneath mine, my self-assured man stripped bare and open. He finally eases his head back, our foreheads no longer touching, but now I can look into his eyes and I can see a clarity that's never been there before. And a small place within me sighs that he just might be able to find some peace now, just might be able to lay the demons to rest.

I smile solemnly at him as he draws in a ragged breath and reaches his hands out and urges me up from my knees and onto his lap, where he wraps his arms around me. I sit there cradled, comforted, and loved by a man capable of so much. I hope he's finally able to see it and accept it. A man who swears he doesn't know how to love and yet that's exactly what he's giving me right now—love—in the midst of being in the darkest of despairs. I press a kiss to the underside of his jaw, his stubble tickling my sensitive lips.

The dust of a broken past settles around us as hope rises from its remnants.

"*Why tell me now?*"

He draws in a quick breath and tightens his arms around me, pressing a kiss to the top of my head and chuckles softly. "Because you're the fucking alphabet."

What? My head shakes back and forth, and I lean back so I can look at him. And when I meet his eyes, when the smile that spreads on his face lights up the green in the dark around us, my heart tumbles to new depths of love for this man. "*The alphabet?*"

I'm sure it's the look on my face that has his grin widening, dimple winking, and his head shaking. "Yep, A to motherfucking Z." A spark of his personality that he'd lost shines through fleetingly, and it warms my heart to hear that touch of amused arrogance in his voice. He chuckles again and says "Fucking Becks" before leaning forward and pressing his lips to mine without answering my question.

He pulls back and looks at me, eyes intense. "Why now, Ry? Because of you. Because I've pushed and pulled and hurt you way too much … and despite all of that, you've fought for me—to keep me, to help me, to heal me, to *race* me—and for once in my life, I want someone to do that for me. And I want to be free to do that for someone else. I …" He sighs trying to find the words to match the emotion swimming in his eyes. Eyes still haunted on the fringes but so much less now than ever before, and that alone eases the ache in my soul. "I want the chance to prove I'm capable of it. That all of this …" he says with an irrelevant wave of his hand, "didn't rob me of that. That I can be who you need and give you what you want," his voice pleads.

I hear the sadness from his confessions still tingeing his voice, but I can also hear hope and possibility woven in there as well. And it's such a welcome sound that I purse my lips and press them against his.

I can still feel the emotion shuddering through him as he slips his tongue between my parted and willing lips to deepen the kiss. I can still sense him trying to grasp this new ground he's trying to find his footing on, but I know that he'll find it.

Because he's a fighter.

Always has been.

Always will be.

Chapter Thirty-Six

I GLANCE OVER TO HIM watching the light of the streetlights play over the angles of his face as I sing softly to Lifehouse's *Everything* on the radio. It's late, but time was of no importance as we sat together in the grandstands laying old wounds to rest and bringing new beginnings to the table. Sammy's driving my car to the house but as Colton and I exit the freeway in the Range Rover, I realize we're not going home just yet.

Home.

What a crazy notion. That I'm going home with Colton, because right now, after tonight, the word means so much more than just a brick and mortar building. It means comfort and healing and Colton. *My ace.* I sigh, my chest tightening with love.

I look over at him again and he must feel the weight of my stare because he glances over at me with eyes still slightly red from crying. They lock on mine momentarily as he smiles softly and then shakes his head subtly, as if he's still trying to process the events of the past few hours before looking back at the road. But I keep my eyes on him because I know deep down that's where they'll always land no matter where else they look.

I'm so deep in thought I don't even recognize our location when Colton pulls into a parking lot and puts the car in park. "There's something I've gotta do. Come with me?"

I look at him confused about what we're doing at eleven o'clock at night in some random parking lot in the outskirts of Hollywood. Obviously it's important because after tonight all I can think of is that he's probably exhausted and just wants to go home. "Of course."

We exit the car and I look around, a little leery leaving such a nice car in this rundown, poorly lit lot, but Colton is completely unfazed. He pulls me in close to his side and leads me toward a very formidable wooden door that looks like it came straight out of the medieval times. Colton opens it and I'm immediately confronted with bright lights, music playing softly, and a strangely unique buzzing sound.

I whip my head over to Colton, who's watching me with a bemused curiosity. He just chuckles and shakes his head at my slack jawed reaction and widening eyes.

I've never even stepped foot in one of these places before. Deep down a part of me knows why we're here, but it doesn't make sense.

Colton links his fingers with mine as we walk down a narrow hallway toward a room where there are bright lights. Colton crosses the threshold ahead of me and stops momentarily until the buzzing ceases.

"Well motherfucking cocksuck! The fucking wonder boy pays a visit," a rumbling voice yells out, and Colton laughs before being pulled farther into the room. "Well goddamn, you're a sight for sore eyes, Wood!"

I watch as arms, sleeved in a variety of colors and images, wrap around Colton and bring him in for a quick hug. I see a pair of hazel eyes catch sight of me over Colton's shoulder.

"Oh fucking shit! I'm so sorry about all of the fucking cussing," the voice belonging to the eyes says as he shoves Colton backwards and steps toward me. "Dude, if you bring a fucking lady in here you need to make sure to give me warning so I can be respectable and shit!"

Colton laughs as the man wipes his hand off on his jeans before reaching it out to shake mine. My eyes roam over the heavy set, tattoo riddled man with closely cropped hair and a long unruly beard, but what I find the most endearing is the blush staining his cheeks. It's actually quite adorable, but I doubt he'd be amused if I said that right now.

"So fucking sorry! Christ, I just did it again," he shakes his head with a wheeze of a laugh and I can't help but smile.

"No worries," I tell him, lifting a chin over toward Colton. "His mouth's just as bad. I'm Rylee."

"Okay, well I'll try to keep *the fucking* to a minimum," he says and then blushes again. "I mean—not with you of course—well unless you wanted to because then—"

"Don't even think about it, Sledge," Colton warns with a laugh as Sledge, I assume, shakes his head and just laughs that unique laugh of his again before ushering us into the tattoo parlor.

"So, dude, really?" Sledge asks Colton.

"Yeah." He looks over to me and smiles. "Really." And I'm completely lost.

"Whatever yanks your dick man," he says, shaking his head as he walks over to a counter and starts rifling through some papers. "Speaking about yanking dicks and shit ..." He glances over at me and his face scrunches up in apology before continuing to look for something. "How's that fine ass sister of yours that I'd love to have yank mine, among other things."

I expect Colton to freak out, but he just throws his head back and bellows out a laugh. His reaction makes me realize these two go way back.

"She'd eat you alive and you know it, dude ... you're such a pussy."

"Fuck you!" Sledge laughs as Colton starts pulling his shirt over his head. And even with so many new sights to take in here, I can't tear my eyes from his chiseled abdomen. I take in the four symbols—representations of his past—and wonder what he's going to do now.

"Yeah ... quite the hard ass," Colton teases as he ushers me to a chair and presses a chaste kiss on my lips. He looks me in the eye for a moment, as if to say *trust me*, before sitting down in a chair himself. "The inked up man who listens to Barbara Streisand and keeps his five pussies in the back room." *What in the hell is he talking about?* "Didn't you know, if you're gonna pretend to be a badass you need to listen to death metal and have a man-eating pit bull instead of enough cats to rival an old spinster." Colton is laughing, carefree even, and I love that whoever this contradiction of a man is brings this out in Colton.

"I'm a delicate flower!" Sledge quips before yelling out, "A-ha!"

"Flower my ass!" Colton says, shaking his head and laughing as Sledge walks over to him with a piece of paper in his hand. "That it?" Colton asks, and I straighten my posture to try and see what's on it. He stares at it a moment, lips pursing, head subtly bobbing as he considers it. "You sure? It'll really work?" He flicks his eyes up at Sledge, his expression reinforcing the question.

"Like you have to fucking ask. Oops, there I go again with the fucking." He raises his eyebrows as he glances over to me in a silent apology. "Dude, if I'm gonna stain you, I'm gonna research it to make sure."

"Like Google research or bottom of a bottle research?" Colton asks.

"Get out of my fucking chair!" Sledge teases, throwing his arm toward the direction of the door before looking over at me. "You really put up with this shit on a daily basis?"

I nod my head and laugh as Colton leans forward and stares at me, and for a second I see sadness flicker there but it goes away just as quickly as it came. "Ryles?"

"Yeah?" I scoot to the edge of my seat, still curious what the paper has on it.

"Time to lay the demons to rest," he says, his eyes locked on mine, "and move on."

I force myself to look away from his eyes and down to the sketch of curved, interlinking lines. I know the symbol is a Celtic knot and it's similar but different to the others, but I don't know why it's significant.

I look up from the paper, my eyes beseeching Colton's for an explanation. "New beginnings," he says, his eyes telling me he's ready, "...rebirth."

I suck in a breath, my eyes burning with tears, the significance of the symbol is so poignant I can't find the words to speak so I just nod.

"Okay, I get you're all fucking lovey-dovey and shit, but I'm itching to cause you some fucking pain, Wood, so scoot your ass back," he says, pressing Colton's shoulders back and winking at me with a smirk. "Because you ain't gonna have a chance to be reborn, motherfucker, if you sit and stare at her so long that you fucking die in the meantime."

I laugh, my love for this man I just met is already profound. Colton complies but not without a comeback. "Dude, you're just jealous!"

"Fuck yeah, I am. I'm sure that she can..." he stalls, eyes darting back to me and then down to where he's busy setting up his supplies "...whip up a mean bowl of macaroni and cheese." He chortles out that laugh again.

"Damn straight," Colton says, slapping him on the shoulders. "Nice and creamy."

I choke on my breath the same time Sledge does, both of our faces staining red with embarrassment. I give Colton a disbelieving look and shake my head while mischief glimmers in his eyes. And the sight of it—troublemaker in full effect—makes me smile even brighter.

"Just for that I oughta give you a fucking pansy instead ..." He shakes his head as the needle buzzes to life and Colton jolts at the sound. Sledge throws his head back and laughs a deep belly rumble. "Pansy ass motherfucker! Oops, there's a heart. Oops, there's a vagina. Oops, there's a daisy!" Sledge teases pretending to place the needle on Colton's body.

I am dying with laughter, so desperately needing this humor after the heaviness of our night.

"Oops, there's a boot up your ass, is more like it." Colton starts laughing but stops the minute Sledge angles the needle near his side. I've never seen anyone get a tattoo before and I'm quite curious. I stand and walk over to an empty chair next to Colton so I can watch.

I don't even look at first—can't as I see Colton's body tense and his breath hiss out as the needle touches him for the first time.

"God nothing changes," Sledge says, exasperation in his voice. "Once a puss, always a puss." The buzzing stops and he lifts his head to look up at Colton. "Seriously, dude? If I've gotta worry about you shivering like a fucking chihuahua, then we're gonna have some serious fucking issues and I'm not gonna claim this job as mine."

Colton just lifts a hand and flashes Sledge his middle finger before flicking his eyes over to me and then closing them as the needle starts again. This time the buzz remains steady, and after Colton relaxes some, I move around to the other side of Sledge to test if I can handle watching him draw Colton's blood. And when I get the courage to finally look down, I'm confused.

Sledge's needle is working over the symbol for vengeance. He's cut dark red lines that make me cringe at the thought of what that must feel like against Colton's rib cage. I look up to find Colton's eyes locked on mine as I try to figure out what's going on.

"Sledge figured out how to overlay the new knot on top of vengeance."

"Vengeance is gone," I whisper, and for some reason this concept is so moving to me that I just stand there, lips parted, head shaking, and eyes watching Sledge reconfigure a concept that would only destroy Colton further and give him one filled with hope instead.

"Time to lay the demons to rest."

I swallow over the lump in my throat at Colton's words and reach out to hold his hand as we watch the slow transformation of one of his inked scars. One that is now a symbol of hope and healing.

After some time and more ribbing between the two of them—along with me falling further in love with Sledge—Colton's tattoo has been transformed.

"I want to see it before you bandage it up," Colton says as Sledge slathers it with petroleum jelly. "Go pet your pussies and make sure you didn't sneak any hearts or rainbows in there somewhere since you kept blocking my view, you fucker." Colton stands from the chair and I notice the time it takes to steady himself from the after effects of his accident is a lot shorter now. He heads off to the back room where the mirror is.

And I don't know what it is—maybe the events of the night or maybe the hope weaving its way into our lives—but my decision's made before Colton even clears the door to the back. I have to act now before I lose the courage, before my rational head catches up with my irrational heart.

Before I chicken out.

"Hey, Sledge," I say as I sit down in the chair Colton's vacated, pulling the elastic band of my exercise pants down over my hip bone, and point there. "I think it's the perfect time to get my first tattoo. I want the same thing only a lot smaller."

He looks over at me, eyes dancing and startled. "Darlin', when I said fucking, I didn't think you'd offer, much less bring your pants down for it with Wood in the back fucking room." He winks at me and smiles before staring into my eyes. "You trying to get me killed?"

I laugh. "He'll go easy. I think he has a soft spot for you, Sledge."

"Yeah soft spot in his head more like it." He just licks his lips and looks down at my hip before back up to my eyes, concern and uncertainty in his. "You sure? It's kinda permanent," he questions with an amused raise of an eyebrow. I nod my head before I lose the courage to go through with it—to prove to Colton that I want to be there for him every step of the way on this journey.

Sledge laughs and rubs his hands together. "I always love being the first to touch virgin skin. Makes my fucking balls tighten up and shit ..." He blows out a breath. "Fucking shit, I'm sorry. Again." He shakes his head as he starts to trace the image on my hipbone after looking up at me to make sure it's where I want it.

"You positive?" he asks again, and I nod because I'm so frickin' nervous I can barely force a swallow down my throat.

I'm not a tattoo type of girl, I tell myself, so why am I doing this? And then I realize I'm not a bad boy kind of girl either. Look how wrong I was with that assumption.

I jolt when the needle buzzes on, my breath hitching and body vibrating with anxious anticipation. I bite my bottom lip and fist my hands as the first sting hits me. Holy shit! It hurts so much more than I expected. *Don't wimp out, don't wimp out,* I repeat over and over in my head to try and drown out the needle that's stinging my hip like a bitch. And my chant doesn't ease the pain so I close my eyes and exhale a breath, nodding at Sledge to continue because I'm okay when he stops and looks up to check on me.

I don't hear him or see him, but I know the minute that Colton re-enters the room because I can feel him. His energy, our connection, his pull on me has me opening my eyes and lock on his instantly.

The look on his face is priceless—shock, pride, disbelief—as he steps closer to see around Sledge's hands. I know when he sees it because I hear him suck in a startled gasp before his eyes flash up to mine.

"New beginnings." It's all I say as I watch the emotion dance in his sparks of green.

"You know that's permanent, right?" he murmurs, shaking his head at me, still floored by what I'm doing.

"Yeah," I say, reaching out to lace my fingers with his, "kinda like we are."

Chapter Thirty-Seven

I CAN'T HELP BUT LAUGH and feel sentimental as Colton finishes explaining the whole alphabet comment he'd made earlier. The lighthearted sound from Colton makes me content, causes me to remember the dark days in the hospital when all I wanted was to hear that sound again, and the request is out of my mouth before I think twice. "Can we have ice cream for breakfast?"

Colton's hand stills on my thigh as he stutters out a laugh. "What?" I love the look on his face right now. Carefree, careless, and unburdened from the secrets that are no longer between us.

I just smile at him lying on his side next to me as I adjust the pillow behind me and lie back, sighing, his amused eyes still staring at me. Music plays overhead as I shrug at him, suddenly feeling silly for my comment. It's just that I feel like everything is coming full circle. Things I said I wanted to do, I needed to do, promises I made when he was lying in that hospital bed, I need to keep.

"Yes, ice cream for breakfast," I tell him, wincing as I move and my panties tug on the bandage over my new tattoo—the tattoo my mother is going to kill me over when she finds out about it. But the sudden startled look in his eyes pulls me from my thoughts and causes me to lean forward to look at him closer, curious as to what just put it there. He stares back at me momentarily, and then after blinking his eyes a few times as if he's trying to figure something out, he just shakes his head and smiles at me, melting my heart, and confirming that I have absolutely no regrets.

About being with him or the tattoo I just got to prove it.

Of the ups and the downs that our relationship has gone through, endured, persevered, and come out stronger for.

None of it, because it brought us here to this point—right here, right now.

Healing together and loving one another.

Taking the first steps toward our future.

He angles his head on his hand propped on his elbow beneath him and quirks his lips. "Well, what the woman wants, the woman gets."

"I like the sound of that," I say, wiggling my hips, "because I have a whole lot of wants, Mr. Donavan."

"Oh really? And what might those be?" He raises his eyebrows, a lascivious smile tugging at one corner of his mouth as he leans forward and presses a soft kiss to the edge of my bandage. He looks up at me, lust and so much more dancing in the depths of his eyes as he slowly crawls his way up my body until his lips are inches from mine.

And my God, do I want to lean in and taste those lips and feel my skin hum to life from his touch, but I opt for one more request before losing myself in him, to him. "For dinner, I want—"

"Pancakes." Colton finishes my sentence. "Ice cream for breakfast and pancakes for dinner. I remember hearing you say that." His voice is filled with awed reverence as my heart soars at the revelation that he heard me when he was unconscious in the hospital. I watch him try to process everything with a soft shake of his head. "You talked a lot," he murmurs, leaning closer to my lips but not touching, and I know he's smiling because I can see the lines bunch around his eyes.

"So we have our menu planned for tomorr—"

Colton leans forward and captures my mouth with his in a soft kiss. "It's time to stop talking, Ryles," he says as he leans back to look me in the eyes, humor and unguarded love reflected in them.

"Colton," I say, arching my back to try and brush my breasts against his bare chest because everything in my body at this moment is desperate for his touch, his taste, the connection between us. And when he stays still and doesn't move, I reach out and grab the back of his neck, trying to pull him into me, but he doesn't move.

He just remains motionless, staring at me with such intensity. And for the first time I understand what he meant when he told me I was the first one to ever really see him—to see into the depths of his soul—because right now there's nothing I can hide from him. Absolutely nothing. Our connection is that strong, that irrefutable.

It's been such an emotional evening, more so for him than for me, but my body is humming for a physical release. It's vibrating with need and all I want is him.

"Rylee ..." It's that one word plea of my name on his lips that gets me every time.

"Don't *Rylee* me," I implore as I watch concern edge the desire from his eyes. I move my hands to frame his cheeks and hold him still so he has no option but to hear me. "I'm *fine*, Colton."

"I'm so afraid I'm going to hurt you ..." His voice fades and the concern that floods it makes every part of me slip further under his tidal wave of love.

"No, baby, no. You're not going to hurt me." I lean forward and brush my lips to his and then lean back until I can see his eyes again. "You not wanting to be with me, that hurts me. Destroys me. I need you, Colton, every side of you—physical and emotional. After tonight, after we've stripped away everything that's been keeping us apart, I need to share this with you. Connect in every way possible because it's the only way I can truly show you how I feel about you. Show you what you do to me."

I can hear his shuddered exhale moments before the heat of it hits my lips. His hand flexes on my bicep and then softens as if he wants and then doesn't want at the same moment. He just stares at me, indecision written across his face. And then that muscle pulses in his jaw, his last tell of resistance, because the desire clouding his eyes tells me his decision has already been made.

When he leans in to kiss me, I don't think victory has ever tasted so sweet.

His lips brush softly against mine, once, twice, and then his tongue delves between my lips and licks against mine. He slides his hands behind my back and gathers me against him while our tongues dance a seductive ballet. His hands find their way beneath the hem of my shirt and then tease my bare skin as he draws my shirt up and over my head.

A soft sigh escapes my lips as we part so my shirt can clear my face and then our lips find each other's again. I release my tangled grip on the back of his hair and scrape my fingernails down the steeled muscles of his biceps, his body responding, tensing to my touch. The guttural moan he emits from the back of his throat turns me on, entices me, has me wanting and needing more.

Desire coils and need springs with each passing second, my thighs clenching together, my breath coming faster. "Colton," I murmur as his lips travel down my jawline to the pleasure point just beneath my ear that has me arching my back and moaning out loud on contact, heated warmth on willing flesh. His hands scrape over my rib cage and cup my breasts, already weighted with desire. Sensations spiral into and then through every part of me.

"Fuck, Ry, you test a man's control. I've been craving the taste of that sweet pussy of yours. That sound you make when I bury my cock in you. The feel of you coming around me."

He groans as I slide my hands between his shorts and grip his heated flesh. And as incendiary as his words are, as much as they stoke the fires already raging out of control, there's an added tenderness in his touch that's a stark contrast to their explicitness.

"I want every inch of you trembling, *fucking shaking*, begging for me to take you, Ry, because fuck if I won't be doing the same. I want to be your sigh, your moan, your cry out in pleasure and every fucking sound in between." He leans in and nips my lip, and I can feel him quiver, and know that he's just as affected as I am.

"*I want to feel you.* Your fingernails digging into my shoulders. Your thighs tense around mine as I drive you closer." He breathes out, the dominance of his tone fringed with a raw necessity has my entire body vibrating with need. "I want to see your toes curl as they push against my chest. Want to watch your mouth fall open and your eyes close when it becomes too much—the pleasure so fucking intense—because, baby, I want to know I make you feel that way. I want to know you feel just as fucking alive inside as you make me."

And I can't take it anymore, his words the most seductive foreplay for my body that's already craving his touch. I pull him toward me, hesitancy a distant memory. Our bodies and hearts crash together as we fall back on the bed beneath us as hands and mouths explore, taste, and tempt.

I force him on his back by scoring my nails down his chest, his muscles tensing and throat humming with a desperate groan. My mouth traces a languorous trail down the line of his neck, over the ridged muscles of his abdomen scrunching and flexing with each lick of my tongue or scrape of my fingers. I kiss my way down one side of his sexy as hell V and then back up the other side, cautious of his freshly tattooed rib cage as my fingertips find and encircle his steeled length through his shorts.

I look up and meet his eyes, clouded with desire and weighted with emotion, as I pull down his shorts. I kiss my way down the tiny line of hair and then move down and tease the crest of his dick with the wet, warmth of my lips. His cock pulses against my lips as he hisses out, "*Fuck!*" The drawn out way he says the word encourages me to take him further into my mouth, and press my tongue to the underside as I slide down and take him deeper.

His hands sitting idly on the bed clench into fists, and his hips twitch as I slide him back out until just his tip is in my mouth. I roll my tongue around it, paying special attention to the nerves on the underside, before sliding back down until he hits the back of my throat. In an instant, his hands are fisting my hair as pleasure overtakes him. "Sweet Christ," he pants out between labored breaths as I continue to work him with my mouth. "So fucking good."

Fingertips tease his sensitive skin beneath, tickling and pressing, as I hollow my cheeks out with each slide down and subsequent suck back out. I look up at him and can't help the satisfied smile that tries to form despite his place in my mouth. Colton's head is thrown back, lips pulled tight in pleasure, and the muscles are strained in his neck. The sight of him slowly coming undone would have me wet and wanting if I wasn't already.

I fist my hand around him and work it in circular motions while I bob my head up and down over the remainder of him. He groans, turning to steel in my mouth, and in an instant he is dragging me up the length of him, my nipples aching from the skin on skin contact.

His mouth is on mine the minute my lips are within reach, a greedy clash of lips, tongues, and teeth as he dominates the kiss, taking what he wants even though I'm giving it up more than willingly. He shifts our position in the blink of an eye so I am on my back, atop the pillows propped behind me. He scrapes his eyes down the length of my torso, a mischievous grin lighting up his face as he looks at my panties and then back up at me.

"I'm out of practice," he says with a shake of his head and a flash of his lone dimple. And then despite the carnal need raking through every one of my nerves, I can't help the laugh that falls from my lips as the fabric of my panties is ripped in half. "There," he says, lowering his mouth to my abdomen and pressing a kiss there. "Much better."

And it's not the kiss in itself, but the unexpectedness of his lips holding still momentarily, just below my navel, that sobers the moment for me. But at the same time, makes it that much sweeter. His eyes are closed and his lips are pressed atop the womb that held his child, and chills immediately race across my anticipatory flesh.

After a moment, his lips make their torturously slow ascent up my rib cage to my breast. I can feel his heated breath, the slide of his tongue, the suction of his mouth as he closes over my nipple, and I cry out involuntarily. The sensations his mouth evokes are like a lightning strike to my sex, my inhibitions singed and body lit afire.

"Colton," I pant as the ache in my core intensifies and fingernails score the skin on his shoulders as his mouth pleasures and hints at things to come. When my nipples are tightened and teased so thoroughly they're on the edge of pain, he moves back up my body. One of his hands fists in the back of my hair, holding my curls hostage, while the other slides down my body and slips between my legs.

I hold my breath in that space of time between feeling his fingers move my thighs apart and them actually touching me. Lungs robbed of air and body full of anticipation, Colton brands his mouth to mine in a soul-searing, gravity-defying kiss, and just when it leaves my head spinning and desire spiraling out of control, his fingers part me and stake their claim. His mouth captures the moan he coaxes from me as my nerves are expertly manipulated. Heat ignites and a rapturous moan emanates from the back of my throat as I am entirely consumed and completely undone by Colton.

His fingers coated in my arousal slide back out and up to add friction to my already throbbing clit. "Ah!" I can't help the garbled cry as his fingers connect, sensations overwhelm, and emotions swell. His fingers stroke and his mouth tempts the skin along my neck as my body climbs the wave at a rapid pace. My nipples tighten and thighs tense as desire ricochets through me and then comes back to hit me ten times harder.

And I am lost. Stepping into an oblivion that's assaulting all my senses, and overwhelming all thoughts. My hands grip his arms and my hips buck as my body detonates into a million splinters of pleasure. The only thing I hear besides my pulse thundering in my ears is a satisfied groan falling from his lips.

Within a second of riding out the last wave of my orgasm, Colton is shifting, pushing my thighs apart with his knees as he places the head of his cock against my still pulsing entrance.

And then it hits me—breaks through my hazy state of desire—and shocks me back to my senses. I push against his chest, shaking my head. "Colton ... we need a condom ..." I tell him, reality hitting me stronger than the climax tremors still rumbling through me.

Colton's body tenses and his head snaps up from where he's watching our connection. He angles his head and just stares at me, the only sounds in the room are my still shuddered breathing and the soft strains of *Stolen* on the speakers overhead. But the way he looks at me—as if I am his next draw of breath—halts any further protests from my lips.

"*I don't want to use a condom, Rylee.*" His words startle me but more than that, it's the way he says them, resigned disbelief laced with irritation.

But why?

Disbelief because I ruined the mood to ask? Irritation because he has to now? "C'mon, Colton, don't be such a guy. I know it doesn't feel the same but we need to be smart and—"

Colton's sudden shift in the bed, pulling me up and into him so I straddle his lap, surprises me so much that I abandon my protest. His hands find the nape of my neck, thumbs framing the sides of my face, and his eyes bore into mine with a reverent intensity that I've never seen before. "No, Ry. I don't want to use a condom and it's not because of lack of feeling. Fuck, baby, I could have burlap wrapped around my dick and I'd still feel you."

I want to laugh as my mind tries to figure out just what Colton is telling me. "What do you—what are you trying to say?" And even though he hasn't answered me yet, my heartbeat quickens and my fingers start to tremble.

I watch him swallow, his Adam's apple bobbing, and his lips turn up in a ghost of a smile. He shakes his head slightly as that smile deepens. "I don't know how to explain it, Ry. *That night* was horrible. It was something that will forever be etched in my mind—you, me

... the baby ..." His voice fades as he shakes his head softly, looking down for a moment because I know he's still trying to come to terms with the fact that we lost a baby together. He exhales a shaky breath, and when he looks up the raw honesty in his eyes has me holding my own. "I was scared shitless," he says, leaning in and brushing the most tender of kisses against my lips before kissing my nose and then leaning back. "It still scares me every time I think about it and what could have happened. I—I'm just not sure how to even explain it." He blows out a loud breath, and I can see the need in his face to try and capture the right words to express how he feels.

"Take your time," I whisper, knowing I'd give him all the time in the world if he asked for it.

He rubs his thumbs back and forth on my cheek, goose bumps dancing over my skin at the poignancy of the moment. "A part of me ..." His voice breaks and I can see the muscle in his jaw tic as he attempts to control the emotion I see swimming in his eyes. "... a part of *us* died that day. But it was the part of me that I've been holding on to."

When he refers to the baby as *ours*, my breath catches in my chest and my hands reach out to hold onto his biceps.

"I sat in that waiting room, Ry, with your blood, our baby's blood, on my skin and I don't think ... I don't think I've ever felt so fucking alive." That soft smile is back on that magnificent mouth of his, but it's his eyes that captivate me. Those sparks of green that are pleading, asking, and searching to make sure I understand the words—spoken and unspoken—that he is telling me right now.

He looks down at his hands for a beat, emotion flickering over his face as he remembers how he felt before looking back to me. "The blood of a baby I'll never meet, but that was something we'd created together ..." The gravel of his voice breaks on his last words, but his eyes remain steady on mine, making sure I see everything in his—grief, disbelief, loss.

"All the emotions ... everything that was happening ... trying to process it all felt like taking a sip of water from a fucking fire hose." He exhales another breath, closing his eyes momentarily as he becomes overwhelmed with the memory and how to best explain it. "And I still don't know if I'll ever be able to process it, Ry. But the one thing I do know," he says, his fingertips tightening on my cheeks to reinforce the certainty of his words, "is that when I sat in that waiting room and the doctor told me ... about the baby ... feelings I never thought possible filled me," he says, eyes unflinching and complete reverence in his voice that causes my heart to swell with hope for things I never thought I could imagine.

His thumb wipes away a tear that runs down my cheek I didn't even know I'd shed and he continues on. "And sitting there in that damn hospital room, waiting for you to wake up ... I realized what you meant to me, what we had created together—the best parts of us combined. And then it hit me," he says with so much tenderness in his eyes that when I go to open my mouth to say something nothing comes out. He smiles softly at me, darting his tongue out to wet his bottom lip. "I realized that what *she* did to me *doesn't have* to happen again. That I can give someone the life I never had, Rylee. The life you showed me is a possibility."

I bite back the comments that rush into my head as Colton's words break down every last form of protection I've ever woven around my heart. My fingers tense on his biceps and my chin quivers from the emotions coursing through me.

"No, don't cry, Ry," he murmurs as he leans in and kisses the tracks of tears coursing down my cheeks. "You've cried enough already. I just want to make you happy because fuck, baby, it's you that's the difference. It's you that allowed me to see that my biggest fear— darkest goddamn poison—wasn't really a fear at all. It was an excuse for me to not open myself up by saying all I could do was bring pain and pass my demons on. But I know—*I know*—that I could never hurt a child—a baby that is my own flesh and blood. And I sure as fuck know you could never hurt one just to spite me."

Tears well in his eyes as he lowers them for a moment and shakes his head, the confession and cleansing of his soul finally taking its toll. But when he looks up at me, despite the tears swimming in his eyes I see such clarity, such reverence, that my breath is stolen. My heart that was robbed long ago is undeniably his. "It's like out of the horrible darkness I've had to live with my whole life came this incredible ray of light."

His voice breaks and a tear drops as we sit in this beast of a bed, bodies bare, pasts no longer hidden, hearts naked and completely vulnerable, and yet I have never felt more certain about any other person in my life.

He tilts my head back up to look at him. "So are you okay with this?"

I look at him not sure what he's asking, but hoping my assumptions are true.

Chapter Thirty-Eight

COLTON

"**G**OD, I NEED TO KNOW you're okay with this, Ry?" I search her face for any indication that she's along for the ride, because right now, my fucking heart's pounding and my chest is constricting with each damn breath.

Those violet eyes of hers—the only ones that have ever been able to see straight into my soul and see everything I've hidden—blink back tears and try to process what I've been telling her I've never wanted, I now want with her.

Tomorrows.

Possibilities.

A fucking future.

The ultimate motherfucking checkered flag.

And deep in my heart I know with absolute certainty how I feel about this woman who crashed into my damn life, grabbed me by the balls—and apparently my heart—and never let go. I can't resist one brief taste to calm the apprehension coursing through me, to ease the upheaval of a soul I always thought was doomed to Hell. I lean in and press my mouth to hers using her soft lips as a silent reassurance she doesn't even know she's giving me.

I look at my hands trembling on her cheeks, and I know this tremor has nothing to do with the fucking accident and everything to do with the healing of wounds so old and scarred I never thought they could be mended. I lift my eyes to meet hers again because when I tell her, I need her to know that there may have been many before her, but she is the only fucking one who will ever hear this.

"I told you in Florida that I've always used adrenaline—the blur, women—to fill the void I've always felt. And now ..." I shake my head, not sure how I'm going to get the words racing laps around my fucking head to sound coherent. I take a deep breath because these words are the most important ones I've ever spoken. "Now, Ry, none of that matters. All I need is you. Just. You. And the boys. *And whatever it is we create together.*"

Chills dance on my skin and I'm so overwhelmed with everything—the moment, the feeling, the fucking vulnerability—that I have to force a swallow as I close my eyes momentarily. And when I open them, the compassion and love in hers—and the simple notion that I see her love, accept it— has my pulse racing from the euphoria it brings, and it breaks the final barrier of my past.

"*I love you, Rylee.*" I whisper the words. The weight in my chest fractures, splinters into a million fucking pieces freeing my soul like a 747 taking flight.

Chapter Thirty-Nine

*H*E LOVES ME.

The thought races around my mind, over and over as adrenaline surges through me.

He just told me he loves me.

Words escape me as a swell of love and pride for this man engulfs me, wraps me in its cocoon of possibilities, and quiets any remaining doubt I might have had. "Colton ..." I'm so overcome with emotion I can't even find the words to tell him what I've waited so long to say.

"Shhh," he says, bringing a finger to my lips while a shy smile forms on his. "Let me finish. *I love you, Rylee.*" His voice is more certain now in his declaration, as he finds his footing in this new-found world. His smile widens and so does mine with his finger still pressed against my lips. "I think I always have ... from that first damn night. You were that bright spot—that fucking spark—I couldn't hide from even when the darkness claimed me. My God, baby, we've been through so fucking much that I ..." His voice fades as the moisture pooling in his eyes leaks, a single tear sliding down the side of his face.

I hiccup the sob I've been holding back because it's impossible to keep it at bay. I reach up and hold his cheeks, his stubble coarse and comforting beneath my palms, and press my lips to his as his arms wrap around me and pull me in tight against his body. I lean my forehead against his as my fingers fist in his hair so I can pull his head back to see his eyes. "I love you, Colton. I've wanted to say those words to you again for so long." I laugh, unable to contain the happiness bubbling inside of me. "I love you, you brave, amazing, complicated, stubborn, gorgeous man that I can't seem to ever get enough—"

His lips capture mine, our mouths joining in a kiss packed with so much emotion I can't contain my tears that fall or the repeated murmurs of the words I've had to withhold for so long finally being set free.

The calluses on his fingers rasp across my back as he presses me into him, his steeled skin against the softness of my breasts reigniting the licks of desire deep in my belly. Tongues delve, sighs expel, needs intensify as we slide into a slow but utterly body-tingling, mind-numbing kiss. Every nerve in my body itches for his fingers to graze and stake its claim anywhere and everywhere.

I rock my aching apex over the tip of his erection at the same time his tongue leaves me weak and defenseless, branding his indelible mark on me from his kiss alone. My fingers stroke absently over the hard edged muscles of his shoulders before I thread them in his hair, holding his head captive like he's already done to every single piece of me.

He pulls back, breaking our kiss, and I cry out in protest feeling like I'll never fully sate my desire for him. I take in his mussed hair and sparkling eyes before being drawn down to his lips curled up in a smile that completely knocks my world off balance. His fingertips trace feather-light lines down the column of my spine as I try to gauge what it is his eyes are telling me.

"Let me make love to you, Ry," he says, the huskiness of his voice laced with affection.

How many more times tonight is he going to leave me breathless? How many more times is he going to give me the broken pieces of him so I can hold them and heal with him to make him whole again?

I just stare at him, my lips forming a smile as I say, "I *always* have been." I shake my head as emotion stains my cheeks. It's silly really, to

Crashed

be embarrassed by my confession when everything else between us has been shared, but I love the spark in his eyes and parting of his lips as my words hit him. I run a hand up his arm and rest it over his heart. "I've always made love to you, you just never knew."

He breathes out a laugh, that grin deepening as he shifts and lays us down on the pillows behind me. His face is inches from mine, his body supported on his elbows, and his knees between my thighs.

"Well this time, we'll both know," he says, inhaling a shaky breath as his steeled length presses at my opening.

I close my eyes as my body trembles beneath his, needing and wanting the bombardment of the all-consuming sensation I know is coming. "Look at me, Ry." My eyes flutter open and look up to lose myself in the beauty of his face. "I want to watch you as I take you. I want to watch you as you let me love you." He leans his head down and teases my lips with the whisper of a kiss before finding my eyes again. "I love you."

As he says the three words he pushes his way into me, and I swear sparks ignite with our union because this time it's more than just the physical connection. It's the joining of our hearts, souls, and everything in between. I watch his eyes cloud with desire and darken with emotion as he seats himself fully into me.

"Sweet Jesus!" He groans as he begins to move, raking over every interior nerve possible. My body reacts instinctively, hips angling and back arching so I can draw every possible ounce of pleasure from this incredible man.

I feel bombarded by sensation. The slide of his skin across mine. The unhindered lust and unfettered love in his eyes. The soft groan of pleasure from the back of his throat. The rush of heat enveloping me as he grinds into me circling his hips before slowly pulling back out only to start all over again.

My body vibrates from this sensual high—a collision of everything with the most perfect timing that I couldn't escape even if I wanted to.

373

Pressure builds and pleasure catapults me to a dizzying high as Colton finds a slow but steady cadence that allows him to draw out and drag over every last nerve. His eyes still hold mine, but I can see the pleasure start to edge out the need to watch me as his eyes close momentarily, his jaw set tight in concentration, his eyelids heavy, and nostrils flared.

"Colton ..." I moan as a desirable devastation begins to rock through me, my muscles tense in preparation for the onslaught of sensation just within reach. With the call of his name, he shifts, drawing his hands down the length of my body as he sits back onto his knees. His hands sweep over the top of my sex, thumb grazing over my clit making me buck my hips up asking for more.

The lines of concentration on his face ease as his lips curl into a lascivious smirk. "You want more of that?"

All I can do is nod, my words lost to the onslaught of sensation. His fingers, careful of my newfound ink, grip the flesh at the sides of my hips, holding me firmly as his smile still plays over his face but his hips continue their painfully exquisite surge in and subsequent withdrawal. There is nothing I can do but focus, try to manage the all-consuming attack on my senses as he holds my gaze, driving me higher and higher. My thighs tense and my head falls back as the force of my impending climax heightens.

And then nothing.

Colton stops all movement stealing my orgasm with his sudden lack of motion. My head snaps up to look at him, frustrated, to meet green eyes dancing with mirth and full of restraint.

He leans forward, his heated length surging to unimaginable depths inside of me, dragging out an insuppressible moan I don't even attempt to stop. His hands push the backs of my thighs forward as his face fills my entire line of sight. I can feel the heat of his panting breath on my face and see his muscles tighten as he controls his need to pound into me with reckless abandon and drive us to the brink fast and hard, the way I know he likes.

"Fuck, baby, you feel like Heaven," he says as he leans forward and brushes his mouth to mine. He surprises me as he pushes his tongue between my lips and dominates the kiss in much the same fashion as he dominates my heart. I can sense his restraint slipping, can feel every sweet inch of him expand inside of me, can taste the desire mounting, need edging out all reason.

His mouth brands and claims me while his body slowly starts moving again—taking, taunting, pushing mine to accept his challenge. Liquid fire flickers to life again, molten lava singeing and refueling the inferno he's just forced me to abandon. I swallow his groan as he rocks deeper into me, throbbing sparks of pleasure igniting my nerve endings.

He nips my bottom lip and breaks the kiss as he starts to pick up his tempo, drives into me with a passionate desperation as he drops his forehead to my shoulder. My body begins to tremble from the intense pull at my core while he continues his punishing rhythm. The room is filled with my soft moans, his inarticulate grunts, and the slap of skin against skin as he edges me higher and higher.

The scrape of his teeth along my collarbone is my undoing. Mindless pleasure seizes me as my body tightens all around him and free falls into rapturous oblivion as I surrender myself to him.

I have forgotten everything—he has made me forget everything—except for his scent, his sounds, his taste, his touch. My body crashes into the wave of sensation, his name on my lips, our bodies united as one.

"So fucking hot to watch you come undone," he whispers as his stubble scrapes against my neck, his body stilling and then moving in and out of me ever so slowly to draw out the last remnants of my orgasm still firing through me. I pulse and tighten around his cock, my fingernails scoring his shoulders as I hold tight with each surge of pleasure.

"Fuck, Ry, that feels so fucking good!" He groans out as his hips start jerking, my own orgasm starting to milk his from him. And within a moment Colton is back on his knees, hands pushing my thighs up, and his hips are pounding into me as he chases his own climax.

"Come on, baby," I pant out as I try to meet him thrust for thrust, surrendering myself completely to his needs.

His guttural groan fills the room as he hits his peak, his shuddering and body tensing while he rides out his own high. After a beat, he rolls us over, our hips remaining connected in the most primal of ways so that I'm lying atop him, my cheek on his chest where I can hear his thundering heartbeat.

And we sit like this for a moment, fingers drawing lazy lines over each other's bare flesh, regaining our breaths, and calming our pounding hearts. The silence around us is so comfortable without the demons haunting the shadows. Yes, he'll always have a part of him haunted and damaged, but for the first time ever he has someone he can share them with. Someone to help ease the burden, to help heal.

I sigh at the thought and am completely content as he presses a kiss to the top of my head. "I love you," I whisper the words still overwhelmed with everything that has transpired this evening. His fingers continue tracing aimlessly over my spine. I close my eyes and enjoy the feeling of our bodies pressed against one another's and the simplicity of his touch. And then my OCD kicks in as I mentally trace what his fingers are spelling, and I shift my head so my chin rests on my hands covering his sternum.

"What?" he asks innocently, despite the smile tugging at the corner of his mouth and eyes reflecting the mischief I've come to love and expect from him. When all I do is raise my eyebrows, I feel the rumble of his chuckle through his chest and into mine.

"The alphabet, Ace?" I raise an eyebrow and try to bite back my own smile, but it's useless.

"Yep. I'm seeing the alphabet in a whole new light these days," he says, abandoning his letter tracing and trailing his finger down the top of my backside.

My laugh is overtaken by a sigh as his hand palms my ass. I can feel that ache he always has on low burn start to simmer anew. He starts to harden inside of me again and moisture starts to pool as desire is heightened by the complete connection of our bodies.

"And just what might your favorite letter be?"

He emits a full bodied laugh, his shaking body reverberating all the way down to his cock, now alert and fully buried within me. "Oh, baby, I'm kind of partial to your V. That's the only place that I want to B."

I can't even laugh at his corny line because he chooses this moment to thrust his hips upward, my body moving with it, his skin rubbing my nipples and coaxing a pleasurable groan from my throat. My eyes close and body softens as his movements draw heightened responses from the flesh already swollen from him.

"Good God!" I sigh as he pulls me out of my post-catatonic orgasmic state and drags me under his spell once again.

Chapter Forty

COLTON

THE SUN FEELS JUST AS good as the ice cold beer sliding down my throat and the sight of Rylee bending over in front of me. *Fuck* is my only thought as I adjust myself and think thoughts I shouldn't be thinking with the boys here.

Will this ever end? To want her near? The want to watch her sleep and wake up next to her? My need to be buried in her? It's been only three damn hours since we've left my bed and fuckin' A, I'd love to drag her upstairs right now and have her again.

"Down boy!"

And there's the voice that will make me go limp.

"'Sup, Becks."

"Apparently you, if you don't stop looking at her like you want to bend her over that lounge chair and fuck her into oblivion," he says, taking a long sip of his beer.

Well, that's always a thought.

I groan. "Thanks for the visual, dude, because that's really not helping right now," I reply with a roll of my eyes and shake of my head, before looking around to make sure the boys are far enough away they can't hear us talking about how I want to defile their sexy-as-fuck guardian. And my God is she a walking wet dream. I shift in my chair again as I watch her squat down and adjust the top of her suit before slathering sunscreen all over Zander.

I shake my head thinking about her concern earlier in picking which swimsuit to wear with the boys coming over for a pool party. Even in the red one piece that she deemed matronly, every curve of hers is on display like a goddamn road map tempting me to take it out for a test drive.

Dangerous curves ahead? Fuckin' A. *Bring. It. On.* I'm a man that lives for danger. The thrill I get from it. And hell if I'm not itching for the keys, right now.

Talk about revved and raring.

"By that sappy ass look on your face, I take it things are going good?" Becks asks as he sits down beside me and snaps me from my dirty thoughts.

"Pretty much." I pop the top off of another bottle with the opener and take a drink.

"Please don't tell me you're gonna get all domesticated and shit on me now."

"Domesticated? Fuck no." I laugh. "Although the woman is hot as hell in her heels pushing that grocery cart in front of me." I can visualize it now and damn if the thought's not making me ache to take her.

"*You*—Colton Donavan—stepped foot into a grocery store?" he sputters.

"Yep." I raise my eyebrows and smirk at the look of shock on his face.

"And it wasn't just to buy condoms?"

I can't help it now. I love fucking with him. It's just too goddamn easy. "Nah, no longer a requirement when you hold a frequent flier card to the barebacking club."

"Jesus Christ, dude, are you trying to get me to choke on my beer?" He wipes beer off his chin that he spit out.

"I got something else you can choke on," I murmur as my eyes are drawn back to Rylee bending over, my constant semi wanting to fly full staff. I'm so focused on her and my corrupt but oh-so-fucking awesome thoughts of what I can do to her later that I don't hear what Becks says. "Huh?" I ask.

"Dude, you are one whipped motherfucker, aren't you?"

I look over at him ready to defend my manhood when I realize it's right where I want it to be, held in Rylee's hands—the perfect mixture of sugar and spice. So I laugh out and just shake my head, bring the beer to my lips and shrug. "As long as it's her pussy doing the whipping, I'm fucking game all day long."

Becks chokes again but with laughter this time, and I pat him on the back as Ry looks over at us making sure he's okay. "My God! That must be the best voodoo pussy ever to tame Colton fuckin' Donavan."

"*Tame?* Never." I chuckle and shake my head, leaning back on the chair behind me to look over at him. "But some asshole—er friend— made me realize how much I like the fucking alphabet."

"That *friend* deserves a shitload of beer as a thank you then." He shrugs. "That, or a mighty fine piece of ass in return."

I snort out a laugh, grateful for his sarcasm to avoid talking about deep feelings and shit that I'm not really comfortable discussing. I'm just getting used to saying this kind of shit to Ry, I'm sure as shit not going to be getting touchy-feely with Becks.

"*She's got a hot friend,*" I tell him with a raise of my eyebrow, earning me a snort in return as I repeat what I said the night I talked him into inviting Ry to Vegas with us.

"She sure does," he murmurs, but before I can respond, Aiden cannonballs into the pool and the splash hits us full on. We start laughing, comment forgotten, sunglasses now splashed with water.

"Hey," he says, and I look back over at him. "I have to give you shit because that's just the way we roll … but I'm really happy for you, Wood. Now don't fuck it up."

I grin at him. *The fucker.* "Thanks for the vote of confidence, dude."

"Anytime, man. Anytime." We sit in silence for a moment, both watching the boys around us acting like they're supposed to be, kids. "So you ready?"

Becks' voice pulls me from my thoughts and back to what I should really be focusing on: the race next week. First time back in the car since the accident. Pedal to the floor and the next left turn. And just the thought makes my blood pressure spike.

But I got this.

"Fuck, I was born ready," I tell him, tapping the neck of my beer bottle to his. "Checkered flag's mine for the taking."

"Fuck yeah it is," he says as he looks down at his phone that's received a text, and my eyes drift back to Rylee and thoughts of a particular pair of checkered panties I never did get to claim. I sure as hell need to fix that.

I shake my head as I sink back into my chair and watch the boys jumping in the pool and chicken fight one another. I sit and wait for it, but it doesn't happen. That fucking pang of jealousy I used to get when I saw boys acting their age, acting how I never got to. Because even after I was adopted, the fear was still there, still raw as fuck.

Rylee catches my eye from across the deck and those sexy-as-sin lips spread wide. Fuck me running. My balls tighten and chest constricts at the notion that I put that smile on those lips. The woman is my fucking kryptonite.

Who else would I allow to invite seven boys to my house for a pool party to celebrate summer being here? What other woman could I share my demons with and instead of running like a banshee, she looks me in the eyes and tells me I'm brave? Who else would scar their skin to prove to me she's in it for the long haul?

Motherfucking checkered flags and alphabets and sheets. When did all of this become okay with me?

I shake my head, pretending I don't want it but fuck if I can't look away from her for one goddamn second before my eyes find her again.

I lift the fresh beer Becks hands me and start to take a sip and look over at him as he shakes his head laughing at me. *"What?"*

"You are so going to fucking marry her."

It's my turn to choke on my beer. I double over in a coughing fit as Becks pounds me a little too hard on the back. "He's fine!" I hear him say as I try to control the choking mixed with laughter burning its way up my throat. "He's fine," he says again, and I can hear the amusement in his voice.

"Fuck off, Becks!" I finally manage to get out. "Not gonna happen! *No rings, no strings,*" I say our old motto with a laugh. And then I look up to find Ry. She's across the patio sitting on the edge of the pool, Diet Coke in hand, and is playing referee to the boys' game of Marco Polo. Ricky gets caught as a fish out of water, and Rylee throws her head back in laughter at something Scooter says to him.

And there's something about her right now—hair highlighted from the sun, a carefree sound to her laugh, and obviously in love with everyone around her. Something about her being with the boys, making life normal for them at a place that has never really been a home until now—until her—hits me harder than that fucking rookie Jameson did in Florida. Has me thinking about the forevers and shit that six months ago would have never once crossed my mind.

It's just gotta be Becks getting in my head. Mucking it up. The bastard needs to shut the hell up about shit that's not gonna happen.

Never.

So why the fuck am I wondering what Ry'd look like wearing white? Why am I wondering how *Rylee Donavan* sounds out loud?

Never. I try to shake the thoughts from my head, but they linger, spooking the shit out of me.

"So not gonna happen." I laugh, not sure if I'm repeating the words to convince Becks or myself. I look back over at Ry for a second. Talk about jumping the gun when I haven't even found the bullets to load it yet. Fucking Beckett. "Taming's one thing, fucker. Ball and chaining?" I whistle out. "That's a whole 'nother ball game I have no interest

in playing." I shake my head again at that shit-eating grin on his face as I rise from the chair. "Never."

"We'll see about that," he tells me with that smirk I want to wipe from his face.

"Dude, do you feel that?" I ask, raising my arms out from my side and lifting my face to the sun before looking back down at him.

"Huh?"

"That's called heat, Daniels. Hell can't freeze if it's still hot outside," I toss over my shoulder before walking to the edge of the pool. Conversation over. No more discussion of marriage and shit like that.

Is he trying to give me a heart attack?

Fuck.

"Cannonball!" I yell before jumping in, hoping to create more turmoil in the pool than what Becks is trying to create in my head.

Chapter Forty-One

DÉJÀ VU HITS ME LIKE a runaway train as I step from the RV ahead of Colton. The humid heat of Fort Worth hits me instantly, but the sweat trickling in a line down my back has nothing to do with the weather and everything to do with the anxiety coursing through every nerve.

Over Colton.

And over the car we're walking toward.

I know he's nervous, can feel it in the tightened grip of his fingers laced with mine, but his outward appearance reflects nothing but a man preparing to do his job. People around us chatter incessantly but Colton, Becks, and I walk off the infield as one unit, completely focused.

I attempt to push away the memories bombarding my mind, to appear calm even though every fiber of my being is vibrating with absolute trepidation.

"You okay?" His rasp washes over me, the concern in it tugs on my guilt since it should be me reassuring him.

I can't lie to him. He'll know if I am and it will only cause him to worry more. The last thing I want is him to be thinking of me. I want him focused and confident when he buckles into the car and takes the green flag all the way to the checkered one.

"I'm getting there," I breathe and squeeze his hand as we reach the pits and the mass of photographers waiting to record Colton's first race back after the accident. The click of shutters and shouting of questions drowns out the response he gives me. And as I tense up further, Colton seems to relax some, comfortable in this environment like it's his second skin.

And I realize that while all of this is uncomfortable and foreign to me, this is part of the blur that Colton used to permanently reside in. Surrounded by the shouts and the flashes of light, he's one hundred percent back in his element. The utter chaos is allowing him to forget the worry I know is plaguing his thoughts, and for that I'm so thankful.

I step to the side and watch him answer questions with a flash of his disarming smile that gets me every time. And as much as I see the cocky bad boy shining through with each answer, I also see a man in utter reverence of the sport he loves and the role he plays in it. A man gaining back bits and pieces of the confidence he left on the track in St. Petersburg with each response.

As much as I'm dreading the familiar call of *"gentlemen start your engines,"* a part deep down within me sags in relief that he's back. My reckless, rebellious rogue just found his footing and is stepping back in his place.

Silence descends around us—the constant noise fading to a white humming as the minutes tick away, bringing us closer and closer to the start of the race. I can feel Colton's restlessness rising, can see it in his constant movement, and wish I could ease it somehow, someway, but fear he'll sense mine and that will only make matters worse.

I see him toss his empty Snickers wrapper into the trash beside him as he goes over pit stop scheduling with Becks and some of the other crew members, his face intense but his body language fluid. I watch him step away and look at his car, his head angling to the side as he stares at it for a beat—a silent conversation between man and machine. He walks up to it slowly; the crew, still making last minute adjustments, steps back. He reaches a hand out and runs it up the nose to the driver's cockpit, almost a caress of sorts. Then he raps his knuckles on the side, his customary four times. The last time he holds his fist there, resting against the metal for a second before shaking his head.

And even with the chaos of all the last minute preparations happening around me, I can't tear my eyes away from him. I realize how wrong I was to hope he'd give this all up as I sat beside his hospital bed. How asking him to give up racing would be like asking him to breathe without air. To love without me being the one he's loving. Racing is in his blood—an absolute necessity—and that has never been more evident than right now.

I wonder how different this race will be for him without the constant pressure of the demons on his heels, of the need to drive faster, to push harder to outrun them. Will it be easier or harder without the threat he's had his whole life?

The PA hums to life shattering my thoughts and Colton's moment of reflection. When he looks over his shoulder, his eyes immediately lock with mine. A shy smile spreads over his lips, acknowledging that our connection is so deep that we don't need words. And that feeling is priceless.

People scramble around us but with his eyes on mine, he wraps his knuckles two more times on the hood before turning and walking toward me.

"Starting a new tradition?" I ask with a quirk of my brow, a smile a mile wide and a heart brimming with love. "Two more for extra luck or something?"

"Nah." He smirks, scrunching his nose up in the cutest way—such a contrast to the strong lines of his face—that my heart melts.

"All the extra luck I need is right here," he says as he leans in and presses the tenderest of kisses to my lips and just holds his mouth against mine for a moment.

Emotions threaten—war really—inside of me as I try to tell myself his sudden affection isn't because the fates above are giving me one last memory with him because something bad is going to happen again. I try desperately to fight the burn of tears and enjoy the moment, but I know he knows, know he senses my unease, because he lifts his hands up to hold my face as he draws back and meets my eyes.

"It's gonna be okay, Ry. Nothing is going to happen to me." I force myself to hear the absolute certainty in his voice so I can relax some, be strong for him.

I nod my head subtly. "I know ..."

"Baby, Heaven doesn't want me yet, and fuck if Hell can handle me, so you're kinda stuck with me." He flashes me a lighting fast grin that screams everything I never thought was sexy—unpredictable, adventurous, arrogance—and now can't help the ache it creates.

"Stuck with you, huh?"

He leans in and brings his mouth to my ear. "Stuck *in you* is more what I'm thinking," he murmurs, his heated breath against my ear sending shivers down my spine. "So please, *please*, tell me you're wearing some type of checkered flag I can claim later because fuck if I don't want to throw you over my shoulder and take a test lap right now."

Every part of my body clenches from his words. And maybe it's my heightened adrenaline and excessive emotion being back in the moment so precious yet stolen so brutally from us months ago, but fuck if I don't want him to do just that.

"I love a man willing to beg," I tease, my fingers playing with the hair curling over the neck of his fire suit.

"You have no idea the things I'm willing to beg for when it comes to you, sweetheart." He disarms me with that roguish grin of his, his words causing my breath to catch in my throat. "Besides, my begging leads to you moaning and fuck if that's not the hottest sound ever."

I exhale a small groan of frustration, needing and wanting him desperately when I can't have him … and I know that's exactly why the ache is so intense. I start to speak, but am cut off by the opening chords of the Star Spangled Banner. Colton holds tight to the sides of my face and looks at me a moment longer before pressing one more kiss to my lips, and then nose, before turning toward the flag, removing his lucky hat, and placing his hand over his heart.

As the song plays on, its last notes sounding, I take a deep breath to prepare myself for the next few moments—to be strong, to not show him my fear's still there, regardless of how certain he feels. And then chaos descends around us the minute the crowd cheers.

Colton gets suited up, taped down, zipped up, gloves on. Engines start to rev farther down the line, and the rumble vibrates through my chest. He's in the zone, listening to Becks and getting ready for the task at hand.

Superstition tells me to make this race different. To step back over the wall without Davis' help. To do anything to not let time repeat itself. And then his voice calls to me. Shattering all my resolve with the shards of nostalgia.

"*Rylee?*"

My eyes flash up immediately, the breath knocked clear from my chest with his words and the bittersweet memories they evoke, and lock onto his as he strides toward me, shrugging off a groan from Beckett about running out of time.

My mouth parts and my eyebrows furrow, "Yeah?"

He reaches out, the short barrier of a wall between us and yanks my body to his so our hearts pound against one another's. "Did you actually think I was going to let you walk away this time without telling you?"

The smile on my face must spread a mile wide because my cheeks hurt. Tears pool in my eyes and this time it's not from fear.

But from love.

Unconditional adoration for this man holding me tight.

"I love you, Ryles." He says the four words so softly in that rasp of his, and even with everything around us—revved engines, a packed grandstands, the crackle on the PA system—I can hear it clear as day.

His words wrap around my heart, weave through its fibers, and tie us together. I exhale a shaky breath and smile at him. "I love you too, Ace."

He smirks before pressing a toe-tingling kiss to my lips and says, "Checkered flag time, baby."

"Checkered flag time," I repeat.

"See you in victory lane," he says with a wink before turning and walking back toward a crew standing motionless, waiting for their driver.

I watch them help him slide his helmet on, mesmerized with both love and fear, and then allow Davis to lead me up the stairs to the pit box so I can watch from an elevated level. I place the headset on as I look down over the sill and watch them fasten Colton's HANS device, yank on his harnesses, and tighten the steering wheel down.

"Radio check, Wood." The disembodied voice of Colton's spotter fills my ears, startling me. "Check one, two. Check one, two."

There's silence for a moment and I look down as if I'd be able to actually see him through his helmet and the surrounding crew.

The spotter tries again. "Check one, two."

"Check, A, B, C." Colton's voice comes through loud and clear.

"Wood?" The spotter calls back, confusion in his voice. "You okay?"

"Never better," he laughs. "Just giving a shout out to the alphabet."

And the nerves eating at me dissipate immediately.

"*The alphabet?*"

"Yep. A to motherfucking Z."

Quinlan grips my hand as I look up at the ticker on the top of the screen counting down the laps left to go.

Ten.

Ten laps to go through the gamut of emotions—nervous, excited, frantic, hopeful, enamored—just like I have the past two hundred and thirty eight laps. I've stood, I've sat, I've paced, I've yelled, I've prayed, and have had to remind myself to breathe.

"He's gonna pull it off," Quinlan murmurs beside me as she squeezes my hand a little tighter and while I agree with her—that Colton is going to win his comeback race in a flurry of glory—I won't say it aloud, too afraid to jinx the outcome.

I look down below to where Becks is talking furtively with another crew member, their heads so close they're almost touching as they scribble on a piece of paper. And I don't know much about racing, but I know enough that they're worried their fuel calculations are so slim in margin that Colton may literally be running on fumes on the final lap.

I watch as the lap number gets lower, my pulse racing and heart hoping as it hits five. "You've got Mason coming up hard and fast on the high side," the spotter says, anxiety lacing his usually stoic voice.

"Ten-four," is all that Colton says in response, concentration resonating in his voice.

"He's going for it!" the spotter shouts.

I glance at the monitor in front of me to see a close up version of what I'm seeing on the track, and my body tenses in anticipation as they fly into turn three, masses of metal competing at ungodly speeds. I swear that everyone leans forward from their position in the booth to get a closer look. I fist my hands and rise up on my toes as if that will help me see more, quickly pushing my prayers out to Colton as

Mason challenges him for the lead.

I hear the crowd the same time my eyes avert back to the monitor, just in time to see rear tires touching together, Mason overcorrecting and slamming into the wall on the right of him, while Colton's car swerves erratically on the bank of asphalt from the force of their connection.

Everyone in the box is on their feet instantly, the same sound, different track, wreaks havoc on our nerves. My hands are covering my mouth, and I'm leaning out of the open-windowed booth to see the track.

"Colton!" Becks shouts out as I gasp, a blaze of red car sliding out of control onto the apron. Colton would normally reply instantly, but there is absolute radio silence. And I think a little part of me dies in that instant. A tiny part forever lost to the notion that there will always be this trickle of unease and flashback of the riotous emotions from Colton's crash every time I see smoke or the wave of the yellow flag.

I see Beckett pull on the bill of his baseball cap as his eyes fixate on the track. Anxiety rules over my body right now, and yet I still feel those seeds of certainty Colton planted with his confidence earlier ready to root and break through. And I can't imagine what's going through his head—the mix of emotions and memories colliding—but he doesn't let up. The car doesn't slow down one bit.

And yet he still hasn't spoken.

"C'mon, son," Andy murmurs to no one in particular down the line from me, hands gripping the edge of the table he stands behind, knuckles turning white.

Only seconds pass but it feels like forever as I watch Colton's car aim erratically toward the grass of the infield, heading straight for the barrier, before miraculously straightening out.

And then the whole booth lets out a collective whoop when the telltale red and electric blue nose of the car flies back up the apron and onto the asphalt, under control. And still in the lead. Colton's voice comes through the speaker. "Fuckin' A straight!" he barks, the overflow of emotion breaking through both his voice and the radio, followed by a "Woohoo!" The adrenaline rush hitting him full force.

"Bring it home, baby!" Becks shouts at him as he paces below us and blows out a loud breath, taking off his headset and hat for a moment to regain his composure before putting them back on.

Four laps left.

I feel like I can breathe again, my fingers twisting together, my nerves dancing, and my hopes soaring to new heights. *C'mon, baby. You can do this,* I tell him silently, hoping he can feel my energy with the thousands in the stands pushing for him to claim this victory.

Three laps left. I can't stand it anymore. My body vibrates from more than the rumbling of the engines as the cars pass us one after another in an endless sequence. I shove back from the counter and shrug at Quinlan when she gives me a questioning look about where I'm going. I want to be as close to him as possible so I make my way to the stairs and start running down them.

"Two to go, baby!" Becks shouts into the mic as I make it to the bottom step and stay close to the wall below on the inside border of the pits. I can't see the track very well from here but I smile as I watch Becks look at the monitor and shake his head back and forth, body moving restlessly, energy palpable.

I look up at the standings and see that Colton is still in the lead before my eyes are drawn to the flag stand where the flagger is getting the white flag denoting last lap ready. And then it waves and my heart leaps into my throat. Becks pumps a fist in the air and reaches over to squeeze the shoulder of the crew member next to him.

Someone brushes against my shoulder and I look over to see Andy beside me, cautious smile ready to light up his face when the checkered flag takes flight. I look back up but my view of the flag stand is obstructed by the row of red fire suits standing atop the pit row wall, watching, waiting, anticipating.

And then I hear it.

The crushing roar of the crowd and the jubilant whoops of the crew as they jump off the wall hooting and hollering in victory. I'm so overcome with emotion I don't even remember who grabbed who, but all I know is that Andy and I are hugging each other out of pure excitement. He did it. He really did it.

The next few minutes pass in a blur as hugs and high fives are given all around, headsets are removed, and we all move quickly in a big mass toward victory lane. The motor revs as Colton pulls into his spot fresh off his victory lap.

And I don't know what the protocol is for non-crew members, but I'm right in the thick of it, fighting my way to see him. Wild horses couldn't keep me from him right now.

My view is blocked temporarily by camera crews and I'm so anxious—heart pounding, cheeks hurting from smiling so wide, heart overflowing with love—that I want to push them out of the way to get to him.

When they shift to get a better shot, I see him standing there, accepting congratulations from Becks, bottle of Gatorade to his lips, hand running through his sweat soaked hair sticking up in total disarray, and the most incredible expression on his face—exhaustion mixed with relief and pride.

And then as if he can feel my gaze on him, he locks his eyes on mine, the biggest, most heart-stopping grin blanketing his face. My heart stops and starts as I take him in. I swear the air zings with sparks from our connection. He doesn't even say a word to Beckett but leaves him behind and starts pushing through the crowd, the mass moving with him, his eyes never leaving mine, until he's standing before me.

I'm against him in an instant, his arms closing around me and lifting my feet off the ground as he throws his head back and emits the most carefree laugh I've ever heard before crushing his mouth to mine. And there is so much going on around us—utter chaos—but it's nothing compared to the way he's making me feel inside right now.

Everyone and everything fades away because I'm right where I belong—in his arms. I feel the heat of his body pressed against mine rather than the press jostling us to and fro to get the perfect shot. I inhale his smell, soap and deodorant intermingled with a hard day's work—and it has my pheromones snapping to attention, has them silently urging him to take me, dominate me, own me so I'm marked by that scent. I taste Gatorade on his lips and it's nowhere near enough to satiate the desire coursing through me, because with Colton, one taste will never be enough. I hear his laugh again as he breaks from our kiss and presses his forehead to mine for a moment, his chest rumbling from the euphoric sound.

"You did it!"

"No," he disagrees, pulling his head back to look in my eyes. "We did it, Ry. It was us together because I couldn't have won without you."

My heart tumbles in my chest and crashes into my stomach that's jolted up as if I'm free falling. *And in a sense I am.* Because my love for him is endless, bottomless, eternal.

I smile at him, tears blurring my vision as I press one more chaste kiss on his lips. "You're right," I murmur. "We did it."

He squeezes me tight one more time and lowers me to the ground with another heart-stopping grin as the world around us seeps back. I step away, allowing everyone else their five seconds with him, and yet all I can think of are his words, *we did do it.*

And I watch him—the man I love—and know his words have never been more true. We've really done it. We've faced our demons together.

His past, his fears, his shame.

My past, my fears, my grief.

He looks over in the midst of an interview question and winks at me with a smirk. Pride, love, and relief flow through me like a tidal wave.

Holy shit.

We really did do it.

Chapter Forty-Two

I SIT BACK AND WATCH Zander and his counselor work together, and my heart surges at seeing him so actively engaged. He's talking so much now and beginning to heal. I allow the pride I feel to swell and the tears to blur my vision because he's doing it.

He's actually doing it.

I walk from his room where they're having their session and out toward the kitchen, listening to the music in Shane's room and the chatter of the rest of the boys building a Lego city out on the backyard patio. Dane's emptying the last of the silverware from the dishwasher when I walk into the kitchen and plop down on a stool with an exhausted sigh.

"I agree!" he says, closing a drawer and sitting down beside me. "So," he says when I don't say anything. "How's it going with the panty melting Adonis?"

I roll my eyes. "You just wish he was a boxer-brief melting Adonis." I snort.

"Hell to the yeah I do, but I've given up hope that I can turn him to the better side. Only a blind man would miss the way he looks at you."

"Oh, Dane." I sigh, a smile spreading on my lips at just the thought of Colton and how great things have been over the past few weeks. At the comforting rhythm we've settled ourselves into without even speaking about it. Things just feel natural. Like they were meant to be. No more drama, no more lack of communication, and no more hiding secrets. "Things are great. Couldn't be more perfect."

And when I say it, I really believe it. I'm not waiting for the other shoe to drop like before. I'm not expecting anything anymore because if being with Colton has taught me anything, it's that our love isn't patient, nor is it kind, it's just uniquely ours.

"So living together hasn't been a horrible disaster?"

"No," I say with a softness as I think of how it's been quite the opposite. "It's been pretty incredible actually."

"C'mon, the man has to have something that's horrific about him," he teases.

"Nah, he's pretty damn *perfect*," I reply, loving the chance to say perfect again when it comes to Colton and me.

"I don't believe it," he says, smacking a fist to the counter. "He's got to pick his nose or snore horribly or fart like a rhino."

"Nope!" Laughter rocks through me and he tries incredibly hard to not crack a smile but his resolve is short lived.

"You have to be lying, Ry, because no man can be that fucking perfect." He shrugs. "Well, unless of course, it's me."

"Well, of course," I say, laughing and shaking my head. "Let's see …" I smirk, thinking of something to satisfy him. "He did refuse to buy me a box of tampons on the way home from work the other day."

The look on his face is priceless, lips lax and eyes wide. "The prick!" he spits out in mock disgust before shaking his head. "Shit, he just went up twenty points in my book. Sweetie, you can't ask an alpha-Adonis like him to buy your girly shit. That's the equivalent of asking him to hand over his balls on a platter."

The water in my mouth almost comes out my nose I'm laughing so hard. "Dane!"

"Well it's true." He shrugs. "I'm glad to see they're still firmly attached."

"Yeah." I snort. "Just 'cause you want them."

"Well," he draws out, "we would make a cute couple, and fuck if I don't like balls firmly attached to the people I date."

And my next sip of water isn't as lucky as my last one. I spit it out as laughter forces a spray causing us to laugh even harder. It takes a few minutes for us to settle down because each time one of us looks at the other, we start laughing again.

I'm hung up at the office again. Haddie's picking you up for me. Call you on the way home. Crash My Party, Luke Bryan. - Xx C

My heart soars and soul warms at the song he's texted. My sentimental, alpha male full of continuous contradictions. I sigh to push away my disappointment because I missed him terribly today, but I'm ecstatic about spending a little time with Haddie. I haven't seen her much lately.

I pick up my phone and reply. **I miss you. Hurry home. All of Me, John Legend. -XXX**

I check the clock and realize time's gotten away from me, so I start getting my stuff together and saying my goodbyes to the boys.

When I exit the house she's sitting in her car outside. I open the passenger side door to her squeal of delight. "Well fuck me sideways it's so good to see you!"

"I know!" I tell her as she pulls me in for a quick hug across the console, before gunning the motor and taking off with a laugh.

I throw my head back in a laugh that matches hers and close my eyes for a minute, letting the wind of the open window rush over my face. The wind dissipates as she rolls the window up, and I turn to see her eyes glancing from the road ahead of her over to me.

"Thanks for picking me up. If I had known Colton was going to work late, I wouldn't have let him drop me off. Sorry."

"I know, you're such a pain in the ass!" she says as she flicks her blinker and makes a left turn. "So since Mr. Fine-as-fuck has dumped you for now, how about a few drinks to catch up on things? Like why even though all your things are in our house, you never are … despite you adamantly denying that you've "officially" moved in with him."

I laugh and shake my head. "I don't want to jinx things." I shrug. "You know how I am."

"Yep, I sure do. So that's why we're going to knock back a few so you relax, get loosey-goosey and talk to me."

As much as I want to catch up with her, I'm dead tired. "Why don't we go to his house and we can sit on the deck, look out at the water, and have some wine. Besides," I say, looking down at my T-shirt and jeans, "I'm not dressed for a bar."

"Exactly what I thought you'd say," she says, reaching behind my seat and grabbing something. She places a tote bag on my lap. When I look over at her, she just smirks. "Nice try, Ry, but we're going out for drinks." She nods her head at the bag. "A shirt, sexy shoes, and makeup."

"What?" I say, surprised but at the same time not surprised that she's going to get her way.

"Hussy-up baby! I'm a driving and time's a wasting." I laugh and shake my head at her. "You'll thank me before the night is through." We slow to a stop at a light and she picks up her phone and sends a quick text, before putting it down and looking over at me. "You're not getting out of this, Thomas. I miss my friend, I want a drink, end of story."

The light changes and she takes off as a smile spreads on my lips. God, I love her.

I don't really pay attention to where we're going because I'm looking in the visor mirror and fixing my makeup and primping my hair. Haddie's only input is "Leave it down," when I try to put it up in a clip. We chat about this and that, to catch each other up on the day to day. I'm zipping up my pouch of makeup when my phone rings.

I fumble with it clumsily when I see it's Colton. My immediate thought is that he's done with work and can meet up with us for a drink.

"Hi!" I say as I shove everything back into the bag at my feet on the floor.

"Hey, sweetheart."

And just the sound of his voice causes a wave of love to wash over me. "Are you done with work?"

"I lied," he says, and I'm immediately confused. "I'm not working because I'm busy planning the perfect date for you, so look up because that date starts right now."

I snap my head up and cannot contain the sob that catches in my throat as I take in the dirt field and the quiet carnival in front of me. The motionless Ferris wheel, the vacant Midway, the locked turnstiles

"Colton ... what ... why?" I attempt to ask as astonishment passes through me, his amused chuckle resonating through the line.

"We haven't been on a real date since our night at the carnival, so I thought this would be the most fitting way to start this one. I know you're not good with the unknown, but promise me you'll go with it. For me."

What? Holy hell! "Yes ... of course," I stutter.

"See you soon," he says and the line goes dead.

I immediately look to Haddie who has the hugest grin on her face. "You!" I say to her, my voice breaking from so many overwhelming emotions. "You knew?"

"Do men have penises?" She laughs with mock abhorrence. "Of course I'm in on it!"

I just sit in the car with my mouth hanging open, as I look around and my mind tries to process this. Tries to process how the man that swears he isn't romantic is a hopeless romantic at heart. "How ... what?" I try to spit out the questions my head is forming, but they're not coming out.

"Colton thought you deserved a real date—a night out to thank you for hanging with him through everything so he asked for a little help." She shrugs. "I agreed with him, so here we are."

Tears well in my eyes as I breathe in deeply, still trying to comprehend that I'm sitting at the same carnival seven months later. While I sit stunned, Haddie reaches behind my seat and produces a box larger than a shoebox.

I laugh. "Do you have a whole store back there?"

"Nope. This is the last thing." She places the box in my hand and I cough out a nervous laugh, not because I'm actually nervous, but because of my dislike for the unknown and my need for control.

Colton knows me so well.

I sit there and stare at the rectangular gray box and can't help the soft smile that graces my lips as I recall something Colton told me a long time ago—*sometimes not being in control can be extremely liberating.*

"Jesus, woman, open the damn box already, will you? The suspense is killing me!" Haddie says beside me, her body vibrating with anticipation.

I let out a deep breath and crack open the top like something is going to jump out at me. And when I lift the top off, an envelope sits atop some black and white checkered tissue paper, my name written on it. I lift it up and slide the paper out of it.

Ryles-

I know you're probably wondering what in the hell is going on, so let me try and explain. You always put everyone else first—me, the boys, the stray dog on the corner—so I thought it was time to switch places and let you be the one front and center. So with the help of others, I've put together a bit of a scavenger hunt for you. In order to get to the prize, you have to follow and answer all of the clues.

Good luck.

Here's your first clue: The carnival is the place I knew you were so much more than I'd ever expected. I knew sitting atop the Ferris wheel with you that no matter how hard I was fighting it, I couldn't do casual with you and that you deserved so much more than that from me. So the first item is waiting for you at the first ride we went on.

Love,

Colton

I wipe away the tears that slide down my cheeks without messing the makeup I'd just put on, but it's damn near impossible. Haddie reaches over and squeezes my forearm to help steady my trembling hands. I look over at her trying to comprehend what it took for Colton to organize all of this, as well as put the words he has a hard time expressing verbally to paper.

"Get your ass out of the car and go find your man before I have a heart attack from the anticipation," she says as she pushes my shoulder toward my open car door.

I slide out of the car, my heart pounding and head trying to understand that he cares enough about me to do this. I walk up to the gated entry to find a single turnstile unlocked. I walk through it and into the eerily deserted carnival, my pace starting to quicken with each step as memories flood back to me. Stuffed dogs, stolen kisses, and cotton candy. Dares to a bad boy who had already captured my heart even though I didn't want to admit it just yet. Fears and firsts and a shy, lopsided grin on his magnificent face.

I reach the ride section and head for the Tilt-A-Whirl. I let out a gasp as Shane and Connor step out of the shadowed ticket booth with huge grins on their faces and a box in their hands.

My hand presses to my chest from utter shock and absolute adoration at Colton for including my boys in his scavenger hunt. For allowing them to help him do something nice for me. "You guys!" I exclaim as I jog over to where they stand and take in the mischievous looks in their eyes. "You kept this from me?" I step forward and hug both of them tightly as we all laugh.

"We were sworn to secrecy," Shane says, blushing.

"Colton said we wouldn't get in trouble for lying to you either,"

Connor adds, shaking his head.

"No." I laugh, completely overwhelmed by everything. "You'd never get in trouble for something like this."

Shane clears his throat and I look over to him. "We have your next clue."

"Oh, okay," I say with a laugh, my nerves returning.

"You have to answer this question right in order to get the next clue, okay?" I nod. "When you see this item, which Con is going to hold up, what one word answer comes to your mind?"

Connor holds up a yellow, rubber ducky and I erupt into a fit of giggles, fresh tears appear at the corners of my eyes. I shake my head trying to staunch my laughter but can't when I say, "Quack!"

And more recollections hit of shouting and hurt cutting through the morning chill on the front lawn of the Palisades house to a hotel room in Florida and my menagerie of animals I threw at Colton when trying to preserve my heart from misconceived truths. Of being so stubborn I didn't really listen, didn't hear what he was telling me.

But I'm listening now. He's not the only one who's learned during our time together.

Connor and Shane let out a little cheer and they hand me another envelope in which I hurriedly tear open. It says:

The memories this next clue remind me of are burned in my mind just as much as the ink of my tattoos. And you were sexy as fuck. Damn! "In case you need a little sweetener after I dirty you up." Where exactly would you buy that?

Everything below the waist tightens at the memory of Colton and cotton candy and I smile at the thought and then feel weird thinking those thoughts near the boys. "Are you guys going to be okay?" I ask them immediately.

They roll their eyes. "We're not here alone," Shane says. "Now go figure out the clues!"

"Okay," I say as my excitement mounts. I kiss both boys on the top of their heads and jog through the fair looking everywhere for a vendor cart that has cotton candy on it. And with every step, I look for and expect to find Colton and his impish grin waiting to surprise me.

But there's nothing.

I start to get panicked at the quiet calm of the grounds. After a bit of wandering I turn a corner and look up to see a lone funnel of cotton candy hanging from a stand. As I get closer I cry out when I see Ricky and Jackson standing in aprons and smiles.

"I can't wait any longer!" Ricky says, fidgeting behind the counter and handing me another box as both Jax and I laugh at his excitement to be a part of this.

I set the box down and open it to find an auction paddle that says: **Go back to where it all began. Where I learned defiance can be pretty damn sexy.**

I shake my head again, feeling like I'm having an out of body experience as I say goodbye to them. I walk as fast I can out to the parking lot, to where Haddie is sitting behind the wheel, eyebrows raised and fingers drumming in anticipation.

I slide into the car to her repeating "Tell me, tell me." Over and over. I tell her to drive where the date auction charity gala took place and then fill her in on the two clues I'd received at the carnival. She's bouncing in her seat with enthusiasm while I sit here wide-eyed and shocked at Colton's sweet surprise.

"Well shit, that bonk on the head at the race in Florida sure as fuck helped him in the romance department." She laughs. "I think it might become a mandatory thing for the penis-poking gender!"

I laugh with her. "You really didn't know about this part?" I ask Haddie several times.

"Ry, he told me he had a cool date planned for you and asked if I'd be your chauffeur for part of it. So I'm here, and I so can't wait to see what else he has in store for you!" she says, reaching over and running her hands over the words of the auction paddle. It's sitting on my thigh and I can't stop staring at it.

The stars must be aligned because we avoid Los Angeles traffic and make it to the old theater in record time. "I'll be waiting right here!" she yells as I climb out of the car with the paddle in my hand and jog to the grand front doors of the old theater to find one of them ajar.

I enter the familiar foyer and look around as I walk toward the door to the right of the stage like I did that night so many months ago. I start humming out of habit to Matchbox Twenty's *Overjoyed* playing softly on the speakers overhead. It has to be a complete coincidence because even Colton couldn't time my arrival this perfectly, but it makes me smile at how perfect it is that *my group* is playing. I blink back tears as the significance of this moment takes hold—Colton leading me back here after all this time where something I never really wanted to happen, actually started.

And look at us now.

I swallow the burn of tears in my throat as I push through the door and into the lit backstage hallway. And suddenly my tears are replaced with an uncontrollable fit of giggles when I see caution tape over the little alcove where Bailey tried to seduce him. And more hilarious than the caution tape is the little sign that says "Beware, piranhas lurking."

I'm still laughing as I turn the corner to see *the* storage closet door propped open and a light on inside. My heeled boots click on the linoleum as I try to figure out who is going to meet me this time. A part of me wants it to be Colton so I can kiss him and hug him and thank him for all of this, but at the same time I don't think I'm ready for this walk down memory lane to end just yet.

And the giggles return when I see Aiden and my co-counselor Austin sitting in chairs just inside the closet playing Uno. Aiden jumps up with a squeal when he sees me, and Austin and I laugh at his enthusiastic reaction.

"Hi, guys!"

"Rylee," he shouts out in excitement. "Here! This is for you!"

He fumbles as he hands an envelope and two boxes to me. One very small on top of a larger one. I look at both Aiden and Austin, their anticipatory grins matching mine as I set the boxes on the table and tear open the envelope. Colton's familiar penmanship greets me: **You were the first person to ever look at me and really see into my soul. And it scared the ever-loving shit out of me. Where did this happen? If you need a clue, it's in the top box. (Open the larger box once you leave the theater.) – C**

My heart is pounding and my hands are trembling with excitement. I know the answer. He's referring to the Penthouse where we had sex for the first time after the Merit Rum party, but nothing prepares me for what is inside the first box.

My breath catches and I instinctively lift a hand to cover my mouth before I reach out and lift the lone earring from it. The earring I couldn't find that night as I tried to gather my dignity and leave the hotel room. The earring I left, never caring if I saw it again or the man now giving it back to me.

Something about the sight of the earring and the fact that he kept it all this time, kept it when I walked out on him, causes so many emotions to surface I can barely speak as I thank Aiden and Austin before picking up the other box and hurrying back to Haddie and our next destination.

I climb in the car, stunned and bewildered, as I tell Haddie about the significance of the earring. She starts to drive to the hotel as I tear open the larger of the two boxes. And the air punches from my lungs from laughter as I look into a box of all the panties that have been ripped off me. Included in the box is another envelope that takes me a minute to open because I'm laughing so hard at the memories they evoke, and the fact that he actually kept them all.

"Geez, woman! You weren't kidding when you said the man put a dent in your drawers!" she teases as she nods her head, urging me to open the envelope.

I tear it open and a gift card falls out to La Perla for a ridiculous amount of money. The note wrapped around the gift card is worth ten times more to me though. It says: **You better buy a large supply, Ry, because I don't see my need to have you when, where, and how I want stopping any time soon.**

The blatant sensuality of his words causes an ache of desire to coil and spring to life between my thighs that I don't even bother to ignore.

"Wow!" Haddie drawls, breaking me from my less than pure thoughts as she looks over and reads the card while we're at a stoplight. "The man is that fucking hot *and* has a dirty, dominant mouth like that?" She draws in a shaky breath. "Shit, Ry ... I'd tell him to handcuff me to the bed and let me be his sex slave for life." She laughs.

I'm feeling a little blown away that this man is most definitely mine. "Who says I haven't?" I say with a smirk on my lips and a raise of eyebrows.

"Well hot damn!" she says, slapping my thigh. "That's my girl talking!"

We laugh together and try to figure out what the next clue at the hotel is going to be until she pulls up into the valet circle. "I'm assuming I'll be right back," I tell her as I climb out and jog into the lobby before I suddenly stop. I just can't go up to the Penthouse and knock on the door.

I head over to the front desk and when I approach, a woman eyes me up and down. "Ms. Thomas, I presume?"

"Yes ..." I reply, a little astounded she knows who I am.

"This way please," she says, leading me to a private elevator on the side of the lobby. She takes out a key card and presses it to the scanner causing the door to open. "There you go," she says, her stoicism breaking as she grins broadly at me before walking back to her desk.

"Thank you," I call out to her before stepping in. The familiar décor inside the car causes memories to flood back from our first time, my nerves heighten from the dark promise of the words Colton said to me as we made the same ascent in a different elevator. The car dings when I reach the top floor and I exit, unable to fight my smirk over the desperation-filled, clumsy exit we made that night.

I knock on the Penthouse door and hear a giggle from behind it as the knob starts to turn. Zander opens the door with Avery standing behind them, both have beaming smiles as they look at me. And the carefree giggle that falls from Zander's mouth warms my overflowing heart even more.

"Hi, guys! Let me guess, you have a clue for me?"

Zander nods his head frantically as he looks over at Avery to see if it's okay to give me what's in his hands.

"Hey, Rylee."

"Hi!"

"Okay, our clue is, what one word first comes to your mind when you see what Zander has?"

I look down as Zander produces a small black box from behind his back and holds it out to me. I look down at it, as perplexed as the look on Avery's face, until Zander flips it over.

And then I laugh.

The box contains a fire engine red pocket square for a tuxedo. My senses are suddenly assaulted with every sensation Colton evoked from me in the limo that night, when we were overdressed and underdressed. But that can't be the answer because that's two words. "Anticipation!" I almost shout when the word hits me like lightning, images of that more than memorable evening flashing through my mind.

"Bingo!" Avery cries out as Zander hops up and down.

"Good job, Ry!" he says as he holds out another box and envelope to me. I look at him with a furrowed brow that has him giggling again before I take it from him.

"This is for me?" I ask him.

"Uh-huh!" he says, nodding his head.

"You're sure?"

"Yes! Just open it!" he says with amused exasperation.

I slide my finger across the envelope and smile before I even know what it says because I know Colton's words are going to touch me.

Ry- I always knew you were different than the others ... but this is the night you became my checkered flag. Without a doubt. Here's to the night I knew the one thing I never wanted, I'd fight like hell to keep. Go where you first became familiar with the object in the box. – C

I cautiously open it and roll my eyes and shake my head when I see a scale model of a red F12 Ferrari. I know exactly where I'm going next because that night is most definitely one I'll never forget.

I say my goodbyes and vibrate with anticipation as I ride the elevator down to the lobby and hurry past a smirking hostess at the front desk and out to the car. I slide in and tell Haddie about the clue and laugh when she shakes her head as she drives the few blocks to the hotel where the other gala I attended with Colton is.

I direct her to drive to the top floor of the parking garage and instinctively suck in a breath when Sex comes into view. Images and emotions fill me and I don't even try to stifle the sigh they evoke in me.

"Damn that car is like a fucking visual orgasm," she says with a hum of appreciation.

"You have no idea," I drawl then whistle and am left blushing as I slide out and walk the short distance to its isolated spot in the garage. As I get closer I see a figure behind one of the columns beside the car and my heart leaps in my throat. I hope it's Colton. I've had enough of memory lane, and as much as I love this right now, I just want him. Desperately.

I laugh as Beckett steps out, a shit-eating grin spread wide across his handsome face. He looks over my shoulder at Haddie and nods his head subtly at her, his grin softening to a smolder that has my curiosity piqued, but my attention is diverted quickly when Becks talks.

"Well, I'm not sure what you've done to my man," he says, giving me a quick hug, "since his balls seem to have retracted, judging by this overt display, but fuck if I don't love it!"

"I'm sure you're giving him tons of shit," I tell him, and he just angles his head and looks at me for a second, a softness settling over his features.

"It's the happiest I've ever seen him," he says with a nod.

And before I even think of what I'm saying, the words are out of my mouth. "But why do you think that is?" I ask.

He just laughs that low chuckle of his and holds out a white plastic bag with humor in his eyes. I take the bag from him and look into it. It takes my mind a moment to figure out what I'm looking at. "Because I'm the whole alphabet," I whisper as I gaze at the plastic preschool letters.

"A to motherfucking Z, Ry," he says, causing my head to snap up so I catch the wink that he gives me mixed with a lazy, lopsided grin. I just look at him, a stupid smile on my face. "So, I am in charge of getting you to your next destination," he says.

I immediately look over my shoulder and am surprised to see Haddie's car gone. I was so caught up with Becks that I didn't even hear her leave. He motions for me to get in and I oblige. The minute that our seat belts are fastened and the engine roars to life, Becks looks over at me. "Where is the one place you proved to Colton that rookies can drive for the win?"

I laugh immediately, thinking of our intimate exchange about rookies and racing before realizing that Colton's referring to a more innocent time with the boys. "Go-kart track!" I shout as we head out of the parking garage and onto the side streets.

"Yes, ma'am," he tells me as we merge onto the freeway and lose the traffic behind us. We talk about this and that, but regardless of how hard I try, I can't get Becks to tell me what the rest of the clues are or the end game for this evening. He just smirks at me and shakes his head.

In no time, we arrive at the industrial park where Colton took the boys and me go-karting. "I'll be right here," Becks says as I hop out and enter through the glass door.

My smile widens as I see Dane and Scooter leaning against the counter. "Rylee!" Scooter yells and runs to hug me.

I squeeze him tight and kiss the top of his head before I arch an eyebrow at Dane. "You knew and didn't say anything to me!" I tell Dane, eliciting a belly-giggle from my sweet Scooter.

"Some things are worth being secretive about," he says with a shrug and a smirk before pushing off the counter to hand Scooter a bag.

I shake my head at him with a fake glare that makes him laugh. I don't say anything further because Scooter is basically bouncing out of his shoes with excitement. "Okay, Scoot ... you gonna help me figure this one out?"

"Can I?" he asks.

"Of course!" I tell him as I reach in the bag and lift out a plastic action figure of Spiderman. Tears immediately prick the back of my eyes, despite the soft smile forming on my lips.

"What's the answer? What does Spidey make you think of?"

And I think for a second because there are two possible answers, but given that Scooter's way of saying I love you was the catalyst that started all of this, I say, "I Spiderman you!" And I know immediately when his face falls that I got the answer wrong, but I don't care because I still got to tell him I love him. So then I try my other guess. "Spiderman. Batman. Superman. Ironman."

"Yay!" he shouts, jumping up and down before hugging me tightly as Dane and I laugh.

Dane looks up and meets my eyes as he holds out an envelope. "I guess things are as *perfect* as they seem."

"Imperfectly perfect," I tell him with a quiet smile as I open up the envelope.

Why the superheroes? Because after that night at the track, I'm not scared anymore. My childhood comfort isn't needed because I have you, Ry. It's your name I chant now, not theirs. The

clue to your next location: "Welcome to the big leagues, Ace."

I laugh at the memory of him telling me this, of turning my lame attempt at seduction back around on me, all the while reeling from the other words that he's written. That he holds me in as high of a regard as he does his beloved superheroes. My heart is so swollen with love that it's bursting at the seams. When I look up to meet Dane's eyes through my tear blurred vision, he says nothing but his eyes say it all. *He's the one.*

I say my rushed goodbyes and hurry outside to the sexy purr of the F12. I slide into the seat and look over at a grinning Beckett. "Where to next, Ry?"

"The Surf Shack," I tell him with a shake of my head as we just stare at each other for a beat.

"*What?*" he asks as he angles his head at me.

I breathe in deeply and stare out the windshield for a moment, taking it all in. "Nothing, I'm just trying to process all this ... it's just overwhelming."

"Yeah well," he says, gunning the engine at the stoplight, "it appears Hell sure as fuck has frozen over." He laughs and I join in, laying my head back on the head rest. I'm thankful that Becks allows me the silence to collect my thoughts and reflect on everything Colton's told me so far today.

We pull into the parking lot and my mind immediately remembers taking Tanner here and Colton's near fight with him. Of the overabundance of testosterone and the shocked look on his face when I left him standing alone outside in rejection. I look over at Becks and the look on his face seems to be saying "*Well, go on then.*"

I climb out and enter the restaurant to find Rachel standing at the hostess podium. Her grin is huge and she immediately says, "Your table is waiting for you."

"Thanks, Rachel," I say as I hurry past her to see what my next surprise is. I assume it's Kyle since he's the one boy I haven't seen yet. I walk out onto the patio and think back on getting to know Colton during our first time here, learning about his past, his family, and how he likes me *laid-back*.

When I look up through the cloud of memories I see Quinlan and Kyle sitting at the table—our table—with grins as wide as the ocean at their back. "Hi, guys!"

"Hey, Ry," Quinlan says the same time Kyle greets me. "So … we have another clue for you."

"Your brother is something else," I say affectionately.

"Yeah, I think so," she says with a laugh. "But then again, love will do that to you." Her eyes well with tears as they meet mine, and I see a softness there, an acceptance, a thank you.

Kyle interrupts our silent exchange by shoving another box toward me. "Open it, open it!" he says. "You have to give the right answer to get the next clue!"

I slide the lid off the box and start laughing when I see a set of sheets, sheets with the alphabet on them. Quin looks at me oddly and says, "I sure hope there's a good explanation for that one because it seems rather odd to us outsiders."

"Oh there is definitely a good explanation." I laugh, impressed that he didn't forget anything on this scavenger hunt. I look over at Kyle. "Nothing between us but sheets."

"Woohoo!" he says, jumping up and almost knocking over the table. Quinlan steadies the table and wraps an arm over his shoulders with a laugh. "She got it right!" he tells Quin. She responds with a nod and he hands an envelope over to me.

"Should I open this?" I ask, although my fingers are already itching to rip it apart.

"Yes!" he cries, startling other patrons in the restaurant.

I tear it open and read the note inside:

Ry- I knew more than ever when I couldn't have you, how much I couldn't live without you. I might not have said it with words, but I thought about it often. Where were we when we talked about "Nothing between us ever again except for sheets?"

Crashed

I feel like I have a permanent smile plastered to my face as I say my goodbyes and make my way back out to Beckett in the waiting car. "Well?" he asks with a tilt of his head.

"Broadbeach Road!"

We head up the coast, and as we draw closer, my excitement rises. I'm certain Colton is waiting for me.

Chapter Forty-Three

A S WE DRIVE DOWN BROADBEACH, I'm excited and nervous and every emotion in between. The gates open before we reach them, and I don't even give Beckett a chance to stop completely before I'm out of the car and running toward the front door where Sammy stands.

"Hi, Sammy!" I say almost out of breath as I wait for him to move away from the door.

"Don't you want your next clue?" His deep voice rumbles and I think my mouth falls lax and shoulders sag because I thought there were no more clues. I thought I was in the homestretch and on my way to see Colton.

"Sure," I force out. Without thinking, I suddenly cover my face to block it from whatever Sammy is throwing up into the air. For a minute it doesn't register with me. The tiny sparkles of silver reflecting against the sun's rays and then it hits me. Every part of my body stands at attention as goose bumps blanket my body. And it seems so funny really, that this strong, intimidating man is standing amid a rainfall of sparkle. It's priceless in more ways than one, because it's *glitter in the air.*

The sob strangles in my throat as a smile spreads across Sammy's face as he holds out a box to me. I take it from him, words robbed, and my heart tumbling fearlessly. When I open the box, the tears I have held don't stand a chance because inside is a coffee mug filled with sugar cubes.

And it may be corniness at its finest but the thought that Colton heard me that night, heard me tell him the significance of the bridge of Pink's song and is saying it back to me right now on top of all of the other gestures he's made tonight wrecks me.

Undoes me, lays me wide open, and completes me with a single, ugly pink coffee mug filled with sugar cubes.

"So?" Sammy asks, trying to suppress the grin on his face at my overemotional reaction to this tacky clue.

"*You called me sugar,*" I tell him with a wavering voice and a smile on my face.

"Attagirl!" He laughs and steps aside, opening the door behind him. "Last clue." My eyes flash up to his. "Go where you first heard this with Wood."

"Thanks, Sammy!" I yell over my shoulder as I run like a madwoman through the house and up the stairs. My heart is pounding and my hands are shaking and my mind is reeling, desperate to see him, touch him, kiss him, thank him, but when I reach the patio it's empty except for hundreds of lit candles sprinkled over every imaginable surface.

I gasp at the beauty of the soft lights twinkling amidst the darkening sky as I walk into the upstairs terrace. I run my finger over the top of a chaise lounge as I hear *Glitter in the Air* floating softly on the speakers above and laugh.

"Fuckin' Pink." It's his amused voice, that rasp that washes over me, holding me a willing hostage, and as much as it startles me, it makes me feel at home.

"Fuckin' Pink," I repeat as I turn to face Colton—the man I love with all of my heart—standing before me with the sunset at his back haloing his dark features in its soft light. So many emotions surge through me as he stands there, hands shoved deep in the pockets of his worn denim jeans, his favorite T-shirt covering his shoulders leaning casually against the doorjamb, and that half-shy smile that melts my heart gracing his lips.

"Did you have a good day?" he asks casually as his eyes rake up and down the length of my body, his tongue darting out to wet the lips he's fighting not to turn into a full blown smirk.

And God how I want to run into his arms and kiss him senseless, my body vibrating with both an emotional and physical need so strong that I squeeze my hands around the coffee mug to prevent myself from giving in. "I was kind of sent on a wild goose chase, but I'm pretty sure I'm right where I belong now."

"Hmm …" He pushes off the wall and saunters slowly my way, sex personified and then some. "And where would that be?" he asks with an arch of his brow.

His nonchalance is killing me, burning a hole right through the fire raging inside of me. All I want to do is devour this man. This man who put thoughts and words and mementos of our time together and wrapped them up in one neat package for me to unravel piece by piece, allowing me to remember the significance of each and every one. And more importantly, he remembered each and every one. That they all matter to him as much as they do to me.

"Right here," I breathe. "I belong right here with you, Colton." I step toward him—my need, my fix, my eternal addiction—and reach out to place my hand on his cheek when all I really want is to pull him to me and hold on forever. "Thank you," I tell him, our bodies mere inches apart but our hearts undeniably connected. "I'm speechless."

He lets his smile spread and reaches out to play with a curl resting on my shoulder. I watch as his eyes follow his fingers. The fact that he seems nervous over my compliment, makes him that much sweeter, and this whole evening that much more meaningful.

After a beat, his eyes move slowly back to mine, crystal green swimming with emotion, a soft shrug of his shoulders. "You are the most selfless person I know. I just wanted to do something to show you how much it means to me. I wanted the boys to be a part of it all so they can show you how much it means to them too."

Tears well in my eyes for the hundredth time today, and I swallow down the lump in my throat as I look at this man so beautiful inside and out. A man I once thought arrogant, who only looked out for himself. A man that proved me wrong in spades.

Or I guess I should say in aces.

I rub my thumb back and forth on his cheek and smile at him. "I'm floored ... overwhelmed really ... by everything you put into this." I look down for a minute to try and steady the waver in my voice. "No one's ever done something like this for me before."

He leans in and brushes the sweetest of kisses against my lips. I try to deepen the kiss, ravenous for the rest of him, the sound of his sigh, the heat of his touch, but he pulls back, kisses the top of my nose, and then rests his forehead against mine. He brings his other hand up to match the first, fingertips tangled in my hair while palms cradle my jaw.

"So a first of sorts," he says, the heat of his breath warming my lips.

"Yes." I release a shaky breath, my heart pounding.

"Good, because, Ry, I want to be your first, your last, and every fucking thing in between." He emphasizes each word as if it almost pains him to say them.

My heart squeezes because the hopes and dreams I've wished for us are now a possibility, but before I can truly grasp the reality of this, he leans back and looks into my eyes. He stares at me with such intensity, that it's like he's seeing me for the first time, and then he asks me a question that I wasn't expecting. "Why do you love me, Rylee?"

I jostle my head and look back at him, so many things passing through my mind that I can't get the words out, so I just laugh. He looks at me oddly, and I take advantage of the break to catch him off guard and grab the back of his neck to pull him down to me.

My lips are on his in a heartbeat, my tongue slipping between his parted lips and melding with his. I can feel his surprise in the tightening of his lips, but it dissipates in seconds as his hands reach out to mimic mine and tangle in my curls as we slip into the gentle tenderness of the kiss. I show him why I love him with the caress of my tongue, the satisfied moan in my throat, my unrequited need to always have more from him.

And although it's not nearly enough for me, I pull back with his taste on my tongue and look him in the eyes. "I love you, Colton Donavan, for so many reasons." I have to stop because emotion overwhelms me and I want him to see my eyes when I say this to him so that he knows with certainty why I feel how I feel.

"I love you for who you are, for everything you aren't, for where you came from, and for where you want to go." I let a soft smile play over my lips as I look at him, the man I love so much, and allow myself to feel everything that I'm telling him. "I love your little boy smirk hidden beneath your bad boy sneer. I love you because you've let me in, handed me your heart, trusted me with your secrets, and let me see the side of you that no one else has gotten to ... *you've let me be your first.*" My voice breaks on the last words and tears pool in my eyes as I stare at him, overcome with emotion.

"I love that you have an affection for cotton candy and sexy-ass cars. I love this dimple right here..." I lean up and lay a kiss where it's hiding "...and I love this right here," I say, running my hand over the stubble on his face. "And I love these right here when you're hovering over me, about to make love to me," I say, squeezing his biceps as he flexes them for me and flashes me a smile. "But more than anything, I love what's in here." I lean forward and press a kiss to his chest where his heart thunders beneath my lips. I keep them pressed there momentarily before I look up at him beneath my eyelashes and finish the most important reason of all. "Because what's in here, Colton, is pure and good and untouched and so incredibly beautiful it leaves me speechless, like it did today ... like it is right now."

He stares at me, muscle pulsing in his jaw as he tries to accept everything that I've just said to him. Our eyes are locked, our souls are bared, and our hearts are so accepting of everything the other is that we're lost in our unspoken words.

Within a heartbeat he pulls me into him, wraps his arms around me, and holds on tight. "*Fuck, I love you,*" he says, his face is buried in the curve of my neck, and I can feel the unevenness of his heated breath as he tries to compose himself.

The desperation of his touch and in his words cements everything between us as we cling to each other.

"This is what I mean," he murmurs, pressing a kiss to the side of my neck, his mouth a whisper from my ear. "Tonight's supposed to be about you—completely about you—and yet you just gave me so much that I can barely fucking breathe right now."

He leans back and the emotion in his eyes is overpowering. Little boy, grown man, and rebellious rogue are all looking at me right now, all telling me they love me. He takes in a deep breath and forces a swallow.

"It's impossible to be around you, Ry, and not be moved by you somehow, someway. You leave me tongue-tied and make my goddamn stomach twist in knots half the time." He shakes his head and I smile at him, so touched by his compliments. He reaches out and moves a piece of hair from my face. "You loved me at my darkest," he whispers, and steals my breath.

The stark reality of his words cause goose bumps to dance over my flesh and I'm speechless. His eyes glisten with moisture as he bites his bottom lip, before finding the words he needs to finish expressing himself.

"You loved me when I hated myself. When I pushed you away and tried to hurt you so that you couldn't see … everything from my past. You accepted my fear and loved me because of it." He shakes his head. "And then you grabbed my balls and told me *non-negotiable.*" We both laugh at his words, the levity of the comment allowing us to expel some of the pent up energy from this unexpectedly intense conversation.

"That still goes by the way," I say to him with a smirk, and he leans forward and brushes his lips against mine.

"I ..." He sighs. "Ry, you have given me so fucking much and today I just wanted to let you know that I get it. That I accept it now and feel it in return." He shoves a hand through his hair and closes his eyes for a beat, followed by that shy smile I love returning to his lips.

He starts to speak and then stops to clear the emotion strangling his words before he looks back up and meets my eyes. "You gave me hope when I thought I was hopeless. You taught me that defiance is sexy as fuck, that curves are definitely my kryptonite, and that *fuck blondes*, because brunettes are way more fun." I laugh, enjoying the return of my arrogant bad boy as he scrubs his hands over his face, the scratch of stubble grating through the air. "I'm fucking rambling here ... not making much sense, so bear with me."

"There's nowhere else I'd rather be, Colton," I tell him as he leads me to a chaise lounge. I sit down and he leans on his knees, on the ground in front of me, his body between the V of my thighs, his hands holding onto my waist.

"Ry, I asked you why you love me, but what I really wanted was to tell you all the reasons I love you. It's important for me to know you don't doubt my feelings for you ... because fuck, Ry, you've knocked me on my ass. You were the one thing I never wanted—never, ever expected in my life—and fuck if I can live without you now." He laughs at his admission while my smile widens. "You test me and tempt me and make me look at the truths I don't want to face and are stubborn as hell, but God, baby, I wouldn't want you any other way. Wouldn't want *us* any other way." He places his hands on my shoulders, his thumbs caressing the hollow between my collarbones as he shakes his head and continues.

"I think I always knew you were so much *more* ... but I knew I was in love with you the night of the Kids Now event ... you stood in that garden and pushed me to take a chance ... dared me to love you." His voice breaks with the emotion from remembering that night.

"And then we had sex on *Sex,*" I add in with a laugh that earns me a sexy as hell groan from deep in his throat.

"Fuck, Ry, between stairwells and car hoods and cotton candy, I'll never be able to escape thinking about you," he drawls.

"That was my plan all along," I tease with a smirk.

"Oh really? You've been playing me this whole time?"

"Uh-huh," I say. "Hate the game and not the player, right?" I laugh. "Welcome to the big leagues, Ace." The comment is off my tongue in a flash, and my sarcasm is rewarded by the grin I love spreading wide on his lips. He shakes his head, leans in to tease my lips with his, and surprises me by deepening the kiss. His tongue tempts and tantalizes me, desire coiling and need clenching every muscle south of my waist before he pulls back.

"See," he whispers, "this is why I love you. It's not the big things you do but the million fucking little things that you don't even know you're doing. It's making me laugh because you know I'm uncomfortable talking about this kind of shit and being okay with it. It's for making me see the world in a different light, like ice cream for breakfast and pancakes for dinner type of light." He shakes his head and looks down momentarily.

"And this is why I love you," I tell him. "Because no matter how uncomfortable you are expressing yourself, you know I need to hear it and you're trying … hell you knocked it out of the park today. It was—you are—perfect."

"I'm so far from perfect, Ry" he says with a self-deprecating laugh.

I reach out and touch him, run my hand over the line of his jaw. "You're my kind of perfect, Colton."

He smiles softly at me, his eyes suddenly becoming so intense and serious. "No, I don't think you get it, Ry, and I don't know how else to say it …" He reaches out and cups my face again, holding my head with unsteady hands so that my eyes lock with his. "I want to be your motherfucking checkered flag, Rylee. Your pace car to lead you through tough times, your pit stop when you need a break, your start line, your finish line, *your goddamn victory lane.*"

His words have stolen mine and feed the need I've had since our first meeting. As much as I tried to fight the feeling that fateful night, I wanted to be his. Wanted so much more than a make-out session in a backstage hallway. I wanted the whole frickin' race with him.

"Your trophy," I muse with a soft smile, thinking back to our conversation the morning after our first time together, and I know he remembers, because he returns the same smiles back at me.

"No," he whispers as he leans forward and presses his lips to mine. "You're so much more than a trophy, Rylee. Trophies are inconsequential when all is said and done … but you? *You could never be inconsequential.*" I can feel his lips curve up to a smile.

"No, you and me together … *that would make you mine,*" I tell him with a smile of my own as I contribute a memorable moment from our past myself.

"Good one," he concedes, leaning back with a devilish smirk on his handsome face. "My turn," he says, licking his lips before his grin returns. "Is there anyone whose ass I have to kick before I can make it official?" he says with a laugh, his words challenging me to remember.

I shake my head, smiling as his fingers trail up my arms and his eyes dare me to recall my line. His touch is distracting, but I remember. I bat my eyelashes at him. "Make what official, Mr. Donavan?" I ask, and when I meet his eyes, I'm surprised by his intense gaze.

"*This, Rylee.*" He breathes. "Make *this* official," he says.

I gasp, my hand flying up to cover my mouth as I look down at the sparkling engagement ring. I'm so thankful I'm sitting because the world is moving around me in a blur. All I can focus on is the brilliance of the man in front of me, asking to make my world complete. A world I never thought would exist for me.

I remind myself to breathe, even though I still can't trust myself to form words properly, so I just stare at him, my body covered in goose bumps despite the warmth of his love pulsing through me. I stare at him through tear blurred eyes and nod subtly in shock. I don't move my eyes from his, because I can see this moment means as much to him as it does to me.

"Make this official with me, Rylee," he says, his voice certain but hands are unsteady. I love the fact that he's nervous, that I mean so much to him that he's worried I might say no.

"I told you once that if I couldn't say the words, I'd do anything I could to prove to you how I feel about you. Well I can say the words now, baby. You showed me how. I love you." His eyes hold mine but I can't help but look down at that shy smile of his that owns my heart. "I love who you are and what you make me. I love that your spark has stopped the blur. That you wanted to race with me. That I don't need the superheroes anymore because I need you instead." He shakes his head slightly and nervously laughs before he begins again.

"Shit, we've already done the *for better or worse* part and the *in sickness and health*, so let's do the *'til death do us part* too. Make a life with me, Ryles. Start with me. End with me. Complete me. Be my one and only first. Be my goddamn victory lane and my fucking checkered flag because God knows I'll be yours if you'll let me. Marry me, Ry?"

Tears are coursing down both of our faces, and I'm so overwhelmed by the beauty of his words and the outpouring of his soul that I can't speak, so I show him instead. I lean forward and press my lips to his, the taste of salt mingling on our lips as I pour myself into the kiss.

And then I start giggling as my lips are pressed against his, and emotions run rampant through me. I can't help it. I lean back and dash away my tears as he looks at me.

"You're killing me here, Ry..." His voice wavers, a mix of exasperation and anxiety. His eyes hold mine—beseeching, imploring, pleading—and I realize that I know the answer without a doubt, but never told him.

"Yes, Colton." I say, my voice escalating with excitement as more tears form. "Yes, I'll marry you."

"Thank Christ!" He sighs and shakes his head, total adoration in his eyes as he looks at me. My eyes are still locked with his, but his hand reaches out to take mine. He breaks our connection and looks down, drawing my eyes down to watch him slip the cushion cut canary diamond, framed by smaller diamonds, onto my ring finger.

We're silent as we stare at it, the enormity of the moment hitting us. The ring is beautiful and huge but a simple gold band would have done the trick, because when I look up, there's my real prize. Dark hair, green eyes, stubbled jaw, and a heart that owns me: mind, body, and soul.

"I love you," I whisper.

"I love you too," he says and presses a kiss to my lips and then throws his head back and laughs before yelling at the top of his lungs, "She said yes!"

I'm startled by his shout, but then I understand when I hear a roar of cheers and rush to the edge of the terrace. When I look down I'm shocked to see everyone looking up at us from the patio below. Everyone from today, including both sets of our parents.

They're all cheering and whistling and all I can do is shake my head and accept their happiness. I wave at them all, holding my hand out to show off my ring and celebrate with them.

I look over at Colton and the emotions swallow me whole. I love him with all my heart. No questions. No doubts. No fears.

"Hey, Ryles," he says, pulling me into him. "If they're gonna stare …" He raises an eyebrow and smiles when he sees the ring on my left hand resting on his bicep.

I throw my head back and laugh before completing the line for him. "Might as well give them something good to stare at."

He raises an eyebrow at me. "Fuck, I love you, soon-to-be-Mrs. Donavan," he drawls out, chills dancing on my spine and a smile spreading on my lips, as he leans forward and kisses me.

The cheers rise to a riotous level down below, but all I hear is Colton's soft groan. All I feel is every place our bodies are touching.

All I know is that the warmth spreading inside of me, taking hold, is finding permanence.

Everything else fades away.

The crowd below.

The world beyond.

Because I have everything I need right here in my arms.

The one thing neither of us ever wanted turned out to be the one thing we don't ever want to live without.

Each other.

Chapter Forty-Four

1 year later

YOU'RE LATE. WHO DO YOU think you are, the bride or something?

It's all the text says and I laugh as I try to type a text back but can't because my hands are shaking. I can't steady them and yet I need to. If my mom walks in she's going to think I'm nervous. She's going to think I have doubts and that my feet are getting cold.

And that's the farthest thing from the truth.

Because I am so ready to dive in headfirst. So excited to see him, to kiss him, to become *officially* his, I'm bouncing up and down with excitement. My stomach churns because I can't wait to see his face— the best part of a wedding I think—when he'll see me for the first time.

I look down at my phone and reply. **I can be late if I want to. It's my wedding. Rule number one. The bride—the wife—is always right. Non-negotiable.**

I look out the window of our bedroom to the deck below and take in the tropical paradise the terrace has been transformed into. Our close family and friends are milling around, the boys are all dressed in matching tuxedos, ushering them to their seats.

I enjoy this quiet moment away from the frenzy that ruled my morning and the chaos I know will ensue shortly. *My last few moments as Rylee Thomas.* Dressed in white—every ounce of me ruched and inlayed and princessed to perfection—with one simple exception that I refused to budge on.

I look in the mirror at the black and white checkered sash that wraps around my waist and falls down the back of my dress. My little ode to Colton and our private joke.

My phone dings. **Already giving rules and we're not even married yet? A certain wife just might need to be fucked into submission later.** *My* **rule number one: You can have any rule you want, baby, but in the bedroom I'm the one making the rules.**

I laugh, my body already strung so tight with need that I know his simple touch will set me off. I smirk, thinking of the checkered flag theme that's carried over to my undergarments and the groan I'll hear when Colton discovers it later. And I'm so desperate for that part, considering I've not let him touch me for the past month, regardless of how much he begged and pleaded. But when I decided to screw my own rules—give in to my own desire of wanting him to make love to him, he rejected me. *"Welcome to the big leagues"* his preferred comment of choice.

Ace, you already dominate my mind, heart, and soul ... in the bedroom's just an added bonus. Besides, since when do you follow rules?

I hit send as I breathe in deeply and smile at my reflection. Hair swept up with loose curls falling haphazardly, eyes bright and without doubt, so ready to walk down the aisle to the man I want to spend the rest of my life with. My gaze catches the glimmer of the wedding traditions I'm wearing. And I pick my phone back up.

I love my gift. You didn't have to. Thank you. Can't wait to see you. I go to hit send and then stop myself, needing to tell him in *our way.* So I add to the text, ***Unconditionally,*** **Katy Perry.**

Tears blur my vision as I think of him and run my fingers over the bracelet around my wrist. The gift he left for me on my dresser. When

I opened it my mom's brow furrowed, but I laughed at the alphabet letters linked together with alternating diamonds and sapphires.

My something blue and something new.

My eyes focus on the diamond studs in my ears that my mom wore when she married my dad and I hope we can have a marriage as successful and loving as theirs.

My something old.

My heart aches remembering the look on Had's face last night when she offered the simple tiara for me to wear. "You're the only sister I have left now. I'd like for you to wear it."

My something borrowed.

I close my eyes for a moment, emotions threatening to overwhelm me as I take this all in. As I etch in my brain what this feels like—life changing and yet so full of excitement all at once. And then my mind drifts toward the man I can't wait to spend my life with. The man who caught me that first day, and despite a few bumps, has never let me fall—except for more in love with him. Every single day.

What is Colton thinking and feeling right now? Is he jittery? Nervous? Does he feel as certain as I do?

My phone alerts me again.

Get used to being spoiled. Not too much longer now. You know how much I love you because I'm handing over my balls momentarily to type the next song title, but fuck if it's not true –Halo, Beyonce. Whew. Balls back in place now. And hey, there's a lot of dressed up women down here, how will I know which one is you?

The words to the song hit me the same time as his sarcasm, and I emit a sobbing laugh, my body unsure which emotion it should let rule. And I decide to let them all rule—every single one—because this is a once in a lifetime kind of day.

And because I allow myself to feel everything right now, all I want is him, desperately. I appreciate all of the guests being here, but I couldn't care less about all of the pomp and circumstance because what matters most is the man that's going to be waiting for me at the end of the aisle.

I pick up my phone one last time, a soft smile on my face and type, **I'll be the one in white.**

The knock on the door pulls me back from my thoughts. "Come in."

"You ready, sweetheart?"

My mom's voice tugs at all of the emotions rolling through me, and I have to fight the burn in the back of my throat. I keep telling myself not to cry—that I'll mess up my makeup—but I know it's futile. I've shed a lifetime of tears over the past three and a half years; I'm entitled to ruin my makeup with tears of joy now.

"Yeah, I am." I look over at my mom and my lips curve into a soft smile that reflects hers. She holds my gaze, the pride along with a tinge of sadness that she's letting me go, is evident in her blue eyes. "Don't start," I warn her, because I know if she begins crying, so will I.

"I know." She sniffles and then laughs as places her hands on both sides of my cheeks and stares into my eyes. "He's the one, Ry. A mother knows these things." She shakes her head, a soft smile on her face before she answers the question in my eyes. "*He dances in the rain with you. That's how I know.*"

I swallow back the tears again as I recall her advice the day we left the hospital. About how life isn't how you survive the storm, but how you dance in the rain. And if I had any doubt about what I was about to do, it would have vanished in an instant with her simple comment.

Nothing like a mother's stamp of approval to make my moment that much sweeter.

I'm about to say something when Haddie comes barreling through the door. "Time to fly the flag, baby, because it's altar time!" she says with a whistle. "Hot damn, woman!"

"Thanks." I laugh as she and my mom start to gather my dress up and we move toward the staircase, the soft notes of *A Thousand Years* is being played on an acoustic guitar down below. The words reveal everything I feel about the man waiting for me.

Quinlan gives us the go-ahead from downstairs that signals Colton is in position and can't see me. My mom and Haddie help me walk down the stairs with my train so I don't trip and break my ankle. We reach the bottom floor and my mom pulls me into a tight hug before pulling back and smiling at me with so many emotions swimming in her eyes.

"I know," I whisper to her with a nod as Shane comes to escort her to her seat.

I feel a hand on my arm and turn to find the soft smile of my brother looking so handsome in his tux. Tanner locks eyes with me and just shakes his head. "It's definitely not dress up at Nana's house," he teases, love reflected in his eyes as he reaches out and grabs my hands. "You ready to do this, Bubs?"

I nod my head vigorously, emotion clogging my throat as I think back to when we were little and used to play wedding at our Nana's house. Gummy lifesavers for wedding rings and stuffed animals for guests. "Never been more ready," I tell him, kissing him on the cheek as my usually stoic brother's eyes well up with tears.

"You look stunning." He shakes his head in disbelief one more time, before placing a soft kiss on my cheek.

"Dad?" I ask, looking over his shoulder for our father.

"Trying to compose himself," he says with a wink. "It's not every day you give your baby girl away. He'll be here in a second." I nod to him and then he turns to go stand beside Quinlan who's already a blubbering mess. She meets my eyes and shakes her head, a silent acknowledgment that if we talk right now we'll both be crying so hard we won't recover.

"And there's the woman who's responsible for hundreds of females crying in their coffee today." I turn my head to find the man I've grown to love over the past year.

"Becks." It's all I can say, but the admiration in my tone tells him all he needs to know. I adore him in so many ways, least of all for pushing Colton and me together when all we wanted was to break apart.

"Hey, gorgeous," he says. "You've got time to skip out if you want. His ego's only going to get bigger after he claims the ultimate prize today."

My heart squeezes at his words. "Only if you're driving," I tease as I take in a deep breath to tame my emotions.

"Nah, he might actually kick my ass for that." He laughs softly as he pulls me into a hug. "He's waiting for you," he whispers into my ear before stepping back and nodding to me.

His words hit their mark as everything around me comes into crystal clear focus. The music. Haddie and Quinlan in their classic black dresses and vibrant bouquets. Tanner rocking on his heels, trying to be patient, but anxiously awaiting the reception so he can take off his bow tie. The strings of the guitar. The hum of everything swirling around me. My heart thundering with anticipation beyond words.

I am so ready for this.

Haddie steps closer, my kick-ass friend has tears in her eyes, and starts to fix my train around me. She finishes and looks at me with a smile. "Just remember, marriage is gonna be tough sometimes. When it is, wear a dress with a zipper up the back."

I laugh as I look at her like she's crazy.

"He'll have to touch you to help you undress and what's underneath will make him forget whatever it is he's pissed at." She raises her eyebrows. "Then will come the best part, *make-up sex*." She laughs causing me to roll my eyes.

"Thanks, Had," I tell her with a shake of my head, because even though I'm sure about what I'm about to do, my stomach's just dropped to my feet.

"I love you, Ry." She presses a kiss to my cheek as I bite my lip and nod. "One for luck," she whispers to me.

"And one for courage," I whisper back and kiss her cheek in turn, not needing the tequila this time because I'm high enough on emotion as it is.

She starts to walk toward Beckett as Quinlan and Tanner start their walk down the aisle, but stops and turns back. "Hey, Ry?"

"Yeah?"

"Today's going to go incredibly fast. Everything is going to hit you at a hundred miles an hour. Make sure you stop and take it all in so you can really remember the first day of the rest of your lives together."

I can't even breathe I'm trying so hard not to cry right now. I nod and blow out a loud breath, trying to compose myself. Our eyes hold, unspoken words passing between us, before she turns and loops her arms through Becks' and starts their walk.

I peek around the curtain, wanting to see everything, take it all in, but all my eyes do is search for him. And from where I stand, I can't see him. So I look over our family and friends. Colton's crew, my co-counselors, our families fill the chairs and watch as our best friends walk down the aisle together. I catch Dorothea's eyes, her smile widening as she mouths "gorgeous" to me before nudging Andy. He turns his head immediately and our gazes lock before he nods his head subtly, the expression on his face filled with awe and gratitude.

"You ready, kiddo?"

The voice of the man who I used to compare all men to is behind me, and I know I'm going to lose it. I turn around and stare at my father, so incredibly handsome, and my whole body trembles with the thought that I'll no longer be his little girl after today. I breathe out a shaky sigh as he looks at me, unable to hide the tears pooling in the corners of his eyes.

"You did good, Ry." He nods his head, strong chin quivering with emotion.

And my first tear slips down my cheek after I hear what every little girl wants from their daddy, approval–especially about the person I've chosen to spend the rest of my life with.

"Thank you, Dad." I can't manage much more without the floodgates opening and I know he feels the same way because we both look away.

Pachelbel's Canon begins and chills cover my body. That's my cue. My dad holds his elbow out to me, and I weave my hand through it, holding on one last time. He'll always be my hero and the one I look to for advice, but it's time to step toward the man whom I'll make new memories with.

My future.

My once upon a time.

My happily ever after.

"You've never looked more beautiful," he whispers to me as we step into the doorway and my eyes blur with unshed tears. "Your husband is waiting."

Those bittersweet words—a daddy letting his little girl go—nearly break me as I force a swallow down my throat to keep the waterworks at bay.

I draw in a deep breath and look at the colorful rose petals scattered on the white fabric aisle in front of me. I blink away the moisture from my eyes, because when I raise them to see Colton for the first time, I want this moment to be crystal clear. Unhindered. Perfect.

Just like the love I feel for him.

We take the first step. I hear the rustling of our guests as they strain to see me and hushed murmurs when they do. I hear the violin strings and the click of cameras. I feel my pulse thunder through my veins and feel the trembling in my dad's arm as we take this most important of walks together. I smell the flowers that litter the terrace mingled with the soft ocean breeze. I try to take it all in, take Haddie's advice and memorize every single detail.

And above all that, I hear Colton inhale as I come into view, and I can't wait any longer. Every part of my body is vibrating with anticipation.

I look up.

And my feet move.

But my heart stops. And beats again.

My breath is punched from my lungs as I lock eyes with Colton and take in the stunned look on his face. The man who is always so sure of himself looks like the world has stopped, tilted, and spun off course.

And the funny thing is … *it has*, starting the minute he caught me in his arms.

Our eyes remain locked. Even when I kiss my dad on the cheek and he shakes Colton's hand before going to sit with my mom. Even when Colton takes my hands in his and shakes his head with a little chuckle and says, "Nice checkered flag."

"I was afraid you wouldn't know which one I was," I tease and I feel like I can breathe for the first time all day. My heart's pounding and my hands are shaking, but he's got me now.

"Baby, I'd know where you are even if I were blind." And that smile, the one that lights up his eyes and warms my soul, spreads across his lips. I get so lost in his eyes and the unspoken words they're communicating that I don't even realize our officiate has begun the ceremony until Colton looks over at her and then back at me. The green of his eyes glisten with emotion, and his smile softens as he stares at me.

"Rylee," he says, shaking his head subtly as he looks down at our hands and then back up to me. "I was a man racing through life, the idea of love never crossing my radar. It just wasn't for me. And then you *crashed* into my life. You saw good in me when I didn't. You saw possibility when I saw nothing. When I pushed you away, you pushed back ten times harder." He laughs softly. "You showed me your heart, time and again. You taught me checkered flags are so much more valuable off the track than on. You brought light to my darkness with your selflessness, your temerity …" He reaches up and rubs a thumb over my cheek to wipe away the tears that are silently sliding down my cheeks now.

His personal vows signify the depth of his love for me—the man who swore he couldn't love, does whole-heartedly.

"You've given me a life I never even knew I wanted, Ry. And for that? I promise to give myself to you—the broken, the bent, and every piece in between—wholeheartedly, without deception, without outside influences. I promise to text you songs to make you hear me when you just won't listen. I promise to encourage your compassion because that's what makes you, you. I promise to push you to be spontaneous because breaking rules is what I do best," he says with a smirk as a lone tear slides down his face. "I promise to play lots and lots of baseball, making sure we touch each base. *Home run!*" He says the last word softly so only I can hear, and I laugh through my tears.

And I can't hold back anymore so I reach out and rub my hand over the side of his jaw, not caring one bit about the assumptions people might be making about that vow.

"And that right there ... that laugh? I promise to make you laugh like that every single day. *And sigh.* I like hearing your sighs too." He winks at me. "I promise nothing will be more valuable in my life than you. That you will never be inconsequential. That those you love, I'll love too," he says and then looks over to the row where all of the boys sit. "As I stand here promising to be yours, to give you all of me, I already know that a lifetime will never be long enough to love you. It's just not possible." He shrugs, my heart swelling as his voice wavers slightly. "But, baby, I've got forever to try, if you'll have me."

"Yes!" I choke out as Colton slips my ring on my finger, my body trembling, my heart never more steady, my head completely clear.

"I love you," he whispers.

My tears fall and I don't even try to stop them. He looks so conflicted, wanting to draw me in his arms and comfort me. He looks over to our officiate, silently asking for permission to touch me. And it's so cute that my man, who always disregards rules, is afraid to break them now.

I wipe my eyes with a Kleenex that Haddie hands me and draw in a deep breath to prepare myself for getting through my vows. "Colton, as much as I tried to fight it, I think I've been in love with you since

I fell out of that storage closet and crashed into your arms. *A chance encounter.* You saw a spark in me when all I'd felt for so long was grief. You showed me romance when you swore it wasn't real. You taught me I deserve to feel when all I'd been for so long was numb." I shake my head and look down at our hands, before looking back up to meet his eyes.

"You showed me scars—inside and out—are beautiful and to own them without fear. You showed me the real you—*you let me in*—when you always shut others out. You showed me such fortitude and bravery that I had no choice but to love you. And even though you never knew it, you showed me your heart time and time again. Every bent piece of it." I breathe, my trembling hands holding his.

And the look in his eyes—filled with acceptance, adoration, reverence—is one I will never forget. Tears slide silently down his cheeks, in such stark contrast to the intensity on his face but I see his vulnerability. I feel the love.

"You say I brought light to your darkness, but I disagree. Your light was always there, I just showed you how to let it shine. You're giving me the life I've always wanted. And for that? I promise to give myself to you—the defiance, the selflessness, the whole damn alphabet—wholeheartedly, without deception, without outside influences."

And I can't help it, even though I know it's against the rules, I lean forward and press a soft kiss to his lips, and when I lean back, the look in his eyes and the lopsided smile on his face is one I'll remember for the rest of our lives.

"Rule breaker," he teases with a raise of his eyebrow as I prepare to finish my vows.

"I learned from the best." I shake my head and look back at him with clarity. "I promise to encourage your free spirit and rule breaking ways because that's what makes you, you. I promise to challenge you and push you so we can continue to grow into better versions of ourselves. I promise to be patient and hold your hand when you want it held the least, because that's what I do best. I promise to text you songs too so we can keep the lines of communication open between us. And I promise to wear dresses with zippers up the back," I throw in on a whim, prompting Colton to look over at Haddie who is laughing behind me. He shakes his head, before focusing back on me.

"I promise a lifetime of laughter, ice cream breakfasts and pancake dinners. And as much as I love waving that checkered flag? *Batter-up, baby*." My smile matches his as my love for him swells and soars to new heights. "I promise that nothing will be more valuable in my life than you—because everything else is inconsequential—and you, Colton, are most definitely not. I remember sitting in a Starbucks watching you and wondering what it would be like to get the chance to love you, and now I get a lifetime to find out. And I still don't think that will be enough time." I take his ring from Haddie, the band etched with a checkered design, and slip it on his finger.

Becks starts mocking and all the guests laugh. As much as I want to throttle him, I never could. This is my life now and he's a part of it.

"You're next, fucker," Colton mutters to him under his breath, causing him to choke more and me to laugh louder. It takes a minute for the laughter to abate and for everyone to settle down so that the focus is back on us.

"Colton, we've got forever to try, if you'll have me?"

"You know this is permanent, right?" he says softly, reminding me of the symbol forever marking my hip. I nod my head subtly as he looks at me, head angled, eyes dancing, lips smiling, and says, "I wouldn't have you any other way." He looks down at his hand, the new band on his ring finger and shakes his head for a moment as he accepts what's just happened. The look on his face is priceless. And with impatience rivaling that of one of my boys, his eyes dart over to the officiate.

"Yes, Colton." she chuckles, knowing exactly what he wants. "You may kiss your bride!"

Wonderment and love flow through me.

"Thank Christ!" He exhales as he steps into me and frames my face with his hands. "This is one checkered flag I'm forever claiming."

And then his lips are on mine, our connection irrefutable, as I hear the officiate announce, "Friends and family, may I present to you Mr. and Mrs. Colton Donavan."

Epilogue One

10 Years Later

THE VIBRATION OF THE MOTOR rumbles in my chest long before the car slings into turn four. I track the car, my eyes glued to it as he fights traffic on his second to last lap, and I wonder if it will always be this way. If I'll always be a nervous wreck when he's out there.

Definitely. Without a doubt.

I hear him shift gears as he enters into turn two, the only turn I can't see from my place in the box along pit row, so I turn to look at the monitor in front of me. I hear the announcer growing frantic as the end of the race nears, and I don't fight my pride or smile.

"Donavan's flying through turn three. One more to go and he's claiming the checkered flag here today, race fans, as well as taking the lead in the current points standings. Traffic moves aside as he enters turn four and now Donavan's on the homestretch with no one even challenging him." His excitement is contagious as I look up from the screen to watch the car fly toward the start/finish line.

And even though the outcome is unfolding in front of me, my rising anxiety won't be soothed until I can wrap my arms around him again.

"And it's Donavan across first! Donavan takes the checkered flag here today at the Indy Lights Grand Prix, ladies and gentleman! Another one in the bag for this talented driver I know we'll see so much more of in victory lane."

The box around me buzzes with excitement, but I don't even stop to chat because my headset's off and I'm jogging down the stairs. Everyone knows the drill by now, so I'm not worried about who's with whom or where we'll meet up again. I fight through the crowd just in time to see his car slowly enter the black and white checkered staging area of victory lane.

My body vibrates with excitement, and my heart is in my throat as I see the crew descend around him, reaching their hands into the open capsule of the car and squeeze his shoulders or pat the top of his helmet in congratulations. I stand back letting them have their team moment, anxious to congratulate him myself.

I see the steering wheel get passed out, and then I watch as he unfolds his body from the car. Hands help steady him as he climbs out and finds his legs after sitting for the past five hours.

The crew steps back as one man approaches. This has been the good luck routine for the past year. Love swells as I watch the man I fall in love with more and more every single day step forward and start to help unbuckle his helmet.

The media pushes their way around me to get closer, but I remain rooted and watch the moment that chokes me up every single time I see it. A moment that will never lose its impact.

The helmet and white balaclava comes off in one smooth stroke, allowing me to see Zander's eyes sparkle with the same pride and excitement I feel over his win. Colton takes his helmet from him and grabs *our son* in a quick embrace packed full of so many emotions. And I know what Colton is saying to him. The same thing he's told him countless times over the years. *"I'm proud of you, son. I love you."* These are the words he wants him to never forget, or ever be ashamed to say. I swallow the lump in my throat as Colton ruffles Zander's sweat-soaked hair and then steps back to let him have his moment in the sun.

Colton gets lost in the crowd as Becks steps forward and slings an arm around Zander to praise him before the media descends around them.

I stand in the crowd of people around me and wait, knowing he'll find me. It takes only minutes before I feel his hands slide around my waist and pull me back against him, my softness to his steel, at the same time I feel his mouth against my ear.

"Zander did good today, huh?" The rasp of his voice has me closing my eyes momentarily and wondering how over ten years later that sound can still get to me. Can still cause every feeling to flood back like the first night we met.

I angle my head sideways, his stubble tickling my skin as I move my mouth closer to his ear so he can hear me above the announcers and craziness around us. "He gets better with each race," I tell him as I press a kiss to the underside of his jaw and hold it there for a moment. "He has a great teacher," I say, my lips pressed against his skin. "It's your turn to take the checkered flag now." I lift my head up just in time to catch him raise an eyebrow and flash a roguish smirk, and I know he's most definitely not thinking about his race next week. I can't help the laugh that falls from my lips. "On the track, Ace! You already claimed this one!"

"Damn straight I did." He laughs before pressing another chaste kiss to the side of my head, leaving his lips there momentarily before murmuring, "I gotta get back to the team. See you in a bit?"

"Mmm-hmm. Tell everyone dinner's at six-thirty sharp tomorrow, okay?"

"Yep," he says as he turns me around in his arms to face him and then looks at me for a beat with that soft smile I love. The years have been kind to him, a few more lines around his eyes perhaps, but he still has the same Adonis-like looks that stop my heart.

He leans forward and presses a kiss to my lips, and it takes everything I have to not sink a little farther into it, into him. Because even after all this time, I simply can't get enough of him.

Like everything else about me, he senses my need for him and I can feel his smile on his lips before he brushes one last kiss against mine. He leans forward and whispers into my ear, "There'll be plenty of that later."

"Whatever happened to when I want, where I want, huh, Ace?" I challenge him.

I love the carefree sound that falls from his lips as he throws his head back in a full-bodied laugh. He shakes his head and just looks at me, his eyes darting over to a meeting room over my shoulder. "I believe I already proved that theory earlier this morning, Mrs. Donavan." His words cause the ache he'd sated earlier on the desk in that room to come back with a vengeance. He trails a finger down my cheek. "I'll be more than happy to prove that point to you again a little later tonight though."

"Oh no worries." I smirk. "Your *point* was more than proven."

"Baby, this point was most definitely more than proven," he murmurs suggestively as he splays his hand across my lower back and pulls me hard against him so I can feel every single inch of that point pressed against my lower belly. All I can do is breathe out as every part of my body craves him again. "Fuck, I love you," he says, pressing a chaste kiss to my lips before winking at me and walking back toward Zander and the race team.

And all I can do is watch his back as he walks away—strong shoulders, head held high, and still sexy as hell. I shake my head, reminded of when all those years ago as he walked away from me in a race suit. How he called out my name, found the courage to tell me he raced me, and changed more than just our lives, forever.

Epilogue Two
COLTON

THE HOUSE IS BUZZING WITH noise like a goddamn beehive.

Just how Ry likes it. Though fuck if I know why, because it's filled with high powered testosterone, overtaking her tiny bit of estrogen.

I glance out on the patio as I walk down the stairs to see Shane talking to Connor about how he's doing with his new job, his arm around his wife and a bottle of beer to his lips.

All of the boys are here for our once a month *family dinner* as Ry calls it, even though some of the boys—shit, men now—are starting families of their own.

"Hey, Shane," I call out to him through the open pocket doors. "I have a few more beers in here if you want them," I tease and he snorts and rolls his eyes in response.

"No thanks. I'm good with just one," he says, holding the bottle up to me in a mock toast with a wide smirk. I laugh, the memory of him green and hungover making me smile.

I walk through the hallway and take it all in. Aiden in his UCLA baseball jersey fresh from practice shooting the shit with Zander in his board shorts and backwards baseball hat, a relaxed grin on his

face. Scooter sitting on the deck outside playing with Spiderman fig-
urines with Shane's two year old son. *Shit.*

The sight makes me feel like I'm older than dirt.

Everyone's here but Kyle and Ricky. I feel sorry as fuck for the
freshman girls at Stanford those two are currently unleashing their
charm on. Or maybe it's their own type of voodoo. The women don't
stand a chance against them. Hearts are gonna be breaking.

Fuck 'em and chuck 'em.

Thinking of those two has the old term hitting me like a ton of
bricks as the memories of that first night flash back. I don't even fight
my smile as I think of the hearts I used to break … damn I was good—
until a certain wavy haired vixen crashed into my damn life, grabbed
hold, and never let go. Defiance and curves and my world got turned
upside down when I opened up that damn storage closet.

And thank Christ for that.

My fucking Rylee.

And then I hear her voice in the kitchen, and my feet head toward her without a second thought. I clear the doorway and every
ounce of love I never thought I could have, never thought a possibility, fucking sucker punches me like it does every goddamn time I see
them like this.

Pots are boiling on the stove, the microwave is dinging, and the
Goo Goo Dolls are playing overhead, but I don't notice any of that because my eyes are fixed on the sight before me, my heart beating like
a damn freight train. They're sitting cross-legged on the floor, knees
touching, giggling uncontrollably over some shared secret, flour coating their hair and faces, and complete adoration reflected back at one
another.

I stand there and watch them, my soul aching in the best fucking
way possible at how I'm the luckiest son of a bitch on the face of the
earth. I've been to Hell and back, but it was worth every goddamn
second for what I feel right now … feelings that aren't so fucking foreign any more.

The ones I can't imagine living a lifetime without.

The giggles stop as a pair of green eyes look up at me from beneath dark lashes, freckles on his scrunched nose dusted with flour, and a lopsided smirk on his lips. He just looks at me, gauging if I'm going to get upset at the mess he obviously played a part in.

Then violet eyes look up at me, that soft smile, on those lips I love, directed straight at me. And I silently marvel at how that simple smile gets me every fucking time, no matter how many years have passed. It has me wanting to pull her into my arms, share all my secrets, and fuck her senseless simultaneously.

Her voodoo powers still in full fucking effect.

And fuck if I'd want it any other way.

I fight the smile creeping onto my lips because I'm the biggest fucking softie when it comes to him—a fact I deny regularly—and try to act tough. "What's going on here?" I ask, stepping into the room as Rylee pats her hands together and a plume of flour flies into the air like a dust cloud around her, causing them to erupt into another fit of giggles.

I walk over to them, flour coating the soles of my bare feet, and squat down beside them. My eyes dart back and forth over them before I reach out and place a dot of flour on his nose with my finger. "Looks like you guys made quite a mess," I say, trying to play the part of disciplinarian but failing miserably.

"Well thanks, *Captain Obvious!*" he giggles at me, sarcasm in full swing.

"*Ace Thomas!*" Ry reprimands our son, but his words have already knocked me on my ass.

I look at him, search his face over and over, studying it like a fucking road map to see if he has any clue, any goddamn inkling what he's just said to me, but there's nothing looking back at me but mischievous green eyes and a heart-breaking smile. My spitting image.

"*Hey?*"

That telephone-sex rasp of a voice pulls me back from flashes of plastic helicopters, superhero Band-aids covering an index finger, and the sound of thwacking. Thoughts I don't really remember but that seem clear as fucking day somehow. I shake my head and try to clear out the confusion before I look over to her. "Yeah?"

"You okay?" She reaches out, touches my cheek, and stares at me.

And then he starts giggling, breaking the thoughts holding me hostage. He points to the flour she's now transferred to my own cheek. "What?" I growl in a monster voice, causing the almost six year old to squeal like a little girl as my fingers reach out to tickle him.

"You're a flour monster too now!" he says between panted breaths as he tries to squirm away from me.

Our tickle fest lasts for a few more seconds as I let him escape, chase him, and then hug him. And he wiggles for a bit more before I feel his arms slide around my neck and hold on tight.

Those tiny arms pack the biggest punch of all because they hold everything I am in their fucking hands. I take a moment and breathe him in—little boy, flour, and a bit of Ry's vanilla all mixed in one— and close my eyes.

I guess it was *in the cards after all.*

Fuck me running.

He saved me.

Then. And now.

Just like his mother did.

I feel her hand on my back, feel her lips press against my shoulder, and open my eyes to look at her—*my whole fucking alphabet*— and smile.

"I think our flour monster here needs to take a quick bath before dinner," she says.

"Nah." I reach up to ruffle his hair, flour flying again. "Nothing a cannonball in the pool won't wash off, right, Ace?"

He shouts out a "Woohoo!" and gives me a high five before running out of the kitchen at full speed. I watch him run and jump into the pool, Zander yelping as the splash soaks him.

"He's got you wrapped around his little finger," she says as she walks over to the sink to wash the flour from her hands.

"And you don't?" I ask with a shake of my head as I walk up behind her and slide my arms around her waist, pulling her back into me. And fuck if that ass of hers pressed against my dick doesn't make me ache to take her, throw her over my shoulder, and haul her upstairs right now.

I press a kiss to that spot beneath her neck, and even after all this time, her body responds instantly to me. Goose bumps appear on her exposed skin, her breath hitches and the fucking sigh that turns me on, as if her hands are wrapping around my dick, falls from her lips. And if her beautiful body doesn't turn me hard as fucking steel, her responsiveness does without a fucking hesitation.

That and how much I know she loves me, faults and all.

How in the fuck did I get so lucky?

I shake my head as all of the shit that's happened in my life flashes through my mind. I chuckle, the things that hit me the hardest—that mean the most—all started with a damn storage closet and this defiant-as-fuck woman in my arms who called me to the carpet, grabbed me by the balls, and told me our outcome was non-negotiable.

And fuck me, we've still got a lifetime left for her to call all the shots she wants because my balls are still nestled exactly where they're supposed to be, right in her hands.

"What are you laughing about?" she asks.

"Just thinking of the look on your face when you found out I'd won the auction," I tell her, the memory clear as fucking day. "You were so pissed."

"What woman wouldn't have been when you came off as arrogant as you did?" She snorts out a laugh and then sighs softly.

And the sigh alone makes my dick start to get hard.

"Arrogant? Me? *Never*," I tell her.

"Whatever! I know you fixed that auction, Ace."

And I laugh. God, I love this woman. Ten years later and still feisty as fuck.

"Baby, that answer I'll hold on to forever," I tell her, pressing a kiss to the back of her head.

"That's not possible," she whispers, looking up to press a kiss to the underside of my jaw, "because you'll be busy holding on to me."

Fuckin' A straight I will.

I squeeze her a little tighter, not wanting to let her go just yet because, fuck, what racer doesn't want to hold on to their checkered flag a little longer?

At least I know mine waves only for me.

My kryptonite.

My alphabet, motherfucking A to Z.

My fucking Rylee.

THE END

Acknowledgements

Wow! Where do I even begin to start? I was criticized for the length of my acknowledgments for Fueled…so if you were one who thought I was verbose, I suggest you skip this next part.

A little over nine months ago, I pushed publish on Driven. I wasn't sure what I expected to happen. I just know that both my mom and my husband kept telling me to not get my hopes up. I could lie and tell you I had grand visions that people would love it and my writing career would take off overnight. In reality, I was scared to death. I'd never done something that put me 'out there' in the public realm to be scrutinized, criticized, or possibly praised. I hoped people would buy the book about this cocky, self-assured race car driver and a feisty yet believable heroine. Yes, I did use the formulaic story line of good girl, bad-boy, but I hoped that people would pick the book up for that reason alone and discover that I could actually write, spin a tale, draw you into a different world, and make you feel. And people did buy. And people did criticize my thematic plot. But people also fell in love with Rylee and Colton and the boys.

A little over six months ago I pushed publish again on Fueled with different expectations and a determination to prove that I could make this storyline my own. That I could put my own spin on the cursed 'second book' of a trilogy and make it stand apart from the other books it was being compared to. I rewrote most of what I already had written: added Colton point of view chapters, incorporated the superheroes, the 'I race you.' And when I hit publish, I had a little more confidence and the knowledge that this book could possible make or break my attempt at becoming a 'real' author.

I could have never expected what would happen next, could have never imagined that agents would be calling—agents mind you that had rejected my query letters previously—that other authors I admired would be emailing me, that readers wouldn't be able to get enough of this world and the story I'd created. The only word I can use to even come partially close to the last five months has been surreal. Completely, incredibly surreal.

I set out to write Crashed with my eighty page outline and the pressure of readers to get it written fast. Nothing like motivation, right? But at the same time, how lucky was I that people wanted more? I know that authors work their whole lives for this moment, so no way in hell was I going to take for granted the opportunity I'd been given. I started Crashed and struggled big time on how to make it live up to Fueled. How was I going to leave something that resonated with the readers as loudly as the chant of the superheroes or the *I race you* did? It was a tough first two months of writing. And then I realized that Crashed didn't have to live up to that cliffhanger high you got at the end of Fueled because it was a different part of Rylee and Colton's story. So with that epiphany, things started coming together and forming into what you just read.

I truly hope you enjoyed the conclusion to Rylee and Colton's story. I am beyond proud of their journey, their healing, where they ended up, and yet feel bittersweet over its conclusion because just as you have grown to love them and the boys, I have too.

On that note, I have had an outpouring of correspondence from readers who have been touched by Colton's story of abuse and how I wrote about it…whether it be from a personal experience or that of a loved one. I am truly heartbroken by your stories and yet humbled that you feel I depicted the situations and the psychological effects accurately. I wish that you didn't have the knowledge to tell me that. For those that are surviving…hour by hour, day by day…your strength amazes me. I know the memories will never disappear, but I hope one day soon, like Colton, your 747 can take flight too.

There are some people that helped make this last book what it turned out to be, and I would like to take a moment to mention them. First and foremost, my husband and three young children who have been the ones to make the biggest sacrifice to get you Crashed as quickly as possible. They went from having a mom/wife who was always present, who never forgot anything, and was always ready for everything, to one who often gets lost in her thoughts, has become quite absent-minded, and sometimes fights the spontaneous because she wants to finish this chapter while it's still clear in her head.

Secondly, I have to thank Beta Biggs and Beta Yeti. Crashed came a long way from their initial reaction that Chapter 15 felt like it was still in Chapter 6 (i.e. slow moving) and for that and so many other things, I will forever be grateful. Thanks for pushing me, daring me to make you 'feel more', and all of those comments saying "I know you can do better." Your input was monumental, the PM's unforgettable, and the entire process painless (well, sometimes)…and you too, should take some of the credit for this book because you helped make the conclusion of Rylee and Colton's story a memorable one we can be proud of.

I also need to thank Beta Who and Beta Haw for giving me much appreciated advice and dead honesty at all times. For that I will forever be grateful and will never be upset even if I choose to go a different route. Friends before books, always.

To my other proofers/readers, thank you for all of your help.

And then there's a crazy group of ladies—all 7,500 and counting of them—that call themselves the V.P. Pit Crew on Facebook. You guys astound me with your support, your motivation, the friendships started, and the overall community that you've created around these books. Your unending support and involvement makes me the luckiest author in the world. Rest assured the Driven Trilogy may be over, but the group is not. Oh and ladies, did you see my shout-outs to you in Crashed?

I'd also like to thank my #WickedAwesomeAdmins (Cara Arthur, Amy McAvoy, and Christina Hernandez) as well as Colton's assistant (aka Lara) for everything they do for me without asking for anything in return. Ladies, the friendships we have made are so much more valuable than the books that brought us together and for that, I will forever be grateful. #Beckspert #TheRealMrsDonavan #WalkersChristinas #LaraMetHimFirst…Thank you from the bottom of my heart. I couldn't do it without you.

To Maxanne Dobbs of The Polished Pen…thank you once again for polishing my words and making them shine. I also must thank you for answering my numerous questions and giving me the knowledge to withstand the whirlwind you predicted would come. I am forever grateful and will never write another 'action beat' again without thinking of you fondly.…well and probably cursing you, but it's all from a place of love.

To Deborah with Tugboat Designs, thank you for having the gumption to speak up, go against the grain, and tell me I was wrong in my original choice for Crashed's cover. I am so blessed to have so many people such as yourself in my corner, looking out for me for reasons other than to benefit themselves. I'm glad you spoke up because you were right, Crashed needed to have a couple on the cover. And when you look at three together, it's perfect.

To Stacey with Hayson Publishing, thank you for being patient as I edited a little bit more and for making Crashed look beautiful and professional. And checkered flag-ish.

To Amy Tannenbaum, thanks for being patient with this leery Indie author who was a little brusque with you during our first few conversations. I appreciate your knowledge, your guidance, and I look forward to seeing where we can take the next step of this ride.

To the bloggers...I have no words that can adequately express my gratitude for the support you've given me and the books. Some of you have been with me from my original requests to read Driven way back in April of 2013. You guys are the reason that our books are seen by readers. Our free publicity, if you will...I will never forget that. Thank you so much for everything you have done helping promote the books and participating in whatever random ideas I have.

Thanks to Jodi Ellen Malpas for letting me ask questions about what comes next, answering honestly, and understanding how ridiculously emotional saying goodbye to a fictional man can be. Thank you to Raine Miller, Laurelin Paige, BJ Harvey, and the various other authors for answering random questions from this newbie. Thanks to Trisha and Carla for teaching me to laugh at this whole experience that can only come with double digit years of friendship.

To sweet Parker, hey, your superheroes finally came too!

And lastly, thank you to my readers...you are amazingly wonderful and leave me speechless on a daily basis with your little notes, emails, and comments. I know you're sad that The Driven series is over, but rest assured you have not seen the last of Colton and Rylee. In the meantime, a book for Becks and Haddie is up next. And if you're still missing Rylee and Colton in the meantime, I have a little something to keep their magic alive for you called C.R.A.S.H. Dash...for more information head on over to:

www.kbromberg.com/?page_id=743
or
www.facebook.com/Crash13Dash

As always, thanks for reading and for your unending support.

About the Author

New York Times and *USA Today* Bestselling author K. Bromberg writes contemporary novels that contain a mixture of sweet, emotional, a whole lot of sexy and a little bit of real. She likes to write strong heroines and damaged heroes who we love to hate and hate to love.

She's a mixture of most of her female characters: sassy, intelligent, stubborn, reserved, outgoing, driven, emotional, strong, and wears her heart on her sleeve. All of which she displays daily with her husband and three children where they live in Southern California.

On a whim, K. Bromberg decided to try her hand at this writing thing. Since then she has written **The Driven Series** (*Driven, Fueled, Crashed, Raced*), the standalone **Driven Novels** (*Slow Burn, Sweet Ache, Hard Beat* (releasing 11/3/15), and a short story titled *UnRaveled*. She is currently working on new projects and a few surprises for her readers.

She loves to hear from her readers so make sure you check her out on social media.

http://pinterest.com/kbrombergwrites/
@KBrombergDriven
@ColtonDonavan

CPSIA information can be obtained
at www.ICGtesting.com
Printed in the USA
LVOW01s0050170816

500681LV00015B/598/P